MOONRISE

*The Golden Age
of Lunar Adventures*

edited by

MIKE ASHLEY

BRITISH LIBRARY

First published 2018 by
The British Library
96 Euston Road
London NW1 2DB

Cataloguing in Publication Data

A catalogue record for this book is available from the British Library

ISBN 978 0 7123 5275 8

Frontispiece from *Astronomie populaire* by Camille Flammarion, Paris, 1880.

Typeset by Tetragon, London
Printed and bound by CPI Group (UK) Ltd, Croydon CR0 4YY

MOONRISE

CONTENTS

INTRODUCTION

For as long as humans have lived we have looked up to the skies and seen the Moon—and wondered: what is it? Is it like the Earth? Does life exist there? Can we get there?

The Sun may have inspired similar thoughts, but you can't stare at the Sun. You can look at the Moon. You see its phases which help measure the passing of time—the word "month" comes from the Nordic word for the Moon. On clear nights, you could see many features and make out images, such as the face of the Man in the Moon. Yet we only see the same face of the Moon all the time, never the far side—the Dark Side!

The Moon has inspired our imagination and the desire to explore it has gone hand in hand with writers and visionaries speculating about how to get there and what we might find. The Moon was a major factor in encouraging what we now call science fiction. Up until we finally fulfilled our desire to reach the Moon in July 1969 with the Apollo 11 mission, there had been over two thousand years of writing and speculation about the Moon.

And perhaps, to many, the triumph of reaching the Moon was also the start of the end of that love affair. In December 1972, just three years after Neil Armstrong stepped on to the Moon, Eugene Cernan was the last to leave. Only twelve astronauts actually walked on the Moon. Their footprints remain, unchanging, waiting for us to return.

But our love affair in fiction continues. People still write books and make films about the Moon, but the Golden Age of Lunar Fiction was before the first landing when the mystery let our imaginations run wild.

This collection brings together some of the most original and ingenious ideas from that Golden Age. This began in the late Victorian period when scientific advance was sufficient to make us believe a lunar voyage was possible, and the stories selected here range from the 1880s to the 1960s. The intention is to show how writers have viewed the moon and its potential for life and colonization, the mysteries it might conceal or the hope it might hold for the future. It includes works by some of the giants of the field from H.G. Wells to Arthur C. Clarke, and Judith Merril to John Wyndham as well as much rare fiction which has been forgotten over the years.

Inevitably some of the ideas and concepts included have dated wildly, but that should come as no surprise. Indeed, one of the determining factors in assembling this volume was to show how our understanding of the Moon has changed. For example, no one envisaged how every minute of the lunar missions would be monitored by television, though it is not entirely true that writers did not forecast coverage by television. These stories, therefore, do not feature the cutting edge of technological advance or scientific knowledge. There is a quaintness in our vision in the past which emphasizes just how far we advanced during the twentieth century. No one could really have imagined that after landing on the Moon we would desert it three years later. One day we will return, but in the meantime these stories show the hopes and dreams that we once held and, maybe, still do.

THE LUNAR PIONEERS

Few of the stories from centuries ago are easily readable today, but I did not want to ignore them completely, as I thought it important to appreciate the development of lunar fiction over the centuries. It is, after all, one of our oldest fields of the imagination. Some might believe that it began with H.G. Wells or Jules Verne, but almost two thousand years before them, the Greeks and Romans were speculating about the Moon. In the centuries since, the Moon has been explored by writers as diverse as Johannes Kepler, Cyrano de Bergerac, Daniel Defoe and Edgar Allan Poe.

So, where did it all begin?

In the five centuries before Christ, the Greek philosophers and astronomers were trying to make sense of the heavens and rationalize them away from the myths and legends that continued to abound. Philolaus, who was one of the first to write down his thoughts, around the middle of the fifth century BC, believed that the moon was Earth-like and inhabited by giant creatures. Because the lunar day lasts fifteen times longer than that on Earth, Philolaus believed that the lunar creatures could be as much as fifteen times larger than on Earth. Along with others of the Pythagorean school of philosophy, Philolaus believed the Moon was like a mirror, smooth and perfect, reflecting light from the Sun which in turn reflected it from a central fire at the heart of the universe. Philolaus proposed that all the heavenly bodies, including the Moon, Earth and Sun, orbited that central fire.

A few early astronomers were getting a feel for the size of the cosmos. In around 150 BC, Hipparchus of Rhodes, regarded as the greatest of the Greek astronomers, used detailed observations and geometry to work out the distance to the Moon. He estimated it was thirty times the diameter of the Earth. A century earlier, the astronomer Eratosthenes, head librarian at Alexandria in Egypt, had calculated that the Earth's circumference was about 25,000 miles, so the diameter was roughly 7,950 miles (it's actually 7,926 at the equator). Hipparchus's calculation thus meant that the moon was 238,500 miles distant—the actual average figure is 238,856. Between them Eratosthenes and Hipparchus were pretty much spot on.

Unfortunately, few accepted Eratosthenes's calculation because that made the Greeks feel their world was only a small part of the globe, and they were far more important than that. So, when in around 90BC Poseidonius came up with a figure of 18,000 miles for the Earth's circumference they accepted that, though it still meant the moon was 172,000 miles away. Poseidonius also calculated that the distance to the Sun was 9,893 times the Earth's radius, or just over 28 million miles. It is, in fact, around 93 million miles, but let's not quibble. It shows that the ancient Greeks did not think the Moon or the Sun were just over the horizon. They were getting into serious figures.

Hipparchus also considered that the Earth and planets revolved about the Sun—the heliocentric model—but found it difficult to prove. In around 150AD, Claudius Ptolemaios drew upon Hipparchus's work for his own astronomical treatise, *Mathematica Syntaxis*, now known by its Arab name as the *Almagest*, but he stated that the Earth was the centre of the universe and everything revolved around it, including the Sun. This view prevailed for fifteen hundred years.

Before Ptolemy's observations, Plutarch, in *Peri tou emphain- omenou prosōpou to kuklō tēs selēnes* ("On the Face That Can be Seen in the Orb of the Moon", written about 80 AD), had considered these huge distances and concluded that the Universe must be infinite, thus raising a question about exactly where was its centre. Plutarch's dialogue effectively summarized contemporary beliefs, including the idea that when people died their soul ascended to the Moon. Plutarch suspected the Moon was inhabited and believed those creatures would need to adapt to the Moon as we adapt to the Earth.

Plutarch chose not to consider how we might reach the Moon. Those distances were difficult to ignore. Well, not by everyone. The ancient Greeks and Romans loved a good travellers' tale. This wasn't just Homer's *Odyssey* or Apollonius's *Argonautica* or Virgil's *Aeniad*. There were scores of them, probably hundreds, many now long lost though a few are summarized in later Greek texts. The Greek satirist Lucian of Samosata (in modern-day Turkey but then in the Roman province of Syria), writing in around 150AD, decided to lampoon all these travellers' tales and write the most extreme example. His title, *Alêthês historia* or *True History*, was a deliberate joke since in his preface Lucian says that everything he is about to tell is a lie. The story starts with the narrator (Lucian) and his crew setting sail from the Pillars of Hercules to explore the oceans. They encounter such oddities as an island where the rivers run with wine and all the fish are alcoholic. A waterspout sucks the ship into the air and they sail on for seven days and nights until they reach the moon.

Lucian and his men are confronted by soldiers mounted on giant three-headed vultures—their size clearly in keeping with Philolaus's philosophy. They are taken before Endymion, King of the Moon. In Greek legend, Endymion was a shepherd boy who had been cast into a deep sleep by Selene, the Moon goddess, who loved him dearly, and he was spirited away to the Moon. The Moon is at war with the Sun over ownership of the morning star, Venus. Endymion has assembled a vast army and Lucian and his comrades agree to join them. A force of giant spiders spins a web between the Moon and Venus, providing a route for Endymion. The army of the Sun is nevertheless victorious and Lucian is captured, but released after a peace treaty is agreed. Eventually, after learning more about the wonders of the Moon, including a mirror which displays everything

happening on Earth, they are escorted into space by the giant vultures and return to Earth.

True History is often cited as the earliest work of science fiction,
but there's no science in it. It is one giant tall story, a genre which
has its own wonderful pedigree and includes Rudolf Eric Raspe's
Baron Munchausen's Marvellous Travels (1786) which likewise includes
a trip to the Moon (in fact, two), one by climbing a beanstalk.

Lucian wrote one other lunar journey, *Ikaromenippos*, which takes
a satirical swipe at philosophers. Menippos had been a satirist who
lived several centuries before Lucian. In the dialogue, Menippos
wishes to explore the heavens so straps an eagle's wing to one
arm and a vulture's wing to the other and launches himself off the
Acropolis. According to Menippos, it is only 350 miles to the Moon
but he still arrives exhausted. He meets the philosopher Empedocles
who had lived in the fifth century BC. Empedocles had committed
suicide by jumping into Mount Etna and Lucian has him thrown to
the Moon when the volcano erupts.

References are sometimes made to *Ta huper Thulēn apista* ("Of
Wonderful Things Beyond Thule") written by Antonius Diogenes
around the year 100AD. It is now lost but the text survived long
enough to be summarized by the scholar Photius in the 9th century.
It is another travel tale and explorers, venturing beyond Thule, the
northernmost place known to the ancients, possibly Iceland, see the
giant Moon before them but the summary does not say whether they
actually reached it. Lucian's fictions, therefore, are the only ancient
stories we know that took travellers to the Moon and it would be
almost fifteen centuries before anyone else explored the possibility,
but when they did the floodgates opened.

*

The doctrine of the Catholic Church, maintaining the Ptolemaic geocentric model, was so powerful that scholars were cautious about advancing any alternate theories. The Polish astronomer Nicolaus Copernicus had been working on his calculations, which proved the heliocentric model, since 1512 but did not publish his work until 1543 just weeks before his death. Although banned by the Church, it was recognized by fellow mathematicians and astronomers and effectively began the Scientific Revolution. Galileo was able to prove the Copernican system through his use of the telescope, particularly when he observed the moons of Jupiter orbiting their planet. Galileo published his findings in *Sidereus Nuncius* ("Starry Messenger") in 1609 and though it brought him into conflict with the Church, most of the scientific world was converted.

And so was the literary. When Galileo had observed the Moon through his telescope he discovered that far from being flat and smooth, it was rugged and uneven, with mountains and plains, just like the Earth. In other words the Moon was not some untarnished sphere, it was a real world. The playwright Ben Jonson penned a masque, *Newes from the New World Discover'd in the Moone*, first performed for King James I of England on 7 January 1620. In the banter between heralds we learn that the Moon is earthlike, with seas, rivers, forests and meadows, inhabited by "lunatics" who communicate by sign language. Jonson reports there are only three ways to reach the Moon—in dreams, by wings or by volcanic eruption. Jonson had clearly read Lucian's *Ikaromenippos* in the Latin.

He would soon be able to read it in English. Scholar Francis Hickes had translated many of Lucian's works, including *True History*, but they were not published until 1634, three years after Hickes's death. This was true of another work published that year in Latin: *Somnium* ("Dream") by the German astronomer Johannes

Kepler. He had died in 1630 and had worked on *Somnium* since 1609, revising it extensively in 1620. He had set out to provide a scientifically rigorous description of the Moon (which he calls Levania), along with how the Earth (which he calls Volva) would appear from the Moon. Unfortunately, this brief treatise is wrapped up in a story of daemons and witchcraft. Kepler's narrator has his vision of the Moon in a dream, but the dream takes his explorers (a mother and son) to the Moon with the aid of a daemon. Seen through a dream we can, perhaps, excuse this fantasia, which has added gravitas in that Kepler's mother had in fact been arrested and tried for witchcraft in 1615. Kepler deduced there can be little, if any, atmosphere between the Earth and the Moon—this was not proved conclusively until experiments by Blaise Pascal in 1646—and he showed how the Moon suffered extremes of temperature between day and night, such that any inhabitants prefer to live underwater. Kepler places the Moon at 50,000 German miles away (about 230,500 miles), yet the daemons reach it in four hours. They obtain their initial speed with an explosion. Kepler does not refer to rockets, but the idea of an explosive propellant was clearly in his thoughts.

Somnium was only a brief work, with footnotes longer than the story itself, and was pretty much ignored. There was a German translation in 1898, but no English version until 1950. As a consequence it had little influence at the time but was, in its own idiosyncratic way, the first true work of science fiction.

Others were also turning their thoughts to a serious study of the Moon. Amongst astronomers mapping the Moon, none were more thorough than Johann Hevelius who, in *Selenographia* (1647), introduced the word *mare* ("sea") for the dark plains, which has stuck ever since. The theologian and later Bishop of Chester, John Wilkins, was fascinated in developments in all matters of natural philosophy, and collected his thoughts on the Moon in *The Discovery of a New World* in 1638. This was not a story but an analysis of various propositions regarding the Moon and Wilkins concluded, so far as he was able, that the Moon was a distinct world with an atmosphere. He suspected there would be inhabitants, to whom our Earth was their Moon, but he had no idea of their nature. He was also certain that one day humans would reach the moon and, looking back at the benefits that had arisen from explorers on Earth, notably Columbus and Magellan, he believed it would be advantageous for trade and commerce.

At the time he wrote *Discovery*, Wilkins had clearly read Lucian and Kepler but, no sooner had he published his work than he saw a new book, just published, *The Man in the Moone, or a Discourse of a Voyage Thither by Domingo Gonsales the Speedy Messenger*. It was written by Francis Godwin, the late Bishop of Hereford, who had died in 1633. It has been speculated that Godwin wrote this as early as the 1580s when he was a student at Oxford, but more recent scholarship has suggested it was probably written in the late 1620s. The book, introduced by an anonymous "E.M.", purports to be a manuscript by a Spaniard, Domingo Gonsales, of noble parentage but who had fallen on hard times. After various travels, in which he regains his wealth, he falls ill and is left on the island of St. Helena. He becomes fascinated by the wild swans, which he calls *gansas*, and succeeds in training some to carry a device in which he can sit. His plan is that the swans will take him home, but instead they migrate to the Moon, a journey of 50,000 miles which takes eleven days. (When Apollo 11 went to the Moon it took 8 days.)

Godwin meets the Lunarians and their king. He finds the inhabitants, who in true tradition are giants, living in a world of harmony and pleasure, but also discovers they hardly eat any food, even though they live to a great age. He tries to learn their language which is musical rather than speech. He tries to adapt to the colours on the Moon which defy definition. The Lunarians have an innate skill for detecting whether any newborn children are imperfect and, if so, they exchange them with good children on Earth—an early example of alien abductions—though Gonsales has no idea how they do this. Gonsales remains on the Moon for six months and then, worried about his swans, returns to Earth to have further adventures.

When Wilkins read Godwin's story he decided to add an extra chapter to his *Discovery of a New World* and this second edition, in 1640, considers how we might reach the Moon. The result is a remarkable work of conjecture where he analyses all the problems and whether they can be overcome. He is naturally limited by the scientific knowledge of his day and still speculated that maybe man could perfect wings to enable him to fly or train a giant bird to carry a man. Wilkins was sure that the atmosphere became too attenuated to breathe at some stage, but suspected that, because of the cold, humans would go into some kind of torpor, as animals do when they hibernate, so that you could pass through space without having to eat or breathe much. Of course, precautions needed to be taken against the severe cold. Wilkins believed that if you could reach an altitude of twenty miles you would escape the influence of the Earth. It is now generally believed that the point at which you leave the Earth's atmosphere and enter space is 100 kilometres or 62 miles, known as the Kármán Line. Wilkins's third option for reaching space was a flying chariot, "in which a man may sit, and give such a motion unto it, as shall convey him through the aire." Wilkins did not believe the size of the chariot mattered provided it had a sufficiently strong "motive force", but he was unable to consider what that motive force may be except perhaps the flapping of giant wings.

Between them, Wilkins and Godwin proved an inspiration to generations of writers and, like a set of falling dominoes, each work inspired the next. The key player in this was the French author Savinien Cyrano de Bergerac. There is more myth than fact surrounding Cyrano, best remembered from the 1897 play by Edmond Rostand, but that he was a renowned wit and swordsman is not disputed. He lived from 1619 to 1655 and died as a result of injuries caused from what was probably a botched assassination attempt. He had previously received two near fatal injuries that forced him to turn from soldiery to writing. Amongst his surviving works was *Histoire comique des états et empires de la lune* ("Comical History of the States and Empires of the Moon"), which was probably completed around 1650 but was not published until after his death, in 1657, and then in an abridged form to tone down the heretical and irreverent views.

Cyrano had clearly read Godwin's story as he includes Gonsales as a character, held like a pet on the Moon, with whom he discusses the nature of the universe. Cyrano also meets the prophet Elijah who had reached the Moon centuries before by sitting in an iron vessel and throwing a giant magnet above him so that it drew the vessel up—thus reaching the Moon by his bootstraps! As in Godwin's story the native Lunarians are giants and communicate via a musical language. Food is inhaled. On the Moon is the Garden of Eden from which Cyrano is expelled for his irreverent views. Much of the story allows Cyrano to explore various theological and philosophical arguments which were still heretical in Cyrano's day, including the vehement view held by the Lunarians that the Moon is a world and the Earth its moon. Where Cyrano differs from Godwin and Wilkins is in his consideration of how to reach the Moon. In addition to Elijah's magnetic chariot, Cyrano proposes two ideas, one farcical and one revolutionary. His first attempt was to cover his body in bottles containing dew so that as the Sun drew up the dew, it took Cyrano with it. That method only got Cyrano as far as Quebec. Then he built a machine which he hoped might take him to the Moon but this was stolen by soldiers who attached fireworks to it and were about to burn it when Cyrano found it and leapt in. As the fireworks were lit so the rockets lifted him skyward. The rockets had been fixed in tiers so as one set finished another set lit and took him beyond the Earth's attraction. Cyrano was thus the first author to consider the idea of rocket power to lift a machine from the Earth.

Cyrano wrote two other works, but only part of *L'Histoire comique des états et empires du soleil* (1662) survives and none of *L'Etincelle* ("The Spark"), so we have lost much of the fruits of his fertile imagination. But such as was published inspired others. There were several stage productions which drew upon Cyrano and Godwin including *Emperor of the Moon* (1687) by Aphra Behn and the comic operas *World in the Moon* (1697) by Elkanah Settle and *Wonders of the Sun* (1706) by Thomas d'Urfey, the last two extravagant failures. The French writer Gabriel Daniel continued Cyrano's philosophical discussions in *Voyage du monde de Descartes* ("Voyage to the World of Descartes" 1690) whilst Murtagh McDermot's *A Trip to the Moon* (1728), which clearly lampoons Lucian and Godwin, takes the narrator to the Moon by whirlwind. McDermot did, though, consider the power of gunpowder and his adventurer is blasted back to Earth via a violent explosion.

Of particular interest in these Cyrano-inspired works was *Iter Lunare, or a Voyage to the Moon* (1703) by the outspoken ship's chandler David Russen. Russen had read Cyrano's book in the 1659 English translation by Thomas St. Serf, *Selenarchia*, and revelled in its possibilities. *Iter Lunare* is one long review of Cyrano's ideas peppered with new thoughts and proposals by Russen, who was pragmatic enough to realize that "to ascend to the Moon is a matter of no small difficulty." Russen reviewed the suggestions by Cyrano and others, and even proposed a deliberately preposterous idea of his own—that man be catapulted to the Moon via a giant spring fixed on a mountain top—but was uncertain that any would work. He saw the drawbacks as being the difficulty of breaking free of the Earth's "magnetic attraction" and the distance to the Moon with the likely attenuated atmosphere. Moreover, the need to take food and clothing would add to the weight to be transported and thus make it more difficult. Russen concludes that even if all the mechanical and technical problems are overcome, human nature with all its vices, might limit the chances of any such journey. Russen had predicted, quite correctly, that the prospect of reaching the Moon was such a vast undertaking that it needed a determined and supportive humanity to make it work. Which, of course, is exactly what happened in the early space programme.

For the most part, the eighteenth century saw the Moon as an alternate Earth allowing for satirical comments upon the institutions and beliefs of Earth (i.e. Britain) with only some scientific speculation. Very little thought went into any realistic method of transport. In *The Consolidator* (1705), for instance, which Daniel Defoe wrote over a decade before *Robinson Crusoe*, we find that the eponymous Consolidator is a machine, originally invented centuries before by the Chinese, powered by liquid-fuelled engines which flap enormous feathered wings. But this is all a metaphor for the British Parliament, with each feather representing a Member of Parliament. Defoe proposes several wonderful inventions, all created by the Chinese who have long had contact with the Lunar civilization. These include one that writes down speeches, and one that helps enhance thoughts.

There are also references to super "tellescopes" and although in Defoe's case it is a sarcastic reference to people seeing what they want to see, it was the development in optics, coupled with the arrival of balloon flight, which would move lunar fiction on beyond the many reworkings of Lucian, Godwin and Cyrano.

It is, perhaps, surprising that no writer had yet considered the idea of a lighter-than-air vessel for flight especially as in 1670 Francesco Lana de Terzi, an Italian Jesuit mathematician and naturalist, had proposed the principle in his book *Prodromo*. His design was essentially a ship with a sail supported by four evacuated globes. It was later realized that the principle was flawed and that the ship would be too heavy, but had the properties of hydrogen been known, his air-ship would have flown. Hydrogen was not isolated until the experiments of Henry Cavendish in the 1760s. Until then the only substance known to be lighter than air was hot air. In 1709 the Brazilian Jesuit Bartolomeu de Gusmão had demonstrated a model hot-air balloon to King John V of Portugal in Lisbon. Gusmão worked further on his design hoping to create one capable of carrying people but he died of a fever before he could complete it. So it was not until November 1783 that, following earlier unmanned demonstrations by the brothers Joseph and Jacques Montgolfier, the first untethered manned flight took place. The honour as the first aeronauts goes to Pilâtre de Rozier and the Marquis d'Arlandes. They reached a height of 3,000 feet and travelled over five miles. Soon afterward, the scientist Jacques Charles ascended to over 500 feet in a balloon filled with hydrogen. The age of aeronautics was born.

It should therefore be no surprise if the first fictional use of balloons for a lunar voyage would be by a Frenchman, but in fact it was by a Belgian, and a lady at that, Cornélie Wouters, the Baroness de Vasse. In her highly philosophical novel *Le Char Volant; ou, Voyage dans la lune* ("The Flaming Chariot; or, a Voyage in the Moon", 1783) two men manage to reach the Moon and discover it is ruled by women. There are five realms each with a woman in charge creating a Universal Monarchy. Wouters shows the analogy between the five realms and the five human senses which together create a unified whole. The women of the Moon find the two humans repellent, because of their smell and vices. The Moon is a feminine utopia whilst the Earth is a masculine hell.

The first French lunar balloon voyage was *Le Retour de mon pauvre uncle* ("The Return of my Poor Uncle", 1784), published anonymously but by the architect Jacques-Antoine Dulaure. It is somewhat spoiled by the absurd notion that the explorer reaches the Moon by filling *himself* with hydrogen, though he does have the sense to return in a more orthodox balloon. Unfortunately the rest of the short work is a typical satire, with the lunar civilization being much like Earth's.

An Account of Count D'Artois and His Friend's Passage to the Moon (1785) by the young Connecticut Yankee, Daniel Moore, is something of a religious monograph. Two Frenchmen lose control of their balloon and are taken to the Moon which is populated by Hebrew-speaking humans who have remained in a perfect state of Grace. There they learn how they might regain their lost innocence and create a utopia on Earth.

In similar vein, though more vitriolic, is *A Voyage to the Moon* (1793), subtitled "Strongly Recommended to All Lovers of Real Freedom", with an introduction signed by the pseudonymous Aratus. The narrator travels to the Moon by balloon and lands in the continent of Barsilia near its capital Augustina. Barsilia is a thinly disguised England which Aratus portrays as a dystopian regime overlorded by the Great Snake. There are several tiers of Snakes, all of whom walk upright like humans, and the vast majority toil like slaves. The book, a little over forty pages long, appearing at the same time as both the French and American Revolutions, is a clear exhortation to rebellion.

Whilst the balloon now became the de rigueur mode of lunar transport, it disregarded the long-established fact that there was no atmosphere between the Earth and the Moon, though there remained a belief that there must be some form of medium called the "ether", the existence of which was not categorically disproved until 1887. Until then writers had an excuse, and an ether ship appears in *Aleriel, or a Voyage to Other Worlds* (1883) by W.S. Lach-Szyrma. This book is unusual both because it is narrated by a Venusian, an explorer who is visiting all the planets, and because it gives an image of a dead Moon. "Not a city, not a house, not a tree, not even a blade of grass was to be seen," Aleriel reports. "All horror, desolation, death!"

Scientific research continued to further our understanding of the Moon. At the end of the eighteenth century the most famous astronomer in the world was William Herschel, German born but long resident in England. With the help of his sister, Caroline, they ground the most accurate lenses yet produced and with them created the most superior telescopes. As a result in 1781 Herschel became the first astronomer to discover a new planet, later called Uranus.

Despite this and other remarkable discoveries, he also became the victim of his own achievements. He caused a stir in 1780 with his paper "Observations on the Mountains of the Moon" where he claimed he had observed forests on the Moon and believed that the

Moon was inhabited. His notes also contained thoughts that the small craters on the Moon were towns built in this circular formation (he called them "Circuses") to help refract the light. His beliefs rather disturbed the then Astronomer Royal, Nevil Maskelyne, who visited Herschel and reprimanded him, but when Herschel discovered Uranus a year later there was no stopping his reputation.

That reputation extended to his son, John, who continued his father's work after his death in 1822, methodically cataloguing the distant stars and nebulae. Having completed this for the Northern Hemisphere in November 1833 he moved south, setting up base in the Cape Colony, South Africa, to map and catalogue the southern skies, a project that would take four years. With his powerful new telescope and his by now legendary status everything was expected of him, so it was no surprise when the *New York Sun* published a series of reports in the last week of August 1835 declaring that Herschel had discovered life on the Moon.

The story broke in the *Sun* for 25 August 1835 with the headline:

GREAT ASTRONOMICAL DISCOVERIES LATELY MADE BY SIR JOHN
HERSCHEL, LL.D., F.R.S., &C. AT THE CAPE OF GOOD HOPE

It claimed to be reprinted from the Supplement of the Edinburgh *Journal of Science* and to be written by Dr. Andrew Grant, a colleague of Sir John Herschel and a former pupil of William Herschel. The first report held back the main story and instead gave details of the nature of Herschel's magnificent new telescope with a magnifying power of 6,000, meaning that he could observe the Moon as if it were only forty miles away and could discern objects as small as 22 yards across. None of this was true, but it was delivered with such technical verisimilitude that there was no reason for anyone to doubt it. Having ensnared its readers, the next day the Sun began the full revelations with the headline NEW LUNAR DISCOVERIES. Over the next five days the paper revealed the discovery of all forms of life on the Moon, from forests and grazing animals to human-like beings with batwings.

The reports took not only North America by storm but most of Europe. The newspaper reissued the details in a pamphlet along with a set of lithographs showing the scenes on the Moon. Sales of these were reported to be around 60,000 copies. Further pamphlets were reprinted in Great Britain, France and elsewhere. It was only when the New York *Journal of Commerce* planned to reprint the story that the reporter who had perpetrated the hoax admitted it was all a fabrication.

That reporter was an Englishman, Richard Adams Locke (1800–71), a native of Somerset. Raised as a farmer he turned his back on his patrimony to become a writer and journalist but most papers shunned him because of his radical views. He emigrated to the United States with his wife and young child in January 1832, and rapidly established himself. His fame did not last, however. He remained a writer for much of his life but in his later years he became a Customs Officer for which he had to fabricate his birth as being in New York. Locke was evidently a hoaxer to the end. His story was reprinted many times, taking on the title *The Moon Hoax* in an edition in 1859. It has remained what many claim to be one of the most elaborate and successful of all newspaper hoaxes, the equivalent of today's "fake news".

Sir John Herschel first accepted it as a joke though soon tired of it but his wife, Margaret, thought it "a very clever piece of imagination" and rather hoped it had been true. As such, just like the later reports of the discovery of canals on Mars, "The Moon Hoax" may be seen as the start of the public's modern fascination with the possibility of extraterrestrial life.

An author who was rather annoyed at the Moon Hoax was Edgar Allan Poe. He had only just published his story "Hans Phaall—A Tale" in the June 1835 *Southern Literary Messenger*. Phaall needed to escape from his creditors and creates a large balloon filled with a new form of "atomic hydrogen" which is lighter than normal hydrogen. This whisks him away in a sealed basket (with an air condenser) to the Moon where he is greeted by the Lunarians, who are all dwarves. The story ends there but Poe had planned a sequel which he now found impossible to write, thanks to Locke's hoax. Poe later wrote his own hoax story, usually reprinted as "The Balloon Hoax". in 1844, about the first transatlantic balloon crossing, but this did not cause the same sensation as Locke's.

Although the balloon continued to be used in fiction as a mode of lunar transport, the increasing belief that there was no atmosphere in space meant authors looked for other ideas. The first original concept had already appeared in *A Voyage to the Moon* (1827) by George Tucker, the Professor of Moral Philosophy at the University of Virginia. The book is narrated by and credited to Joseph Atterley who, on his travels, is shipwrecked off Burma. He discovers, thanks to a local Brahmin, that inland is a deposit of "lunarium", a metal which repulses the Earth and is attracted to the Moon. A vessel partly coated with this and with various controls can thus leave the Earth and be drawn to the Moon. Tucker makes the vessel airtight and with compressed air on board. Unfortunately, the rest of the novel is a lunar travelogue and satire. Nevertheless, lunarium is the first suggestion of antigravity.

A more rigorous scientific proposal for antigravity was put forward by the naturalist John L. Riddell in 1847, another form of hoax.

Orrin Lindsay's Plan of Aerial Navigation purports to be a lecture by
Riddell who had received an account by Lindsay of his trip to, but
not landing on, the Moon. Lindsay had developed a special amalgam
from mercury and steel which, when placed in a strong magnetic
field, negates the pull of the Earth. He constructs a sphere coated in
the amalgam with shutters to cut off the forces as required—a system
just like H.G. Wells used in *The First Men in the Moon*. The story is
full of intricate technical and scientific measurement to ensure not
only a safe journey but one that can be accurately recorded. After
a test flight Lindsay and a companion take a journey into space but
rather than land on the Moon they orbit it. They recognize that it is
a dead world, though on the far side they witness an active volcano.
In its detail and thoroughness it is reckoned as the first true work
of "hard" science fiction.

Despite being a landmark work, Riddell's story was little known
and thus influenced few, if any. Nevertheless, authors continued to
experiment. Charles Rumball's children's book *The Marvellous and
Incredible Adventures of Charles Thunderbolt on the Moon* (1851), written
under the alias of Charles Delorme, features the first steam-powered
spaceship. In *A History of a Voyage to the Moon* (1864), the pseudonymous Chrysostom Trueman further developed the antigravity material with his *repellante* which is mined in Colorado. On the moon
they discover an ideal society whose people are only four-feet high
and appear to be reincarnations of people from Earth, though they
have no memory of their Earthly existence.

What followed next is where many believe science fiction began.
In *De la terre à la lune* ("From the Earth to the Moon", 1865) and its
sequel *Autour de la lune* ("Round the Moon", 1869) Jules Verne gave
an intricate description of how a lunar journey could be developed, organized and fulfilled. Verne took no notice of balloons or

anti-gravity but seriously considered how a projectile might be fired from a huge cannon. Verne chose as his launch site Tampa, Florida, not too far from Cape Canaveral. It was not originally intended to fire a manned capsule, but rather send a projectile to the Moon to alert any inhabitants of America's advanced technology. However, the Frenchman Michel Ardan insists he wants to be the world's first man in space so the capsule is adapted to accommodate not only Ardan but the two leading members of the Baltimore Gun Club who have planned the mission, Impey Barbicane and Captain Nicholl. The first book is filled with detailed technical descriptions and ends with the missile being fired into space, fate unknown. There was, even then, much debate over whether the humans would withstand the pressure of the launch, which Verne deliberately sidestepped. He eventually wrote the sequel, but realized that there was no way he could have the capsule return to Earth if it landed on the Moon, so the second novel has them orbit the Moon, taking such observations as they could, and returning to Earth. They believed the Moon was lifeless. Verne sensibly has the capsule land in the sea from whence the lunarnauts are rescued, which is what happened to the Apollo astronauts a century later.

It is apparent that despite various ways of reaching the Moon, the principle of the rocket had not been seriously explored. Although Cyrano de Bergerac had included firework rockets in his story, no one had taken that to the next stage. At least, not to the moon. There was a juvenile book, *Gulliver Joi* (1852) by Elbert Perce which was a clear derivative of *Gulliver's Travels*. A descendant of Gulliver is shipwrecked on an island where dwells an old scientist who happens to have a powerful telescope, a big cylinder, large enough for the narrator to enter, and a reddish powder which ignites sufficiently to power the cylinder. So, it's getting close to being a rocket. The narrator visits a new planet, Kailoo. In the book, he has further adventures, but by balloon, so the potential of rocketry was soon abandoned.

John Munro took us one step nearer in *A Trip to Venus* (1897). He explores several methods one of which is a compound cannon (operated by electro-magnetism), each one firing a smaller cannon until escape velocity is reached and then, once in space, rockets control the ship's speed and direction. As an alternative, Munro also proposes an anti-gravity device. Munro is represented in this anthology with one of his shorter pieces.

It is not clear in H.G. Wells's *The War of the Worlds* (1898) whether the Martian invaders use rockets or whether their space cylinders are fired by giant cannon. In fact, neither British nor American writers showed much interest in rockets. Writers continued to consider balloons, or antigravity, or astral/psychic/dream travel. When the French film director Georges Méliès made the first significant sf film in 1902, *Le voyage dans la lune*, the space vessel was fired from a giant gun, à la Verne.

There was the occasional attempt by US writers to consider rocket propulsion. A rather feeble early example is the humorous "Bagley's Inter-planet Skyrocket" (1908) by Howard Dwight Smiley. Bagley has built a space rocket and dupes his friends into believing he has taken them to the Moon when in fact they've ended up in South Dakota! At the other extreme was "The Planeteer" (1918) by Homer Eon Flint where Martians create a giant rocket out of a volcano to move their planet out of orbit. Curiously, in *Number 87* (1922) by Eden Phillpotts (writing as Harrington Hext) a scientist develops an atomic-powered rocket plane, The Bat, capable of reaching 180,000 miles an hour "in our atmosphere". Since the velocity required to escape Earth's gravity is just over 25,000mph, The Bat should have been well on its way into space but Phillpotts chose to keep it Earthbound! So, generally, no British or American writers gave the rocket serious consideration.

It was down to Russian and German visionaries to pursue the concept. The Russian scientist Konstantin Tsiolkovsky had suggested as early as 1883 that the only way into space was by some form of jet propulsion and he put his thoughts in a series of papers, most importantly "The Probing of Space by Means of Jet Devices" in 1903 which foresaw multi-stage rockets. Tsiolkovsky was also writing fiction though none was published at that time. The most important was *Vne Zemli* ("Out of the Earth") which he had started as early as 1896 and continued to revise, publishing one version in a newspaper in 1916 and a longer version in 1920. He tells of an international team of scientists working in seclusion in Tibet and creating the world's first rocket. It launches them into space, first into orbit and then on to the Moon. They have a moon buggy with which they explore the dark-side of the Moon, where they find a primitive but mobile form of vegetable life. They also discover giant diamonds!

Vne Zemli was eventually translated and published as *Beyond the Earth* in 1960 by which time it had lost its glitter of originality. During his lifetime—Tsiolkovsky lived until 1935—his work became known to others, notably the German scientist Hermann Oberth who wrote his own book about rocketry, *Die Rakete zu den Planetenraumen* ("By Rocket into Planetary Space", 1923). That book inspired many scientists including the rocket pioneer Max Valier, and the young student Wernher von Braun who went on to develop the V-2 rocket during the Second World War. After the War, von Braun was taken to the United States where he helped develop the American space programme.

Oberth's book also inspired the science popularizer Otto Willi Gail. He wrote three science-fiction novels starting with *Der Schuss*

ins All ("The Shot Into Infinity", 1925), where Russians are the first
to launch a rocket into space. It becomes trapped by the moon's
gravity and the Germans launch their own rocket to rescue the
Russians. Oberth was consulted by Fritz Lang for his film *Frau im
Monde* ("Woman in the Moon", 1929) based on the 1928 novel *Die
Frau im Monde*, by his wife Thea von Harbou. The film, released in
the USA as *By Rocket to the Moon*, was the first an audience would
see of a multi-stage rocket.

The Germans had organized the German Rocket Society in June
1927 and it encouraged interest from American and British enthusi-
asts. An American Interplanetary Society was formed in March 1930
and the British Interplanetary Society, of which Arthur C. Clarke
was a member, in October 1933.

By then, Hugo Gernsback had started the first science-fiction
magazine, *Amazing Stories* in April 1926 and he encouraged writers
to explore new ideas and inspire others in turn. One young hopeful,
Charles Cloukey, was, so far as I can ascertain, the first American
to write a story of a rocket flight to the Moon and that story, "Sub-
Satellite" (1928), is included here.

Such were the lunar pioneers. From Lucian to Francis Godwin,
John Wilkins and Cyrano de Bergerac, down through Daniel
Defoe, William Herschel, the Baroness de Wasse, Daniel Moore,
Richard Adams Locke, John L. Riddell, Jules Verne and Konstantin
Tsiolkovsky, amongst many others, each one a rung on a ladder that
took our imagination and later humans to the Moon.

MIKE ASHLEY

DEAD CENTRE

Judith Merril

No one expected that the pioneering journeys to the Moon would go without a hitch. There have been many fatalities during the American and Russian space programmes, the first major tragedy occurring in January 1967 when a pre-flight test in Apollo 1 *ended in a fire which claimed the lives of three astronauts, including Gus Grissom, who had been America's second astronaut in space in July 1961.*

Whilst many writers were producing stories about the adventures of astronauts on the Moon, Judith Merril (1923–1997) considered the effects upon their friends and relatives. "Dead Centre", first published in 1954, was an especially powerful evocation of emotions, hope and pride. So powerful, in fact, that unusual for most science fiction at that time, it was selected by Martha Foley for inclusion in the 1955 volume of her landmark series The Best American Short Stories.

Merril was one of the early post-war women writers of science fiction and was also one of the few at the time to give thought to lunar exploration. Merril also became one of the field's leading editors, compiling twelve volumes of her own S-F: The Year's Greatest Science Fiction and Fantasy *between 1956 and 1968. She was one of the first American authors to champion the New Wave in science fiction which was emerging in Britain in the mid-1960s. She relocated to Canada in 1968 and in 1970 she donated her collection of books to the Toronto Public Library. Initially called the Spaced-Out Library it became* The Merril Collection of Science Fiction, Speculation and Fantasy *in 1990.*

I

T HEY GAVE HIM SWEET ICES, AND KISSED HIM ALL ROUND, and the Important People who had come to dinner all smiled in a special way as his mother took him from the living room and led him down the hall to his own bedroom.

"Great kid you got there," they said to Jock, his father, and "Serious little bugger, isn't he?" Jock didn't say anything, but Toby knew he would be grinning, looking pleased and embarrassed. Then their voices changed, and that meant they had begun to talk about the important events for which the important people had come.

In his own room, Toby wriggled his toes between crisp sheets, and breathed in the powder-and-perfume smell of his mother as she bent over him for a last hurried goodnight kiss. There was no use asking for a story tonight. Toby lay still and waited while she closed the door behind her and went off to the party, click-tap, tip-clack, hurrying on her high silver heels. She had heard the voices change back there too, and she didn't want to miss anything. Toby got up and opened his door just a crack, and set himself down in back of it, and listened.

In the big square living room, against the abstract patterns of grey and vermilion and chartreuse, the men and women moved in easy patterns of familiar acts. Coffee, brandy, cigarette, cigar. Find your partner, choose your seat. Jock sprawled with perfect relaxed contentment on the low couch with the deep red corduroy cover. Tim O'Heyer balanced nervously on the edge of the same couch, wreathed in cigar smoke, small and dark and alert. Gordon Kimberly dwarfed the big easy chair with the bulking importance of him. Ben Stein, shaggy and rumpled as ever, was running a hand through his hair till it too stood on end. He was leaning against a window frame, one hand on the back of the straight chair in which his wife Sue sat, erect and neat and proper and chic, dressed in smart black that set off perfectly her precise blonde beauty. Mrs. Kimberly, just enough overstuffed so that her pearls gave the appearance of *actually* choking her, was the only stranger to the house. She was standing near the doorway, politely admiring Toby's personal art gallery, as Allie Madero valiantly strove to explain each minor masterpiece.

Ruth Kruger stood still a moment, surveying her room and her guests. Eight of them, herself included, and all Very Important People. In the familiar comfort of her own living room, the idea made her giggle. Allie and Mrs. Kimberly both turned to her, questioning. She laughed and shrugged, helpless to explain, and they all went across the room to join the others.

"Guts," O'Heyer said through the cloud of smoke. "How do you do it, Jock? Walk out of a setup like this into... God knows what?"

"Luck," Jock corrected him. "A setup like this helps. I'm the world's pampered darling and I know it."

"Faith is what he means," Ben put in. "He just gets by believing that last year's luck is going to hold up. So it does."

"Depends on what you mean by *luck*. If you think of it as a vector sum composed of predictive powers and personal ability and accurate information and..."

"Charm and nerve and..."

"Guts," Tim said again, interrupting the interrupter.

"All right, all of them," Ben agreed. "*Luck* is as good a word as any to cover the combination."

"We're all lucky people." That was Allie, drifting into range, with Ruth behind him. "We just happened to get born at the right time with the right dream. Any one of us, fifty years ago, would have been called a wild-eyed visiona—"

"Any one of us," Kimberly said heavily, "fifty years ago, would have had a different dream—in time with the times."

Jock smiled, and let them talk, not joining in much. He listened to philosophy and compliments and speculations and comments, and lay sprawled across the comfortable couch in his own living room, with his wife's hand under his own, consciously letting his mind play back and forth between the two lives he lived: this, here... and the perfect mathematic bleakness of the metal beast that would be his home in three days' time.

He squeezed his wife's hand, and she turned and looked at him, and there was no doubt a man could have about what the world held in store.

When they had all gone, Jock walked down the hall and picked up the little boy asleep on the floor, and put him back into his bed. Toby woke up long enough to grab his father's hand and ask earnestly, out of the point in the conversation where sleep had overcome him:

"Daddy, if the universe hasn't got any ends to it, how can you tell where you are?"

"Me?" Jock asked. "I'm right next to the middle of it."

"How do you *know*?"

His father tapped him lightly on the chest.

"Because that's where the middle is." Jock smiled and stood up. "Go to sleep, champ. Good night."

And Toby slept, while the universe revolved in all its mystery about the small centre Jock Kruger had assigned to it.

*

"Scared?" she asked, much later, in the spaceless silence of their bedroom.

He had to think about it before he could answer. "I guess not. I guess I think I ought to be, but I'm not. I don't think I'd do it at all if I wasn't *sure*." He was almost asleep, when the thought hit him, and he jerked awake and saw she was sure enough lying wide-eyed and sleepless beside him, "*Baby!*" he said, and it was almost an accusation. "Baby, *you're* not scared, are you?"

"Not if you're not," she said. But they never could lie to each other.

II

Toby sat on the platform, next to his grandmother. They were in the second row, right in back of his mother and father, so it was all right for him to wriggle a little bit, or whisper. They couldn't hear much of the speeches back there, and what they did hear mostly didn't make sense to Toby. But every now and then Grandma would grab his hand tight all of a sudden, and he understood what the whole thing was about: it was because Daddy was going away again.

His Grandma's hand was very white, with little red and tan dots in it, and big blue veins that stood out higher than the wrinkles in her skin, whenever she grabbed at his hand. Later, walking over to the towering skyscraping rocket, he held his mother's hand; it was smooth and cool and tan, all one colour, and she didn't grasp at him the way Grandma did. Later still, his father's two hands, picking him up to kiss, were bigger and darker tan than his mother's, not so smooth, and the fingers were stronger, but so strong it hurt sometimes.

They took him up in an elevator, and showed him all around the inside of the rocket, where Daddy would sit, and where all the food was stored, for emergency, they said, and the radio and everything. Then it was time to say goodbye.

Daddy was laughing at first, and Toby tried to laugh, too, but he didn't really want Daddy to go away. Daddy kissed him, and he felt like crying because it was scratchy against Daddy's cheek, and the strong fingers were hurting him now. Then Daddy stopped laughing and looked at him very seriously. "You take care of your mother, now," Daddy told him. "You're a big boy this time."

"Okay," Toby said. Last time Daddy went away in a rocket, he was not-quite-four, and they teased him with the poem in the book that said, *James James Morrison Morrison Weatherby George Dupree, Took great care of his mother, though he was only three...* So Toby didn't much like Daddy saying that now, because he knew they didn't really mean it.

"Okay," he said, and then because he was angry, he said, "Only she's supposed to take care of me, isn't she?"

Daddy and Mommy both laughed, and so did the two men who were standing there waiting for Daddy to get done saying goodbye to him. He wriggled, and Daddy put him down.

"I'll bring you a piece of the moon, son," Daddy said, and Toby said, "All right, fine." He reached for his mother's hand, but he found himself hanging onto Grandma instead, because Mommy and Daddy were kissing each other, and both of them had forgotten all about him.

He thought they were never going to get done kissing.

Ruth Kruger stood in the glass control booth with her son on one side of her, and Gordon Kimberly breathing heavily on the other side. *Something's wrong,* she thought, *this time something's wrong.* And then, swiftly, *I mustn't think that way!*

Jealous? she taunted herself. Do you *want* something to be wrong, just because this one isn't all yours, because Argent did some of it?

But if anything is wrong, she prayed, let it be now, right away, so he can't go. If anything's wrong let it be in the firing gear or the... what? Even now, it was too late. The beast was too big and too delicate and too precise. If something went wrong, even now, it was too late. It was...

You didn't finish that thought. Not if you were Ruth Kruger, and your husband was Jock Kruger, and nobody knew but the two of you how much of the courage that had gone twice round the moon, and was about to land on it, was yours. When a man knows his wife's faith is *unshakeable,* he can't help coming back. (But: "Baby! *You're* not scared, are you?")

Twice around the moon, and they called him Jumping Jock. There was never a doubt in anyone's mind who'd pilot the KIM-5, the bulky beautiful beast out there today. Kruger and Kimberly, O'Heyer and Stein. It was a combo. It won every time. *Every* time. Nothing to doubt. No room for doubt.

"Minus five..." someone said into a mike, and there was perfect quiet all around. "Four... three..."

(But he held me too tight, and he laughed too loud...)

"... two... one..."

(Only because he thought *I* was scared, she answered herself.)

"... Mar—"

You didn't even hear the whole word, because the thunder-drumming roar of the beast itself split your ears.

Ringing quiet came down and she caught up Toby, held him tight, tight...

"Perfect!" Gordon Kimberly sighed. *"Perfect!"*

So if anything *was* wrong, it hadn't showed up yet.

She put Toby down, then took his hand. "Come on," she said. "I'll buy you an ice cream soda." He grinned at her. He'd been looking very strange all day, but now he looked real again. His hair had got messed up when she grabbed him.

"We're having cocktails for the press in the conference room," Kimberly said. "I think we could find something Toby would like."

"Wel-l-l-l…" She didn't want a cocktail, and she didn't want to talk to the press. "I think maybe we'll beg off this time…"

"I think there might be some disappointment—" the man started; then Tim O'Heyer came dashing up.

"Come on, babe," he said. "Your old man told me to take personal charge while he was gone." He leered. On him it looked cute. She laughed. Then she looked down at Toby. "What would you rather, Tobe? Want to go out by ourselves, or go to the party?"

"I don't care," he said.

Tim took the boy's hand. "What we were thinking of was having a kind of party here, and then I think they're going to bring some dinner in, and anybody who wants to can stay up till your Daddy gets to the moon. That'll be pretty late. I guess you wouldn't want to stay up late like that, would you?"

Somebody else talking to Toby like that would be all wrong, but Tim was a friend, Toby's friend too. Ruth still didn't want to go to the party, but she remembered now that there had been plans for something like that all along, and since Toby was beginning to look eager, and it *was* important to keep the press on their side…

"You win, O'Heyer," she said. "Will somebody please send out for an ice-cream soda? Cherry syrup, I think it is this week…" She looked inquiringly at her son. "… and… *strawberry* ice cream?"

Tim shuddered. Toby nodded. Ruth smiled, and they all went in to the party.

"Well, young man!" Toby thought the redheaded man in the brown suit was probably what they called a reporter, but he wasn't sure. "How about it? You going along next time?"

"I don't know," Toby said politely. "I guess not."

"Don't you want to be a famous flier like your Daddy?" a strange woman in an evening gown asked him.

"I don't know," he muttered, and looked around for his mother, but he couldn't see her.

They kept asking him questions like that, about whether he wanted to go to the moon. Daddy said he was too little. You'd think all these people would know that much.

Jock Kruger came up swiftly out of dizzying darkness into isolation and clarity. As soon as he could move his head, before he fully remembered why, he began checking the dials and meters and flashing lights on the banked panel in front of him. He was fully aware of the ship, of its needs and strains and motion, before he came to complete consciousness of himself, his weightless body, his purpose, or his memories.

But he was aware of himself as a part of the ship before he remembered his name, so that by the time he knew he had a face and hands and innards, these parts were already occupied with feeding the beast's human brain a carefully prepared stimulant out of a nippled flask fastened in front of his head.

He pressed a button under his index finger in the arm rest of the couch that held him strapped to safety.

"Hi," he said. "Is anybody up besides me?"

He pressed the button under his middle finger and waited.

Not for long.

"Thank God!" a voice crackled out of the loudspeaker. "You really conked out this time, Jock. Nothing wrong?"

"Not so I'd know it. You want… How long was I out?"

"Twenty-three minutes, eighteen seconds, takeoff to reception. Yeah. Give us a log reading."

Methodically, in order, he read off the pointers and numbers on the control panel, the colours and codes and swinging needles and quiet ones that told him how each muscle and nerve and vital organ of the great beast was taking the trip. He did it slowly and with total concentration. Then, when he was all done, there was nothing else to do except sit back and start wondering about that big blackout.

It shouldn't have happened. It never happened before. There was nothing in the compendium of information he'd just sent back to Earth to account for it.

A different ship, different… different men. Two and a half years different. Years of easy living and… growing old? Too old for this game?

Twenty-three minutes!

Last time it was under ten. The first time maybe 90 seconds more. It didn't matter, of course, not at takeoff. There was nothing for him to do then. Nothing now. Nothing for four more hours. He was there to put the beast back down on…

He grinned, and felt like Jock Kruger again. Identity returned complete. *This* time he was there to put the beast down where no man or beast had ever been before. This time they were going to the moon.

III

Ruth Kruger sipped at a cocktail and murmured responses to the admiring, the curious, the envious, the hopeful, and the hateful ones who spoke to her. She was waiting for something, and after an unmeasurable stretch of time Allie Madero brought it to her.

First a big smile seeking her out across the room, so she knew it had come. Then a low-voiced confirmation.

"Wasn't it… an awfully long time?" she asked. She hadn't been watching the clock, on purpose, but she was sure it was longer than it should have been.

Allie stopped smiling. "Twenty-three," she said.

Ruth gasped. "What…?"

"*You* figure it. I can't."

"There's nothing in the ship. I mean nothing was changed that would account for it." She shook her head slowly. This time she didn't know the ship well enough to talk like that. There *could* be something. Oh, *Jock!* "I don't know," she said. "Too many people worked on that thing. I…"

"Mrs. Kruger!" It was the redheaded reporter, the obnoxious one. "We just got the report on the blackout. I'd like a statement from you, if you don't mind, as designer of the ship—"

"I am not the designer of this ship," she said coldly.

"You worked on the design, didn't you?"

"Yes."

"Well, then, to the best of your knowledge…?"

"To the best of my knowledge, there is no change in design to account for Mr. Kruger's prolonged unconsciousness. Had there been any such prognosis, the press would have been informed."

"Mrs. Kruger, I'd like to ask you whether you feel that the innovations made by Mr. Argent could—"

"Aw, lay off, will you?" Allie broke in, trying to be casual and kidding about it; but behind her own flaming cheeks, Ruth was aware of her friend's matching anger. "How much do you want to milk this for, anyhow? So the guy conked out an extra ten minutes. If you want somebody to crucify for it, why don't you pick on one of us who doesn't happen to be married to him?" She turned to Ruth before the man could answer. "Where's Toby? He's probably about ready to bust from cookies and carbonation."

"He's in the lounge," the reporter put in. "Or he was a few minutes—"

Ruth and Allie started off without waiting for the rest. The redhead had been talking to the kid. No telling how many of them were on top of him now.

"I thought Tim was with him," Ruth said hastily, then she thought of something, and turned back long enough to say: "For the record, Mr... uh... I know of no criticism that can be made of any of the work done by Mr. Argent." Then she went to find her son.

There was nothing to do and nothing to see except the instrument meters and dials to check and log and check and log again. Radio stations all around Earth were beamed on him. He could have kibitzed his way to the moon, but he didn't want to. He was thinking.

Thinking back, and forward, and right in this moment. Thinking of the instant's stiffness of Ruth's body when she said she wasn't scared, and the rambling big house on the hill, and Toby politely agreeing when he offered to bring him back a piece of the moon.

Thinking of Toby growing up some day, and how little he really knew about his son, and what would they do, Toby and Ruth, if anything...

He'd never thought that way before. He'd never thought anything except to know he'd come back, because he couldn't stay away. It was always that simple. He couldn't stay away now, either. That hadn't changed. But as he sat there, silent and useless for the time, it occurred to him that he'd left something out of his calculations. *Luck*, they'd been talking about. Yes, he'd had luck. But—what was it Sue had said about a vector sum?—there was more to figure in than your own reflexes and the beast's strength. There was the *outside*. Space... environment... God... destiny. What difference does it make what name you give it?

He couldn't *stay* away... but maybe he could be *kept* away.

He'd never thought that way before.

"You tired, honey?"

"No," he said. "I'm just sick of this party. I want to go home."

"It'll be over pretty soon, Tobe. I think as long as we stayed this long, we better wait for... for the end of the party."

"It's a silly party. You said you'd buy me an ice-cream soda."

"I did, darling," she said patiently. "At least, if I didn't *buy* it, I got it for you. You had it, didn't you?"

"Yes, but you *said* we'd go *out* and have one."

"Look. Why don't you just put your head down on my lap and..."

"I'm no *baby!* Anyhow I'm not tired."

"All right. We'll go pretty soon. You just sit here on the couch, and you don't have to talk to anybody if you don't feel like it. I'll tell you what. I'll go find you a magazine or a book or something to look at, and—"

"I don't *want* a magazine. I want my own book with the pirates in it."

"You just stay put a minute, so I can find you. I'll bring you something."

She got up and went out to the other part of the building where the officers were, and collected an assortment of leaflets and folders with shiny bright pictures of mail rockets and freight transports and jets and visionary moon rocket designs, and took them back to the little lounge where she'd left him.

She looked at the clock on the way. Twenty-seven more minutes. There was *no* reason to believe that anything was wrong.

They were falling now. A man's body is not equipped to sense direction *toward* or *from,* *up* or *down,* without the help of landmarks or gravity. But the body of the beast was designed to know such things; and Kruger, at the nerve centre, knew everything the beast knew.

Ship is extension of self, and self is—extension or limitation?—of ship. If Jock Kruger is the centre of the universe—remember the late night after the party, and picking Toby off the floor?—then ship is extension of self, and the man is the brain of the beast. But if ship *is* universe—certainly continuum; that's universe, isn't it?—then the weakling man-thing in the couch is a limiting condition of the universe. A human brake. He was there to make it stop when it didn't "want" to.

Suppose it wouldn't stop? Suppose it had decided to be a self-determined, free-willed universe?

Jock grinned, and started setting controls. His time was coming. It was measurable in minutes, and then in seconds… *now!*

His hand reached for the firing lever (but *what* was she scared of?), groped, and touched, hesitated, clasped, and pulled.

Grown-up parties at home were fun. But other places, like this one, they were silly. Toby half-woke-up on the way home, enough to realize his Uncle Tim was driving them, and they weren't in their own car. He was sitting on the front seat next to his mother, with his head against her side, and her arm around him. He tried to come all the way awake, to listen to what they were saying, but they weren't talking, so he started to go back to sleep.

Then Uncle Tim said, "For God's sake, Ruth, he's safe, and whatever happened certainly wasn't *your* fault. He's got enough supplies to hold out till…"

"Shh!" his mother said sharply, and then, whispering, "I know."

Now he remembered.

"Mommy…"

"Yes, hon?"

"Did Daddy go to the moon all right?"

"Y… yes, dear."

Her voice was funny.

"Where is it?"

"Where's what?"

"The moon."

"Oh. We can't see it now, darling. It's around the other side of the earth."

"Well, when is he going to come *back*?"

Silence.

"*Mommy… when?*"

"As soon as… just as soon as he can, darling. Now go to sleep."

And now the moon was up, high in the sky, a gilded football dangling from Somebody's black serge lapel. When she was a little girl, she used to say she loved the man in the moon, and now the man in the moon loved her too, but if she was a little girl still, somebody would tuck her into bed, and pat her head and tell her to go to sleep, and she would sleep as easy, breathe as soft, as Toby did…

But she wasn't a little girl, she was all grown up, and she married the man, the man in the moon, and sleep could come and sleep could go, but sleep could never stay with her while the moonwash swept the window panes.

She stood at the open window and wrote a letter in her mind and sent it up the path of light to the man in the moon. It said:

"Dear Jock: Tim says it wasn't my fault, and I can't explain it even to him. I'm sorry, darling. Please to stay alive till we can get to you. Faithfully yours, Cassandra."

IV

The glasses and ashes and litter and spilled drinks had all been cleared away. The table top gleamed in polished stripes of light and dark, where the light came through the louvred plastic of the wall. The big chairs were empty, waiting, and at each place, arranged with the precision of a formal dinner-setting, was the inevitable pad of yellow paper, two freshly-sharpened pencils, a small neat pile of typed white sheets of paper, a small glass ashtray and a shining empty water glass. Down the centre of the table, spaced for comfort, three crystal pitchers of ice and water stood in perfect alignment.

Ruth was the first one there. She stood in front of a chair, fingering the little stack of paper on which someone (Allie? She'd have had to be up early to get it done so quickly) had tabulated the details of yesterday's events. "To refresh your memory," was how they always put it.

She poured a glass of water, and guiltily replaced the pitcher on the exact spot where it had been; lit a cigarette, and stared with dismay at the burnt match marring the cleanliness of the little

ashtray; pulled her chair in beneath her and winced at the screech
of the wooden leg across the floor.

Get it over with! She picked up the typed pages, and glanced at
them. Two at the bottom were headed "Recommendations of U.S.
Rocket Corps to Facilitate Construction of KIM-VIII." That could
wait. The three top sheets she'd better get through while she was
still alone.

She read slowly and carefully, trying to memorize each sentence,
so that when the time came to talk, she could think of what had
happened this way, from outside, instead of remembering how it
had been for *her.*

There was nothing in the report that she didn't already know.

Jock Kruger had set out in the KIM-VII at 5:39 P.M., C.S.T., just
at sunset. First report after recovery from blackout came at 6:02-
plus. First log readings gave no reason to anticipate any difficulty.
Subsequent reports and radioed log readings were, for Kruger,
unusually terse and formal, and surprisingly infrequent; but earth-
to-ship contact at twenty-minute intervals had been acknowledged.
No reason to believe Kruger was having trouble at any time during
the trip.

At 11:54, an attempt to call the ship went unanswered for 56
seconds. The radioman here described Kruger's voice as "irritable"
when the reply finally came, but all he said was, "Sorry. I was firing
the first brake." Then a string of figures, and a quick log reading—
everything just what you'd expect.

Earth acknowledged, and waited.

Eighteen seconds later:

"Second brake." More figures. Again, everything as it should be.
But twenty seconds after that call was completed:

"This is Kruger. Anything wrong with the dope I gave you?"

"Earth to Kruger. Everything okay in our book. Trouble?"

"Track me, boy. I'm off."

"You want a course correction?"

"I can figure it quicker here. I'll keep talking as I go. Stop me if I'm wrong by your book." More figures, and Kruger's calculations coincided perfectly with the swift work done at the base. Both sides came to the same conclusion, and both sides knew what it meant. The man in the beast fired once more, and once again, and made a landing.

There was no reason to believe that either ship or pilot had been hurt. There was no way of finding out. By the best calculations, they, were five degrees of arc around onto the dark side. And there was no possibility at all, after that second corrective firing that Kruger had enough fuel left to take off again. The last thing Earth had heard, before the edge of the moon cut off Kruger's radio, was:

"Sorry, boys. I guess I fouled up this time. Looks like you'll have to come and..."

One by one, they filled the seats: Gordon Kimberly at one end, and the Colonel at the other; Tim O'Heyer to one side of Kimberly, and Ruth at the other; Allie, with her pad and pencil poised, alongside Tim; the Colonel's aide next down the line, with his little silent stenotype in front of him; the Steins across from him, next to Ruth. With a minimum of formality, Kimberly opened the meeting and introduced Col. Swenson.

The Colonel cleared his throat. "I'd like to make something clear," he said. "Right from the start, I want to make this clear. I'm here to help. Not to get in the way. My presence does not indicate any—*criticism* on the part of the Armed Services. We are entirely satisfied with the work you people have been doing." He cleared his throat again, and Kimberly put in:

"You saw our plans, I believe, Colonel. Everything was checked and approved by your outfit ahead of time."

"Exactly. We had no criticism then, and we have none now. The rocket program is what's important. Getting Kruger back is important, not just for ordinary humanitarian reasons—pardon me, Mrs. Kruger, if I'm too blunt—but for the sake of the whole program. Public opinion, for one thing. That's your line, isn't it, Mr. O'Heyer? And then, *we have to find out what happened!*

"I came down here today to offer any help we can give you on the relief ship, and to make a suggestion to facilitate matters."

He paused deliberately this time.

"Go ahead, Colonel," Tim said. "We're listening."

"Briefly, the proposal is that you all accept temporary commissions while the project is going on. Part of that report in front of you embodies, the details of the plan. I hope you'll find it acceptable. You all know there is a great deal of—necessary, I'm afraid—*red tape,* you'd call it, and 'going through channels,' and such in the Services. It makes cooperation between civilian and military groups difficult. If we can all get together as one outfit 'for the duration,' so to speak…"

This time nobody jumped into the silence. The Colonel cleared his throat once more.

"Perhaps you'd best read the full report before we discuss it any further. I brought the matter up now just to—to let you know the *attitude* with which we are submitting the proposal to you…"

"Thank you, Colonel." O'Heyer saved him. "I've already had a chance to look at the report. Don't know that anyone else has, except of course Miss Madero. But I personally, at least, appreciate your attitude. And I think I can speak for Mr. Kimberly too…"

He looked sideways at his boss; Gordon nodded.

"What I'd like to suggest now," O'Heyer went on, "since I've seen the report already, and I believe everyone else would like to have a chance to bone up some—perhaps you'd like to have a first-hand look at some of our plant, Colonel? I could take you around a bit...?"

"Thank you. I would like to." The officer stood up, his gold Rocket Corps uniform blazing in the louvered light. "If I may say so, Mr. O'Heyer, you seem remarkably sensible, for a—well, a *publicity* man."

"That's all right, Colonel." Tim laughed easily. "I don't even think it's a dirty word. You seem like an all-right guy yourself—for an *officer*, that is."

They all laughed then, and Tim led the blaze of glory out of the room while the rest of them settled down to studying the R.C. proposals. When they had all finished, Kimberly spoke slowly, voicing the general reaction:

"I hate to admit it, but it makes sense."

"They're being pretty decent about it, aren't they?" Ben said. "Putting, it to us as a proposal instead of pulling a lot of weight."

He nodded. "I've had a little contact with this man Swenson before, He's a good man to work with. It... makes sense, that's all."

"On paper, anyhow," Sue put in.

"Well, Ruth..." the big man turned to her, waiting. "You haven't said anything."

"I... it seems all right to me," she said, and added: "Frankly, Gordon, I don't know that I ought to speak at all. I'm not quite sure why I'm here."

Allie looked up sharply, questioning, from her notes; Sue pushed back her chair and half-stood. "My God, you're not going to back out on us now?"

"I… look, you all know I didn't do any of the real work on the last one. It was Andy Argent's job, and a good one. I've got Toby to think about, and…"

"Kid, we *need* you," Sue protested. "Argent can't do this one; this is going to be another Three, only more so. Unmanned, remote-control stuff, and no returning atmosphere-landing problems. This is up your alley. It's…" She sank back; there was nothing else to say.

"That's true, Ruth." Tim had come back in during the last out-burst. Now he sat down. "Speed is what counts, gal. That's why we're letting the gold braid in on the job—we are, aren't we?" Kimberly nodded; Tim went on: "With you on the job, we've got a working team. With somebody new—well, you know what a ruckus we had until Sue got used to Argent's blueprints, and how Ben's pencil notes used to drive Andy wild. And we can't even use him this time. It's not his field. He did do a good job, but we'd have to start in with somebody new all over again…" He broke off, and looked at Kimberly.

"I hope you'll decide to work with us, Ruth," he said simply.

"If… obviously, if it's the best way to get it done *quick,* I will," she said. "Twenty-eight hours a day if you like."

Tim grinned. "I guess we can let the braid back in now…?" He got up and went to the door.

Another Three, only more so… Sue's words danced in her mind while the Colonel and the Colonel's aide marched in, and took their places, while voices murmured politely, exchanging good will.

Another Three—the first ship she had designed for Kimberly. The ship that made her rich and famous, but that was nothing, because it was the ship that brought Jock to her that made him write the letter, that made her meet him, that led to the Five and Six and now…

"I've got some ideas for a manned ship," he'd written. "If we could get together to discuss it some time…"

"... pleasure to know you'll be working with us, Mrs. Kruger."
She shook her head sharply, and located in time and place.

"Thank you, Colonel. I want to do what I can, of course..."

v

James James Morrison's mother put on a golden gown...

Toby knew the whole thing, almost, by heart. The little boy in the
poem *told* his mother not to *go down to the end of the town,* wherever
that was, unless she took him along. And she said she wouldn't, but
she put on that golden gown and went, and thought she'd be back
in time for tea. Only she wasn't. She never came back at all. *Last seen
wandering vaguely... King John said he was sorry...*

Who's King John? And what time is tea?

Toby sat quietly beside his mother on the front seat of the car,
and looked obliquely at the golden uniform she wore, and could not
find a way to ask the questions in his mind.

Where was James James's *father?* Why did James James have
to be the one to keep his mother from going down to the end of
the town?

"Are you in the Army now, Mommy?" he asked.

"Well... sort of. But not for long, darling. Just till Daddy comes
home."

"When is Daddy coming home?"

"Soon. Soon, I hope. Not too long."

She didn't sound right. Her voice had a cracking sound like
Grandma's, and other old ladies. She didn't look right, either, in
that golden-gown uniform. When she kissed him goodbye in front
of the school, she didn't *feel* right. She didn't even *smell* the same
as she used to.

"'Bye, boy. See you tonight," she said—the same words she always said, but they sounded different.

"'Bye." He walked up the driveway and up the front steps and down the corridor and into the pretty-painted room where his teacher was waiting. Miss Callahan was nice. Today she was *too* nice. The other kids teased him, and called him teacher's pet. At lunch time he went back in the room before anybody else did, and made pictures all over the floor with the coloured chalk. It was the worst thing he could think of to do. Miss Callahan made him wash it all up, and she wasn't nice any more for the rest of the afternoon.

When he went out front after school, he couldn't see the car anywhere. It was true then. His mother had put on that golden gown, and now she was gone. Then he saw Grandma waving to him out of *her* car, and he remembered Mommy had said Grandma would come and get him. He got in the car, and she grabbed at him like she always did. He pulled away.

"Is Daddy home yet?" he asked.

Grandma started the car. "Not yet," she said, and she was crying. He didn't dare ask about Mommy after that, but she wasn't home when they got there. It was a long time after that till dinner was ready.

She came home for dinner, though.

"You have to allow for the human factor..."

Nobody had said it to her, of course. Nobody would. She wondered how much tougher it made the job for everybody, having her around. She wondered how she'd stay sane, if she didn't have the job to do.

Thank God Toby was in school now! She couldn't do it, if it meant leaving him with someone else all day—even his grandmother. As it was, having the old lady in the house so much was nerve-racking.

I ought to ask her if she'd like to sleep here for a while, Ruth thought, and shivered. Dinner time was enough.

Anyhow, Toby liked having her there, and that's what counted.

I'll have to go in and see his teacher. Tomorrow, she thought. I've got to make time for it tomorrow. Let her know... but of course she knew. Jock Kruger's family's affairs were hardly private. Just the same, I better talk to her...

Ruth got out of bed and stood at the window, waiting for the moon. Another ten minutes, fifteen, twenty maybe, and it would edge over the hills on the other side of town. The white hands on the clock said 2:40. She had to get some sleep. She couldn't stand here waiting for the moon. Get to sleep now, before it comes up. That's better...

Oh, *Jock!*

"... the human factor..." They didn't know. She wanted to go tell them all, find somebody right away, and shout it. *"It's not his fault. I did it!"*

"You're *not scared, are you, baby?"*

Oh, no! No, no! Don't be silly. Who, me? Just stiff and trembling. The cold, you know...?

Stop that!

She stood at the window, waiting for the moon, the man, the man in the moon.

Human factor... well, there wouldn't be a human factor in this one. If she went out to the field on takeoff day and told KIM-VIII she was scared, it wouldn't matter at all.

Thanks God I can do something, at least!

Abruptly, she closed the blind, so she wouldn't know when it came, and pulled out the envelope she'd brought home; switched on the bed light, and unfolded the first blueprints.

It was all familiar. Just small changes here and there. Otherwise, it was the Three all over again—the first unmanned ship to be landed successfully on the moon surface. The only important difference was that this one had to have some fancy gadgetry on the landing mech. Stein had given her the orbit calcs today. The rest of the job was hers and Sue's: design and production. Between them, they could do it. What they needed was a goldberg that would take the thing once around low enough to contact Jock, if... to contact him, that's all. Then back again, prepared for him to take over the landing by remote, according to instructions, if he wanted to. If he could. If his radio was working. If...

Twice around, and then down where they figured he was, if he hadn't tried to bring it down himself.

It was complicated, but only quantitatively. Nothing basically new, or untried. And no *human* factors to be allowed for, once it was off the ground.

She fell asleep, finally, with the light still on, and the blind drawn, and the blueprints spread out on the floor next to the bed.

Every day, she drove him to school, dressed in her golden gown. And every afternoon, he waited, telling himself she was sure to come home.

That was a very silly little poem, and he wasn't three, he was six now.

But it was a long time since Daddy went away.

"I'd rather not," she said stiffly.

"I'm sorry, Ruth. I know—well, I *don't* know, but I can imagine how you feel. I hate to ask it, but if you can do it at all... just be there and look confident, and... *you* know."

Look confident! I couldn't do it for Jock, she thought; why should I do it for *them?* But of course that was silly. They didn't know her the way Jock did. They couldn't read her smiles, or sense a barely present stiffness, or know anything except what she chose to show on the front of her face.

"Look confident? What difference does it make, Tim? If the thing works, they'll all know soon enough. If..."

She stopped.

"All right, I'll be blunt. If it *doesn't* work, it's going to make a hell of a difference what the public feeling was at the time it went off. If we have to try again. If—damn it, you want it straight, all right! If we can't save Jock, we're not going to give up the whole thing! We're not going to let space travel wait another half century while the psychological effects wear off. *And Jock wouldn't want us to!* Don't forget that. It was his dream, too. It was yours, once upon a time. If..."

"All *right!*" She was startled by her voice. She was screaming, or almost.

"All right," she said bitterly, more quietly. "If you think I'll be holding up progress for fifty years by not dragging Toby along to a launching, I'll come.

"Oh, Ruth, I'm sorry. No, it's not that important. And I had no business talking that way. But listen, babe, you used to understand this—the way I feel, the way Jock fel—feels. Even a guy like Kimberly. You used to feel it too. Look: the single item of you showing your face at the takeoff doesn't amount to much. Neither does one ounce of fuel. But either one could be the little bit that makes the difference. Kid, we got to put *everything* we've got behind it this time."

"All right," she said again. "I told you I'd come."

"You do understand, don't you?" he pleaded.

"I don't know, Tim. I'm not sure I do. But you're right. I would have, once. Maybe—I don't know. It's different for a woman, I guess. But I'll come. Don't worry about it."

She turned and started out.

"Thanks, Ruth. And I *am* sorry. Uh—want me to come and pick you up?"

She nodded. "Thanks." She was glad she wouldn't have to drive.

VI

He kept waiting for a chance to ask her. He couldn't do it in the house before they left, because right after she told him where they were going, she went to get dressed in her golden uniform, and he had to stay with Grandma all the time.

Then Mr. O'Heyer came with the car, and he couldn't ask because, even though he sat up front with Mommy, Mr. O'Heyer was there too.

When they got to the launching field, there were people around all the time. Once he tried to get her off by himself, but all she did was think he had to go to the bathroom. Then, bit by bit, he didn't *have* to ask, because he could tell from the way they were all talking, and the way the cameras were all pointed at her all the time, like they had been at Daddy the other time.

Then there was the speeches part again, and this time *she* got up and talked, so that settled it.

He was glad he hadn't asked. They probably all thought he knew. Maybe they'd even told him, and he'd forgotten, like he sometimes did. "Mommy," he listened to himself in his mind, "Mommy, are you going to the moon too?" Wouldn't that sound silly!

She'd come back for him, he told himself. The other times, when Daddy went some place—like when they first came here to live, and Daddy went first, then Mommy, and then they came back to get him, and some other time, he didn't remember just what—but when Daddy went away, Mommy always went to stay with him, and then they *always* came to get him too.

It wasn't any different from Mommy going back to be with Daddy at a party or something, instead of staying in his room to talk to him when she put him to bed. It didn't feel any worse than that, he told himself.

Only he didn't believe himself.

She never did tell me! I wouldn't of forgotten that! She should of told me!

She did not want to make a speech. Nobody had warned her that she would be called upon to make a speech. It was bad enough trying to answer reporters coherently. She stood up and went forward to the microphone dutifully, and shook hands with the President of the United States, and tried to look confident. She opened her mouth and nothing came out.

"Thank you," she said finally, though she didn't know just what for. "You've all been very kind." She turned to the mike, and spoke directly into it. "I feel that a good deal of honour is being accorded me today which is not rightfully mine. We gave ourselves a two-month limit to complete a job, and the fact that it was finished inside of six weeks instead…"

She had to stop because everybody was cheering, and they wouldn't have heard her.

"… that fact is not something for which the designer of a ship can be thanked. The credit is due to all the people at Kimberly who worked so hard, and to the Rocket Corps personnel who helped so much. I think…"

This time she paused to find the right words. It had suddenly become very important to level with the crowd, to tell them what she honestly felt.

"I think it is I who should be doing the thanking. I happen to be a designer of rockets, but much more importantly, to me, I am Jock Kruger's wife. So I want to thank everyone who helped…"

Grandma's hand tightened around his, and then pulled away to get a handkerchief, because she was crying. Right up here on the platform! Then he realized what Mommy had just said. She said that being Jock Kruger's wife was more important to her than anything else.

It was funny that Grandma should feel bad about that. Everybody else seemed to think it was a right thing to say, the way they were yelling and clapping and shouting. It occurred to Toby with a small shock of surprise that maybe Grandma sometimes felt bad about things the same way he did.

He was sort of sorry he wouldn't have much chance to find out more about that.

She broke away from the reporters and V.I.P.'s, and went and got Toby, and asked him did he want to look inside the rocket before it left.

He nodded. He was certainly being quiet today. Poor kid—he must be pretty mixed up about the whole thing by now.

She tried to figure out what was going on inside the small brown head, but all she could think of was how *much* like Jock he looked today.

She took him up the elevator inside the rocket. There wasn't much room to move around, of course, but they'd rigged it so that all the big shots who were there could have a look. She was a little startled to see the President and her mother-in-law come up together in the next elevator, but between trying to answer Toby's questions, and trying to brush off reporters, she didn't have much time to be concerned about such oddities.

She had never seen Toby so intent on anything. He wanted to know *everything*. Where's this, and what's that for? And where are you going to sit, Mommy?

"I'm not, hon. You know that. There isn't room in this rocket for..."

"Mrs. Kruger, pardon me, but..."

"Just a minute, *please*."

"Oh, I'm sorry."

"What was it you wanted to know now, Tobe?" There were too many people; there was too much talk. She felt slightly dizzy. "Look, hon, I want to go on down." It was hard to talk. She saw Mrs. Kruger on the ramp, and called her, and left Toby with her. Down at the bottom, she saw Sue Stein, and asked her if she'd go take over with Toby and try to answer his questions.

"Sure. Feeling rocky, kid?"

"Kind of." She tried to smile.

"You better go lie down. Maybe Allie can get something for you. I saw her over there..." She waved a vague hand. "You look like hell, kid. Better lie down." Then she rushed off.

He got away from Grandma when Sue Stein came and said Mother wanted her to show him everything. Then he said he was tired and got away from *her*. He could find his Grandma all right, he said.

He'd found the spot he wanted. He could just about wriggle into it, he thought.

★

The loudspeaker crackled over her head. Five minutes now.

The other women who'd been fixing their hair and brightening their lipstick snapped their bags shut and took a last look and ran out, to find places where they could see everything. Ruth stretched out on the couch and closed her eyes. Five minutes now, by herself, to get used to the idea that the job was done.

She had done everything she could do, including coming here today. There was nothing further she could do. From now on, or in five minutes' time, it was out of anyone's hands, but—Whose? And Jock's, of course. Once the relief rocket got there, it was up to him.

If it got there.

If he was there for it to get to.

The way they had worked it, there was a chance at least they'd know the answer in an hour's time. If the rocket made its orbit once, and only once, it would mean he was alive and well and in control of his own ship, with the radio working, and...

And if it made a second orbit, there was still hope. It *might* mean nothing worse than that his radio was out. But that way they would have to wait...

God! It could take months, if the calculations as to where he'd come down were not quite right. If... *if* a million little things that would make it harder to get the fuel from one rocket to the other.

But if they only saw one orbit...

For the first time, she let herself, forced herself to, consider the possibility that Jock was dead. That he would not come back.

He's not dead, she thought. I'd know it if he was. Like I knew something was wrong last time. Like I'd know it now if...

"Sixty seconds before zero," said the speaker.

But there is! She sat bolt upright, not tired or dizzy any more. Now she had faced it, she didn't feel confused. There was something… something dreadfully *wrong*…

She ran out, and as she came on to the open field, the speaker was saying, "Fifty-one."

She ran to the edge of the crowd, and couldn't get through, and had to run, keep running, around the edges, to find the aisle between the cords.

Stop it! she screamed, but not out loud, because she had to use all her breath for running.

And while she ran, she tried to think.

"Minus forty-seven."

She couldn't make them stop without a reason. They'd think she was hysterical…

"… forty-five…"

Maybe she was, at that. Coolly, her mind considered the idea and rejected it. No; there was a problem that hadn't been solved, a question she hadn't answered.

But *what* problem? What…

"Minus forty."

She dashed down between the ropes, toward the control booth. The guard stepped forward, then recognized her, and stepped back. The corridor between the packed crowds went on forever.

"Minus thirty-nine… eight… thirty-seven."

She stopped outside the door of Control, and tried to think, think, *think!*. What *was* it? What could she tell them? How could she convince them? *She knew,* but they'd want to know what, why…

You just didn't change plans at a moment like this.

But if they fired the rocket before she figured it out, before she remembered the problem, and then found an answer, it was as good as murdering Jock. They could never get another one up quickly enough if anything, went wrong this time.

She pushed open the door.

"Stop!" she said. "Listen, you've got to stop. Wait! There's something…"

Tim O'Heyer came and took her arm, and smiled and said something. Something soothing.

"Minus nineteen," somebody said into a microphone, quietly.

She kept trying to explain, and Tim kept talking at her, and when she tried to pull away she realized the hand on her arm wasn't just there to comfort her. He was keeping her from making trouble. He…

Oh, God! If there was just some way to make them understand! If she could only remember *what* was wrong…

"Minus three… two…"

It was no use.

She stopped fighting, caught her breath, stood still, and saw Tim's approving smile, as the word and the flare went off together:

"*Mark!*"

Then, in a dead calm, she looked around and saw Sue.

"Where's Toby?" she asked.

She was looking in the reserved grandstand seats for Mrs. Kruger, when she heard the crowd sigh, and looked up and saw it happening.

The crash fire did not damage the inside of the rocket at all. The cause of the crash was self-evident, as soon as they found Toby Kruger's body wedged into the empty space between the outer hull of the third stage, and the inner hull of the second.

The headlines were not as bad as might have been expected. Whether it was the tired and unholy calm on Ruth Kruger's face that restrained them, or Tim O'Heyer's emergency-reserve supply of

Irish whisky that convinced them, the newsmen took it easy on the story. All America couldn't attend the funeral, but a representative hundred thousand citizens mobbed the streets when the boy was buried; the other hundred and eighty million saw the ceremonies more intimately on their TV sets.

Nobody who heard the quiet words spoken over the fresh grave—a historic piece of poetry to which the author, O'Heyer, could never sign his name—nobody who heard that simple speech remained entirely unmoved. Just where or when or with whom the movement started is still not known; probably it began spontaneously in a thousand different homes during the brief ceremony; maybe O'Heyer had something to do with that part of it, too. Whichever way, the money started coming in, by wire, twenty minutes afterwards; and by the end of the week "Bring Jock Back" was denting more paychecks than the numbers racket and the nylon industry combined.

The KIM-IX was finished in a month. They didn't have Ruth Kruger to design this time, but they didn't need her: the KIM-VIII plans were still good. O'Heyer managed to keep the sleeping-pill story down to a tiny back-page notice in most of the papers, and the funeral was not televised.

Later, they brought back the perfectly preserved, emaciated body of Jock Kruger, and laid him to rest next to his wife and son. He had been a good pilot and an ingenious man. The moon couldn't kill him; it took starvation to do that.

They made an international shrine of the house, and the garden where the three graves lay.

Now they are talking of making an interplanetary shrine of the lonely rocket on the wrong side of the moon.

A VISIT TO THE MOON

George Griffith

It is interesting to compare the previous story with the following and see how different the vision of travelling to the Moon was just fifty years earlier. Here the Moon is seen as an ideal venue for the start of a honeymoon.

Though practically forgotten today, in the mid-1890s George Griffith (1857–1906) was the most popular writer of scientific romances in Britain, even more than H.G. Wells, and certainly the most prolific. He shot to fame in 1893 with his first serialized novel The Angel of the Revolution, in which a new form of flying machine is taken over by anarchists who agree to help the British government fight an invading force of a Franco-Russian axis, provided the anarchists are given control over Britain. The consequences of their victory are explored in a sequel Olga Romanoff, or the Syren of the Skies (1894). These two novels were part of a growing interest in "future war" fiction which was popular in the decades before the First World War. H.G. Wells evidently read his work because Griffith's third novel, The Outlaw of the Air (1895) was cited as having stimulated the imagination of the lead character in Wells's The War in the Air (1908). Alas by the time that book appeared Griffith had died aged only 49, having become an alcoholic.

Griffith was amazingly prolific, publishing nearly fifty books in a career of just fourteen years, during which time he also travelled extensively. Amongst them was A Honeymoon in Space (1901) which follows the adventures of Lord Redgrave and his young wife Zaidie in his airship Astronef which, powered by antigravity, takes them on a tour of the solar system. Before the book's publication an edited version was serialized in Pearson's Magazine, and the following is the start of their honeymoon.

THE ADVENTURES OF ROLLO LENOX SMEATON AUBREY, Earl of Redgrave, and his bride Lilia Zaidie, daughter of the late Professor Hartley Rennick, Demonstrator in Physical Science in the Smith-Oliver University in New York, were first made possible by that distinguished scientist's now famous separation of the Forces of Nature into their positive and negative elements. Starting from the axiom that everything in Nature has its opposite, he not only divided the Universal Force of Gravitation into its elements of attraction and repulsion, but also constructed a machine which enabled him to develop either or both of these elements at will. From this triumph of mechanical genius it was but a step to the magnificent conception which was subsequently realized by Lord Redgrave in the *Astronef.* Lord Redgrave had met Professor Rennick, about a year before his lamented death, when he was on a holiday excursion in the Canadian Rockies with his daughter. The young millionaire nobleman was equally fascinated by the daring theories of the Professor, and by the mental and physical charms of Miss Zaidie. And thus the chance acquaintance resulted in a partnership, in which the Professor was to find the knowledge and Lord Redgrave the capital for translating the theory of the "R. Force" (Repulsive or Antigravitational Force) into practice, and constructing a vessel which would be capable, not only of rising from the earth, but of passing the limits of the terrestrial atmosphere, and navigating with precision and safety the limitless ocean of Space.

Unhappily, before the *Astronef*, or star-navigator, was completed at the works which Lord Redgrave had built for her construction on his estate at Smeaton, in Yorkshire, her inventor succumbed to pulmonary complications following an attack of influenza. This left Lord Redgrave the sole possessor of the secret of the "R. Force." A year after the Professor's death he completed the *Astronef*, and took her across the Atlantic by rising into Space until the attraction of the earth was so far weakened that in a couple of hours' time he was able to descend in the vicinity of New York. On this trial trip he was accompanied by Andrew Murgatroyd, an old engineer who had superintended the building of the *Astronef*. This man's family had been attached to his Lordship's for generations and for this reason he was selected as engineer and steersman of the Navigator of the Stars.

The excitement which was caused, not only in America but over the whole civilized world, by the arrival of the *Astronef* from the distant regions of space to which she had soared; the marriage of her creator to the daughter of her inventor in the main saloon while she hung motionless in a cloudless sky a mile above the Empire City; their return to earth; the wedding banquet; and their departure to the moon, which they had selected as the first stopping-place on their bridal trip—these are now matters of common knowledge. The present series of narratives begins as the earth sinks away from under them, and their Honeymoon in Space has actually begun.

*   *   *

When the *Astronef* rose from the ground to commence her marvellous voyage through the hitherto untraversed realms of Space, Lord Redgrave and his bride were standing at the forward-end of a raised deck which ran along about two-thirds of the length of the cylindrical body of the vessel. The walls of this compartment, which was about fifty feet long by twenty broad, were formed of thick, but perfectly transparent, toughened glass, over which, in cases of necessity, curtains of ribbed steel could be drawn from the floor, which was of teak and slightly convex. A light steel rail ran round it and two stairways ran up from the other deck of the vessel to two hatches, one fore and one aft, destined to be hermetically closed when the *Astronef* had soared beyond breathable atmosphere and was crossing the airless, heatless wastes of interplanetary space.

Lord and Lady Redgrave and Andrew Murgatroyd were the only members of the crew of the Star-navigator. No more were needed, for on board this marvellous craft nearly everything was done by machinery; warming, lighting, cooking, distillation and re-distillation of water, constant and automatic purification of the air, everything, in fact, but the regulation of the mysterious "R. Force" could be done with a minimum of human attention. This, however, had to be minutely and carefully regulated, and her commander usually performed this duty himself.

The developing engines were in the lowest part of the vessel amidships. Their minimum power just sufficed to make the *Astronef* a little lighter than her own bulk of air, so that when she visited a planet possessing an atmosphere sufficiently dense, the two propellers at her stern would be capable of driving her through the air at the rate of about a hundred miles an hour. The maximum power would have sufficed to hurl the vessel beyond the limits of the earth's atmosphere in a few minutes.

When they had risen to the height of about a mile above New York, her ladyship, who had been gazing in silent wonder and admiration at the strange and marvellous scene, pointed suddenly towards the East and said: "Look, there's the moon! Just fancy—our first stopping-place! Well, it doesn't look so very far off at present."

Redgrave turned and saw the pale yellow crescent of the new moon just rising above the eastern edge of the Atlantic Ocean.

"It almost looks as if we could steer straight to it right over the water, only, of course, it wouldn't wait there for us," she went on.

"Oh, it'll be there when we want it, never fear," laughed his lordship, "and, after all, it's only a mere matter of about two hundred and forty thousand miles away, and what's that in a trip that will cover hundreds of millions? It will just be a sort of jumping-off place into space for us."

"Still I shouldn't like to miss seeing it," she said. "I want to know what there is on that other side which nobody has ever seen yet, and settle that question about air and water. Won't it just be heavenly to be able to come back and tell them all about it at home? But fancy me talking stuff like this when we are going, perhaps, to solve some of the hidden mysteries of Creation and, maybe, to look upon things that human eyes were never meant to see," she went on, with a sudden change in her voice.

He felt a little shiver in the arm that was resting upon his, and his hand went down and caught hers.

"Well, we shall see a good many marvels, and, perhaps, miracles, before we come back, but I hardly think we shall see anything that is forbidden. Still, there's one thing we shall do, I hope. We shall solve once and for all the great problem of the worlds—whether they are inhabited or not. By the way," he went on, "I may remind your ladyship that you are just now drawing the last breaths of earthly air which you will taste for some time, in fact until we get back! You may as well take your last look at earth as earth, for the next time you see it, it will be a planet."

She went to the rail and looked over into the enormous void beneath, for all this time the *Astronef* had been mounting towards the zenith. She could see, by the growing moonlight, vast, vague shapes of land and sea. The myriad lights of New York and Brooklyn were mingled in a tiny patch of dimly luminous haze. The air about her had suddenly grown bitterly cold, and she saw that the stars and planets were shining with a brilliancy she had never seen before. Her husband came to her side, and, laying his arm across her shoulder, said:

"Well, have you said goodbye to your native world? It is a bit solemn, isn't it, saying goodbye to a world that you have been born on; which contains everything that has made up your life, everything that is dear to you?"

"Not quite everything!" she said, looking up at him. "At least, I don't think so."

He immediately made the only reply which was appropriate under the circumstances; and then he said, drawing her towards the staircase: "Well, for the present this is our world; a world travelling among worlds, and as I have been able to bring the most delightful of the Daughters of Terra with me, I, at any rate, am perfectly happy. Now, I think it's getting on to supper time, so if your ladyship will go to your household duties, I'll have a look at my engines and make everything snug for the voyage."

The first thing he did when he got on to the main deck, was to hermetically close the two companion-ways; then he went and carefully inspected the apparatus for purifying the air and supplying it with fresh oxygen from the tanks in which it was stored in liquid form. Lastly he descended into the lower hold of the ship and turned on the energy of repulsion to its full extent, at the same time stopping the engines which had been working the propellers.

It was now no longer necessary or even possible to steer the *Astronef*. She was directed solely by the repulsive force which would carry her with ever-increasing swiftness, as the attraction of the earth became diminished, towards that neutral point some two hundred thousand miles away, at which the attraction of the earth is exactly balanced by the moon. Her momentum would carry her past this point, and then the "R. Force" would be gradually brought into play in order to avert the unpleasant consequences of a fall of some forty odd thousand miles.

Andrew Murgatroyd, relieved from his duties in the wheelhouse, made a careful inspection of the auxiliary machinery, which was under his special charge, and then retired to his quarters forward to prepare his own evening meal. Meanwhile her ladyship, with the help of the ingenious contrivances with which the kitchen of the *Astronef* was stocked, and with the use of which she had already made herself quite familiar, had prepared a dainty little *souper à deux*. Her husband opened a bottle of the finest champagne that the cellars of New York could supply, to drink at once to the prosperity of the voyage, and the health of his beautiful fellow-voyager.

When supper was over and the coffee made he carried the apparatus up the stairs on to the glass-domed upper deck. Then he came back and said:

"You'd better wrap yourself up as warmly as you can, dear, for it's a good deal chillier up there than it is here."

When she reached the deck and took her first glance about her, Zaidie seemed suddenly to lapse into a state of somnambulism. The whole heavens above and around were strewn with thick clusters of stars which she had never seen before. The stars she remembered seeing from the earth were only little pinpoints in the darkness compared with the myriads of blazing orbs which were now shooting their rays across the silent void of Space. So many millions of new ones had come into view that she looked in vain for the familiar constellations. She saw only vast clusters of living gems of all colours crowding the heavens on every side of her. She walked slowly round the deck, looking to right and left and above, incapable for the moment either of thought or speech, but only of dumb wonder, mingled with a dim sense of overwhelming awe. Presently she craned her neck backwards and looked straight up to the zenith. A huge silver crescent, supporting, as it were, a dim, greenish coloured body in its arms stretched overhead across nearly a sixth of the heavens.

Her husband came to her side, took her in his arms, lifted her as if she had been a little child, so feeble had the earth's attraction now become, and laid her in a long, low deck-chair, so that she could look at it without inconvenience. The splendid crescent grew swiftly larger and more distinct, and as she lay there in a trance of wonder and admiration she saw point after point of dazzlingly white light flash out on to the dark portions, and then begin to send out rays as though they were gigantic volcanoes in full eruption, and were pouring torrents of living fire from their blazing craters.

"Sunrise on the moon!" said Redgrave, who had stretched himself on another chair beside her. "A glorious sight, isn't it! But nothing to what we shall see tomorrow morning—only there doesn't happen to be any morning just about here."

"Yes," she said dreamily, "glorious, isn't it? That and all the stars— but I can't think of anything yet, Lenox! It's all too mighty and too marvellous. It doesn't seem as though human eyes were meant to look upon things like this. But where's the earth? We must be able to see that still."

"Not from here," he said, "because it's underneath us. Come below, and you shall see Mother Earth as you have never seen her yet."

They went down into the lower part of the vessel, and to the after-end behind the engine-room. Redgrave switched on a couple of electric lights, and then pulled a lever attached to one of the side-walls. A part of the flooring, about 6ft. square, slid noiselessly away; then he pulled another lever on the opposite side and a similar piece disappeared, leaving a large space covered only by absolutely transparent glass. He switched off the lights again and led her to the edge of it, and said:

"There is your native world, dear; that is the earth!"

Wonderful as the moon had seemed, the gorgeous spectacle, which lay seemingly at her feet, was infinitely more magnificent. A vast disc of silver grey, streaked and dotted with lines and points of dazzling light, and more than half covered with vast, glittering, greyish-green expanses, seemed to form, as it were, the floor of the great gulf of space beneath them. They were not yet too far away to make out the general features of the continents and oceans, and fortunately the hemisphere presented to them happened to be singularly free from clouds.

Zaidie stood gazing for nearly an hour at this marvellous vision of the home-world which she had left so far behind her before she could tear herself away and allow her husband to shut the slides again. The greatly diminished weight of her body almost entirely destroyed the fatigue of standing. In fact, at present on board the *Astronef* it was almost as easy to stand as it was to lie down.

There was of course very little sleep for any of the travellers on this first night of their adventurous voyage, but towards the sixth hour after leaving the earth her ladyship, overcome as much by the emotions which had been awakened within her as by physical fatigue, went to bed, after making her husband promise that he would wake her in good time to see the descent upon the moon. Two hours later she was awake and drinking the coffee which Redgrave had prepared for her. Then she went on to the upper deck.

To her astonishment she found on one hand, day more brilliant than she had ever seen it before, and on the other hand, darkness blacker than the blackest earthly night. On the right hand was an intensely brilliant orb, about half as large again as the full moon seen from earth, shining with inconceivable brightness out of a sky black as midnight and thronged with stars. It was the sun, the sun shining in the midst of airless space.

The tiny atmosphere inclosed in the glass-domed space was lighted brilliantly, but it was not perceptibly warmer, though Redgrave warned her ladyship not to touch anything upon which the sun's rays fell directly as she would find it uncomfortably hot. On the other side was the same black immensity of space which she had seen the night before, an ocean of darkness clustered with islands of light. High above in the zenith floated the great silver-grey disc of earth, a good deal smaller now, and there was another object beneath which was at present of far more interest to her. Looking down to the left she saw a vast semi-luminous area in which not a star was to be seen. It was the earth-lit portion of the long familiar and yet mysterious orb which was to be their resting-place for the next few hours.

"The sun hasn't risen over there yet," said Redgrave, as she was peering down into the void. "It's earth-light still. Now look at the other side."

She crossed the deck and saw the strangest scene she had yet beheld. Apparently only a few miles below her was a huge crescent-shaped plain arching away for hundreds of miles on either side. The outer edge had a ragged look, and little excrescences, which soon took the shape of flat-topped mountains projected from it and stood out bright and sharp against the black void beneath, out of which the stars shone up, as it seemed, sharp and bright above the edge of the disc.

The plain itself was a scene of the most awful and utter desolation that even the sombre fancy of a Dante could imagine. Huge mountain walls, towering to immense heights and inclosing great circular and oval plains, one side of them blazing with intolerable light, and the other side black with impenetrable obscurity; enormous valleys reaching down from brilliant day into rayless night—perhaps down into the empty bowels of the dead world itself; vast, grey-white plains lying round the mountains, crossed by little ridges and by long, black lines which could only be immense fissures with perpendicular sides—but all hard grey-white and black, all intolerable brightness or repulsive darkness; not a sign of life anywhere, no shady forests, no green fields, no broad, glittering oceans; only a ghastly wilderness of dead mountains and dead plains.

"What an awful place!" said Zaidie, in a slowly spoken whisper. "Surely we can't land there. How far are we from it?". "About fifteen hundred miles," replied Redgrave, who was sweeping the scene below him with one of the two powerful telescopes which stood on the deck. "No, it doesn't look very cheerful, does it; but it's a marvellous sight for all that, and one that a good many people on earth would give their ears to see from here. I'm letting her drop pretty fast, and we shall probably land in a couple of hours or so. Meanwhile, you may as well get out your moon atlas and your Jules Verne and Flammarion, and study your lunography. I'm going to turn the power a bit astern so that we shall go down obliquely and see more of the lighted disc. We started at new moon so that you should have a look at the full earth, and also so that we could get round to the invisible side while it is lighted up."

They both went below, he to deflect the repulsive force so that one set of engines should give them a somewhat oblique direction, while the other, acting directly on the surface of the moon, simply retarded their fall; and she to get her maps and the ever-fascinating works of Jules Verne and Flammarion. When they got back, the *Astronef* had changed her apparent position, and, instead of falling directly on to the moon, was descending towards it in a slanting direction. The result of this was that the sunlit crescent rapidly grew in breadth, whilst peak after peak and range after range rose up swiftly out of the black gulf beyond. The sun climbed quickly up through the star-strewn, mid-day heavens, and the full earth sank more swiftly still behind them.

Another hour of silent, entranced wonder and admiration followed, and then Lenox remarked to Zaidie: "Don't you think it's about time we were beginning to think of breakfast, dear, or do you think you can wait till we land?"

"Breakfast on the moon!" she exclaimed, "That would be just too lovely for words! Of course we'll wait."

"Very well," he said, "you see that big, black ring nearly below us, that, as I suppose you know, is the celebrated Mount Tycho. I'll try and find a convenient spot on the top of the ring to drop on, and then you will be able to survey the scenery from seventeen or eighteen thousand feet above the plains."

About two hours later a slight jarring tremor ran through the frame of the vessel, and the first stage of the voyage was ended. After a passage of less than twelve hours the *Astronef* had crossed a gulf of nearly two hundred and fifty thousand miles and rested quietly on the untrodden surface of the lunar world.

"We certainly shan't find any atmosphere here," said Redgrave, when they had finished breakfast, "although we may in the deeper parts, so if your ladyship would like a walk we'd better go and put on our breathing dresses."

These were not unlike diving dresses, save that they were much lighter. The helmets were smaller, and made of aluminium covered with asbestos. A sort of knapsack fitted on to the back, and below this was a cylinder of liquefied air which, when passed through the expanding apparatus, would furnish pure air for a practically indefinite period, as the respired air passed into another portion of the upper chamber, where it was forced through a chemical solution which deprived it of its poisonous gases and made it fit to breathe again.

The pressure of air inside the helmet automatically regulated the supply, which was not permitted to circulate into the dress, as the absence of air-pressure on the moon would cause it to instantly expand and probably tear the material, which was a cloth woven chiefly of asbestos fibre. The two helmets could be connected for talking purposes by a light wire communicating with a little telephonic apparatus inside the helmet.

They passed out of the *Astronef* through an air-tight chamber in the wall of her lowest compartment, Murgatroyd closing the first door behind them. Redgrave opened the next one and dropped a short ladder on to the grey, loose, sand-strewn rock of the little plain on which they had stopped. Then he stood aside and motioned for Zaidie to go down first.

She understood him, and, taking his hand, descended the four easy steps. And so hers was the first human foot which, in all the ages since its creation, had rested on the surface of the World that Had Been. Redgrave followed her with a little spring which landed him gently beside her, then he took both her hands and pressed them hard in his. He would have kissed her if he could; but that of course was out of the question.

Then he connected the telephone wire, and hand in hand they crossed the little plateau towards the edge of the tremendous gulf, fifty-four miles across, and nearly twenty thousand feet deep. In the middle of it rose a conical mountain about five thousand feet high, the summit of which was just beginning to catch the solar rays. Half of the vast plain was already brilliantly illuminated, but round the central cone was a vast semi-circle of shadow impenetrable in its blackness.

"Day and night in this same valley, actually side by side!" said Zaidie. Then she stopped, and pointed down into the brightly lit distance, and went on hurriedly: "Look, Lenox, look at the foot of the mountain there! Doesn't that seem like the ruins of a city?"

"It does," he said, "and there's no reason why it shouldn't be. I've always thought that, as the air and water disappeared from the upper parts of the moon, the inhabitants, whoever they were, must have been driven down into the deeper parts. Shall we go down and see?"

"But how?" she said. He pointed towards the *Astronef*. She nodded her helmeted head, and they went back to the vessel. A few minutes later the *Astronef* had risen from her resting-place with a spring which rapidly carried her over half of the vast crater, and then she began to drop slowly into the depths. She grounded as gently as before, and presently they were standing on the lunar surface about a mile from the central cone. This time, however, Redgrave had taken the precaution to bring a magazine rifle and a couple of revolvers with him in case any strange monsters, relics of the vanished fauna of the moon, might still be taking refuge in these mysterious depths. Zaidie, although like a good many American girls, she could shoot excellently well, carried no weapon more offensive than a whole-plate camera and a tripod, which here, of course, only weighed a sixth of their earthly weight.

The first thing that Redgrave did when they stepped out on to the sandy surface of the plain was to stoop down and strike a wax match; there was a tiny glimmer of light which was immediately extinguished.

"No air here," he said "so we shall find no living beings—at any rate, none like ourselves."

They found the walking exceedingly easy although their boots were purposely weighted in order to counteract to some extent the great difference in gravity. A few minutes' sharp walking brought them to the outskirts of the city. It had no walls, and in fact exhibited no signs of preparations for defence. Its streets were broad and well-paved; and the houses, built of great blocks of grey stone joined together with white cement, looked as fresh and unworn as though they had only been built a few months, whereas they had probably stood for hundreds of thousands of years. They were flat roofed, all of one storey and practically of one type.

There were very few public buildings, and absolutely no attempt at ornamentation was visible. Round some of the houses were spaces which might once have been gardens. In the midst of the city, which appeared to cover an area of about four square miles, was an enormous square paved with flag stones, which were covered to the depth of a couple of inches with a light grey dust, and, as they walked across it, this remained perfectly still save for the disturbance caused by their footsteps. There was no air to support it, otherwise it might have risen in clouds about them.

From the centre of this square rose a huge Pyramid nearly a thousand feet in height, the sole building in the great, silent city which appeared to have been raised as a monument, or, possibly, a temple by the hands of its vanished inhabitants. As they approached this they saw a curious white fringe lying round the steps by which it was approached. When they got nearer they found that this fringe was composed of millions of white-bleached bones and skulls, shaped very much like those of terrestrial men except that the ribs were out of all proportion to the rest of the bones.

They stopped awe-stricken before this strange spectacle. Redgrave stooped down and took hold of one of the bones, a huge thigh bone. It broke in two as he tried to lift it, and the piece which remained in his hand crumbled instantly to white powder.

"Whoever they were," said Redgrave "they were giants. When air and water failed above they came down here by some means and built this city. You see what enormous chests they must have had. That would be Nature's last struggle to enable them to breathe the diminishing atmosphere. These, of course, will be the last descendants of the fittest to breathe it; this was their temple, I suppose, and here they came to die—I wonder how many thousand years ago—perishing of heat, and cold, and hunger, and thirst, the last tragedy of a race, which, after all, must have been something like our own."

"It is just too awful for words," said Zaidie. "Shall we go into the temple? That seems one of the entrances up there, only I don't like walking over all those bones."

Her voice sounded very strange over the wire which connected their helmets.

"I don't suppose they'll mind if we do," replied Redgrave, "only we mustn't go far in. It may be full of cross passages and mazes, and we might never get out. Our lamps won't be much use in there, you know, for there's no air. They'll just be points of light, and we shan't see anything but them. It's very aggravating, but I'm afraid there's no help for it. Come along!"

They ascended the steps, crushing the bones and skulls to powder beneath their feet, and entered the huge, square doorway, which looked like a rectangle of blackness against the grey-white of the wall. Even through their asbestos-woven clothing they felt a sudden shock of icy cold. In those few steps they had passed from a temperature of tenfold summer heat into one far below that of the coldest spots on earth. They turned on the electric lamps which were fitted to the breast-plates of their dresses, but they could see nothing save the glow of the lamps. All about them was darkness impenetrable, and so they reluctantly turned back to the doorway, leaving all the mysteries which the vast temple might contain to remain mysteries to the end of time. They passed down the steps again and crossed the square, and for the next half hour Zaidie, who was photographer to the expedition, was busy taking photographs of the Pyramid with its ghastly surroundings, and a few general views of this strange City of the dead.

Then they went back to the *Astronef*. They found Murgatroyd pacing up and down under the dome looking about him with serious eyes, but yet betraying no particular curiosity. The wonderful vessel was at once his home and his idol, and nothing but the direct orders of his master would have induced him to leave her even in a world in which there was probably not a living human being to dispute possession of her.

When they had resumed their ordinary clothing, she rose rapidly from the surface of the plain, crossed the encircling wall at the height of a few hundred feet, and made her way at a speed of about fifty miles an hour towards the regions of the South Pole. Behind them to the north-west they could see from their elevation of nearly thirty thousand feet the vast expanse of the Sea of Clouds. Dotted here and there were the shining points and ridges of light, marking the peaks and crater walls which the rays of the rising sun had already touched. Before them and to right and left of them rose a vast maze of crater-rings and huge ramparts of mountain-walls inclosing plains so far below their summits that the light of neither sun nor earth ever reached them.

By directing the force exerted by what might now be called the propelling part of the engines against the mountain masses, which they crossed to right and left and behind, Redgrave was able to take a zigzag course which carried him over many of the walled plains which were wholly or partially lit up by the sun, and in nearly all of the deepest their telescopes revealed what they had found within the crater of Tycho. At length, pointing to a gigantic circle of white light fringing an abyss of utter darkness, he said:

"There is Newton, the greatest mystery of the moon. Those inner walls are twenty-four thousand feet high; that means that the bottom, which has never been seen by human eyes, is about five thousand feet below the surface of the moon. What do you say, dear—shall we go down and see if the searchlight will show us anything? There may be air there!"

"Certainly!" replied Zaidie decisively, "haven't we come to see things that nobody else has ever seen?"

Redgrave signalled to the engine-room, and presently the *Astronef* changed her course, and in a few minutes was hanging, bathed in sunlight, like a star suspended over the unfathomable gulf of darkness below.

As they sank beyond the sunlight, Murgatroyd turned on both the head and stern searchlights. They dropped down ever slowly and more slowly until gradually the two long, thin streams of light began to spread themselves out, and by the time the *Astronef* came gently to a rest they were swinging round her in broad fans of diffused light over a dark, marshy surface, with scattered patches of moss and reeds which showed dull gleams of stagnant water between them.

"Air and water at last!" said Redgrave, as he rejoined his wife on the upper deck, "air and water and eternal darkness! Well, we shall find life on the moon here if anywhere. Shall we go?"

"Of course," replied her ladyship, "what else have we come for? Must we put on the breathing-dresses?"

"Certainly," he replied, "because, although there's air we don't know yet whether it is breathable. It may be half carbon-dioxide for all we know; but a few matches will soon tell us that."

Within a quarter of an hour they were again standing on the surface. Murgatroyd had orders to follow them as far as possible with the head searchlight, which, in the comparatively rarefied atmosphere, appeared to have a range of several miles. Redgrave struck a match, and held it up level with his head. It burnt with a clear, steady, yellow flame.

"Where a match will burn a man can breathe," he said. "I'm going to see what lunar air is like."

"For Heaven's sake be careful, dear," came the reply in pleading tones across the wire.

"All right, but don't open your helmet till I tell you."

He then raised the hermetically-closed slide of glass, which formed the front of the helmets half an inch or so. Instantly he felt a sensation like the drawing of a red-hot iron across his skin. He snapped the visor down and clasped it in its place. For a moment or two he gasped for breath and then he said rather faintly:

"It's no good, it's too cold, it would freeze the blood in our veins. I think we'd better go back and explore this valley under cover. We can't do anything in the dark, and we can see just as well from the upper deck with the searchlights. Besides, as there's air and water here, there's no telling but there may be inhabitants of sorts such as we shouldn't care to meet."

He took her hand, and, to Murgatroyd's intense relief, they went back to the vessel.

Redgrave then raised the *Astronef* a couple of hundred feet and, by directing the repulsive force against the mountain walls, developed just sufficient energy to keep them moving at about twelve miles an hour.

They began to cross the plain with their searchlights flashing out in all directions. They had scarcely gone a mile before the headlight fell upon a moving form half walking, half crawling among some stunted brown-leaved bushes by the side of a broad, stagnant stream.

"Look!" said Zaidie, clasping her husband's arm, "is that a gorilla, or—no, it can't be a man."

The light was turned full upon the object. If it had been covered with hair it might have passed for some strange type of the ape tribe, but its skin was smooth and of a livid grey. Its lower limbs were evidently more powerful than its upper; its chest was enormously developed, but the stomach was small. The head was big and round and smooth. As they came nearer they saw that in place of fingernails it had long white feelers which it kept extended and constantly waving about as it groped its way towards the water. As the intense light flashed full on it, it turned its head towards them. It had a nose and a mouth. The nose was long and thick, with huge mobile nostrils, and the mouth formed an angle something like a fish's lips, and of teeth there seemed none. At either side of the upper part of the nose there were two little sunken holes, in which this thing's ancestors of countless thousand years ago had possessed eyes.

As she looked upon this awful parody of what had once perhaps been a human face, Zaidie covered hers with her hands and uttered a little moan of horror.

"Horrible, isn't it?" said Redgrave. "I suppose that's what the last remnants of the lunarians have come to, evidently once men and women something like ourselves. I daresay the ancestors of that thing have lived here in coldness and darkness for hundreds of generations. It shows how tremendously tenacious nature is of life.

"Ages ago that awful thing's ancestors lived up yonder when there were seas and rivers, fields and forests just as we have them on earth; men and women who could see and breath and enjoy everything in life and had built up civilizations like ours. Look, it's going to fish or something. Now we shall see what it feeds on. I wonder why that water isn't frozen. I suppose there must be some internal heat left still, split up into patches, I daresay, and lakes of lava. Perhaps this valley is just over one of them, and that's why these creatures have managed to survive. Ah, there's another of them, smaller not so strongly formed. That thing's mate, I suppose, female of the species. Ugh, I wonder how many hundreds of thousands of years it will take for our descendants to come to that."

"I hope our dear old earth will hit something else and be smashed to atoms before that happens!" exclaimed Zaidie, whose curiosity had now partly overcome her horror. "Look, it's trying to catch something."

The larger of the two creatures had groped its way to the edge of the sluggish, foetid water and dropped or rather rolled quietly into it. It was evidently cold-blooded or nearly so, for no warm-blooded animal could have withstood that more than glacial cold. Presently the other dropped in, too, and both disappeared for some minutes. Then suddenly there was a violent commotion in the water a few yards away; and the two creatures rose to the surface of the water, one with a wriggling eel-like fish between its jaws.

They both groped their way towards the edge, and had just reached it and were pulling themselves out when a hideous shape rose out of the water behind them. It was like the head of an octopus joined to the body of a boa-constrictor, but head and neck were both of the same ghastly, livid grey as the other two bodies. It was evidently blind, too, for it took no notice of the brilliant glare of the searchlight. Still it moved rapidly towards the two scrambling forms, its long white feelers trembling out in all directions. Then one of them touched the smaller of the two creatures. Instantly the rest shot out and closed round it, and with scarcely a struggle it was dragged beneath the water and vanished.

Zaidie uttered a little low scream and covered her face again, and Redgrave said: "The same old brutal law again. Life preying upon life even on a dying world, a world that is more than half dead itself. Well, I think we've seen enough of this place. I suppose those are about the only types of life we should meet anywhere, and one acquaintance with them satisfies me completely. I vote we go and see what the invisible hemisphere is like."

"I have had all I want of this side," said Zaidie, looking away from the scene of the hideous conflict, "so the sooner the better."

A few minutes later the *Astronef* was again rising towards the stars with her searchlights still flashing down into the Valley of Expiring Life, which seemed worse than the Valley of Death. As he followed the rays with a pair of powerful field glasses, Redgrave fancied that he saw huge, dim shapes moving about the stunted shrubbery and through the slimy pools of the stagnant rivers, and once or twice he got a glimpse of what might well have been the ruins of towns and cities; but the gloom soon became too deep and dense for the searchlights to pierce and he was glad when the *Astronef* soared up into the brilliant sunlight once more. Even the ghastly wilderness of the lunar landscape was welcome after the nameless horrors of that hideous abyss.

After a couple of hours rapid travelling, Redgrave pointed down to a comparatively small, deep crater, and said:

"There, that is Malapert. It is almost exactly at the south pole of the moon, and there," he went on pointing ahead, "is the horizon of the hemisphere which no earthborn eyes but ours and Murgatroyd's have ever seen."

Contrary to certain ingenious speculations which have been indulged in, they found that the hemisphere, which for count-less ages has never been turned towards the earth, was almost an exact replica of the visible one. Fully three-fourths of it was bril-liantly illuminated by the sun, and the scene which presented itself to their eyes was practically the same which they had beheld on the earthward side; huge groups of enormous craters and ringed mountains, long, irregular chains crowned with sharp, splintery peaks, and between these vast, deeply depressed areas, ranging in colour from dazzling white to grey-brown, marking the beds of the vanished lunar seas.

As they crossed one of these, Redgrave allowed the *Astronef* to sink to within a few thousand feet of the surface, and then he and Zaidie swept it with their telescopes. Their chance search was rewarded by what they had not seen in the sea-beds of the other hemisphere. These depressions were far deeper than the others, evidently many thousands of feet deep, but the sun's rays were blazing full into this one, and, dotted round its slopes at varying elevations, they made out little patches which seemed to differ from the general surface.

"I wonder if those are the remains of cities," said Zaidie. "Isn't it possible that the populations might have built their cities along the seas, and that their descendants may have followed the waters as they retreated, I mean as they either dried up or disappeared into the centre?"

"Very probable indeed, dear," he said, "we'll go down and see."

He diminished the vertically repulsive force a little, and the *Astronef* dropped slantingly towards the bed of what might once have been the Pacific of the Moon. When they were within about a couple of thousand feet of the surface it became quite plain that Zaidie was correct in her hypothesis. The vast sea-floor was literally strewn with the ruins of countless cities and towns, which had been inhabited by an equally countless series of generations of men and women, who had, perhaps, lived in the days when our own world was a glowing mass of molten rock, surrounded by the envelope of vapours which has since condensed to form its oceans.

The nearer they approached to the central and deepest depression the more perfect the buildings became until, down in the lowest depth, they found a collection of low-built square edifices, scarcely better than huts which had clustered round the little lake into which ages before the ocean had dwindled. But where the lake had been there was now only a depression covered with grey sand and brown rock.

Into this they descended and touched the lunar soil for the last time. A couple of hours' excursion among the houses proved that they had been the last refuge of the last descendants of a dying race, a race which had steadily degenerated just as the successions of cities had done, as the bitter fight for mere existence had become keener and keener until the two last essentials air and water, had failed and then the end had come.

The streets, like the square of the great temple of Tycho, were strewn with myriads and myriads of bones, and there were myriads more scattered round what had once been the shores of the dwindling lake. Here, as elsewhere, there was not a sign or a record of any kind—carving or sculpture.

Inside the great Pyramid of the City of Tycho they might, perhaps, have found something—some stone or tablet which bore the mark of the artist's hand; elsewhere, perhaps, they might have found cities reared by older races, which might have rivalled the creations of Egypt and Babylon, but there was no time to look for these. All that they had seen of the dead world had only sickened and saddened them. The untravelled regions of Space peopled by living worlds more akin to their own were before them, and the red disc of Mars was glowing in the zenith among the diamond-white clusters which gemmed the black sky behind him.

More than a hundred millions of miles had to be traversed before they would be able to set foot on his surface, and so, after one last look round the Valley of Death about them Redgrave turned on the full energy of the repulsive force in a vertical direction, and the *Astronef* leapt upwards in a straight line for her new destination. The unknown hemisphere spread out in a vast plain beneath them, the blazing sun rose on their left, and the brilliant silver orb of the Earth on their right, and so, full of wonder, and yet without regret, they bade farewell to the World that Was.

SUNRISE ON THE MOON

John Munro

One of the most famous photographs ever taken was by William Anders in Apollo 8 *as they orbited the Moon during Christmas 1968. It shows the Earth rising above the Moon, a vision of blue against the blackness of space—what is now called Spaceship Earth. It provided significant impetus to the demand for environmental concerns and, quite simply, shows how beautiful the Earth is compared to the barrenness of the Moon and eternity beyond. Over seventy years before that picture was taken, John Munro (1849–1930) had his own dream of that image.*

Munro was an English engineer, a professor of mechanical engineering at Bristol University, and a visionary. He wrote several books on popular science, particularly electricity, and regularly contributed articles to magazines encouraging interest in the sciences. Sometimes this encouragement shifted from fact to fiction as in the following story, which is in a sense part essay. He also wrote A Trip to Venus *(1897) in which an anti-gravity powered ether-ship travels not only to a paradise-like Venus but onward to a dangerous Mercury.*

I AM ALONE AND SEATED UPON A ROCK, BUT I KNOW NOT WHERE. It is night, and the sky above me wears a strange aspect. There is no shining moon and lustrous clouds; no familiar planet beams like a golden lamp; no brilliant star flashes a living gem in the blue and limpid depths of ether.

I see only an immense black vault—to all appearance, hard, and fretted with pale blue points of light. It is a dead funereal sky; and to compare small things with great, it reminds me of a coal-mine studded with corpse-candles. All about me is buried in darkness that would be absolute, save for the faint glister of the starlight on the white and frozen surface of the ground. Not a living thing is to be seen; an awful stillness reigns; not a breath of air fans my cheek; and the cold is more than Arctic in its rigour.

Suddenly a splendid meteor shoots athwart the sky, its head blazing into green and blue, and its long trail sparkling with fire. It seemed to strike the earth quite near me, for I could hear the shock and the rattle of splintered stones. After a time another followed, and I began to grow alarmed for my safety, when a peculiar light in the distance attracted my attention. It appeared as a bluish-white glow revealing itself in the darkness, like an emanation of some aurora borealis. Dim and vague when first seen, it slowly and surely became brighter, more extensive, and more definite.

At the same time, I was sensible of a growing illumination around me. Spires and pinnacles of hoary granite, tinged with the same blue radiance, stood forth weird and ghostly in the blackness.

One might have thought that day was breaking on the mountain tops but for the electrical blueness of the light and the changeless pall of the heavens.

The luminosity in the distance began to assume a crescent shape, but not like that of the moon; for it was horizontal, not vertical. Moreover, I could now see not one, but several, patches and crescents of the bluish lustre which ere long waxed into complete rings, and appeared to float in the darkness, like purple isles and atolls in a shoreless sea of molten pitch.

Shoreless did I say? No: that was only for a space. Beyond the atolls I began to discern a curving band of light, which broadened imperceptibly until it resembled a wall of high cliffs forming the coast-line of a continent, illuminated by the rising sun and trending away into the gloom. In keeping, too, with the effects of sunrise were the long and luminous beams that shot through great gaps and passes in the mountain range on which I now perceived that I was sitting, and fell in purple splashes on the flood of darkness. I knew from the constellations, however, that the light was coming from the west, and, moreover, its colour was neither the amber tinge of sunrise nor of sunset.

How strange and funereal was the spectacle of that black sea, with its purple archipelago enshrined beneath the black sky and the eternal stars! Funereal, yet magnificent beyond all power of language to express. Even the imagination of a Doré could not have conceived the awful sublimity of that Valley of the Shadow of Death. It seemed to me that I was gazing upon the bier of a dead world within the hushed and solemn sepulchre of the universe.

By-and-by a golden light appeared in the east behind the distant line of cliffs, and a vast orb, resembling the moon, but many times, larger, rose with serene majesty into the heavens. Unlike the moon, however, it seemed to shed no radiance around it, for the sky remained as black as ever. The light from its poles was of a dazzling lustre—owing perhaps to the polar ice-fields—but that from the middle zones was dimmer and more shadowy, and varied in tint from a pale green to a ruddy brown and a clouded blue.

The blue patches were probably seas, the brown and green ones continents, with their deserts and vegetation; and I fancied I could trace a configuration like that portion of the earth comprised between America, Africa, and Europe, even to such details as the British Isles.

The light around me had grown so much brighter that I turned to see where it came from, and beheld a still more marvellous sight. Away to the westward rolled a wild chaos of darkness, commingled with bluish light, which I can only compare to the waves of a stormy sea when tipped with lilac phosphorescence; and above the distant horizon in the funereal sky a strange and glorious meteor was blazing like a comet. Its disc was equal in size to that of the sun, and of blinding intensity, but its colour was a kind of lavender blue, inclining to purple; and a silvery white radiance, like that of the Milky Way, extended from it far into the night. What was that brilliant luminary which reminded me so forcibly of an electric arc-lamp when its carbons are burning blue?

I turned once more to the prospect which had first engaged my attention; but I need not linger on the succeeding phases of the dawn. It is enough to say that as the splendid star mounted up the sky the illuminations became stronger, until a grey-blue daylight showed all the features of the landscape. I then saw that what I have called a sea of darkness was in reality a vast grey plain, and that its purple islands were the peaks and craters of volcanoes. The high cliffs beyond were not the shores of a continent, but part of a stupendous wall of rock, which encircled the plain like a rampart. I discovered that my own station was near the verge of this tremendous precipice; and my brain sickened when I found that its crags dropped sheerly down to the plain, many thousands of feet below.

The summit was jagged with lofty pinnacles of rock, standing as towers along the wall, and enormous gaps like the embrasures of a battlement. It cast a long, sharp, pointed shadow as black as jet athwart the grey plain below, on which the craters of the extinct volcanoes, as yet impenetrated by the light, resembled wells of ink; but as the meteor ascended higher and higher the shadows by degrees drew back or became lighter. Not a vestige of human occupation, or animal life, or vegetation could be seen anywhere. Apparently, there was not a drop of water, stagnant or running, and the rise of a sort of mist from the ground here and there was the only sign of energy.

Although it was broad daylight, the sky, except in the neighbourhood of the luminary, remained as black as ever: or at least an indigo-blue so deep as to appear black; and the stars had a cold, harsh, bluish aspect.

When I looked in the opposite direction I saw a still more unearthly prospect—a weird and rugged wilderness of serrated mountain ranges, extinct volcanoes, conical peaks, isolated hills and bosses of rock, walled plains and cindery deserts, traversed by streams of solid lava, or cleft by deep wide cañons, and interspersed with the cones of exhausted geysers, or the basins of dried mud and mineral springs, like the terraces and "paint-pots" of the Yellowstone. The earth and rocks were of all colours, from the white of a deposit like snow, and a species of granite or milky quartz, to the yellow of sulphur, from the red of a vermilion to the green and blues of other natural pigments of volcanic origin; but the prevailing tint was grey, and the light of the sky so chequered the scoriæ and blistered surface with black shadows, that it seemed to be carved out of ivory and ebony.

Here, too, I could see no trace of life, unless some splintered columns on a hill-side were the petrified trunks of an ancient forest; and again the idea came to me that I was looking on the rigid lineaments of a defunct planet.

Dead, perhaps, but not absolutely free of life, for as time went on I began to observe that low forms of vegetation, such as lichen and cacti, were shooting from the arid soil in the growing heat of the luminary, and even imparting a ruddy or green tinge to the grey plains and mountains. Nor was that all: for I was nearly frightened out of my wits on discovering a huge serpent gliding past me as I lay upon the ground. Another and another followed; and not snakes alone, but monstrous toads and flying insects, as gigantic as crocodiles or the winged dragons of past geological eras.

They were of all colours and patterns, to match the earth and rocks, but the majority were black and white. Occasionally a serpent gobbled up a toad, and a toad snapped at a dragon-fly; but still the legion marched on, like a great army. I wanted to run away, but I was rooted to the spot; and—horror of horrors!—an enormous snake glided over my prostrate body. In an agony of fear I struggled to escape from its bloated and slimy folds, but all in vain. I yelled aloud, and—I awoke.

At first I did not know where I was, for the trail of the serpent was still over me; yet I became aware of my identity, and that I was not really where I had thought myself to be. For a moment it flashed upon me that I was crazed, and then I recollected that I was in bed, and that my gruesome experiences were only a dream, evoked, perhaps, by the rays of the dawn falling across my face.

I believe it was a case of what is known as "double conscious-ness," in which the brain seems to be conscious in two different centres. The Ego had awakened while the rest of the mind was under the influence of sleep. The mystery of my dream became clear to me, for I remembered that before going to bed I bad been reading about the moon in the pages of Proctor, Sir Robert Ball, Mr. A.C. Ranyard, and other eminent writers on astronomy. I found, moreover, that there had been a creative method in my dream—that it was, in fact, a vision of sun-rise in the moon, such as it would appear to an observing eye, placed in the moon itself, and not to an astronomer upon the earth.

My point of view had been on the south-west wall of the great crater, or "walled plain," of Clavius, in the third or south-east quadrant of the moon, and the time was that of sun-rise, when the "terminator" or fringe of daylight was creeping over the surface, and illuminating its salient features.

The azure of our sky on the earth is due to the dispersion of the light in the atmosphere; but if the moon has any atmosphere, it is extremely rare—as rare as that some fifty or sixty miles above the earth. Hence both by night and day the lunar sky appears black. On the summit of Mont Blanc there is a decided darkening of our own blue sky. Again, the golden red light of sun-rise and sun-set on the earth is owing to absorption of the blue rays by our atmosphere, such as may be observed in a gas lamp, which appears redder in a fog.

Seen beyond our atmosphere, the sun would in reality be of a blue colour, like Herschel's lavender, tending to purple, as Professor S.P. Langley has found; and hence, as the moon has little or no absorptive atmosphere, the sun-light there will show a purple tinge. The solar disc will also appear to be enveloped by the chromosphere and white corona with its meteoric extensions, including the zodiacal light.

The crater of Clavius is over 142 miles in diameter, or twice the area of Wales; but the absence or purity of the atmosphere favours length of sight. It is surrounded by a bulwark of rocks, in some places attaining a height of more than 17,000 feet above the floor, which comprises about ninety craterlets. Even from the earth a sun-rise on Clavius, when viewed with a good telescope, is a very sublime spectacle. At first the sun lights up the western wall of the crater, which remains in shadow, and appears as a dark bay encroaching on the bright part, or southern horn. As the sun rises higher his rays strike on the craters of the plain, and makes them shine as "golden atolls in a sea of ink."

The eastern wall of the crater catches his fire, and shafts of light dart through the gaps in the western wall into the bottom of the crater: an effect employed by Mr. Rider Haggard in his celebrated romance to enable "She" and her companions to reach the flame of immortality in the caverns of Kôr, which was also a "walled plain," similar to those on the moon. At last the sunlight reaches the plain, the long black shadows are forced to shrink away, and the entire floor is illuminated.

The moon may be regarded as a mummied world which has died young. The earth is much older as a planet, and many traits of its fiery youth have disappeared; but in the aspect of the moon we are able to read what it has once been like. On the volcanic surface of our satellite we see long mountain ranges, but none so high as the Andes or the Himalayas. Those of the moon are evidently the works of Plutonic forces.

The Andes and the Himalayas, on the other hand, are built of rocks which have been deposited under water, and upheaved by the

sinking in of the neighbouring areas. In some terrestrial ranges, however, the original core or back-bone is volcanic, and comparable to
the ranges of the moon, but it has become overlaid by sedimentary
materials: just as a primitive trait of human character is sometimes
disguised by later habits or experience.

There are few great craters, rings, or walled plains on the earth,
and these are not so large as some on the moon. Probably those of
the earth have nearly all been denuded away by wind and water,
frost and fire; but examples can still be seen in Java and elsewhere,
and the crater of Kilauea, in the Sandwich Islands, is one still active,
where the molten lava is forming a ridgy floor or grey plain, dotted
with craterlets which are the last vents of the expiring volcano. The
so-called "seas" of the moon, such as the "Sea of Serenity," the "Lake
of Corruption," and the "Bay of Rainbows," are apparently dry flats
or deserts, like the prairies and the pampas of America, and their
greenish-grey or reddish hue probably comes from the earth and
ashes, or from vegetation.

The "pits" or cup-like depressions are perhaps old craters which
have lost their rings; the "clefts" are long narrow gorges or cracks
remaining open, and the "faults" are doubtless closed cracks, both
the result of shrinkage as the moon parted with its internal heat.

The "bright streaks" which radiate from some of the craters across
valleys and mountains are perhaps frozen lava streams, and the "long
banks" are probably intruded lavas similar to the "trap dykes" of our
own planet. The sulphur plains, extinct geysers, and mineral springs
which I saw in my dream have not yet been recognized on the moon,
because, of course, they would be difficult to discern; but we can hardly
doubt that such-like products of volcanic action are present there.

The seeming absence of air and water in the moon has been
accounted for in several ways. It is more likely that the particles of

air have stolen away into space during the lapse of ages—as Mr. S.T. Preston has supposed—than that it has frozen in the extreme cold or been absorbed by the crust. The water may have been absorbed or frozen out rather than evaporated, but there is a growing tendency amongst astronomers to believe that both an atmosphere and water exist in the moon, though in a diminished quantity. During the long night, lasting two weeks, this water would undoubtedly be frozen, and the peculiar whiteness of the moon's surface, especially at the poles, may be caused by ordinary snow, as well as by frozen carbonic acid or chemical salts, such as borate of lime. If there be some air and water on the moon—and this is the view which I have taken—the long day of two weeks would, of course, vaporise it; rains would follow, and probably the lower species of plants would flourish. That vegetable and animal life of the higher grades once existed on the moon is questionable. Probably there was never any man in the moon, although the likeness of a very beautiful woman and a very ugly man have been traced by some astronomers.

There is no reason to doubt, however, that many of the lower kinds of animals once haunted the grey plains and wooded slopes of the mountains, and it is even possible that some of these yet linger on in more or less modified types, and migrate with the sunshine, like our swallows, thus elevating my awful nightmare to the rank of a prophetic vision.

FIRST MEN IN THE MOON

H.G. Wells

Along with Jules Verne, H.G. Wells (1866–1946) is without doubt the best known of the pioneers of science fiction and, more than Verne, Wells rightly holds the epithet, the Father of Science Fiction. He managed to crystallize the reader's understanding of events by focusing on how the individual coped with major, often unfathomable circumstances, rather than explore the broad canvas. In all his major early works, it is the man-in-the-street who relates the unfolding events and tries to explain to the reader, so far as he can, what is happening. Who can forget how the narrator in The War of the Worlds *(1898), for example, describes and somehow survives the Martian invasion, or how Bert Smallways comes to terms with and ends up the hero in the conflagration in* The War in the Air *(1908).*

Much the same applies to Bedford, the narrator of First Men in the Moon *(1901). Bedford had taken lodgings near Lympne in Kent with a view to finding solitude for his writing but he is interrupted by the eccentric scientist Cavor, who takes Bedford into his confidence. Cavor has discovered a material which repels Earth's gravity, which he calls Cavorite. He has built a sphere coated in Cavorite with shutters that allow the antigravity effects to be switched on and off. They travel to the Moon in the sphere and discover, much as Kepler described in* Somnium *and John Munro in the previous story, that the flora and fauna is quiescent at night but comes alive with the long lunar day. They witness some native Selenites, small insect-like but roughly humanoid creatures, herding animals they call moon-calves. They lose their way and are taken prisoners by the Selenites, and are taken under the lunar surface—hence the book's title of first men in the Moon. The two explorers manage to escape from the Selenites but they lose track* of each other. *Bedford makes it back to the surface, finds the space-sphere and, believing that Cavor is dead, manages to return to Earth. Alas, the sphere is stolen and, not knowing the secret of Cavorite, Bedford is unable to make another to return to the Moon. He writes up his adventures for* The Strand Magazine *and believes that is the end of it. But then, as we learn in the following, he discovers that Cavor is not dead after all and the full story of Cavor's adventures in the Moon is now revealed via radio signals received by a Dutch engineer, Mr. Wendigee. Bedford then relates the message he received from Cavor about his adventures inside the Moon.*

I T IS WELL THE READER SHOULD UNDERSTAND THE CONDITIONS under which it would seem these messages were sent. Somewhere within the moon Cavor certainly had access for a time to a considerable amount of electrical apparatus, and it would seem he rigged up—perhaps furtively—a transmitting arrangement of the Marconi type. This he was able to operate at irregular intervals: sometimes for only half an hour or so, sometimes for three or four hours at a stretch. At these times he transmitted his earthward message, regardless of the fact that the relative position of the moon and points upon the earth's surface is constantly altering. As a consequence of this and of the necessary imperfections of our recording instruments his communication comes and goes in our records in an extremely fitful manner; it becomes blurred; it "fades out" in a mysterious and altogether exasperating way. And added to this is the fact that he was not an expert operator; he had partly forgotten, or never completely mastered, the code in general use, and as he became fatigued he dropped words and misspelt in a curious manner.

Altogether we have probably lost quite half of the communications he made, and much we have is damaged, broken, and partly effaced. In the abstract that follows the reader must be prepared therefore for a considerable amount of break, hiatus, and change of topic. Mr. Wendigee and I are collaborating in a complete and annotated edition of the Cavor record, which we hope to publish, together with a detailed account of the instruments employed, beginning with the first volume in January next. That will be the full and scientific report, of which this is only the popular first transcript. But here we give at least sufficient to complete the story I have told, and to give the broad outlines of the state of that other world so near, so kin, and yet so dissimilar to our own.

An Abstract of the Six Messages First Received from Mr. Cavor

The two earlier messages of Mr. Cavor may very well be reserved for that larger volume. They simply tell with greater brevity and with a difference in several details that is interesting, but not of any vital importance, the bare facts of the making of the sphere and our departure from the world. Throughout, Cavor speaks of me as a man who is dead, but with a curious change of temper as he approaches our landing on the moon. "Poor Bedford," he says of me, and "this poor young man," and he blames himself for inducing a young man, "by no means well equipped for such adventures," to leave a planet "on which he was indisputably fitted to succeed" on so precarious a mission. I think he underrates the part my energy and practical capacity played in bringing about the realization of his theoretical sphere. "We arrived," he says, with no more account of our passage through space than if we had made a journey of common occurrence in a railway train.

And then he becomes increasingly unfair to me. Unfair, indeed, to an extent I should not have expected in a man trained in the search for truth. Looking back over my previously written account of these things I must insist that I have been altogether juster to Cavor than he has been to me. I have extenuated little and suppressed nothing. But his account is:—

"It speedily became apparent that the entire strangeness of our circumstances and surroundings—great loss of weight, attenuated but highly oxygenated air, consequent exaggeration of-the results of muscular effort, rapid development of weird plants from obscure spores, lurid sky—was exciting my companion unduly. On the moon his character seemed to deteriorate. He became impulsive, rash, and quarrelsome. In a little while his folly in devouring some gigantic vesicles and his consequent intoxication led to our capture by the Selenites—before we had had the slightest opportunity of properly observing their ways…"

(He says, you observe, nothing of his own concession to these same "vesicles.")

And he goes on from that point to say that "We came to a difficult passage with them, and Bedford mistaking certain gestures of theirs"—pretty gestures they were!—"gave way to a panic violence. He ran amuck, killed three, and perforce I had to flee with him after the outrage. Subsequently we fought with a number who endeavoured to bar our way, and slew seven or eight more. It says much for the tolerance of these beings that on my recapture I was not instantly slain. We made our way to the exterior and separated in the crater of our arrival, to increase our chances of recovering our sphere. But presently I came upon a body of Selenites, led by two who were curiously different, even in form, from any of those we had seen hitherto, with larger heads and smaller bodies and much more elaborately wrapped about. And after evading them for some time I fell into a crevasse, cut my head rather badly and displaced my patella, and, finding crawling very painful, decided to surrender—if they would still permit me to do so. This they did, and, perceiving my helpless condition, carried me with them again into the moon. And of Bedford I have heard or seen nothing more, nor, so far as I can gather, has any Selenite. Either the night overtook him in the crater, or else, which is more probable, he found the sphere, and, desiring to steal a march upon me, made off with it—only, I fear, to find it uncontrollable, and to meet a more lingering fate in outer space."

And with that Cavor dismisses me and goes on to more interesting topics. I dislike the idea of seeming to use my position as his editor to deflect his story in my own interest, but I am obliged to protest here against the turn he gives these occurrences. He says nothing about that gasping message on the blood-stained paper in which he told, or attempted to tell, a very different story. The dignified self-surrender is an altogether new view of the affair that has come to him, I must insist, since he began to feel secure among the lunar people; and as for the "stealing a march" conception, I am quite willing to let the reader decide between us on what he has before him. I know I am not a model man—I have made no pretence to be. But am I *that*?

However, that is the sum of my wrongs. From this point I can edit Cavor with an untroubled mind, for he mentions me no more.

It would seem the Selenites who had come upon him carried him to some point in the interior down "a great shaft" by means of what he describes as "a sort of balloon." We gather from the rather confused passage in which he describes this, and from a number of chance allusions and hints in other and subsequent messages, that this "great shaft" is one of an enormous system of artificial shafts that run, each from what is called a lunar "crater," downwards for very nearly a hundred miles towards the central portion of our satellite. These shafts communicate by transverse tunnels, they throw out abysmal caverns and expand into great globular places; the whole of the moon's substance for a hundred miles inward, indeed, is a mere sponge of rock. "Partly," says Cavor, "this sponginess is natural, but very largely it is due to the enormous industry of the Selenites in the past. The enormous circular mounds of the excavated rock and earth it is that form these great circles about the tunnels known to earthly astronomers (misled by a false analogy) as volcanoes."

It was down this shaft they took him, in this "sort of balloon" he speaks of, at first into an inky blackness and then into a region of continually increasing phosphorescence. Cavor's despatches show him to be curiously regardless of detail for a scientific man, but we gather that this light was due to the streams and cascades of water—"no doubt containing some phosphorescent organism"—that flowed ever more abundantly downward towards the Central Sea. And as he descended, he says, "The Selenites also became luminous." And at last far below him he saw as it were a lake of heatless fire, the waters of the Central Sea, glowing and eddying in strange perturbation, "like luminous blue milk that is just on the boil."

"This Lunar Sea," says Cavor, in a later passage, "is not a stagnant ocean; a solar tide sends it in a perpetual flow around the lunar axis, and strange storms and boilings and rushings of its waters occur, and at times cold winds and thunderings that ascend out of it into the busy ways of the great ant-hill above. It is only when the water is in motion that it gives out light; in its rare seasons of calm it is black. Commonly, when one sees it, its waters rise and fall in an oily swell, and flakes and big rafts of shining, bubbly foam drift with the sluggish, faintly-glowing current. The Selenites navigate its cavernous straits and lagoons in little shallow boats of a canoe-like shape: and even before my journey to the galleries about the Grand Lunar, who is Master of the Moon, I was permitted to make a brief excursion on its waters.

"The caverns and passages are naturally very tortuous. A large proportion of these ways are known only to expert pilots among the fishermen, and not infrequently Selenites are lost for ever in their labyrinths. In their remoter recesses, I am told, strange creatures lurk, some of them terrible and dangerous creatures that all the science of the moon has been unable to exterminate. There is particularly the Rapha, an inextricable mass of clutching tentacles that one hacks to pieces only to multiply; and the Tzee, a darting creature that is never seen, so subtly and suddenly does it slay…"

He gives us a gleam of description.

"I was reminded on this excursion of what I have read of the Mammoth Caves; if only I had had a yellow flambeau instead of the pervading blue light, and a solid-looking boatman with an oar instead of a scuttle-faced Selenite working an engine at the back of the canoe, I could have imagined I had suddenly got back to earth. The rocks about us were very various, sometimes black, sometimes pale blue and veined, and once they flashed and glittered as though we had come into a mine of sapphires. And below one saw the ghostly phosphorescent fishes flash and vanish in the hardly less phosphorescent deep. Then, presently, a long ultra-marine vista down the turgid stream of one of the channels of traffic, and a landing-stage, and then, perhaps, a glimpse up the enormous crowded shaft of one of the vertical ways.

"In one great place heavy with glistening stalactites a number of boats were fishing. We went alongside one of these and watched the long-armed fishing Selenites winding in a net. They were little, hunchbacked insects with very strong arms, short, bandy legs, and crinkled face-masks. As they pulled at it that net seemed the heaviest thing I had come upon in the moon; it was loaded with weights—no doubt of gold—and it took along time to draw, for in those waters the larger and more edible fish lurk deep. The fish in the net came up like a blue moon-rise—a blaze of darting, tossing blue.

"Among their catch was a many tentaculate, evil-eyed black thing, ferociously active, whose appearance they greeted with shrieks and twitters, and which with quick, nervous movements they hacked to pieces by means of little hatchets. All its dissevered limbs continued to lash and writhe in a vicious manner. Afterwards when fever had hold of me I dreamt again and again of that bitter, furious creature rising so vigorous and active out of the unknown sea. It was the most active and malignant thing of all the living creatures I have yet seen in this world inside the moon....

"The surface of this sea must be very nearly two hundred miles (if not more) below the level of the moon's exterior; all the cities of the moon lie, I learnt, immediately above this Central Sea, in such cavernous spaces and artificial galleries as I have described, and they communicate with the exterior by enormous vertical shafts which open invariably in what are called by earthly astronomers the 'craters' of the moon. The lid covering one such aperture I had already seen during the wanderings that had preceded my capture.

"Upon the condition of the less central portion of the moon I have not yet arrived at very precise knowledge. There is an enormous system of caverns in which the mooncalves shelter during the night; and there are abattoirs and the like—in one of these it was that I and Bedford fought with the Selenite butchers—and I have since seen balloons laden with meat descending out of the upper dark. I have as yet scarcely learnt as much of these things as a Zulu in London would learn about the British corn supplies in the same time. It is clear, however, that these vertical shafts and the vegetation of the surface must play an essential *rôle* in ventilating and keeping fresh the atmosphere of the moon. At one time, and particularly on my first emergence from my prison, there was certainly a cold wind blowing *down* the shaft, and later there was a kind of sirocco upward that corresponded with my fever. For at the end of about three weeks I fell ill of an indefinable sort of fever, and in spite of sleep and the quinine tabloids that very fortunately I had brought in my pocket, I remained ill and fretting miserably, almost to the time when I was taken into the palace of the Grand Lunar, who is Master of the Moon.

"I will not dilate on the wretchedness of my condition," he remarks, "during those days of ill-health." And he goes on with great amplitude with details I omit here. "My temperature," he concludes, "kept abnormally high for a long time, and I lost all desire for food. I had stagnant waking intervals, and sleep tormented by dreams, and at one phase I was, I remember, so weak as to be earth-sick and almost hysterical. I longed almost intolerably for colour to break the everlasting blue…"

He reverts again presently to the topic of this sponge caught lunar atmosphere. I am told by astronomers and physicists that all he tells is in absolute accordance with what was already known of the moon's condition. Had earthly astronomers had the courage and imagination to push home a bold induction, says Mr. Wendigee, they might have foretold almost everything that Cavor has to say of the general structure of the moon. They know now pretty certainly that moon and earth are not so much satellite and primary as smaller and greater sisters, made out of one mass, and consequently made of the same material. And since the density of the moon is only three-fifths that of the earth, there can be nothing for it but that she is hollowed out by a great system of caverns. There was no necessity, said Sir Jabez Flap, F.R.S., that most entertaining exponent of the facetious side of the stars, that we should ever have gone to the moon to find out such easy inferences, and points the pun with an allusion to Gruyère, but he certainly might have announced his knowledge of the hollowness of the moon before. And if the moon is hollow, then the apparent absence of air and water is, of course, quite easily explained. The sea lies within at the bottom of the caverns, and the air travels through the great sponge of galleries, in accordance with simple physical laws. The caverns of the moon, on the whole, are very windy places. As the sunlight comes round the moon the air in the outer galleries on that side is heated, its pressure increases, some flows out on the exterior and mingles with the evaporating air of the craters (where the plants remove its carbonic acid), while the greater portion flows round through the galleries to replace the shrinking air of the cooling side that the sunlight has left. There is, therefore, a constant eastward breeze in the air of the outer galleries, and an up-flow during the lunar day up the shafts, complicated, of course, very greatly by the varying shape of the galleries and the ingenious contrivances of the Selenite mind...

The Natural History of the Selenites

The messages of Cavor from the sixth up to the sixteenth are for the most part so much broken, and they abound so in repetitions, that they scarcely form a consecutive narrative. They will be given in full, of course, in the scientific report, but here it will be far more convenient to continue simply to abstract and quote as in the former chapter. We have subjected every word to a keen critical scrutiny, and my own brief memories and impressions of lunar things have been of inestimable help in interpreting what would otherwise have been impenetrably dark. And, naturally, as living beings our interest

centres far more upon the strange community of lunar insects in
which he is living, it would seem, as an honoured guest than upon
the mere physical condition of their world.

I have already made it clear, I think, that the Selenites I saw
resembled man in maintaining the erect attitude and in having four
limbs, and I have compared the general appearance of their heads
and the jointing of their limbs to that of insects. I have mentioned,
too, the peculiar consequence of the smaller gravitation of the moon
on their fragile slightness. Cavor confirms me upon all these points.
He calls them "animals," though of course they fall under no divi-
sion of the classification of earthly creatures, and he points out "the
insect type of anatomy had, fortunately for men, never exceeded a
relatively very small size on earth." The largest terrestrial insects,
living or extinct, do not, as a matter of fact, measure 6in. in length;
"but here, against the lesser gravitation of the moon, a creature
certainly as much an insect as vertebrate seems to have been able
to attain to human and ultra human dimensions."

He does not mention the ant, but throughout his allusions the ant
is continually being brought before my mind, in its sleepless activity,
in its intelligence and social organization, in its structure, and more
particularly in the fact that it displays, in addition to the two forms,
the male and the female form, that almost all other animals possess,
a number of other sexless creatures, workers, soldiers, and the like,
differing from one another in structure, character, power, and use,
and yet all members of the same species.

For these Selenites have a great variety of forms. Of course these
Selenites are not only colossally greater in size than ants, but also, in
Cavor's opinion, in respect to intelligence, morality, and social wisdom
are they colossally greater than men. And instead of the four or five
different forms of ant that are found there are almost innumerably

different forms of Selenite. I have endeavoured to indicate the very considerable difference observable in such Selenites of the outer crust as I happened to encounter; the differences in size, hue, and shape were certainly as wide as the differences between the most widely-separated races of men. But such differences as I saw fade absolutely to nothing in comparison with the huge distinctions of which Cavor tells. It would seem the exterior Selenites I saw were, indeed, mostly of one colour and occupation—moon-calf herds, butchers, fleshers, and the like. But within the moon, practically unsuspected by me, there are, it seems, a number of other sorts of Selenite, differing in size, differing in form, differing in power and appearance, and yet not different species of creatures, but only different forms of one species. The moon is, indeed, a sort of vast ant-hill, only, instead of there being only four or five sorts of ant, worker, soldier, winged male, queen, and slave, there are many hundred different sorts of Selenite, and almost every gradation between one sort and another.

It would seem the discovery came upon Cavor very speedily. I infer rather than learn from his narrative that he was captured by the mooncalf herds under the direction of those other Selenites who "have larger brain-cases (heads?) and very much shorter legs." Finding he would not walk even under the goad, they carried him into darkness, crossed a narrow, plank-like bridge that may have been the identical bridge I had refused, and put him down in something that must have seemed at first to be some sort of lift. This was the balloon—it had certainly been absolutely invisible to us in the darkness—and what had seemed to me a mere plank-walking into the void was really, no doubt, the passage of the gangway. In this he descended towards constantly more luminous strata of the moon. At first they descended in silence—save for the twitterings of the Selenites—and then into a stir of windy movement. In a little while the profound blackness had made his eyes so sensitive that he began to see more and more of the things about him, and at last the vague took shape.

"Conceive an enormous cylindrical space," says Cavor in his seventh message, "a quarter of a mile across, perhaps; very dimly lit at first and then bright, with big platforms twisting down its sides in a spiral that vanishes at last below in a blue profundity; and lit even more brightly—one. could not tell how or why. Think of the well of the very largest spiral staircase or lift-shaft that you have ever looked down, and magnify that by a hundred. Imagine it at twilight seen through blue glass. Imagine yourself looking down that; only imagine also that you feel extraordinarily light and have got rid of any giddy feeling you might have on earth, and you will have the first conditions of my impression. Round this enormous shaft imagine a broad gallery running in a much steeper spiral than would be credible on earth, and forming a steep road protected from the gulf only by a little parapet that vanishes at last in perspective a couple of miles below.

"Looking up, I saw the very fellow of the downward vision: it had, of course, the effect of looking into a very steep cone. A wind was blowing down the shaft, and far above I fancy I heard, growing fainter and fainter, the bellowing of the mooncalves that were being driven down again from their evening pasturage on the exterior. And up and down the spiral galleries were scattered numerous moon people, pallid, faintly self-luminous insects, regarding our appearance or busied on unknown errands.

"Either I fancied it or a flake of snow came drifting swiftly down on the icy breeze. And then, falling like a snowflake, a little figure, a little man-insect clinging to a parachute, drove down very swiftly towards the central places of the moon.

"The big-headed Selenite sitting beside me, seeing me move my head with the gesture of one who saw, pointed with his trunk-like 'hand' and indicated a sort of jetty coming into sight very far below: a little landing-stage, as it were, hanging into the void. As it swept up towards us our pace diminished very rapidly, and in a few moments as it seemed we were abreast of it and at rest. A mooring-rope was flung and grasped, and I found myself pulled down to a level with a great crowd of Selenites, who jostled to see me.

"It was an incredible crowd. Suddenly and violently there was forced upon my attention the vast amount of difference there is amongst these beings of the moon.

"Indeed, there seemed not two alike in all that jostling multitude. They differed in shape, they differed in size! Some bulged and overhung, some ran about among the feet of their fellows, some twined and interlaced like snakes. All of them had a grotesque and disquieting suggestion of an insect that has somehow contrived to mock humanity; all seemed to present an incredible exaggeration of some particular feature: one had a vast right fore-limb, an enormous antennal arm, as it were; one seemed all leg, poised, as it were, on stilts; another protruded an enormous nose-like organ beside a sharply speculative eye that made him startlingly human until one saw his expressionless mouth. One has seen punchinellos made of lobster claws—he was like that. The strange and (except for the want of mandibles and palps) most insect-like head of the mooncalf-minders underwent astounding transformations: here it was broad and low, here high and narrow; here its vacuous brow was drawn out into horns and strange features; here it was whiskered, and divided, and there with a grotesquely human profile. There were several brain-cases distended like bladders to a huge size. The eyes, too, were strangely varied, some quite elephantine in their small alertness, some huge pits of darkness. There were amazing forms with heads reduced to microscopic proportions and blobby bodies; and fantastic, flimsy things that existed it would seem only as a basis for vast, white-rimmed, glaring eyes. And oddest of all, as it seemed to me for the moment, two or three of these weird inhabitants of a subterranean world, a world sheltered by innumerable miles of rock from sun or rain, *carried umbrellas* in their tentaculate hands!—real terrestrial-looking umbrellas! And then I thought of the parachutist I had watched descend.

"These moon people behaved exactly as a human crowd might have done in similar circumstances: they jostled and thrust one another, they shoved one another aside, they even clambered upon one another to get a glimpse of me. Every moment they increased in numbers, and pressed more urgently upon the discs of my ushers"— Cavor does not explain what he means by this—"every moment fresh shapes forced themselves upon my astounded attention. And presently I was signed and helped into a sort of litter, and lifted up on the shoulders of strong-armed bearers and so borne over this seething nightmare towards the apartments that were provided for me in the moon. All about me were eyes, faces, masks, tentacles, a leathery noise like the rustling of beetle wings, and a great bleating and twittering of Selenite voices...."

We gather he was taken to a "hexagonal apartment," and there for a space he was confined. Afterwards he was given a, much more considerable liberty; indeed, almost as much freedom as one has in a civilized town on earth. And it would appear that the mysterious being who is the ruler and master of the moon appointed two Selenites "with large heads" to guard and study him, and to establish whatever mental communications were possible with him. And, amazing and incredible as it may seem, these two creatures, these fantastic men-insects, these beings of another world, were presently communicating with Cavor by means of terrestrial speech.

Cavor speaks of them as Phi-oo and Tsi-puff. Phi-oo, he says, was about 5ft. high; he had small, slender legs about 18in. long, and slight feet of the common lunar pattern. On these balanced a little body, throbbing with the pulsations of his heart. He had long, soft, many-jointed arms ending in a tentacled grip, and his neck was many-jointed in the usual way, but exceptionally short and thick. His head, says Cavor—apparently alluding to some previous description that has gone astray in space—"is of the common lunar type, but strangely modified. The mouth has the usual expressionless gape, but it is unusually small and pointing downward, and the mask is reduced to the size of a large flat nose-flap. On either side are the little hen-like eyes.

The rest of the head is distended into a huge globe, and the chitinous leathery cuticle of the mooncalf herds thins out to a mere membrane, through which the pulsating brain movements are distinctly visible. He is a creature, indeed, with a tremendously hypertrophied brain, and with the rest of his organism both relatively and absolutely dwarfed."

In another passage Cavor compares the back view of him to Atlas supporting the world. Tsi-puff, it seems, was a very similar insect, but his "face" was drawn out to a considerable length, and, the brain hypertrophy being in different regions, his head was not round but pear-shaped, with the stalk downward. There were also litter-carriers, lop-sided beings with enormous shoulders, very spidery ushers, and a squat foot attendant in Cavor's retinue.

The manner in which Phi-oo and Tsi-puff attacked the problem of speech was fairly obvious. They came into this "hexagonal cell" in which Cavor was confined, and began imitating every sound he made, beginning with a cough. He seems to have grasped their intention with great quickness, and to have begun repeating words to them and pointing to indicate the application. The procedure was probably always the same. Phi-oo would attend to Cavor for a space, then point also and say the word he had heard.

The first word he mastered was "man," and the second "Mooney"—which Cavor on the spur of the moment seems to have used instead of "Selenite" for the moon race. As soon as Phi-oo was assured of the meaning of a word he repeated it to Tsi-puff, who remembered it infallibly. They mastered over one hundred English nouns at their first session.

Subsequently it seems they brought an artist with them to assist the work of explanation with sketches and diagrams—Cavor's drawings being rather crude. He was, says Cavor, "a being with an active arm and an arresting eye," and he seemed to draw with incredible swiftness.

The eleventh message is undoubtedly only a fragment of a longer communication. After some broken sentences, the record of which is unintelligible, it goes on:—

"But it will interest only linguists, and delay me too long, to give the details of the series of intent parleys of which these were the beginning, and, indeed, I very much doubt if I could give in anything like the proper order all the twistings and turnings that we made in our pursuit of mutual comprehension. Verbs were soon plain sailing—at least, such active verbs as I could express by drawings; some adjectives were easy, but when it came to abstract nouns, to prepositions, and the sort of hackneyed figures of speech by means of which so much is expressed on earth, it was like diving in cork jackets. Indeed, these difficulties were insurmountable until to the

sixth lesson came a fourth assistant, a being with a huge, football—
shaped head, whose *forte* was clearly the pursuit of intricate analogy.
He entered in a preoccupied manner, stumbling against a stool, and
the difficulties that arose had to be presented to him with a certain
amount of clamour and hitting and pricking before they reached his
apprehension. But once he was involved his penetration was amazing. Whenever there came a need of thinking beyond Phi-oo's by
no means limited scope, this prolate headed person was in request,
but he invariably told the conclusion to Tsi-puff, in order that it
might be remembered; Tsi-puff was ever the arsenal for facts. And
so we advanced again.

"It seemed long and yet—a matter of days before I was positively
talking with these insects of the moon. Of course, at first it was an
intercourse infinitely tedious and exasperating, but imperceptibly it
has grown to comprehension. And my patience has grown to meet
its limitations. Phi-oo it is who does all the talking. He does it with
a vast amount of meditative provisional 'M'm—M'm,' and he has
caught up one or two phrases, 'If I may say,' 'If you understand,'
and beads all his speech with them.

"Thus he would discourse. Imagine him explaining his artist.

"'M'm—M'm—he—if I may say—draw. Eat little—drink little—
draw. Love draw. No other thing. Hate all who not draw like him.
Angry. Hate all who draw like him better. Hate most people. Hate
all who not think all world for to draw. Angry. M'm. All things mean
nothing to him—only draw. He like you….if you understand… New
thing to draw. Ugly—striking. Eh?

"'He'—turning to Tsi-puff—'love remember words. Remember
wonderful more than any. Think no, draw no—remember. Say'—
here he referred to his gifted assistant for a word—'histories—all
things. He hear once—say ever.'

"It is more wonderful to me than I ever dreamt that anything ever could be again to hear these extraordinary creatures—for even familiarity fails to weaken the inhuman effect of their appearance— continually piping a nearer approach to coherent earthly speech, asking questions, giving answers. I feel that I am casting back to the fable-hearing period of childhood again when the ant and the grasshopper talked together and the bee judged between them…"

And while these linguistic exercises were going on Cavor seems to have experienced a considerable relaxation of his confinement. The first dread and distrust our unfortunate conflict aroused was being, he says, "continually effaced by the deliberate rationality of all I do."… "I am now able to come and go as I please, or I am restricted only for my own good. So it is I have been able to get at this apparatus, and, assisted by a happy find among the material that is littered in this enormous store-cave, I have contrived to dispatch these messages. So far not the slightest attempt has been made to interfere with me in this, though I have made it quite clear to Phi-oo that I am signalling to the earth.

"'You talk to other?' he asked, watching me.

"'Others,' said I.

"'Others,' he said. 'Oh, yes. Men?'

"And I went on transmitting."

Cavor was continually making corrections in his previous accounts of the Selenites as fresh facts flowed in upon him to modify his conclusions, and accordingly one gives the quotations that follow with a certain amount of reservation. They are quoted from the ninth, thirteenth, and sixteenth messages, and, altogether vague and fragmentary as they are, they probably give as complete a picture of the social life of this strange community as mankind can now hope to have for many generations.

"In the moon," says Cavor, "every citizen knows his place. He is born to that place, and the elaborate discipline of training and education and surgery he undergoes fits him at last so completely to it that he has neither ideas nor organs for any purpose beyond it. 'Why should he?' Phi-oo would ask. If, for example, a Selenite is destined to be a mathematician, his teachers and trainers set out at once to that end. They check any incipient disposition to other pursuits, they encourage his mathematical bias with a perfect psychological skill. His brain grows, or at least the mathematical faculties of his brain grow, and the rest of him only so much as is necessary to sustain this essential part of him. At last, save for rest and food, his one delight lies in the exercise and display of his faculty, his one interest in its application, his sole society with other specialists in his own line. His brain grows continually larger, at least so far as the portions engaging in mathematics are concerned; they bulge ever larger and seem to suck all life and vigour from the rest of his frame. His limbs shrivel, his heart and digestive organs diminish, his insect face is hidden under its bulging contours. His voice becomes a mere squeak for the stating of formulae; he seems deaf to all but properly enunciated problems. The faculty of laughter, save for the sudden discovery of some paradox, is lost to him; his deepest emotion is the evolution of a novel computation. And so he attains his end.

"Or, again, a Selenite appointed to be a minder of mooncalves is from his earliest years induced to think and live mooncalf, to find his pleasure in mooncalf lore, his exercise in their tending and pursuit. He is trained to become wiry and active, his eye is indurated to the tight wrappings, the angular contours that constitute a 'smart mooncalfishness.' He takes at last no interest in the deeper part of the moon; he regards all Selenites not equally versed in mooncalves with indifference, derision, or hostility. His thoughts are of mooncalf pastures, and his dialect an accomplished mooncalf technique. So also he loves his work, and discharges in perfect happiness the duty that justifies his being. And so it is with all sorts and conditions of Selenites—each is a perfect unit in a world machine...

"These beings with big heads, to whom the intellectual labours fall, form a sort of aristocracy in this strange society, and at the head of them, quintessential of the moon, is that marvellous gigantic ganglion the Grand Lunar, into whose presence I am finally to come. The unlimited development of the minds of the intellectual class is rendered possible by the absence of any bony skull in the lunar anatomy, that strange box of bone that clamps about the developing brain of man, imperiously insisting 'thus far and no farther' to all his possibilities. They fall into three main classes differing greatly in influence and respect. There are the administrators of whom Phi-oo was one, Selenites of considerable initiative and versatility, responsible each for a certain cubic content of the moon's bulk; the experts like the football-headed thinker who are trained to perform certain special operations; and the erudite who are the repositories of all knowledge. To this latter class belongs Tsi-puff, the first lunar professor of terrestrial languages. With regard to these latter it is a curious little thing to note that the unlimited growth of the lunar brain has rendered unnecessary the invention of all those mechanical aids to brain work which have distinguished the career of man. There are no books, no records of any sort, no libraries or inscriptions. All knowledge is stored in distended brains much as the honey-ants of Texas store honey in their distended abdomens. The lunar Somerset House and the lunar British Museum Library are collections of living brains...

"The less specialized administrators, I note, do for the most part take a very lively interest in me whenever they encounter me. They will come out of the way and stare at me and ask questions to which Phi-oo will reply. I see them going hither and thither with a retinue of bearers, attendants, shouters, parachute-carriers, and so forth—queer groups to see. The experts for the most part ignore me completely, even as they ignore each other, or notice me only to begin a clamorous exhibition of their distinctive skill. The erudite for the most part are rapt in an impervious and apoplectic complacency from which only a denial of their erudition can rouse them. Usually they are led about by little watchers and attendants, and often there are small and active-looking creatures, small females usually, that I am inclined to think are a sort of wife to them; but some of the profounder scholars are altogether too great for locomotion, and are carried from place to place in a sort of sedan tub, wabbling jellies of knowledge that enlist my respectful astonishment. I have just passed one in coming to this place where I am permitted to amuse myself with these electrical toys, a vast, shaven, shaky head, bald and thin-skinned, carried on his grotesque stretcher. In front and behind came his bearers, and curious, almost trumpet-faced, news disseminators shrieked his fame.

"I have already mentioned the retinues that accompanied most of the intellectuals: ushers, bearers, valets, extraneous tentacles and muscles as it were, to replace the abortive physical powers of these hypertrophied minds. Porters almost invariably accompany them. There are also extremely swift messengers with spider-like legs, and 'hands' for grasping parachutes, and attendants with vocal organs that could well-nigh wake the dead. Apart from their controlling intelligence these subordinates are as inert and helpless as umbrellas in a stand. They exist only in relation to the orders they have to obey, the duties they have to perform.

"The bulk of these insects, however, who go to and fro upon the spiral ways, who fill the ascending balloons and drop past me clinging to flimsy parachutes, are, I gather, of the operative class. 'Machine hands,' indeed, some of these are in actual nature—it is no figure of speech, the single tentacle of the mooncalf herd is replaced by huge single or paired bunches of three, or five, or seven digits for clawing, lifting, guiding, the rest of them no more than necessary subordinate appendages to these important parts. Some, who I suppose deal with bell-striking mechanisms, have enormous, rabbit-like ears just behind the eyes; some whose work lies in delicate chemical operations project a vast olfactory organ; others again have flat feet for treadles with anchylozed joints; and others—who I have been told are glass-blowers—seem mere lung-bellows. But every one of these common Selenites I have seen at work is exquisitely adapted to the social need it meets. Fine work is done by fined-down workers amazingly dwarfed and neat. Some I could hold on the palm of my hand. There is even a sort of turn-spit Selenite, very common, whose duty and only delight it is to supply the motive power for various small appliances. And to rule over these things and order any erring tendency there might be in some aberrant nature are the finest muscular beings I have seen in the moon, a sort of lunar police, who must have been trained from their earliest years to give a perfect respect and obedience to the swollen heads.

"The making of these various sorts of operative must be a very curious and interesting process. I am still very much in the dark about it, but quite recently I came upon a number of young Selenites confined in jars from which only the fore-limbs protruded, who were being compressed to become machine-minders of a special sort. The extended 'hand' in this highly developed system of technical education is stimulated by irritants and nourished by injection while the rest of the body is starved. Phi-oo, unless I misunderstood him, explained that in the earlier stages these queer little creatures are apt to display signs of suffering in their various cramped situations, but they easily become indurated to their lot; and he took me on to where a number of flexible-limbed messengers were being drawn out and broken in. It is quite unreasonable, I know, but these glimpses of the educational methods of these beings has affected me disagreeably. I hope, however, that may pass off and I may be able to see more of this aspect of this wonderful social order. That wretched-looking hand sticking out of its jar seemed to have a sort of limp appeal for lost possibilities; it haunts me still, although, of course, it is really in the end a far more humane proceeding than our earthly method of leaving children to grow into human beings, and then making machines of them.

"Quite recently, too—I think it was on the eleventh or twelfth visit I made to this apparatus—I had a curious light upon the lives of these operatives. I was being guided through a short cut hither instead of going down the spiral and by the quays of the Central Sea. From the devious windings of a long, dark gallery we emerged into a vast, low cavern, pervaded by an earthy smell, and rather brightly lit. The light came from a tumultuous growth of livid fungoid shapes—some indeed singularly like our terrestrial mushrooms, but standing as high or higher than a man.

"'Mooneys eat these?' said I to Phi-oo.

"'Yes, food.'

"'Goodness me!' I cried, 'what's that?'

"My eye had just caught the figure of an exceptionally big and ungainly Selenite lying motionless among the stems, face downward. We stopped.

"'Dead?' I asked. (For as yet I have? seen no dead in the moon, and I have grown curious.)

"'*No!*' exclaimed Phi-oo. 'Him—worker—no work to do. Get little drink then—make sleep—till we him want. What good him wake, eh? No want him walking about.'

"'There's another!' cried I.

"And indeed all that huge extent of mushroom ground was, I found, peppered with these prostrate figures sleeping under an opiate until the moon had need of them. There were scores of them of all sorts, and we were able to turn over some of them, and examine them more precisely than I had been able to do previously. They breathed noisily at my doing so, but did not wake. One I remember very distinctly: he left a strong impression, I think, because some trick of the light and of his attitude was strongly suggestive of a drawn-up human figure. His fore-limbs were long, delicate tentacles—he was some kind of refined manipulator—and the pose of his slumber suggested a submissive suffering. No doubt it was quite a mistake for me to interpret his expression in that way, but I did. And as Phi-oo rolled him over into the darkness among the livid fleshiness again I felt a distinctly unpleasant sensation, although as he rolled the insect in him was confessed.

"It simply illustrates the unthinking way in which one acquires habits of thought and feeling. To drug the worker one does not want and toss him aside is surely far better than to expel him from his factory to wander starving in the streets. In every complicated social community there is necessarily a certain intermittency in the occupation of all specialized labour, and in this way the trouble of an unemployed problem is altogether anticipated. And yet, so unreasonable are even scientifically trained minds, I still do not like the memory of those prostrate forms amidst those quiet, luminous arcades of fleshy growth, and I avoid that short cut in. spite of the inconveniences of its longer, more noisy, and more crowded alternative.

"My alternative route takes me round by a huge, shadowy cavern, very crowded and clamorous, and here it is I see peering out of the hexagonal openings of a sort of honeycomb wall, or parading a large open space behind, or selecting the toys and amulets made to please them by the acephalic dainty-fingered jewellers who work in kennels below, the mothers of the moon-world—the queen bees, as it were, of the hive. They are noble-looking beings, fantastically and sometimes quite beautifully adorned, with a proud carriage and, save for their mouths, almost microscopic heads.

"Of the condition of the moon sexes, marrying and giving in marriage, and of birth and so forth among the Selenites, I have to learn very little. With the steady progress of Phi-oo in English, however, my ignorance will no doubt as steadily disappear. I am of opinion that as with the ants and bees there is a large majority of the members in this community of the neuter sex. Of course on earth in our cities there are now many who never live that life of parentage which is the natural life of man. Here, as with the ants, this thing has become a normal condition of the race, and the whole of such replacement as is necessary falls upon this special and by no means numerous class of matrons, the mothers of the moon-world, large and stately beings beautifully fitted to bear the larval Selenite. Unless I misunderstand an explanation of Phi-oo's, they are absolutely incapable of cherishing the young they bring into the moon; periods of foolish indulgence alternate with moods of aggressive violence, and as soon as possible the little creatures, who are quite soft and flabby and pale coloured, are transferred, to the charge of a variety of celibate females, women 'workers' as it were, who in some cases possess brains of almost masculine dimensions."

Just at this point, unhappily, this message broke off. Fragmentary and tantalizing as the matter constituting this chapter is, it does nevertheless give a vague, broad impression of an altogether strange and wonderful world—a world with which our own must now prepare to reckon very speedily. This intermittent trickle of messages, this whispering of a record needle in the darkness of the mountain slopes, is the first warning of such a change in human conditions as mankind has scarcely imagined heretofore. In that planet there are new elements, new appliances, new traditions, an overwhelming avalanche of new ideas, a strange race with whom we must inevitably struggle for mastery—gold as common as iron or wood...

The Grand Lunar

The penultimate message describes, with occasionally even elaborate detail, the encounter between Cavor and the Grand Lunar, who is the ruler or master of the moon. Cavor seems to have sent most of it without interference, but to have been interrupted in the concluding portion. The second came after an interval of a week.

The first message begins: "At last I am able to resume this—"; it then becomes illegible for a space, and after a time resumes in mid-sentence.

The missing words of the following sentence are probably "the crowd." There follows quite clearly: "grew ever denser as we drew near the palace of the Grand Lunar—if I may call a series of excavations a palace. Everywhere faces stared at me—blank, chitinous gapes and masks, big eyes peering over tremendous nose tentacles, and little eyes beneath monstrous forehead plates; below an undergrowth of smaller creatures dodged and yelped, and grotesque heads poised on sinuous, swanlike, long-jointed necks appeared craning over shoulders and beneath armpits. Keeping a welcome space about me marched a cordon of stolid, scuttle-headed guards, who had joined us on our leaving the boat in which we had come along the channels of the Central Sea. The flea-like artist with the little brain joined us also, and a thick bunch of lean porter-ants swayed and struggled under the multitude of conveniences that were considered essential to my state. I was carried in a litter during the final stage of our journey. It was made of some very ductile metal that looked dark to me, meshed and woven and with bars of paler metal, and about me as I advanced there grouped itself a long and complicated procession.

"In front, after the manner of heralds, marched four trumpet-faced creatures making a devastating bray; and then came squat, almost beetle-like, ushers before and behind, and on either hand a galaxy of learned heads, a sort of animated encyclopædia, who were, Phi-oo explained, to stand about the Grand Lunar for purposes of reference. (Not a thing in lunar science, not a point of view or method of thinking, that these wonderful beings did not carry in their heads.) Followed guards and porters, and then Phi-oo's shivering brain borne also on a litter. Then came Tsi-puff in a slightly less important litter; then myself on a litter of greater elegance than any other and surrounded by my food and drink attendants. More trumpeters came next, splitting the ear with vehement outcries, and then several big brains, special correspondents one might well

call them or historiographers, charged with the task of observing
and remembering every detail of this epoch-making interview. A
company of attendants, bearing and dragging banners and masses of
scented fungus and curious symbols, completed the procession. The
way was lined by ushers and officers in caparisons that gleamed like
steel, and beyond their line the heads and tentacles of that enormous
crowd surged on either hand.

"I will own that I am still by no means indurated to the peculiar
effect of the Selenite appearance, and to find myself as it were adrift
on this broad sea of excited entomology was by no means agreeable.
Just for a space I had something like I should imagine people mean
when they speak of the 'horrors.' It had come to me before in these
lunar caverns, when on occasion, I have found myself weaponless
and with an undefended back, amidst a crowd of these Selenites,
but never quite so vividly. It is, of course, as absolutely irrational a
feeling as one could well have, and I hope gradually to subdue it.
But just for a moment, as I swept forward into the welter of the vast
crowd, it was only by gripping my litter tightly and summoning all
my will-power that I succeeded in avoiding an outcry or some such
manifestation. It lasted perhaps three minutes; then I had myself
in hand again.

"We ascended the spiral of a vertical way for some time and then
passed through a series of huge halls, dome-roofed and gloriously
decorated. The approach to the Grand Lunar was certainly contrived
to give one a vivid impression of his greatness. The halls—all happily
sufficiently luminous for my terrestrial eye—were a cunning and
elaborate crescendo of space and decoration. The effect of their
progressive size was enhanced by the steady diminution in the lighting, and by a thin haze of incense that thickened as one advanced.
In the earlier ones the vivid, clear light made everything finite and

concrete to me. I seemed to advance continually to something larger, dimmer, and less material.

"I must confess that all this splendour made me feel extremely shabby and unworthy. I was unshaven and unkempt: I had brought no razor; I had a coarse beard over my mouth. On earth I have always been inclined to despise any attention to my person beyond a proper care for cleanliness; but under the exceptional circumstances in which I found myself, representing, as. I did, my planet and my kind, and depending very largely upon the attractiveness of my appearance for a proper reception, I could have given much for something a little more artistic and dignified than the husks I wore. I had been so serene in the belief that the moon was uninhabited as to overlook such precautions altogether. As it was I was dressed in a flannel jacket, knickerbockers, and golfing stockings, stained with every sort of dirt the moon offered; slippers (of which the left heel was wanting), and a blanket, through a hole in which I thrust my head. (These clothes, indeed, I still wear.) Sharp bristles are anything but an improvement to my cast of features, and there was an unmended tear at the knee of my knickerbockers that showed conspicuously as I squatted in my litter; my right stocking, too, persisted in getting about my ankle. I am fully alive to the injustice my appearance did humanity, and if by any expedient I could have improvised something a little out of the way and imposing I would have done so. But I could hit upon nothing. I did what I could with my blanket—folding it somewhat after the fashion of a toga, and for the rest I sat as upright as the swaying of my litter permitted.

"Imagine the largest hall you have ever been in, elaborately decorated with blue and whitish-blue Majolica, lit by blue light, you know not how, and surging with metallic or livid-white creatures of such a mad diversity as I have hinted. Imagine this hall to end in an

open archway beyond which is a still larger hall, and beyond this yet
another and still larger one, and so on. At the end of the vista a flight
of steps, like the steps of Ara Cœli at Rome, ascend out of sight.
Higher and higher these steps appear to go as one draws nearer their
base. But at last I came under a huge archway and beheld the summit
of these steps, and upon it the Grand Lunar exalted on his throne.

"He was seated in a blaze of incandescent blue. A hazy atmosphere filled the place so that its walls seemed invisibly remote. This
gave him an effect of floating in a blue-black void. He seemed a small,
self-luminous cloud at first, brooding on his glaucous throne; his
brain-case must have measured many yards in diameter. For some
reason that I cannot fathom a number of blue search-lights radiated
from behind the throne on which he sat, as though he were a star,
and immediately encircling him was a halo. About him, and little
and indistinct in this glow, a number of body-servants sustained and
supported him, and overshadowed and standing in a huge semicircle
beneath him were his intellectual subordinates, his remembrancers
and computators and searchers, his flatterers and servants, and all
the distinguished insects of the court of the moon. Still lower stood
ushers and messengers, and then all down the countless steps of the
throne were guards, and at the base, enormous, various, indistinct,
a vast swaying multitude of the minor dignitaries of the moon.
Their feet made a perpetual scraping whisper on the rocky floor,
their limbs moved with a rustling murmur.

"As I entered the penultimate hall the music rose and expanded
into an imperial magnificence of sound, and the shrieks of the
news-bearers died away...

"I entered the last and greatest hall...

"My procession opened out like a fan. My ushers and guards
went right and left, and the three litters bearing myself and Phi-oo

and Tsi-puff marched across a shiny waste of floor to the foot of the giant stairs. Then began a vast throbbing hum, that mingled with the music. The two Selenites dismounted, but I was bidden remain seated—I imagine as a special honour. The music ceased, but not that humming, and by a simultaneous movement of ten thousand respectful eyes my attention was directed to the enhaloed supreme intelligence that hovered above us.

"At first as I peered into the radiating blaze this quintessential brain looked very much like an opaque, featureless bladder with dim, undulating ghosts of convolutions writhing visibly within. Then beneath its enormity and just above the edge of the throne one saw with a start minute elfin eyes peering out of the blaze. No face, but eyes, as if they peered through holes. At first I could see no more than these two staring little eyes, and then below I distinguished the little dwarfed body and its insect-jointed limbs shrivelled and white. The eyes stared down at me with a strange intensity, and the lower part of the swollen globe was wrinkled. Ineffectual-looking little hand—tentacles steadied this shape on the throne...

"It was great. It was pitiful. One forgot the ball and the crowd.

"I ascended the staircase by jerks. It seemed to me that the purple glowing brain-case above us spread over me, and took more and more of the whole effect into itself as I drew nearer. The tiers of attendants and helpers grouped about their master seemed to dwindle and fade into the glare. I saw that the shadowy attendants were busy spraying that great brain with a cooling spray, and patting and sustaining it. For my own part I sat gripping my swaying litter and staring at the Grand Lunar, unable to turn my gaze aside. And at last, as I reached a little landing that was separated only by ten steps or so from the supreme seat, the woven splendour of the music reached a climax and ceased, and I was left naked, as it were, in that vastness, beneath the still scrutiny of the Grand Lunar's eyes.

"He was scrutinizing the first man he had ever seen....

"My eyes dropped at last from his greatness to the faint figures in the blue mist about him, and then down the steps to the massed Selenites, still and expectant in their thousands, packed on the floor below. Once again an unreasonable horror reached out towards me.... And passed.

"After the pause came the salutation. I was assisted from my litter, and stood awkwardly while a number of curious and no doubt deeply symbolical gestures were vicariously performed for me by two slender officials. The encyclopædic galaxy of the learned that had accompanied me to the entrance of the last hall appeared two steps above me and left and right of me, in readiness for the Grand Lunar's need, and Phi-oo's white brain placed itself about half-way up to the throne in such a position as to communicate easily between us without turning his back on either the Grand Lunar or myself. Tsi-puff took up a position behind him. Dexterous ushers sidled side-ways towards me, keeping a full face to the Presence. I seated myself Turkish fashion, and Phi-oo and Tsi-puff also knelt down above me. There came a pause. The eyes of the nearer court went from me to the Grand Lunar and came back to me, and a hissing and piping of expectation passed across the hidden multitudes below and ceased.

"That humming ceased.

"For the first and last time in my experience the moon was silent.

"I became aware of a faint wheezy noise. The Grand Lunar was addressing me. It was like the rubbing of a finger upon a pane of glass.

"I watched him attentively for a time and then glanced at the alert Phi-oo. I felt amidst these filmy beings ridiculously thick and

fleshy and solid; my head all jaw and black hair. My eyes went back
to the Grand Lunar. He had ceased; his attendants were busy, and
his shining super-fices was glistening and running with cooling spray.

"Phi-oo meditated through an interval. He consulted Tsi-puff.
Then he began piping his recognizable English—at first a little nervously, so that he was not very clear.

"'M'm—the Grand Lunar—wishes to say—wishes to say—he
gathers you are—M'm—men—that you are a man from the planet
earth. He wishes to say that he welcomes you—welcomes you—and
wishes to learn—learn, if I may use the word—the state of your
world, and the reason why you came to this.'

"He paused. I was about to reply when he resumed. He proceeded to remarks of which the drift was not very clear, though I
am inclined to think they were intended to be complimentary. He
told me that the earth was to the moon what the sun is to the earth,
and that the Selenites desired very greatly to learn about the earth
and men. He then told me, no doubt in compliment also, the relative magnitude and diameter of earth and moon, and the perpetual
wonder and speculation with which the Selenites had regarded our
planet. I meditated with downcast eyes and decided to reply that
men too had wondered what might lie in the moon, and had judged
it dead, little recking of such magnificence as I had seen that day.
The Grand Lunar, in token of recognition, caused his blue searchlight to rotate in a very confusing manner, and all about the great
hall ran the pipings and whisperings and rustlings of the report of
what I had said. He then proceeded to put to Phi-oo a number of
inquiries which were easier to answer.

"He understood, he explained, that we lived on the surface of
the earth, that our air and sea were outside the globe; the latter part,
indeed, he already knew from his astronomical specialists. He was

very anxious to have more detailed information of what he called
this extraordinary state of affairs, for from the solidity of the earth
there had always been a disposition to regard it as uninhabitable.
He endeavoured first to ascertain the extremes of temperature to
which we earth beings were exposed, and he was deeply interested
by my descriptive treatment of clouds and rain. His imagination
was assisted by the fact that the lunar atmosphere in the outer galleries of the night side is not infrequently very foggy. He seemed
inclined to marvel that we did not find the sunlight too intense for
our eyes, and was interested in my attempt to explain that the sky
was tempered to a bluish colour through the refraction of the air,
though I doubt if he clearly understood that. I explained how the
iris of the human eyes can contract the pupil and save the delicate
internal structure from the excess of sunlight, and was allowed to
approach within a few feet of the Presence in order that this structure
might be seen. This led to a comparison of the lunar and terrestrial
eyes. The former is not only excessively sensitive to such light as men
can see, but it can also *see* heat, and every difference in temperature
within the moon renders objects visible to it.

"The iris was quite a new organ to the Grand Lunar. For a time
he amused himself by flashing his rays into my face and watching
my pupils contract. As a consequence, I was dazzled and blinded
for some little time....

"But in spite of that discomfort I found something reassuring
by insensible degrees in the rationality of this business of question
and answer. I could shut my eyes, think of my answer, and almost
forget that the Grand Lunar has no face...

"When I had descended again to my proper place the Grand
Lunar asked how we sheltered ourselves from heat and storms, and
I expounded to him the arts of building and furnishing. Here we

wandered into misunderstandings and cross-purposes, due largely, I must admit, to the looseness of my expressions. For a long time I had great difficulty in making him understand the nature of a house. To him and his attendant Selenites it seemed no doubt the most whimsical thing in the world that men should build houses when they might descend into excavations, and an additional complication was introduced by the attempt I made to explain that men had originally begun their homes in caves, and that they were now taking their railways and many establishments beneath the surface. Here I think a desire for intellectual completeness betrayed me. There was also a considerable tangle due to an equally unwise attempt on my part to explain about mines. Dismissing this topic at last in an incomplete state, the Grand Lunar inquired what we did with the interior of our globe.

"A tide of twittering and piping swept into the remotest corners of that great assembly when it was at last made clear that we men know absolutely nothing of the contents of the world upon which the immemorial generations of our ancestors had been evolved. Three times had I to repeat that of all the 4,000 miles of substance between the earth and its centre men knew only to the depth of a mile, and that very vaguely. I understood the Grand Lunar to ask why had I come to the moon seeing we had scarcely touched our own planet yet, but he did not trouble me at that time to proceed to an explanation, being too anxious to pursue the details of this mad inversion of all his ideas.

"He reverted to the question of weather, and I tried to describe the perpetually changing sky, and snow, and frost and hurricanes. 'But when the night comes.' he asked, 'is it not cold?'

"I told him it was colder than by day.

"'And does not your atmosphere freeze?'

"I told him not; that it was never cold enough for that, because our nights were so short.

"'Not even liquefy?'

"I was about to say 'No,' but then it occurred to me that one part at least of our atmosphere, the water vapour of it, does sometimes liquefy and form dew and sometimes freeze and form frost—a process perfectly analogous to the freezing of all the external atmosphere of the moon during its longer night. I made myself clear on this point, and from that the Grand Lunar went on to speak with me of sleep. For the need of sleep that comes so regularly every twenty-four hours to all things is part also of our earthly inheritance. On the moon they rest only at rare intervals and after exceptional exertions. Then I tried to describe to him the soft splendours of a summer night, and from that I passed to a description of those animals that prowl by night and sleep by day. I told him of lions and tigers, and here it seemed as though we had come to a deadlock. For, save in their waters, there are no creatures in the moon not absolutely domestic and subject to his will, and so it has been for immemorial years. They have monstrous water creatures, but no evil beasts, and the idea of anything strong and large existing 'outside' in the night is very difficult for them...

[The record is here too broken to transcribe for the space of perhaps twenty words or more.]

"He talked with his attendant I suppose, upon the strange superficiality and unreasonableness of (man), who lives on the mere surface of a world, a creature of waves and winds and all the chances of space, who cannot even unite to overcome the beasts that prey upon his kind, and yet who dares to invade another planet. During this aside I sat thinking, and then at his desire I told him of the different sorts of men. He searched me with questions. 'And for all sorts of work you have the same sort of men. But who thinks? Who governs?'

"I gave him an outline of the democratic method.

"When I had done he ordered cooling sprays upon his brow, and then requested me to repeat my explanation, conceiving something had miscarried.

"'Do they not do different things, then?' said Phi-oo.

"Some I admitted were thinkers and some officials: some hunted, some were mechanics, some artists, some toilers. 'But *all* rule,' I said.

"'And have they not different shapes to fit them to their different duties?'

"'None that you can see,' I said, 'except perhaps for clothes. Their minds perhaps differ a little,' I reflected.

"'Their minds must differ a great deal,' said the Grand Lunar, 'or they would all want to do the same things.'

"In order to bring myself into a closer harmony with his preconceptions I said that his surmise was right. 'It was all hidden in the brain,' I said; 'but the difference was there. Perhaps if one could see the minds and souls of men they would be as varied and unequal as the Selenites. There were great men and small men, men who could reach out far and wide, and men who could go swiftly; noisy, trumpet-minded men, and men who could remember without thinking—

[The record is indistinct for three words.]

"He interrupted me to recall me to my previous statement. 'But you said all men rule?' he pressed.

"'To a certain extent,' I said, and made, I fear, a denser fog with my explanation.

"He reached out to a salient fact. 'Do you mean,' he asked, 'that there is no Grand Earthly?'

"I thought of several people, but assured him finally there was none. I explained that such autocrats and emperors as we had tried upon earth had usually ended in drink, or vice, or violence, and that the large and influential section of the people of the earth to which I belonged, the Anglo-Saxons, did not mean to try that sort of thing again. At which the Grand Lunar was even more amazed.

"'But how do you keep even such wisdom as you have?' he asked; and I explained to him the way we helped our limited [a word omitted here, probably "brains."] with libraries of books. I explained to him how our science was growing by the united labours of innumerable little men, and on that he made no comment save that it was evident we had mastered much in spite of our social savagery, or we could not have come to the moon. Yet the contrast was very marked. With knowledge the Selenites grew and changed; mankind stored their knowledge about them and remained brutes—equipped. He said this... [Here there is a short piece of the record indistinct.]

"He then caused me to describe how we went about this earth of ours and I described to him our railways and ships. For a time he could not understand that we had had the use of steam only one hundred years, but when he did he was clearly amazed. (I may mention as a singular thing that the Selenites use years to count by, just as we do on earth, though I can make nothing of their numeral system. That however does not matter, because Phi-oo understands ours.) From that I went on to tell him that mankind had dwelt in cities only for nine or ten thousand years, and that we were still not united in one brotherhood, but under many different forms of government. This astonished the Grand Lunar very much, when it was made clear to him. At first he thought we referred merely to administrative areas.

"'Our States and Empires are still the rawest sketches of what order will some day be,' I said, and so I came to tell him...

[At this point a length of record that probably represents thirty or forty words is totally illegible.]

"The Grand Lunar was greatly impressed by the folly of men in clinging to the inconvenience of diverse tongues. 'They want to communicate, and yet not to communicate,' he said, and then for a long time he questioned me closely concerning war.

"He was at first perplexed and incredulous. 'You mean to say,' he asked, seeking confirmation, 'that you run about over the surface of your world—this world, whose riches you have scarcely begun to scrape—killing one another for beasts to eat?'

"I told him that was perfectly correct.

"He asked for particulars to assist his imagination. 'But do not your ships and your poor little cities get injured?' he asked, and I found the waste of property and conveniences seemed to impress him almost as much as the killing. 'Tell me more,' said the Grand Lunar; 'make me see pictures. I cannot conceive these things.'

"And so, for a space, though something loth, I told him the story of earthly War.

"I told him of the first orders and ceremonies of war, of warnings and ultimatums, and the marshalling and marching of troops. I gave him an idea of manœuvres and positions and battle joined. I told him of sieges and assaults, of starvation and hardship in trenches, and of sentinels freezing in the snow. I told him of routs and surprises, and desperate last stands and faint hopes, and the pitiless pursuit of fugitives and the dead upon the field. I told, too, of the past, of invasions and massacres, of the Huns and Tartars, and the wars of Mahomet and the Caliphs and of the Crusades. And as I went on and Phi-oo translated, the Selenites cooed and murmured in a steadily intensified emotion.

"I told them an ironclad could fire a shot of a ton twelve miles, and go through 20 feet of iron—and how we could steer torpedoes under water. I went on to describe a Maxim gun in action and what I could imagine of the Battle of Colenso. The Grand Lunar was so incredulous that he interrupted the translation of what I had said in order to have my verification of my account. They particularly doubted my description of the men cheering and rejoicing as they went into battle.

"'But surely they do not like it!' translated Phi-oo.

"I assured them men of my race considered battle the most glorious experience of life, at which the whole assembly was stricken with amazement.

"'But what good is this war?' asked the Grand Lunar, sticking to his theme.

"'Oh! as for *good!*' said I; 'it thins the population!'

"'But why should there be a need—?'...

"There came a pause, the cooling sprays impinged upon his brow, and then he spoke again."

At this point there suddenly becomes predominant in the record a series of undulations that have been apparent as a perplexing complication as far back as Cavor's description of the silence that fell before the first speaking of the Grand Lunar. These undulations are evidently the result of radiations proceeding from a lunar source, and their persistent approximation to the alternating signals of Cavor is curiously suggestive of some operator deliberately seeking to mix them in with his message and render it illegible. At first they are small and regular, so that with a little care and the loss of very few words we have been able to disentangle Cavor's message; then they become broad and larger, then suddenly they are irregular, with an irregularity that gives the effect at last of someone scribbling through a line of writing. For a long time nothing can be made of this madly zigzagging trace; then quite abruptly the interruption ceases, leaves a few words clear, and then resumes and continues for all the rest of the message, completely obliterating whatever Cavor was attempting to transmit. Why, if this is indeed a deliberate intervention, the Selenites should have preferred to let Cavor go on transmitting his message in happy ignorance of their obliteration of its record, when it was clearly quite in their power and much more easy and convenient for them to stop his proceedings at any time, is a problem to which I can contribute nothing. The thing seems to have happened so, and that is all I can say. This last rag of his description of the Grand Lunar begins, in mid-sentence:—

"interrogated me very closely upon my secret. I was able in a little while to get to an understanding with them, and at last to elucidate what has been a puzzle to me ever since I realized the vastness of their science, namely, how it is they themselves have never discovered 'Cavorite.' I find they know of it as a theoretical substance, but they have always regarded it as a practical impossibility, because for some reason there is no helium in the moon, and helium—"

Across the last letters of helium slashes the resumption of that obliterating trace. Note that word "secret," for on that, and that alone, I base my interpretation of the last message, as both Mr. Wendigee and myself now believe it to be, that he is ever likely to send us.

The Last Message Cavor Sent to the Earth

In this unsatisfactory manner the penultimate message of Cavor dies out. One seems to see him away there amidst his blue-lit apparatus intently signalling us to the last, all unaware of the curtain of confusion that drops between us; all unaware, too, of the final dangers that even then must have been creeping upon him. His disastrous want of vulgar common-sense had utterly betrayed him. He had talked of war, he had talked of all the strength and irrational violence of men, of their insatiable aggressions, their tireless futility of conflict. He had filled the whole moon-world with this impression of our race, and then I think it is plain that he admitted upon himself alone hung the possibility—at least for a long time—of any further men reaching the moon. The line the cold, inhuman reason of the moon would take seems plain enough to me, and a suspicion of it, and then perhaps some sudden sharp realization of it, must have come to him. One imagines him going about the moon with the remorse of this fatal indiscretion growing in his mind. During a certain time most assuredly the Grand Lunar was deliberating the new situation, and for all that time Cavor went as free as ever he had gone. We imagine obstacles of some sort prevented Cavor getting to his electro-magnetic apparatus again after that last message I have given. For some days we received nothing. Perhaps he was having fresh audiences, and trying to evade his previous admissions. Who can hope to guess?

And then suddenly, like a cry in the night, like a cry that is followed by a stillness, came the last message. It is the briefest fragment, the broken beginnings of two sentences.

The first was: "I was mad to let the Grand Lunar know—"

There was an interval of perhaps a minute. One imagines some interruption from without. A departure from the instrument—a dreadful hesitation among the looming masses of apparatus in that dim, blue-lit cavern—a sudden rush back to it, full of a resolve that came too late. Then, as if it were hastily transmitted, came: "Cavorite made as follows: take—"

There followed one word, a quite unmeaning word as it stands: "uless."

And that is all.

It may be he made a hasty attempt to spell "useless" when his fate was close upon him. Whatever it was that was happening about that apparatus, we cannot tell. Whatever it was we shall never, I know, receive another message from the moon. For my own part a vivid dream has come to my help, and I see, almost as plainly as though I had seen it in actual fact, a blue-lit dishevelled Cavor struggling in the grip of a great multitude of those insect Selenites, struggling ever more desperately and hopelessly as they swarm upon him, shouting, expostulating, perhaps even at last fighting, and being forced backward step by step out of all speech or sign of his fellows, for evermore into the Unknown—into the dark, into that silence that has no end…

Charles Cloukey

Charles Cloukey (1912–1931) may be the least known and yet most remarkable author in this anthology, and also the most tragic. He was one of those young, aspiring visionaries and experimenters that Hugo Gernsback had hoped to encourage when he launched the first science-fiction magazine, Amazing Stories, *in 1926. During the preceding decade or so Gernsback, who had emigrated from Luxembourg to the United States to better his career, had become increasingly aware that it was the young generation in America who were fascinated by the growing technologies and discoveries emerging from the experiments and inventions of entrepreneurs like Thomas Edison, Nikola Tesla and Lee de Forest. Gernsback encouraged this generation to experiment and to stimulate their imagination he published fiction—at the outset mostly "gadget" stories about new inventions—in his technical magazines such as* The Electrical Experimenter. *As a result the field of "scientifiction", as Gernsback first called it, grew and, believing there was a substantial market, Gernsback created* Amazing Stories.

Cloukey was hooked on the magazine from the start and though only fifteen submitted stories to Gernsback. The following is his very first, published in March 1928, a quite remarkable work for someone so young. It may lack the sophistication of writers of more mature years but it makes up for that in the sheer exuberance of his ideas. Not only does Cloukey describe a trip to the Moon by rocket, which no one had detailed before, but he also proposes that the journey be monitored by television and although in the end that monitor is not used, Cloukey was the very first to suggest it. The rocket also has an onboard computer. Cloukey then raises a subject that had also not been considered before—what happens if you fire a gun in the Moon's lower gravity.

Cloukey's promising career was cut tragically short. Just three years after this first sale, and the publication of eight further stories, he was dead. He had entered college to study chemical engineering but caught typhoid fever and died.

I LOOKED UP FROM MY BOOK. MY FRIEND AND ROOMMATE, C. Jerry Clankey, in his big easy-chair across the room, was gazing intently at the ceiling and talking out loud to himself. This was a peculiar and often annoying habit of his, but this time I could not help being interested in what he was saying.

"It behaved precisely according to the laws of celestial mechanics," he was saying, "exactly as a satellite. Perhaps one could call it a sub-satellite. And then there was the matter of the Doctor's will. The diamonds!

"It was marvellous," he continued to the ceiling, "one chance out of thousands. Duseau swore he would have his revenge. I wonder if he was satisfied. And Jacqueline—"

Jerry stopped suddenly as he noticed that I was looking at him curiously. He became embarrassed.

"Pardon me," I said, "but if you don't mind, I'd like to know what in the world you are talking about. I'm not particularly dense, but I entirely fail to see any connection between celestial mechanics, satellites, diamonds, and revenge. And who is Jacqueline? Would you mind—"

He interrupted me, smiling slightly. "I suppose," he said, "that even in this enlightened era of the twenty-first century, there are portions of Tibet where news travels rather slowly. As you, Kornfield, have only returned to New York today, you are perhaps still ignorant of the fact that Dr. D. Francis Javis actually succeeded with his plans for reaching the moon."

"I heard a man in Paris mention it yesterday," I informed him, "but I don't know the details. After our plane was forced down in the Dangla Mountains, and Basehore had accidentally broken the only radio with the expedition, we were cut off from civilization for four and a half months. Tell me about the moon trip. What did he find there? And what has that to do with the Doctor's will? And who is Jacqueline?"

"All right," said Jerry, leaning back comfortably in his chair, "I'll tell you. Even the newspapers didn't get it all, though I suppose the reporters thought they did. Listen, and I'll tell you the whole story":

As you know, Kornfield, (said C. Jerry Clankey), I was the chief radio engineer on Javis' staff. I designed the transmitter, and the receiver, too, that he took to the moon, and by means of which he was able to communicate with my installation at Albany. I also supervised the construction of a simplified television outfit, which Javis discarded in the last hour before he left, in order to make room for an additional supply of concentrated food.

But I should start at the beginning. Perhaps you remember that Javis discovered, about ten years ago, how to produce artificial diamonds, of greater hardness, size, brilliance, and beauty than the genuine stone. After he had manufactured almost two billion dollars' worth, he destroyed his invention. Since then, many scientists have tried to rediscover his secret, but without success.

He sold about half of the diamonds to secure capital with which to make his moon trip, and deposited the rest in a specially constructed vault here in New York. He also made a will, in which, for some reason of his own, he left his entire fortune to his elder son, Donald, cutting off the younger, Jack, without a cent. Then he started to work on his project of reaching the moon.

I've often wondered why he wanted to reach the moon. One would hardly think that the love of knowledge would be so great that a man would be willing to work ten years, spend a billion dollars, and finally risk his life in an attempt to reach the moon, merely to satisfy that love. But Javis was a queer man. The money meant nothing to him. Neither, apparently, did the risk. He prepared for his journey and he went, regardless of consequences.

You know, of course, the type of vehicle he chose—a projectile-shaped rocket, of the type proposed by Dr. Goddard over a century ago, propelled, once it was out of the earth's atmosphere, by explosive gases. But I won't go into that. You understand the principle. While in the atmosphere, it was flown as an ordinary plane, by propellers.

The unique feature of the Doctor's rocket, however, was the ingenious construction of the wings, which allowed them to be withdrawn into the body of the rocket, after the atmosphere had been left behind.

This feature had been designed by R. Henri Duseau, the French scientist and engineer, who was one of Javis' most able assistants. Just why they quarrelled will probably never be known. They were both hot-tempered. So when Javis paid Duseau off, and discharged him, the impulsive Frenchman swore revenge.

It had been generally understood, though it appears that there was no written contract or agreement, that Duseau was to be the one to accompany Javis in his attempt to reach the moon, because Duseau had once been an air mail pilot in France, and could attend to the navigation of the craft while it was in the atmosphere. The rocket was, in spite of its great size, only designed to carry two passengers, because the rest of the available space had to be utilized to carry food, fuel, the radio equipment I had designed, the Doctor's scientific instruments, and various other necessary objects.

To be discharged after almost nine years of work was a great disappointment to Duseau. He had a natural craving for adventure, and also, I believe, for fame. He wanted to achieve great celebrity by his part in the moon trip. He was exceedingly temperamental, and perhaps this characteristic, together with his persuasion that he had been treated unfairly by Javis, was responsible for the attitude of jealous enmity he held for the Doctor after his discharge. Just how far he was destined to carry his bitter hate, the world was soon to learn.

To take Duseau's place, Javis hired Richard C. Brown, the famous stunt-flier and dare-devil, paying him in advance a flat sum of one million dollars. Men have risked their lives for less.

Dick Brown was a curious character. He was a happy-go-lucky, devil-may-care kid, game as they make 'em, reckless and foolhardy, only about twenty years old, and had the reputation of bearing a charmed life.

Brown made several test flights in the rocket. He was able to see on all sides by means of an ingenious arrangement of periscopes. As an airplane, the great craft functioned perfectly, having a maximum speed of about 350 miles per hour, and a ceiling of approximately 41,000 feet. How it would behave as a rocket remained to be seen.

After the trouble with Duseau, came the trouble with Donald, the Doctor's oldest son. I had always considered him more or less of a good-for-nothing vagabond. I don't know exactly what happened, but it seems that in an insane moment of drunken anger, he had drawn a revolver and fired, point-blank, at his father. Because he was drunk, he missed completely. The Doctor tried to hush up the affair, but in some way, news of the attempted parricide leaked out, and caused a lot of unpleasant publicity.

Javis told me, in a moment of confidence, that he intended to revise his will before he left, to give his entire fortune, including the diamonds, to his other son, Jack, who was a well-known banker and business man, in spite of his youth. Javis also intended to completely disinherit Donald, but he never changed the will. He went off to the moon without attending to the matter. He didn't have time, I suppose.

He and Brown left for the moon just ten days after his last experimental rocket had burst upon the moon, proving the existence of some, though very little, atmosphere on our satellite. This small rocket he sent to the moon contained a chemical compound which could not explode without oxygen. As it was observed by many astronomers to explode upon hitting the moon, it was obvious that our satellite possessed an atmosphere, however rare.

Javis had another purpose also in sending out these small rockets. By observing them, he could form an idea of the way the large one would act in space. When he had obtained all the data he desired, he made his preparations to depart.

For a week his whole establishment was in an uproar. The food, fuel, radio, and scientific instruments were put aboard, while Brown tuned up his motors to perfection. When I saw Javis dismantling and packing a light-weight Marvite machine gun, I ventured to make an inquiry.

"Surely," I said, "you don't expect to have any use for that on the moon, do you?"

"I hope not," Javis replied, "but we know that there is air upon the moon, so it is highly probable that there is some form of life there. I'm taking this gun because it is the most powerful weapon in the world for its size, and we might meet some monsters." He smiled, and finished packing the shining, deadly little weapon. Yet it seemed to me that there was no necessity for such a powerful gun. But he was taking no chances. If there were monsters on the moon, he would be prepared.

The next day they left. I will never forget it. As dozens of cameras and televisors clicked and buzzed on every side, Javis and Brown entered the rocket. Brown was smiling. It was an adventure to him. If he realized what slim chances he had of ever returning to the earth again, he gave no indication of the fact. But the face of Javis was grave. It was more than a mere adventure to him. This trip meant the realization of his life's ambition.

The field was cleared. The massive air-tight door was closed. Suddenly the three enormous propellers burst into action. With the incomparable skill of the born airman, Brown took off. Quickly he took the great plane as high as the motors would carry it. To the observers on the ground, it was only a speck in the cloudless sky.

Then those who were watching it with binoculars saw a brilliant green flash appear at the tail of the rocket. It darted suddenly upward. It was necessary to develop a speed greater than seven miles a second in order to leave the earth, and it was apparent that Javis was gradually attaining this tremendous velocity.

Through the rarefied upper strata of the atmosphere shot the great rocket. It left the earth.

Jerry was silent for awhile. I waited as patiently as I could for him to resume his narrative. But when his silence grew prolonged, I ventured to speak.

"I think," I said, "that I can guess now what you meant by a sub-satellite. I gather that the rocket, obeying the laws of celestial mechanics was captured by the attraction of the moon, revolving around it as a satellite, or sub-satellite, rather."

"Kornfield," said Jerry, "never jump at conclusions. I noticed that you were reading that remarkable story by Verne, 'A Trip to the Moon.' When you stop to consider that it was written almost two centuries ago, the amount of scientific prophecy and foresight in it is amazing. It's interesting to note how famous that story has become during the short time that has elapsed since Javis' great accomplishment. Before his tragic trip, the story was known to only a few learned men who had made a study of nineteenth century literature. But now it is famous, as an example of dreams coming true, of imagination becoming reality. Yesterday's impossibilities are today's facts. And tomorrow—what? But I am digressing.

"In that story, the author's imaginary projectile is deflected from its course by the moon's attraction. But this didn't happen to Javis. He could steer his rocket, you remember, by exploding his gases at any one of fifty different points on its exterior. He landed all right. When they were within a couple of thousand of miles of the moon, he checked their speed by exploding a charge at the end of the rocket nearest the moon. As it began to fall toward the surface of our satellite, he checked it again in the same manner.

"He had to repeat this process several times. Finally the rocket was only a few hundred feet above the broad summit of a lunar peak. So Javis let it fall. Owing to the elaborate shock-absorbing system, and the inferior force of lunar gravity, no damage was done.

"After working nine years, and spending almost a billion dollars, Javis had succeeded in reaching the moon. He landed on the summit of an exceedingly tall mountain near the Mare Tranquilitatis."

"But, then," I protested, "to what were you referring when you spoke about a sub-satellite? And you haven't told me yet who Jacqueline is."

"Be patient, Bob, be patient," he admonished, "I have not yet concluded my narrative." He smiled quizzically. "All in good time, my lad," he said, "control your impatience and all your questions will be answered." Then he plunged once more into his story:

I have, continued C. Jerry Clankey, gone ahead of my story. I've told you of the landing on the moon. But several very important events occurred before the rocket reached its destination.

The greatest danger, perhaps, that confronted the extra-terrestrial pioneers was the danger from meteors*. These meteors are by no means scarce. There are uncounted millions in this solar system alone. Nor are they all as small as you might assume. Many weigh dozens, and some weigh hundreds of tons. Nor are they slow. Most of them are hurtling many miles through space every second. Nor are they visible, until they enter the earth's great protecting blanket of atmosphere, where they become ignited by friction, and are usually entirely consumed before they reach the ground.

So you can see that to devise an apparatus that would enable Javis to avoid these unseen obstacles was no easy task, though, of course, Javis made his attempt in February, in which month the earth meets comparatively few meteors.

Gibson and I took two years to complete the marvellous apparatus. This work was mostly detail, as the principle is not new. Radio waves, like light waves, and sound waves, reflect upon striking

* Note. In trying to present a truly scientific solution of the problem of reaching the moon, the author has purposely refrained from all mention of the Millikan Cosmic Ray, because so comparatively little is known about this subject at the present time. The reader may assume, however, that Javis' large staff of scientists, backed by a billion dollars, was able to discover some suitable method of neutralizing or counteracting the probably harmful effects that this ray might have upon human beings.

various objects. When any meteor large enough to be dangerous came within fifty thousand miles of the rocket, it reflected the radio signal sent out by the special transmitter at five second intervals. The time which elapsed between the sending and the receiving of the reflected signal was measured by a new German instrument, which can accurately record thousandths of a second.

Because of the remarkable advances that have been made in the last fifty years in the manufacture of automatic calculating machines, the distance of the meteor could be ascertained, and its course automatically plotted on the celestial chart which Javis had prepared. As the course of the rocket was also electrically plotted on this chart, Javis could determine several minutes in advance if there were any danger of a collision. Then he had merely to press the button which exploded his gases at the right point on the rocket to send it off in a new direction, avoiding the meteor.

Of course, Kornfield, you understand that this description I have just given you of the apparatus which enabled Javis to avoid large meteors, is necessarily incomplete, inadequate, and faulty, and perhaps it was stated rather poorly. You cannot describe in two minutes a wonderful piece of mechanism which took two years to construct. But perhaps you can form some idea of the unbelievable complexity of the instrument from what I have told you. It performed its functions perfectly.

The huge rocket had left the earth. Though Javis was strapped in his seat, controlling the gigantic vehicle's course with light touches of his finger on the numerous electric push-buttons which surrounded him, Brown had unstrapped himself, and was roaming around the rocket's interior, enjoying the almost complete absence of gravity. Being thirsty, he obtained a drink of water from the watertank, but he had to suck it through a straw, as without gravity, liquids would not flow. When the two travellers became tired, they took their injections of procaine.

Procaine, you know, is an artificial drug, which, while it possesses the stimulating qualities of cocaine raised to the nth degree, is not habit-forming. Javis and Brown did not intend to lose any time by sleeping.

Seven hours after leaving the earth, Brown reported over the radio that all was well. Ten minutes later he found Duseau.

The dam' fool had somehow managed to get aboard the rocket before the take-off. Perhaps he did it by bribing one of the guards. He had concealed himself between the two tanks which contained the motor fuel intended for use when the rocket should return to the earth's atmosphere.

He must have been insane. I can account for his actions in no other way. He had become a monomaniac, and his one thought was to do all possible injury to D. Francis Javis. And he did not intend to stop at murder. When discovered, he drew an automatic and fired.

The bullets were poisoned. If Brown or Javis had merely been scratched by one of them, the wound would have been fatal. But Duseau missed, although one bullet went through Brown's coat-sleeve. He escaped death by less than two inches. The same bullet demolished the radio receiver. Then, as the gun jammed for lack of proper oiling, Brown leaped upon the cursing stowaway, knocking him over. As there was practically no gravity, Duseau didn't exactly fall, but Brown's blow to the jaw caused his head to strike the protruding valve of an oxygen tank with sufficient force to render him completely unconscious for thirty-five minutes. Brown tied his hands and feet with a piece of rope that had been left aboard the rocket when it was being loaded. When Duseau regained consciousness, he started such a tirade of abuse that Brown gagged him also.

Then Brown reported the whole affair over the radio, adding that it was useless for us to try to reply, as Duseau's bullet had rendered their receiver totally useless.

On the earth, Gibson and I recorded with telegraphones every word received from the moon party. My station at Albany was packed with reporters from newspapers and radio news services, eager for the latest details. The whole world gasped when it heard of Duseau's unsuccessful plan to capture the moon rocket and kill the two men whom he hated. Every nation waited impatiently for more news.

Nothing else of importance, except three narrow escapes from meteors, took place until they reached the moon. I have already told you of their extraordinary landing upon the summit of a lunar peak. After they landed, they ate a hurried meal, and then ventured out upon our satellite's untrodden surface.

I have here, Kornfield, a large composite photographic chart of the moon. Here you see the Mare Tranquilitatis, or "Sea of Tranquillity." What a name for such a scene of violence! You see the jagged mountains, the enormous craters! Dead volcanoes! But are they volcanoes? No one knows positively. If they are, how terrible must have been the eruptions, in the days when the moon was young! Consider the size of those stupendous craters. Many exceed fifty miles in diameter—Theophilus is sixty-four miles! And the largest known terrestrial crater, which is Aso San, in Japan, is less than seven miles in diameter. But I am digressing again.

This peak that I have marked with red ink is the one upon which they landed. You observe that it is not crateriform in shape. It is a mountain, not a volcano. Its summit is remarkably level, and is roughly twelve hundred feet square. On this miniature plateau the moon rocket finally landed and came to rest. The mountain is almost ten miles high.

When Javis and Brown emerged from the rocket, several facts were brought to their attention. One was the inferior gravity. They could leap thirty feet with the greatest ease. Another was the contrast between sunlight and shadow. The rare lunar atmosphere does not diffuse the light to any appreciable degree. It is, of course, entirely too rare to support human life. Javis and Brown were equipped with oxygen masks.

They found no form of life. The moon is dead. Its day of splendour is past. What secrets it still holds, no man can guess. The two explorers were only able to investigate an extremely small portion of the moon's surface, because of their limited food supply, and also because they landed about forty-eight hours after the lunar dawn, and intended to stay for the equivalent of ten earth-days, leaving a couple of days before the lunar sunset. You cannot carry on a very extensive exploration in ten days.

During the seventy-two hours after their landing, they thoroughly explored the peculiar truncated peak upon which they landed. They took many photos, and also collected several samples of the rocks for later analysis. Of course, men found out many years ago, by means of polarization photometers and various other instruments, that the surface rocks of the moon are mostly pumice and other stone high in silica. But Javis intended to bring his samples back to the earth and find out exactly what they contained. Perhaps he had hopes of rare minerals. I do not know.

They returned to the rocket frequently, and Brown reported their discoveries over the radio.

They kept Duseau bound. When they ate, they fed him. He remained sullen, silent, brooding over his misfortune, and planning revenge. The longer he was kept bound, the greater grew his maniacal unreasoning hate.

When Javis was satisfied with his investigation of the mountain upon which they had landed, which he had whimsically named "Mount Olympus," he decided to undertake a similar exploration of the nearest neighbouring peak, which was west of "Mount Olympus" and about the same height as it. I think Javis named this other mountain "Mount Parnassus," but I am not sure.

Javis and Brown took another shot of procaine apiece, and set out. Brown carried the concentrated food and the portable radio sending equipment which I had designed, while the Doctor burdened himself with a spare oxygen apparatus for each of them, a very limited water supply, and a few of his scientific instruments, including a couple of recording thermometers.

Although they intended to be away from the rocket at least seventy-two hours, they left Duseau bound without food. They could not trust him loose. Javis did not intend to give up his chance to explore "Mount Parnassus" out of consideration for the man who had tried to murder him. Brown didn't want to be left out of the adventure either. So they left Duseau bound. He would have to get along without food.

The two explorers reached their destination in a remarkably short time. Even though they were burdened with large packs, they could jump many feet with the utmost ease. They descended "Mount Olympus" by leaps and bounds, and ascended "Mount Parnassus." Even though they were greatly fatigued after many hours of steady jumping, they kept on. They reached the summit, and a bullet passed between them.

How Duseau escaped from his bonds is not known. Perhaps in a moment of desperation, he had summoned enough strength to burst them. Or perhaps he wore them through by steady rubbing against some sharp edge.

He escaped, and set up the machine gun. When his two enemies reached the summit of the neighbouring peak, he fired, using the telescopic sights. Javis and Brown took refuge in a large crevice between two enormous boulders, set up the radio, and reported the matter to the earth. A quarter of a million miles away, my sensitive detectors picked up the signals. Soon the whole world knew of Duseau's triumph.

I've often wondered why he went to so much trouble in order to try to kill Javis and Brown. He was familiar with the operation of the rocket. He could have taken it and departed, leaving them stranded without a possibility of rescue, and his purpose would have been accomplished. Perhaps the idea never occurred to him. Or perhaps it did not agree with his ideas of a fitting revenge. I suppose he was entirely demented. No one can account for the actions of an insane person. The fact remains that instead of taking his opportunity to escape with the rocket, leaving the others to starve, or to freeze to death in the cold of the lunar night, he set up the Marvite gun with the purpose of killing them first, and then returning to the earth with the rocket.

Javis and Brown soon discovered that they could not emerge from their refuge without exposing themselves to Duseau's vision. Whenever either of them even showed his head, Duseau fired. Usually his shots came close. You will remember that the Marvite gun was equipped with very accurate telescopic sights.

I wonder if a queerer situation was ever conceived by the most scatter-brained writer of imaginative fiction. A madman on a mountain of the moon, with an ultra-modern machine gun, attempting to kill two men whom he considered his enemies, who had taken refuge in a crevice between two boulders on the summit of another lunar mountain, from which crevice they dared not emerge.

Yes, it was a curious situation. It was tragic, too. What would Javis have said, had he known, when he performed what he considered the trivial action of discharging an insubordinate assistant, that it would lead to the dire straits in which he now found himself?

Emerging from the station at Albany one day, for the purpose of snatching a bite or two of lunch, I was accosted by a young girl of about eighteen, I should say, who seemed greatly troubled about something, and expressed a desire to speak with me privately. I invited her to lunch with me, and this, briefly, is what she told me.

She was engaged to be married to Jack Javis the following June. But her fiancé had recently suffered very severe financial losses, perhaps because he had less experience in Wall Street than the men who were against him. Jack Javis had foolishly borrowed right and left in a vain attempt to avoid the impending crash, and he had been wiped out. Now he was penniless, and about three million dollars in debt. His creditors were pressing him. His assets were nil.

The girl had come to me to ask if there were any possible way I could get in touch with Dr. Javis, and ask him to lend his son enough money to pay off his debts. She also mentioned the will, saying that the huge fortune in diamonds should really have been left to Jack, not to the worthless Donald, and asking me, if I should succeed in communicating with the Doctor, to suggest that he change the will.

It was with the utmost regret that I was forced to explain to the almost hysterical girl that there was nothing that I could do. The moon explorers had no receiver. There was no possible way for me to get word to them. When I had told her this, the girl asked me to permit her to be at the receiver with me. Of course I granted the request, although it was against the regular rules.

I suppose you can guess now, Kornfield, who Jacqueline is. The fact that she had been crying, did not detract from her loveliness. I caught myself envying Jack Javis as we walked the short distance back to the station. Not always will a rich man's sweetheart remain loyal to him after he has lost all his money and three million dollars more.

When we reached the station, Gibson met us at the door. The peculiar expression I saw upon his long, lean, intellectual countenance made me start.

"It's the beginning of the end, Clankey," he said, "Javis has gone crazy, too."

I ran to the receiving room. From the instrument I heard distinctly Javis' voice, a quarter of a million miles away. What he was saying confirmed Gibson's statement. He was raving incoherently, cursing Duseau, cursing himself for a fool for having brought the machine gun, begging that if Duseau should return to the earth he would be punished for murder, and much more along the same line. It was terrible.

In one corner of the room the silent, efficient, never ceasing telegraphone recorded every word permanently, electro-magnetically.

To make a long story somewhat shorter, let me say that Javis continued to rave like a maniac for many hours. Then suddenly his brain cleared.

"We have food for only a day more," said his voice, emerging from the most sensitive radio receiver in the world, "and our oxygen apparatus will not function for more than thirty-six hours more. I am saying good-bye to the world.

"Duseau has beaten me. If the fates will have it so, so be it.

"It is my wish that my entire personal fortune, including the diamonds in the vault at 198th Street and Fifth Avenue, New York, be left to my younger son, Jack, as he has always—"

The receiver fell silent. So ended the last message ever received by the great station at Albany.

For several minutes the utmost silence reigned in the receiving room. Finally Jacqueline—perhaps I should refer to her as Miss Bowers—who was with me at the receiver at that time, broke the stillness.

"He left them to Jack," she said very slowly, "but can we prove it? How?"

"We can," I said. "Under the new inheritance laws of the State of New York, we have merely to prove that Javis expressed a desire to change his will so that Jack would be his heir. We have his exact words recorded on that telegraphone in the corner. In case there is the slightest doubt upon the part of the authorities that Javis was the man who said those words, I will have one of my associates, Dr. Robert Haines, who happens to be the greatest living expert on pho-nophotographical processes, take a photograph of the vibrations of Javis' voice as he said those words. This photo can then be compared with photos taken of the vibrations of other parts of our telegra-phone record which are known to have been uttered by Dr. Javis, and the identity of the speaker of those words which give the second greatest fortune in the world to your sweetheart can be established beyond the possibility of a doubt. Fingerprints can be forged, but the vibrations of the voice cannot be forged, even though the voice may be disguised. No two human beings have exactly the same voice."

After I had explained this, Jacqueline left me to carry the news to her fiancé. I sat in silence a long time, wondering what had inter-rupted Javis' last message, wondering how the two explorers must feel, waiting for death to overtake them on their mountain. It must be a terrible sensation, Kornfield, to wait for death, without hope, without a chance, knowing that your enemy has triumphed. I sat in silence a long time, and then went home for some much-needed sleep, leaving Gibson at the station, in the vain hope that some further message might be received.

Two days later, Professor John P. Hauser, of Yerkes Observatory, reported that the rocket had left the moon. The newspapers and broadcast stations of every nation informed the people of the world that Duseau was returning. Every minute of every day either Gibson or I or one of our capable assistants was at the receiver, but the moon rocket was silent, as we expected.

Then some one pointed out that if Duseau should succeed in returning to the earth, he could not be punished. Neither the United States nor any other nation could lawfully punish Duseau for a murder committed on the moon. If he returned, he could go free, said the most eminent legal authorities.

Three days after Professor Hauser's announcement, the telegraphonic records I had made were stolen, doubtless by some crook in the employ of Donald Javis. I should have foreseen that he would not give up the enormous fortune without a fight. I should have put the record in the safest safe-deposit vault in Albany, but I left it in the unprotected radio-room, and it was stolen.

Of course I hired the best detectives I could get, and promised them an enormous reward if they could recover the little spool of wire that meant so much to Jack Javis, but I was secretly sure that Donald had totally destroyed it, so that there would be no chance of its recovery. Without it there was nothing but the unsupported word of Jacqueline and myself to prove that Javis had desired to change the will. This would be quite decidedly not sufficient.

I have never seen anybody as depressed as Jack Javis was in the nerve-racking, disappointing days that followed. The court of New York

City, after one of the shortest cases in its history, awarded the fortune to Donald. Jack's creditors began stripping him of every bit of his personal property. Though he said nothing, I knew that he secretly blamed me for his misfortune. I offered him my entire fortune, a matter of about a quarter of a million dollars, but he refused it. It would only have been a drop in the bucket, anyhow.

Then the rocket came down at Chicago Field. As it entered the atmosphere, something seemed to go wrong. It seemed to hesitate, to wobble. It was evident that it was not under control. Then it fell.

It fell, three hundred thousand feet. Those who were watching saw it become red-hot as it entered the denser layers of the atmosphere. They heard the terrible hissing scream it made, as it plunged, ever faster and faster, to the waiting earth. They heard the horrific, cataclysmic swan song of the super-airship, diving with ever-increasing speed to its doom. For it fell, three hundred thousand feet. It crashed.

The terrible concussion was recorded by every seismograph in the world. It is truly remarkable that the rocket fell in the only open space in the densely populated region around Chicago, the Chicago Flying Field. Had it fallen anywhere else in the vicinity, it would have been the cause of many deaths, and incalculable damage to property.

The fire department arrived quickly, and drenched the red-hot, flaming wreckage with floods of water. Then the police began to search for Duseau's body. As they were giving up the search as hopeless, somebody looked up.

High above was a parachute, drifting with the breeze. It supported a limp, unconscious figure, clad in an exceedingly thick flying suit. It came to earth. Someone tore the leather helmet from the tired, haggard face. A thrill of the most intense amazement spread through the crowd.

The man was D. Francis Javis.

Gibson, sitting in his apartment in New York, manipulated a dial. His face assumed a satisfied expression as he tuned in Station WEBQD, the New York station of a world-wide chain of broadcasters that had a television news-service as a daily feature. Adjusting another dial, he gazed at the scene which appeared on the screen of his receiver.

It was Chicago Field. He heard the excited news-announcer's voice telling of Javis' return. He saw the unconscious form gently placed in an ambulance and rushed to the nearest hospital.

Then he called me on the 'phone. The two of us took off in my plane less than ten minutes later. We reached Chicago in a few hours, landed on the Illinois Hotel landing platform, left the plane with the mechanics, dropped two hundred storeys in the express elevator, and were soon at Javis' bedside. He had just regained consciousness, and he told us what had happened.

In the hour of his triumph, Duseau had been killed. Consider the tremendous power of the Marvite gun. Long ago men calculated that a bullet shot from a gun with a muzzle velocity of 6,500 feet a second would, if there were no obstacles in its path, completely encircle the moon! And that is what happened! One of the bullets Duseau shot from the summit of "Mount Olympus" travelled all the way around the moon, and hit him in the back! And that, Kornfield, is what I was thinking about when I spoke of a sub-satellite.

Perhaps you may consider it a rather silly comparison, but I can't help thinking of that tiny projectile as a satellite, faithful to the laws of celestial mechanics, following unerringly its orbit around the moon, and returning to its starting point. I wonder how many other bullets are still circling the moon now!

Brown, exposing his head, saw Duseau fall. He and Javis were so excited by this occurrence that they returned to the rocket without the radio! They reached it less than thirty minutes before their oxygen mask apparatus ceased to function. They had used their reserve supply of compressed air completely during their return journey.

"And that," concluded C. Jerry Clankey, "is about all there is to the story. Because a maniac on the moon was so unfortunate as to stand in the orbit of a minute sub-satellite which he himself had launched, Jack Javis was able to pay off his debt. The Doctor lent him the necessary cash, and has just made a new will. So everything is going to be all right."

"Pardon me, Kornfield, but I didn't quite hear that question. What happened to Brown? Oh, yes, I told you that the lucky fool has a charmed life. He was unable to start the motors when the rocket was entering the atmosphere. Duseau had apparently done something to render them useless. When the rocket fell, Brown and Javis jumped. The wind separated the two men.

"Brown landed almost a hundred miles from Chicago. His chute ripped slightly as he fell, and let him down too rapidly. But he landed in an apple tree, and broke thirteen bones.

"A couple of modern surgeons patched him up, and in less than a month the incurable dare-devil was doing outside loops at six hundred miles an hour in his special monoplane, and making a fortune by recommending and endorsing various makes of spark plugs, motor fuel, cigarettes, and so on.

"By the way, I almost forgot that today is the fifteenth of June. It's too bad, Kornfield, that you're scheduled to speak to the Explorers' Club this evening about your discoveries in Tibet. If you weren't I'd take you to Albany with me to attend the wedding of Jacqueline Bowers and Jack Javis. I must leave at once."

I accompanied C. Jerry Clankey to the roof. He entered his waiting plane. The mechanic touched a button. The powerful catapult shot the streamlined flyer into the air. Jerry zoomed gracefully, and the little red biplane soon disappeared in the northern sky.

William F. Temple

As mentioned in the introduction, the growing interest in the potential of rocketry and space travel had led to the creation first of the German Rocket Society in June 1927 followed by the American Interplanetary Society in March 1930 and the British Interplanetary Society [BIS] in October 1933. There was considerable contact between all three. The BIS had been formed in Liverpool by the structural engineer and science-fiction writer Philip E. Cleator, but he rather dominated proceedings to his own ends and members became frustrated. There was a coup and in March 1937 the headquarters of the Society was transferred to London with Professor A.M. Low as President. Low was a noted engineer and inventor who did considerable work on rocket guidance systems and torpedoes. Also in the Society at that time was Arthur C. Clarke, who served as Treasurer, with William F. Temple (1914–1989) as Publicity Director.

Temple had become fascinated with science-fiction from an early age. He had been born in Woolwich, south London, but the family soon moved to Eltham, in Kent. This was not too far from where H.G. Wells had been born in Bromley and where Edith Nesbit lived. Temple could recall as a very young child buying apples from Nesbit whose house at Well Hall had a large orchard. Much later Temple and his family settled in Folkestone, Kent, also close to where Wells had once lived. These associations served as an inspiration. He became one of Britain's leading science-fiction writers of the 1950s and had a life-long fascination with the Moon. One of his last books, Shoot at the Moon *(1966), is a tense study of a group of people trying to survive* on the lunar surface. At the start of his career, his third published story was the following, written in January 1938. In keeping with his role as Publicity Director he records with true British pluck the BIS's first flight to the Moon.

The Pioneer

In a room over a public-house in the West End of London there used to meet a queer group of people styling themselves the Interplanetary Society. Queer, that is, to outsiders... For these people—mainly enthusiastic young men, though with a sprinkling of thoughtful and learned elders—would sit and discuss over their beer and chips, ways and means of reaching the Moon.

They were no idle dreamers. They believed in themselves and their object, and went ahead with their research ignoring the gibes directed at them. They believed the rocket was the ideal vehicle for space travel, experimented with small rockets that fizzed and buzzed, incontinently exploded or did nothing at all, and certainly nothing that was expected of them.

This was because the Interplanetarians could not hit upon the right fuel. Then, in 1939, Mr. Janns, their research chemist, discovered a fuel that was a gift from the gods.

It was a liquid, the most powerful explosive in the world, yet as stable and easy to handle as milk. A gill of it contained enough power to speed ten one-thousand-ton space-ships off the face of the Earth at seven miles a second, leaving enough in reserve to blow up the Houses of Parliament. Using this fuel, the Society built a rocket exactly nine-and-a-half feet long and fired it—unmanned, of course—at the Moon.

Three nights after the firing of the rocket, an observer at one of the telescopes at Greenwich Observatory saw a little flash of light between the horns of the crescent Moon. A flash… and then a steady white flame—the automatic signal flare on the rocket. Very faint, tiny and remote it was, and it burnt only for a few seconds, a ritual fire in honour of man's conquest of the outer void. Then it went out. But it was enough. The way was clear…

The experiment did not attract the serious attention it deserved. The public is notoriously unimaginative, and at the time it was absorbed in the festivities of Christmas. But the novelty of it caught the fancy of a multi-millionaire, bored with this world's pleasures.

It was a new game to play. He offered to pay for the building of the Interplanetary Society's first man-carrying rocket-ship. It cost him just eight-hundred-thousand pounds. He said that was the last one he would pay for, wished the Interplanetarians luck, and went back to racing.

The Interplanetarians called their ship *The Pioneer* and asked for three volunteers to navigate it. Every soul in the Society volunteered. Finally, the three chosen were Captain Cassel, the best all-round authority on astronautics; Clemence Cassel, his wife, because she argued so strongly that her sex be represented, and because they knew that she could not bear to be separated from the Captain; and one blithering idiot who always pretended to know far more about it than he did—myself.

The very rich and very bored gentleman who had provided the money for *The Pioneer* had also allowed us the run of his vast estate on the west coast of Ireland. Here was laid a wide concrete runway, half-a-mile long, pointing straight at the sea.

Now, imagine if you can a huge torpedo-shaped body on four wheels, spaced like those of a roller-skate, four great wheels of tempered steel in streamlined sheaths. Then two expansive wings, shooting out from the body like an air-liner's; the fins of a tail-plane at the rear; and, sticking out from between them at various angles, the blunt nozzles of rocket exhausts. At the sharp bullet-nose, four more exhausts pointing the opposite way, for retarding the speed, and above them the strong quartz windows of the control-cabin.

There you have an outline picture of *The Pioneer* as it stood at the landward end of the concrete runway on that miserable November morning when it was due to start on its tremendous voyage.

It was chilly and dull. The sky was just a grey blanket of rain-cloud. The morning mists were thinning, but were still dense enough to veil the far end of the runway on which we stood. We sheltered under the towering nose of *The Pioneer* from the impalpable drizzle that was drifting down.

In contrast to the weather were the flushed, eager faces of the Interplanetarians as they chattered excitedly around us like a lot of magpies, on tiptoe with nervous tension.

"Don't forget to bring back that bit of lunar rock," cried Chapman, the enthusiastic geologist.

"Did you want peppermint or pineapple?" smiled the Captain.

"Ask the Man in the Moon what he's grinning about," called someone, while another solemnly warned Clemence against flirting with the Selenites.

"Don't be silly," she replied. "How can we sit and gaze at the Moon when we're on it?"

As we joked and chaffed I was trembling inside like a jelly from stark fear. My mouth was dry, and I had to keep clearing my throat. I hoped my cowardice didn't show…

The Captain took out his watch. "'"The time has come," the Walrus said…'" he quoted gently.

Something within me jumped convulsively. "Well, thumbs up, you fellows," I said, with a fine air of good-humoured ease, while a thousand anticipations of disaster rushed madly about in my mind.

"Thumbs up!" came the cry, as the Interplanetarians jerked their thumbs skyward in a simultaneous expression of good luck. Then they rushed forward to help us up the ladder.

Believe me, I was glad of that help. One by one, Clemence first, then the Captain and I, we went up the short ladder, crawled along the broad sloping wing and wriggled our way into the interior of *The Pioneer*. Safely inside, we waved our last farewells, and a frantic cheering came back in response.

Captain Cassel shut the air-tight door, and abruptly the babel outside was cut off. Dead silence... We would not hear any exterior sounds for a long time now, if ever again.

There were three extremely well-sprung chairs facing the front observation window, below which was the control-board with its switches, levers and dials, looking like the dashboard of a motor-car. It was, indeed, just like sitting in a big, luxurious car.

The Captain took the centre seat and grasped the steering-wheel which controlled the front wheels of *The Pioneer*. Clemence took the farther seat, and I the one near the door. We sat there deep in our thoughts, staring at the rain-blurred window-pane, waiting until the Interplanetarians had retreated to a safe distance.

I glanced at the Captain. His bronzed face was inscrutable, but I noticed how fiercely he was gripping the steering-wheel. I looked past him at his wife, whose face was visible to me in profile.

How can I describe the beauty of Clemence? She was the loveli-est woman I ever saw. Pale golden hair, eyes of clear blue, a warm, sympathetic mouth... these descriptive terms are totally inadequate. Her beauty was ethereal: and yet she had a roguish sense of humour that bubbled up at the most unexpected times.

I watched her now as she sat gazing out of the window. Her face was rather pale, her mouth firmly set. It was plain that she was defying the apprehension she felt. But in those steady eyes there was, wonderfully, a glint of her unconquerable humour. I knew she was inwardly smiling at her keyed-up state.

By heaven, I told myself, there's a woman for you! I must confess I had loved her for years; but I always backed hastily away from such thoughts whenever they crossed my mind, for the Captain was my dearest friend.

"Lord, I *am* scared!" I said, voicing the only other thought in my head.

"So am I!" exclaimed both the others simultaneously.

We all laughed, and felt relieved. There is nothing like admitting to a fear to ease it.

"Well, here we go to glory, one way or the other," smiled the Captain, and quite casually turned the starting switches.

A moment's breathless suspense followed, while the fuel filtered from the main tank along the thin pipes to the firing-chamber of every rocket -at the rear.

Then came a fierce jerk. The springs of my chair squeaked protestingly. The landscape seemed to quiver, then went sliding backwards at an ever-increasing speed until it became a streaming blur. All I could see distinctly was the white ribbon of the runway flying swiftly under our wheels as we sped along it faster than any express train.

The mist ahead receded as fast as we approached it. Then suddenly it thinned, and I glimpsed the end of the runway and the oily sea beyond. An awful vision crossed my mind of *The Pioneer* shooting over the cliff and falling with an almighty splash into the sea...

But suddenly the ribbon narrowed and fell away beneath us. We had taken the air, and were hurtling rapidly up towards the grey pall of heaven. A clammy mistiness swirled outside the window for a moment, and then we came through into the sunlight, soaring high over the clouds.

I caught a split-second's glimpse of a black dot—an aeroplane—floating over that snow-white expanse. I wondered vaguely what the pilot must have thought of the huge rocket which had erupted so suddenly from placid cloud-land.

But the clouds were now but a distant, white haze below us, and I turned my gaze to the empty blue sky above. The Captain gently turned the switch which sent more fuel into the rockets, and as we accelerated the sky deepened into a darker blue, became violet-purple, while faint stars appeared and gleamed more brightly as their setting grew blacker and blacker.

Soon the sky was of a blackness more intense than soot, and dusted with myriads of stars—a vast concourse impossible to perceive from the depths of the sea of atmosphere which covers the Earth.

We were in outer space!

★   ★   ★

We've done it," I said, rather obviously.

"Yes," agreed the Captain tersely, and glanced at the instrument-board. "H'm… Two-and-a-half miles a second. Now let's try a spot of real acceleration. Hold tight!"

The injunction was unnecessary. As we accelerated I was pressed back in my seat by an invisible, but immensely strong hand. The chair became a block of granite, and every bone in my body seemed to be grinding against it as I fought to breathe. My chin was forced back relentlessly until I was staring helplessly at the roof.

This painful state of affairs continued unmercifully for some minutes. Then, just as my neck was on the point of breaking, the

strain eased. I stared dazedly around. Clemence and the Captain
were feeling their necks gingerly.

"Are there any other exercises you would like us to perform?"
Clemence asked of her husband. "A hand-spring or two, or perhaps
a neat knee-bend?"

"The fuel is even more powerful than I thought," the Captain
said ruefully. "We must use it more gently."

After that our acceleration was so gradual that we did not notice
it. And when we had steered the ship on a fair course for the Moon
and set the controls, we found time to look around. One by one, we
slid back the steel shutters over the port-holes in the walls of *The
Pioneer* and peered out into space.

The red dot of Mars fascinated us most. We examined it through
the three-inch refracting telescope, and argued over the canals. For
even through airless space they did not appear clearly, chiefly because
the glass of the port-hole limited our power of magnification.

"One day, perhaps, we shall go there and see for ourselves," said
the Captain. "This trip to the Moon is only the first step—the first,
uncertain step of a child learning to walk. I dream of the time when
man will roam, free and unfettered, far beyond this cramped solar
system into other realms, incredibly remote. Where distance means
nothing and Time alone is omnipotent. Where—"

"Where pigs fly, and Jabberwocks whiffle, and retired Captains
don't act all dramatic," went on the incorrigible Clemence. But I
could see that inwardly she was as enthusiastic as her husband.

Idly, I slid back a port-hole cover on the opposite side of the cabin,
and overawed by what I saw, called my companions. For there was
the Earth, our parent Earth, a weirdly beautiful sight.

It was a globe of colour. The dazzling opalescence that was the
Atlantic Ocean bordered one side of a misty patchwork of quiet

pastel hues, in which olive-green struck the predominant note. Spattered across it were dreamy wisps and islands of cloud. There were no sharp outlines; the colours merged into each other almost imperceptibly, dulling into grey where they approached a dark strip on the eastern side, the widening black crescent that was the coming of night.

The whole effect was oddly unreal. It resembled nothing so much as a delicate, illuminated Chinese lantern hanging against a midnight sky. It was all so different from what I'd expected. I had imagined clearly defined coastlines and acute detail, like the globe map standing on its pedestal in my study.

My study! Where was it on that great sphere? Why, the immense sea of streets and buildings that was London was but an indeterminate, microscopic point somewhere on the slope of that huge, coloured ball. Not only London, but every place I could think of, every place I had longed to visit and thought too far away—New York, Hollywood, Bagdad, Bombay, Shanghai, Cape Town, Sydney—towns, rivers and mountains, even mighty Everest, lay there before me, included in one all-embracing glance.

"To think," said Clemence softly, "that crawling all over that globe, like... like microbes, is the whole of the human race—except us! Going about their business, their silly little stocks and shares and wars and parades, so sure of their importance."

She laid her hands wide apart on the thick glass, as if she would clasp the globe hanging out there against the firmament.

"And I can encompass all mankind with my two hands!"

Silently I slid the cover back. "Gives me the willies to look at it," I said. "It makes me realize what an amazingly risky thing we've done to leave those familiar, safe places and step blindly out into the darkness where none have been before."

The Captain slipped open another window-cover, revealing the crescent Moon, looking small and distant as it does at its zenith on Earth.

"Forget all that," he said, "and keep your thoughts instead on our goal."

II

The Landing on the Moon

Life continued pleasantly enough in *The Pioneer*.

The time came when we approached the neutral field of gravitation between the Earth and Moon, and we lost all weight and floated about like bits of gossamer. This event, of course, had been anticipated, and provision made for it in the form of an electrically magnetized floor and the adjunctive steel-soled boots. But we enjoyed floating about.

Clemence draped herself in a long white sheet and drifted about the cabin, moaning like a disembodied spirit, while the Captain struggled frantically in mid-air trying to fasten up one of his steel-soled boots.

We watched his antics with amusement. He kept trying to brace his foot against something so that he could pull his laces tight, but whatever he set foot on, he almost immediately drifted away from it. He grew more and more breathless and impatient, squirming himself into strangely contorted and very inelegant attitudes.

He noticed us regarding him, and glared at us upside down between his feet. "Wha' you—staring at?" he demanded.

"A tipsy Peter Pan, I think," said I.

"The rudeness of some people!" he remarked bitterly, and grabbed hold of the floor-magnetizing switch. The strong current immediately began to draw us steadily down, feet first.

Clemence, a fighter to the last, clutched a wall bracket and hung on grimly. Just below her on the wall was a row of metal discs of various sizes, each with a handle in the centre and a thick rim of tough rubber. Unwisely, she changed her grip to these things. They immediately came loose, and she drifted floorwards clutching a disc in each hand, for all the world like a cymbal-player in a Salvation Army band.

"What are they—saucepan lids?" she asked.

"It's my own invention," answered the Captain. "I've kept it up my sleeve, for the other silly blighters in the Society would have laughed it out of existence."

"Like they tried to do to my wheels," I rejoined warmly, remembering the merriment first evoked by my suggestion that *The Pioneer* should have wheels.

"Oh, blow your wheels," said the Captain unkindly. "I'll bet we come an awful cropper when we try to use them. Now, *this* idea will work. If we should encounter a small meteor—"

I saw the idea at that, and burst into loud, derogatory laughter.

"You should have known better," I said scornfully. "Why, if even the very tiniest meteor hit us now, the friction heat generated would melt the whole ship in a flash!"

Providence must have been watching us very closely at that moment. "I don't—" began the Captain, when—

Zip! A brilliant streak of light shot between us. For a second we stood there, rather startled. The line of light seemed to hang and glow, then faded as a wave of hot air struck me in the face. There came the faint hiss of escaping air...

The Captain picked up two of the smaller discs, located the tiny holes, and pressed the discs over them. The rubber rims adapted themselves to the curve of the walls and clung there like suckers.

"You see? That meteor, about the size of a grain of sand, passed straight through the ship... Of course, the pressure of the air in here is holding those discs there. They're only temporary patches, but effective enough until we can get the holes welded up. Any questions?"

He smiled at me mockingly. Clemence laughed at the expression on my face.

I tried to carry off the situation with aplomb. I smiled back condescendingly, even with faint approval, as though I thought it quite a good idea, although it *could* have been a little better. Then I strolled with studied carelessness to the control window, racking my brains furiously for an excuse to change the subject.

I found it, so unexpectedly that it gave me a shock. For the whole sky outside the window was full of Moon.

A great, glaring, yellow-white expanse it was, wrinkled and seamed with mountain ranges, and blotted with ring craters half filled with shadows. For a moment it appeared to me that the whole mass was rushing towards us like an immense projectile...

Then suddenly I grasped the fact that it was *we* who were moving so rapidly. *The Pioneer* was falling headlong on to the Moon!

My cry brought the Captain hurrying to the window.

"Gosh!" he exclaimed, and flung himself at the controls. The Moon was suddenly half obscured by boiling gases shooting out from our retarding rockets under the window. The powerful braking effect produced hurled me forwards against the glass and kept me pressed there. I heard an awful clatter behind me as Clemence came to grief amongst the rest of the "saucepan lids," which had been jerked loose.

The Captain manipulated the rocket switches expertly. I sensed that we were sweeping in a wide curve; then the deceleration eased and we were able to crawl into our seats.

The retarding rockets had stopped, and I saw that we were now speeding horizontally over the Moon's surface, perhaps twenty miles above it. The Captain was shutting off our rear rockets one by one, and our speed lessened as the gravitation of the Moon gained effect.

We dropped in a sloping dive towards the *Mare Serenitatis,* which seemed to offer that flat, unbroken area we needed for a landing-place. But as we skimmed over its surface we were dismayed to find it an uneven succession of rolling ridges on which it would be madness to attempt a landing.

At length, on the far side of the old sea bottom, we swooped over the mountains of a small crater, and as the encircled floor came into view we saw that it was as flat as any place we were likely to find on the Moon's scarred surface. Far ahead, towards the other wall of the crater, I imagined I caught a glimpse of a patch of green on the landscape. But before I could make certain of this, the Captain said:

"Now to test your wheels, old man!"

Instantly I was eager to see how my derided invention would work out. All this time, with amazing skill, the Captain had been balancing the impetus of the rockets against the downward pull of gravitation, aided by small supporting rockets under *The Pioneer's* body and the delicate exactness of the controls. By further dexterous manipulation he brought our height down to a few hundred feet, then to a matter of mere feet.

We were on a perfectly even keel. By peering down sideways under our left wing, I could just see one of the wheels hanging motionless a yard above the rushing ground. Slowly it bridged the gap, and touched, and was instantly sent spinning so rapidly that I feared for the bearings.

The finely tempered springs took the shock easily. We bounced, bounded a hundred yards, touched again and jumped again, like a giant frog. The retarding rockets spat fury; our leaps grew less, and eventually we slowed up, came to a halt...

So ended the first space flight.

I remember sitting there dazed, trying to grasp the immense importance of what we had done. I tried to think of some grave and noble words to say, something that children would read in their history-books centuries after. Immortal words like "England expects…" But all I was conscious of was that I'd bitten my tongue in the jolting and bouncing, and so couldn't pronounce any memorable words if I had thought of them.

Clemence said them for me:

"Thumbs up!"

We made the familiar gesture in unison.

We had come to rest a mile or more from the foot-hills of the nearest mountain wall of the crater. On the horizon, clear and sharp against the sable sky, lay the distant saw-teeth of the mountains on the other side of the crater. In between stretched only the rocky floor, veined and drifted, as by a gentle wind, with volcanic dust black as iron filings.

The drift of this dust impelled me to make an immediate test for atmosphere. I discovered that, after all, the Moon *had* an atmosphere, but consisting only of nitrogen, very pure and very attenuated.

"We can't expect to find any life, then," commented the Captain. "No one can live on nitrogen alone."

"Not sentient life," I agreed. "But there may be some sort of plant life." And I told them about the green patch I thought I glimpsed before we landed.

"Pickering's vegetation!"* they exclaimed almost together.

We must investigate that," said the Captain. "Whither away?"

---

*   Professor Pickering, the American astronomer, claimed that he observed the growth of vegetation in certain craters of the Moon, notably Aristillus and Linné.

I pointed to the far side of the crater. The Captain grasped the steering-wheel again.

"Hold tight! I'll try to coast her over."

He switched on a couple of the rear rockets at low power. *The Pioneer* immediately began to roll smoothly forward, her magnificently sprung wheels carrying us without a bump. It was like riding in a huge motor-bus. Faster and faster we went.

"Ah, this is what I've been praying for," muttered the Captain crouching over the wheel like a speed demon. "A straight run, no pedestrians, no traffic-lights and no police cars."

I sat back in my comfortable chair with real contentment. All my life I had been reaching for the Moon. I thought of all those summer nights I had laid back in my deck-chair gazing longingly up at its remote plains and craters, dreaming of the day when I might set foot on them. And the winter nights, too, walking the wet and windy streets while the pale, high globe peered fitfully and mockingly down at me between the hurrying rain-clouds.

Now at last I was there! Could life hold more?

Then, across the Captain's bent shoulders, I saw again that lovely profile of Clemence, and straightway forgot all thoughts of the Moon. She was gazing ahead at the lunar landscape, slightly flushed with eagerness and excitement, with her fair hair still dishevelled from the confusion of our landing. A careless flaxen lock hung over her eyes; she pushed it back abstractedly, but it kept falling.

I became as rapt as she was. I fell into a dream world far more remote than the one I had gained. There was a cottage with a sloping flower-garden that looked out over the sea. And there was Clemence... Clemence smiling over the sunlit breakfast-table and pouring my tea, Clemence walking with me in the mellow evening dusk, Clemence...

Oh, what vain imaginings! This was reaching for the Moon indeed. With aching realization I had reluctantly to accept the fact that to Clemence I was never more than a friend—a dear friend, I hoped. She and the Captain lived in their own private and happy world, needing only each other. I was a welcome visitor, but not a dweller therein.

With an effort I lifted myself out of a mood which was degenerating into mere self-pity, and regained something of my former satisfaction at having achieved a life-long ambition. Inarticulately, I tried to communicate this to the others.

"All our reaching for the Moon," I began, and paused confusedly, struggling for other words. But Clemence smiled across at me with such sweet, understanding sympathy that I knew it was unnecessary to express myself further.

"Vegetation, ho!" bawled the Captain just then.

There, some miles ahead, could be seen a horizontal green line, which broadened visibly as we sped towards it.

"A cabbage patch?" breathed Clemence, peering intently. Then the view was blotted out by whirling clouds of gas, vomiting silently from our retarding rockets. The Captain was putting the brake on.

We sat there for some moments staring at the impenetrable veil and wondering how close we were getting. Presently the Captain switched off, the gaseous veil vanished, and we saw that we were still travelling at a fair pace towards a great stretch of green plants, the edge of which was barely a hundred yards off.

We were heading for a collection of what seemed to be white stones about a yard high. I scanned them rapidly. They were buildings—miniature buildings; and in the streets between them tiny human figures swarmed!

"Stop!" I cried hoarsely. "We're heading for a city!"

III

The City of the Selenites

The Captain had realized this at the same moment. He hauled fever-
ishly at the steering-wheel, striving to avoid the Lilliputian town on
the border of the green patch.

But it was too late. *The Pioneer* crunched in a wide curve over
the city like a pitiless juggernaut. The buildings were ground into
white powder, while the luckless inhabitants, darting this way and
that under our terrible metal wheels, were squashed like beetles or
smothered by flying debris.

Frantically we had been doing all we could to bring our ship to
a standstill, and finally she jerked to a reluctant halt. The carnage
was at an end.

White and shaken, we surveyed the damage we had unintention-
ally wrought. Our path through the miniature city was marked by
a swath of tumbled wreckage and dead and dying Selenites—little
creatures scarcely more than two inches in height. A crowd of them
was retreating rapidly towards the forest of green plants that began
on the outskirts of the city, while a few remained behind to rescue
the injured.

They were so human-looking; it was an amazing sight. From our
view-point at the window of *The Pioneer* it was like gazing down at
some earthly town from a low-flying aeroplane.

But there was something strange about the general appearance
of the town. Then I saw that it was a queer mixture of architectural
styles. Flanking some buildings that might have been lifted out of
Regent Street was a domed Indian temple, minarets and all, while
farther down was a row of glass and chromium erections, then a

turreted castle; and away to the right I glimpsed a fine replica of the Kremlin. And the highest of these buildings was no more than seven feet tall.

Little white vehicles which I instantly recognized as motor ambulances came slowly twisting their way through the ruins, and from under our very wheels the drivers picked up the wounded. I saw a manikin dressed like an Arab stop to shake his tiny fist up at us.

I cleared my throat. "Who could have guessed it?" I muttered huskily.

"I feel like a murderer," said Clemence miserably.

The Captain tried to console her. "We cannot be blamed. We didn't dream there were any living creatures on the Moon. What makes it seem so bad to us is that they are of human shape. If they happened to resemble, say, spiders or lizards we should not be nearly so upset at running over them. Anyway, who's to say that their minds aren't totally lacking in human emotion?"

I thought of the little man's demonstration of anger and of the ambulance attendants risking their lives to save the injured, but kept silent and looked out upon the city once more. I noticed that at every road junction and open space there stood one or more of those peculiar green plants, which, as they stood almost as high as some of the buildings, at first sight appeared to be trees. But they were like no trees on Earth, for they had no leaves—only a few pendant green balls like unripe oranges. These little balls seemed to be expanding very, very gradually, and when they reached a certain size they burst, scattering a shower of seeds in all directions.

"How do these Selenites breathe?" pondered the Captain wonderingly. "Surely they don't breathe nitrogen?"

He took a test of the atmosphere. "It's *air!*" he exclaimed presently.

"Now where the devil does the oxygen come from?"

Neither Clemence nor I was in the mood for puzzles, but the Captain, with the enthusiasm of the scientist, was already getting into his space-suit.

"We must go out and investigate," he decided.

Clemence and I donned our space-suits less hurriedly. These suits resembled diving-suits; there was the same globular head-piece, cylinder of compressed air, and leaden weights on the feet to help the wearer to walk normally under the influence of the weaker gravitation. We were connected together by some yards of telephone wire, and so attired we passed through a small air-lock out on to the Moon.

We stepped gingerly about the half-ruined city, from which the inhabitants had completely vanished, taking their dead and injured with them.

I stooped and peered into one of the houses. It was like look-ing into a very small doll's house. Each room was furnished with exquisite craftsmanship, down to the minutest detail. There was even a meal laid on one of the tables, which had evidently been hastily abandoned.

A tiny, far-away voice whispered in my ear.

"Look, Bill. A set of Chippendale." It was Clemence's voice, sounding faintly over the telephone wire. She was gazing in through the open window of a house timbered in Tudor style.

"I can't understand it," I confessed. "This amazing resemblance to terrestrial things… It's beyond coincidence."

As we explored further, my amazement grew. There seemed no object here that did not have its replica somewhere on Earth. I looked back at all the buildings we had wrecked, and my remorse returned.

The Captain's voice broke into my thoughts.

"I've been examining these plants; they explain the air mystery. What little soil there is here is very chalky, as one would expect an old sea-bottom to be. The plants absorb carbon dioxide from the chalk, and with the aid of their chlorophyll the energy of the intense sunlight is used to separate the carbon from the oxygen. But they do not immediately exhale the oxygen: they use it as an aid to propagation. As they produce it so they store it in little round seed-pods, which expand like toy balloons under the increasing pressure from within, until finally they burst and scatter the seeds just as we have seen them do."

He waved his arm towards the great field of plants that spread beyond the city to the cliff-like wall of the crater, and along it in either direction for as far as the eye could see.

"There must be thousands of these pods bursting every hour to release enough oxygen to keep up the content. The air is far too thin for us to breathe, of course, but it must be just about in the right proportion for *them*."

"Speaking of *them*, where are they?" I said.

"Hiding out among the plants, no doubt."

I looked over the field of plants, growing almost visibly in the bright sunlight, and noticed for the first time a road cutting across them, a wide road that started at the city boundary and went straight as an arrow for the crater wall. What was at the end of it? Another city nestling under the wall?

We were all three curious to know, so we began a trek to satisfy our curiosity.

To the Selenites it must have been an enormously wide road. To us it was but a path that we had to negotiate in single file, or else tread over the plants. We would not do the latter for fear of treading on concealed Selenites, and Clemence especially took great care in setting down her lead-soled shoes even on the road. This anxiety was typical of her; she hated hurting any living creature.

In a clearing among the plants on the right-hand side of the roadway we came across an astounding thing.

It was the biggest building job the Selenites had attempted, and in isolating it like this from the city they evidently meant to make some sort of monument of it. It was a miniature skyscraper, already twenty feet high, but only half finished. The bare girders at the top supported two toy cranes, but there were no workmen upon them.

There was not a soul in sight. The tiny black oblongs of the upper windows looked at us like blind, empty eye-sockets; the lower ones had been glazed, and glittered in the sun. We saw at once what this structure was going to be, and I think we all softly whistled our amazement together. For it was, in the making, *an exact replica of the Empire State Building!*

On we trudged along the road, making no comment, but each trying to grasp the significance of this. Was it a deliberate copy of the famous New York building? How, then, could the Selenites know of such terrestrial achievements? Or were the ideas which we Earthlings believed our own shared by the two races—common inspiration?

I extended this fascinating theory. I thought of the whole cosmos, with its myriads of probably inhabited worlds, and all these various races sharing the same common collection of ideas, thinking the same things, doing the same things, and each imagining itself unique.

My mind played with this daydream for several Lilliputian leagues; actually, we walked about half a terrestrial mile. Then the Captain stopped so suddenly that I bumped into him. He pointed silently ahead, while Clemence, standing behind, tried hard to see around me, almost overbalancing in her eagerness.

We had reached the foot of a great cliff that went sheerly up for a thousand feet, then carried peaks which we could not see upward for many more thousands of feet, up towards the dark sky and the splendour of the stars. I, who had felt a big, clumsy Gulliver ever since we left *The Pioneer*, now felt Lilliputian in my turn.

What the Captain was pointing out was a deep doorway, about man-size, cut squarely in the face of the cliff. The slanting rays of the Sun reached into it for a short distance like a glaring limelight, but beyond the sharp edge of that illumination lay the darkest gloom, and the Selenite road disappeared into a tunnel of black mystery.

I looked up at the slate-grey face of the cliff, and detected on it large, rectangular patches that seemed to be of a different and smoother texture than the rough rock, though of the same dull hue. And at that moment a voice that was neither the Captain's nor Clemence's, but a tired, faded, very gentle voice, spoke in my receiver.

"Welcome, friends! Please come through the doorway, and have no fear."

It was the English language, but it was not an English voice. The Moon had an apparently inexhaustible stock of surprises for us, and custom had not yet staled her infinite variety, for once again I could only stare blankly and speechlessly at the others. From their expressions I gathered that they also had heard the voice in their receivers.

"Well?" croaked the Captain, at last.

Clemence indicated the doorway, then cocked her thumbs up and nodded vigorously. I made signals of assent, too. So the Captain led the way in.

As we passed out of the intense sunlight into the intense darkness, green and red patches swam in the void before me; but this was only my overworked retinæ playing tricks. We shuffled slowly along in the stygian gloom until presently a thin, vertical line of light appeared in front of us and to the right. It widened rapidly, revealing its cause to be a metal door that was sliding open and showing beyond a brightly lit room.

A powerful draught came blowing along the passage. It was like being in the slip-stream of a giant air-liner. We battled our way against it, and finally got into the room almost breathless from exertion. The metal door slid back behind us, and the pitch-black hole of the tunnel vanished as though it had never existed.

We were in; but it might not prove so easy to get out...

IV

The Last of the Lunarians

The place we were in was a fair-sized chemical laboratory. The ceiling lifted to a high dome, illuminated with concealed lights, and a long glass-topped bench, covered with the paraphernalia of the chemist, ran down the centre of the room. All around the walls were shelves of bottles and retorts, except the farther wall, which was one big window looking out on to a scene so dimly lit that we could not make out what it was.

All this was the impression we received at first glance; then our attention was immediately absorbed by the lone creature sitting by a control panel, facing us.

"My goodness!" breathed Clemence. "What is it?"

I find it hard to describe this creature without seeming absurd and fantastic. We have a tendency to laugh at anything which goes strikingly against our notion of the fitness of things; and the appearance of this creature (if he resembled anything at all) was like that of the fabulous griffin... a sort of humanized griffin.

There was the same eagle head, with the sharp, downward-curved beak. Yet, when you saw them more closely, the eyes did not have that piercing look of the eagle, but a soft and kind regard, and the eyes themselves seemed very weary. Drab feathers covered the throat and upper chest, but merged into grey fur lower down. The arms and legs were like those of an ape, but far more delicate, and the fingers were long and supple. All the queer being wore in the way of clothing was a thin metal belt with cloth pouches.

The Creature spoke, and I fancy there must have been a microphone and some sort of broadcasting apparatus behind that panel, for his words came dearly over our wires.

"I suppose your sense of humour must be aroused by my strange appearance; but you will become familiar with that, as you have with the kangaroo and giraffe. That habit of mind which you humans call your sense of humour has always baffled me... But you can trust me when I say it is safe for you to take off your helmets. There is breathable air here."

We did, and there was.

"There is a bench behind you," came the voice. "Sit down."

There was, and we did.

"And now, sir," said Clemence, suddenly taking over the reins in her eager fashion, "tell us the story of your life."

"I expect," replied the Creature, "that this impetuosity is another part of human nature which I cannot reconcile with my conception of reason. But, nevertheless, I realize that your curiosity must be appeased before we discuss matters which arise from your conquest of space..."

Straightway he began an account of the history of himself
and of his race. We sat there entranced for hours as we listened.
Our bench became hard and uncomfortable; we abandoned it and
squatted on the floor at the feet of the Creature like disciples of an
ancient philosopher.

Didactically, but interestingly, he unfolded to us a tale so unearthly
that while I sat there lapping it up, knowing from what we had seen
and experienced that it could hardly be other than true, one detached
part of my mind kept doubting the reality of all this—not only of
this creature and this room, but the whole business of our trip to
the Moon, the Selenites' city and the green plants, that unforgettable
view of the Earth from space, *The Pioneer* and the Interplanetarians.

"Gosh!" that obstinate, incredulous part of my mind kept repeating. "This is *Alice in Wonderland* gone crazy!"

In this narrative I can give only a brief and concise account of
the wondrous story which we heard.

The Creature, whose name, phonetically, was Larn, was the last
of a race of similar beings, called Gend, which inhabited the Moon in
the unbelievably distant past, although only yesterday in the vastness
of astronomical time. But in his day the race was already beginning
to dwindle, for the Moon was growing old; the atmosphere was
thinning, and the seas had almost completely dried up.

For a time the botanists of the Gend had tried to stave off the
atmosphere peril by cultivating the oxygen-producing plants. But,
through lack of moisture, the soil began to get as hard as rock or
crumble into dust, and those plants we had seen were among the
few patchy but hardy survivors. Presently the atmosphere became
so thin that the dying population could no longer remain out in it
unprotected. They had either to build air-tight cities on the surface
or bore them out underground.

But the Selenites were not great builders, whereas they had a ray which was ideal for boring. It had the effect of annihilating all matter on which it was directed, with controllable intensity. Actually, it crowded the atoms of matter so closely together that the material within the orbit of the beam shrank to an incredibly minute size. Again, the Gend were creatures of the Sun, and did not relish living in the depths of the ground. So some genius conceived the idea of using the ray to hollow out mountains and making dwelling-places therein.

Then a period of intense engineering activity took place. The Gend chose some of the craters which were complete rings of mountains, and hollowed out the interiors of these mountains all the way round the circle. They let expansive windows into the slopes and cliffs of the mountains; these were the rectangular patches I had seen from outside, now silted over with volcanic dust and in many places obliterated by land-slides. So they evolved great circular cities, planned, like modern blocks of flats on Earth, to cover a lot of ground compactly and yet admit the maximum amount of sunlight.

They inhabited these cities for many hundreds of years, but still the population lessened, and the survivors began to abandon their half-empty cities and congregate in this one at the edge of the dried-up bed of the Sea of Serenity. Time dragged on, and in a thousand years the population of this last lunar city had dropped to a sterile handful, despite all the attempts of the biologists to stop the decline.

It seemed that the end of the race was inevitable, But they decided on one more great effort. If they could only reach the Earth, that green and virgin planet, conditions there might give them a new, lease of life. And so they built a space-ship, much on the lines of *The Pioneer,* but big enough to take the whole seventy Gend that remained.

"They wanted me to go," said Larn, "but I was deep in a biological experiment, and too fascinated to leave it unsolved, whatever the cost. I had been working a long time on the problem of prolonging life, especially the life of our race. But they had little faith in me and were impatient to go, so they left regretfully, promising to return later to fetch me.

"I well remember the ship rushing over the plain within the city and rising into the sky. Your choosing that plain on which to land was not wholly coincidence; it is one of the very few flat stretches on the Moon... I watched the progress of the ship across space through the large telescope here in the city—I will show it to you presently—until, suddenly, it disappeared. One moment it was there, and then there was a great flash of light and it vanished instantly, utterly; all there was in the field of the telescope were the remote, unblinking stars.

"Just a flash in space—and I was the last of the Gend! A great meteor must have struck the ship. I felt appallingly lonely. I buried myself desperately in my work—and found what I had been seeking, *the elixir of life*! The irony of it!" added Larn, bitterly.

The last of the Gend went on to explain to us how he had treated himself in a manner that would prolong his life for—as far as he knew—ever. "Though sometimes now I seem to feel the burden of the centuries," he interpolated, as though doubting his immortality.

After this, he set himself to develop the experiment further and actually create life so as to re-populate the empty cities and provide the companionship he craved. But he suffered an interminable series of disappointments, and an era had passed before he got the cells of life to flourish at all.

Then all the creatures which he tried to evolve into beings like the Gend invariably died at a certain stage in their development. He spent an eternity trying to find the reason for this, but the problem remained obstinately insoluble, and eventually he abandoned these attempts to resurrect his own species and tried to develop other forms of life. Every attempt failed...

"I almost went mad at that," said Larn. "I wandered about this dead city like a lost soul and cried to the desolation of it, 'Am I to remain alone like this for ever?' Then I came to the telescope and gazed through it at the Earth. Why, that world was teeming with life! The most intelligent species was *homo sapiens*, I decided to start new experiments along these lines, and finally I evolved that race of pigmy creatures you have seen. They would not grow larger because of a deficiency in their pituitary glands."

Apparently this was not the only deficiency: the creatures seemed to be devoid of reasoning power. They lived only by imitation. Larn's attempts to educate them were fruitless. They could not conceive themselves repeating any action of his, because he and they were so dissimilar in appearance. They remained dull and listless.

But when Larn built a special attachment to the huge telescope which enabled them to see the Earth and its inhabitants, they woke up amazingly. They saw creatures which appeared to be reflections of themselves busily doing things, and at once their imitative instincts were aroused. They took charge of the telescope and promptly commenced to copy all mankind's deeds. They watched the Earth constantly, and their memory and grasp of detail were unfaltering.

"This laboratory became a busy confusion," Larn went on. "It became impossible for me to continue my work. I had discovered that nitrogen was filtering slowly up from the depths of fissures in the Moon, and that outside in the crater the surviving plants were still giving off enough oxygen to make quite a passable supply of air. So, realizing that these midgets would never develop much power of creative thinking, I turned them out into the crater. There they flourished and built their imitation city—a muddle of buildings they had seen at various times on the Earth.

"But they still have access to the telescope. I arranged that, because I must admit I still have some affection for the little creatures. That road you came along branches off in the dark tunnel and runs down to a cavern beneath this laboratory where they live through the cold lunar nights... Now I will show you the telescope."

He made as if to rise, but Clemence broke in hastily:

"Just a minute, please. How is it that you know our language so well?"

Larn quietly turned a switch on the control-panel beside him, and instantly a familiar voice filled the room.

"... at times. Further outlook, unsettled. Here is the First News, copyright by Reuter, Exchange Telegraph and Central News..."

We laughed. The answer was obvious. A mind like Larn's would have no difficulty in analysing the meanings of the languages he heard on the radio. He had a wonderful set there. In rapid succession he tuned in Rome, Moscow, Berlin, Cracow, Pittsburg, and others.

"I can speak all these languages," he said, "and they are all primitive, clumsy attempts at definition. But..."

He tuned in a French station, and the melody of a small string orchestra stole into the laboratory. It was a sad, bitter-sweet air—the Minuet from Debussy's *Petite Suite*.

"There is the true voice of man," said Larn. "There he expresses every nuance of his thought and emotion. Your music has greatness!"

He switched off the radio, rose on his curious, furry legs and walked slowly across the laboratory. Amid the maze of shelving was a small door, and he opened this and stood on the threshold of another room.

"Come," he said. "I would show you some of the greatness of my own race."

v

The Deserted City

We arose stiffly and followed him. The room in which we found ourselves was like the interior of an observatory. Down from the roof loomed the thick barrel of a telescope. It was like some great gun poking into the room, and the upper part of it was lost in shadow.

Yet, as Larn explained, the part we saw in this observatory was but a small portion of the eye-piece alone! The main body of the telescope went reaching up for thousands of feet before even the pivot was passed, and somewhere up in the peak of the mountain above were situated the immense lenses. A thin tube ran from the eyepiece to a glass case on the floor. I peered into this case, and was startled to see one of the Lilliputians, a tiny figure in a white smock, run down a miniature spiral staircase and disappear under the floor.

"Their observer," said Larn. "The air in that case is maintained at the low pressure suitable for them."

He detached the thin tube, leaving the eye-piece free. At his invitation, I applied my eye to the lens; and there, seen at a sloping, sideways angle, but clear and sharply etched in the noon sun, was the Empire State Building rising out of the busy streets of New York! So this was what the Lilliputian had been observing! Larn did mysterious things to levers and wheels, and New York rapidly shrank and became just an island off a long coastline. The island slid suddenly to one side, and the telescope swept eastward across the grey-green waves of the Atlantic. It halted at the west coast of Ireland; then the landscape rushed up at me so quickly that I involuntarily jerked my head back. When I looked again, there was a long white band running across some green fields in the light of a rosy sunset. It was the concrete runway from which *The Pioneer* had taken off.

"I have for long watched your activities with interest," murmured Larn, and slid the field of the telescope rapidly across Ireland and the sea to southern England.

He focused some large open space in South London. It was Blackheath in twilight, and across it crawled, like glow-worms, the tiny, fore-shortened buses with their lights already on. We swooped down upon one of them like an eagle and followed it along the road. I could read the advertisements on it and see through the window's a sedate row of passengers sitting there, all unconscious of the eye that watched them across a quarter of a million miles of space.

The telescope left the bus and took to the grass by the wayside. Then Larn showed me the really amazing quality of the instrument. He focused one errant blade of grass so clearly that I could perceive traces of an early frost upon it. A blade of grass in the dusk two hundred and fifty thousand miles away!

"In the building of this telescope," Larn explained, "we used a new light-gathering system, on the refractive principle, with a transparent material far more effective than glass. Of course, at the height at which the lenses are, the absence of atmosphere allows of an almost unlimited degree of magnification."

Now he swung the view over the trees of Greenwich Park and picked out the main dome of the Observatory.

"I happen to know that some of your London Interplanetarians are there already, gazing up at this satellite shining in their eastern sky. They think they are looking at a world devoid of cities or life, and both are here before their eyes. But the cities are camouflaged and the life is too small for their poor instrument to distinguish."

Clemence and the Captain had their turn at seeing these things, and then Larn directed the telescope to other worlds. In time I shall be writing a separate treatise on some of the astronomical marvels we saw, so they must now be left. But the mystery of the Martian canals was solved for us, and the far-flung suns of this galaxy became as neighbours, revealing secrets to that all-seeing eye which my pen is incapable of describing.

Sufficient to say that there are other inhabited worlds than this, and strange is the life upon them. But from what we saw it was evident that there is a power which moves the Universe, and beside it all life is a weak, meaningless thing...

Afterwards, Larn let us into the city of his lost people. He would not come himself, saying he had other work to get on with. Perhaps this was so, but I imagine there was another reason—that the melancholy journey would affect him too much emotionally. He was an extremely sensitive being.

"You will find a railway," he said, "which is about the only mechanism still able to work. There is enough power in the City Accumulator left to drive it."

He gave us further particulars, then we donned our helmets and passed from the observatory through an air-lock—for the city was airless—and down a flight of metallic steps to the city floor.

The view had been dimly discernible from the window of Larn's laboratory. Imagine the largest cathedral interior you ever saw, with the beams of a setting Sun striking through the stained-glass windows across the nave like bars of old gold, and multiply that scene a hundred-fold. Only in this case the windows were so dust-grimed as to be barely translucent, so that the sun-rays which did penetrate them were of a dull amber, and in places almost invisible.

There you have an idea of the first general effect that we gathered. The farther wall of this vast interior was too remote to see in the feeble light. Up the sloping wall that leaned out over us the windows mounted one above the other, and became converging lines of brown squares, steadily diminishing as they went up, to meet and vanish at an indefinite point near the invisible roof.

To left and right along the gallery stretched an immensely long row of these sloping, foggy beams, becoming small in the distance and disappearing round the gradual curve of the crater. And in all that lengthy perspective not a thing stirred. The silence and stillness of the tomb reigned over all. It was a place of solemn mystery...

The light from Larn's window streamed out above us, a solitary white torch-light in the golden-brown gloom, and picked out the shine of metal rails on the floor. We walked forward and found the railway. There was a train of open trucks on the lines, and in the foremost was a lever like the "Dead Man's Handle."

"It's a Tube as ever was," said Clemence over the telephone.

We entered the foremost truck, and the Captain started it up by depressing the handle. So began a tour which I shall never forget, although in this narrative I have not space to describe in detail the ancient city of the Gend. That, too, must be the subject of a special treatise.

At first, as we rolled along at steady speed, we exclaimed aloud at the things we saw, and discussed them vigorously. But as the miles reeled on, our conversation died into contemplative silence. The brooding atmosphere seeped into our inner thoughts.

There were the houses of the Gend, endless rows of them. They were simply screens of walls, high enough for privacy; few of them had roofs, because the Gend had not wished to block, out any of the precious daylight. There were areas that had been parks, and tall monuments worked with a queer technique of art dotted the ways.

I sat there taking in all this and trying to visualize the city as it was when it was inhabited. But it was hard to imagine this desolate place teeming with life, or that the griffin-like creatures had ever occupied those seats in the string of trucks that rolled smoothly along behind us.

Some of the windows in the mountain-side had been cracked and starred by meteorites, and one was completely smashed in. At some time a great mass of rock had crashed down, ploughed across the city's floor, and driven many travelling machines into a deep crater. Thank heavens it had missed the line! I should not have wished to walk back from that spot, for it was on the far side of the mountain ring.

The Captain stopped the train at this window and we peered out through the jagged aperture. This was the inner rim of the circle of mountains, and the flat plain of the crater floor stretched away like the asphalt surface of a giant school playground. Only an expanse of bare grey rock; no green plants here.

On the verge of the horizon we could just make out a line of cliffs and peaks. That was where we had left Larn in his hidden observatory, diametrically opposite to us.

"Phew! Haven't we come a distance!" muttered the Captain.

We leaned on the rail of the truck and gazed at the scene in silence. Over all, like a pall, hung the nearly black sky. The Earth was behind us, and invisible; the Sun was a fiery ball, and the hard, sharp points of the stars glittered like millions of bits of quartz.

What I had seen in those stellar depths through the giant telescope stirred in my memory, and suddenly an intense realization of the magnitude of the cosmos swept over me. A wave of strange emotion that stranded me, a lonely mite, on a solitary spur of rock, from which all space and time fell away in bottomless gulfs in every direction. Our voyage in *The Pioneer* had been just a hop between two specks of dust! Man on his planet was a newly-born, blind kitten, crawling along the edge of the infinite with its billion mysteries unexplored, unguessed at...

The Captain's rapt, solemn face told me that he, too was moved by some similar profound feeling, and for once even Clemence was not able to be facetious.

Presently we continued on our way, and in time a white light appeared ahead under the leaning columns of faded sun-beams, telling us that we had almost completed the circuit of the crater. As we came up to it, Clemence remarked that the long, lighted window overhanging the railway line reminded her of a signal-box at night.

I had a ludicrous vision of Larn in a railwayman's peaked cap, and this seemed to bring into my head all the railway jokes I had ever heard. The others were in a lighter mood, too, and as we climbed the steps and stood waiting in the air-lock for the automatic pumps to fill the place with air, we exchanged sallies and witticisms, laughing explosively.

I think this was because of the relief we felt at leaving that great mausoleum behind us. When the air was of sufficient density for us to remove our helmets, we opened the door of the lock and passed into the observatory, still laughing.

Then we stopped short. For on the floor beneath the eye-piece of the telescope lay Larn, on his back, his beak-mouth agape and eyes staring emptily. Quickly the Captain knelt and examined him.

"The poor fellow's dead," he said, almost immediately; and Clemence, who a moment before had been almost choking with merriment, suddenly melted into tears.

VI

The Lilliputians' Revenge

We came down the dark passage with a gale tearing behind us, for we knew not how to shut the sliding door of the laboratory from outside, and the air in the room was rushing out.

Somewhere in the darkness we found the Lilliputian road, and followed it out into the light. There was the spreading field of green plants, silently waving in the wind that burst from the tunnel's mouth with us.

The lunar day was drawing to a close. The opposite crater wall was just a black shadow, hardly discernible from the jet sky. The Sun was sinking towards it, and in that tenuous atmosphere the solar prominences were clearly visible, radiating from the great disc like red-tinged fronds.

We went along the road, past the half-completed replica of the Empire State Building, our minds still dazed with the thought of Larn's death. That a being who had lived for millions of years, and apparently expected to live for many more, should suddenly collapse and die during our brief visit, seemed more than a mere coincidence. Or was it only coincidence after all?

After the shock of the discovery had passed, we had carried Larn's body into the laboratory and laid it on the couch beneath the window. What could we do further? It was impossible to think of burying him in that rocky place.

"This laboratory will have to be his crypt," the Captain had said, as we took our last look at him lying there with the light (which we found no way of extinguishing), shining on him and reaching out above him through the window, out into the shadowy city of his people. Then we had left.

We plodded on...

The Captain's voice sounded suddenly in my telephone receiver.

"Did you notice that Lilliputian observer in the glass case as we came in from the city?"

"No."

"There was one. He was staring at Larn's body on the floor. He bolted underground when we entered. I wonder whether he has gone to the town to tell the others?"

I looked up and down the long, narrow road. The higher spires of the Lilliputian town were just visible ahead over the multitudinous, closely packed spore-cases, which were continually bursting here and there like miniature bombs. A dazzle of reflected sunlight near the town shewed where *The Pioneer* stood.

"No sign of him, though," I said.

"They had cars, you know," interpolated Clemence. "He may have driven to the town already."

"Possibly. I wonder if they will think we had anything to do with Larn's death...?"

"And I wonder, too, if we really had," said the Captain, slowly. "The effect of that elixir was fading, I'm sure. The fellow was dead tired—worn out; you could see that. I think the excitement of encountering real, *responsive* life at last, after an unbelievable age of solitude, was a bit too much for his old heart. He concealed his feelings pretty well while we were there, but I observed signs that all the time he was emotionally upset—all on edge. And the shock—"

On that very word we received a shock ourselves.

Absorbed in our discussion, we had reached the border of the plain of plants, where a stretch of bare ground separated us from *The Pioneer* standing on the outskirts of the town. At least, it *had* been a stretch of bare ground. Now it was covered by an army of Lilliputians.

Yes; a real army! Dense phalanxes of troops were drawn up in orderly array behind a line of field-guns, rows of little pink faces all turned towards us, rows of sharp little rifle-bayonets directed towards us. The guns looked like scale models of howitzers to our eyes, but they completely dwarfed the tiny gunners who stood at the ready beside them; and the muzzles were elevated at a high angle to cover us.

"Good Lord!" exclaimed the Captain, in a whisper. "They've pinched the British Army uniform!"

I had been thinking that they looked somehow very familiar, and the Captain had hit upon the reason. They had meticulously copied the uniforms of the British Army—of all possible armies!—and were neatly clad in khaki. An officer with a Sam Browne belt, carrying a cane—or what passed for one—stepped forward between the guns and stood looking boldly up at us.

It would have been laughable if it were not for those pitiful ruins in the town at the back of them, where *The Pioneer* stood immobile, a giant shell on wheels, like some mechanical beast crouching over its prey.

For a moment longer we stood staring at each other, we three Gullivers and the toy army that challengingly barred the way to our rocket-ship.

"Can't we outflank them?" I suggested. "Get round them to the ship?"

"No, I think they would fire if we attempted to escape that way," said the Captain. "We must try to talk to them. Some of them may possibly have heard Larn's radio often enough to know a little English. For all we know, they may even have radio themselves. It's worth trying, anyway."

He had in a pocket of his space-suit a spare telephone-receiver with an amplifier that made of it a powerful loud-speaker, small though it was. This instrument had been constructed by a thoughtful Interplanetarian against the chance that we might want to speak to possible outsiders while unable to remove our suits. Now that foresight was justified.

The Captain joined the instrument up with the wires that connected us, and held it out towards the Lilliputians as if about to speak. Whereupon, Clemence calmly took it from him.

"*I'm* going to do the announcing, Cap.," she told him. "You're sure to lose your temper and start shouting at them; and Bill here is about as eloquent as a deaf and dumb oyster. What they need is soothing down, then a little peaceful persuasion. Leave it to me. I'll talk to them like a mother."

The Captain demurred for a moment, and muttered something I couldn't catch about "apron strings," but let Clemence have her way. Holding the receiver out, she stepped forward a pace.

There came a stir in the ranks of the midget army; but the officer raised his tiny arm, and instantly the agitation subsided. Then Clemence began to speak in her serene, sweet voice, which sounded in our receivers, faintly but very distinctly.

"Dear people, I find it very hard to express our sorrow for the harm we have done you. We are shocked and dismayed to think of that awful accident; our feelings cannot be put into words. But we do wish you to understand that it *was* only an accident. There was nothing we wished less than to harm you. We have only the kindliest intentions—"

The little officer's arm dropped. Whether or not it was meant as a signal I cannot say for sure; but instantly the line of artillery fired a salvo. We could not hear it, hut we saw all the little guns jerk back on their wheels in recoil and long clouds of smoke, like flour dust, roll out towards us.

"The little fools!" I cursed, thinking they had missed us. "Come on, Cap., let's—"

But the Captain did not hear me for Clemence had swayed and fallen back limply into his arms.

"My God! They've hit her!" I heard his agonized cry, and in an instant reaction of rage, grief and panic, lest the Lilliputians fire and harm Clemence again, I blundered heavily forward and charged the line.

I must have been a frightening sight to those tiny creatures. They broke ranks straightway and fled before me like startled mice. I careered after them as they streamed towards the ruins of the town. Then that confounded telephone wire pulled me up like a tethered dog and I could only stand and swear like mad at them, and in blind rage kick their pieces of artillery after them with my leaden-soled boots.

In the midst of this senseless outburst of fury I thought of Clemence, and hurried back to assist her.

One of those miniature shells, about the size of a small pistol bullet, had caught her on the left shoulder. Fortunately, the steel buckle of the strap which fastened her air cylinder had taken the direct force of the impact, but the missile had exploded, and a fragment of it had penetrated the material of the space-suit and entered her body just above the heart.

The Captain was supporting her, with one hand over the rent in her suit to stop the air from escaping. She was pale and unconscious.

"Help me with her," said the Captain, hoarsely.

We lifted her and carried her gently towards *The Pioneer*. Out of the corner of my eye I could see the scattered midget army swarming about the city, confusedly hesitating between fleeing farther and staying to watch.

To get the unconscious Clemence into the air-lock of the ship and through it to the cabin was a task of constant anxiety and fearful impatience. But at last we got her into her bunk under the curving wall, took off her helmet and cut away her suit. As we were binding her wound, she began to murmur. Her long eyelashes fluttered, and presently she half-opened her eyes and regarded us, at first dully, then questioningly, then finally with recollection and faint amusement.

"Don't try to talk, dear," said the Captain softly.

"You're right, Cap.," she whispered, "I shouldn't. That last little speech was an awful flop... wasn't it? Got the bird... properly. You said... I'd talk myself... to death one day, Cap. Looks as though... you may be right."

"Nonsense, Clem, you'll be all right," said the Captain, almost fiercely, and for the first time since the shooting I noticed his face. It was as pale as his wife's, and set in rigid lines. His eyes were burning with the terrible conflict of emotions that seized and tortured him. Utter despair fought with tentative hope, and tenderness with bitter rage.

I saw that he was stricken to the heart; and it was starkly apparent to me that my love fur Clemence, though it consumed me, was flaccid and insensitive beside the Captain's passionate worship. Instantly, those silly dream castles of mine collapsed like the unsubstantial things they were, and I knew they would never be rebuilt. If Clemence lived, all I craved was the continued warmth of her friendship.

If Clemence lived! My throat went dry with fear at the thought that I might lose her for ever. I touched her hand timorously, and she smiled wanly up at me and closed her eyes.

"I think she will sleep now," the Captain whispered tensely. Then he arose, walked over to the rear port-hole and looked grimly out.

I followed him. The fortnight-long lunar day was steadily, though imperceptibly, closing. The enormously elongated shadow of the opposite crater wall was creeping towards us, a sluggish tide of darkness.

But still the Lilliputians were out and about. Between the jutting tubes of our rear rocket exhausts I saw them reforming their ranks among the ruins, righting their overturned guns, and apparently preparing for an offensive.

The Captain's mouth tightened at this. For the first time in my life I saw him in a cold rage, silent and white with anger; and I was in sympathy with him. The callous shooting of Clemence had aroused in me an intense hatred for the Lilliputians that I had not known was in my nature.

The tiny gunners were busying themselves again. Suddenly one of the guns ejected a wisp of smoke and—crash! the glass window starred before Our eyes. Air immediately began to seep out. The Captain slammed the air-tight shutter over the port-hole.

"They've asked for it," he said grimly. "We've got to get Clem back to Earth, Bill, and we're going to start right now. Notice our rear tubes are pointing right at that refuse-heap and its crawling inhabitants? When we start, the exhaust gases will wipe them out like a spray of insecticide. That'll be poetic justice, if you like!"

It shows what a mental state I was in, for I agreed fervently. We took our seats at the control panel. Then the Captain, with a face as merciless as a condemning judge's, reached for the switch that would release the scorching, rushing gas to shrivel that tiny army behind us.

And at the crucial moment came the voice of Clemence, sharp and clear.

"Stop it, you idiots!"

We spun round in our seats. Clemence had raised herself on an elbow and her drawn face regarded us anxiously. We rushed over to her. The Captain tried to get her to lay back; but she was obdurate.

"I've got to get another speech off my chest first," she said, and I was relieved to note the firmness of her voice. "You two are behaving like a pair of silly boys. Going to take a grand revenge, eh? You'd exterminate all those little mites just because they knocked me stupid for a few minutes?"

She paused for breath, then continued in gentler tones.

"We are to blame—not them. They are only a reflection of ourselves. Their action was an imitation of war as they have seen it on Earth. We destroyed their city, and naturally they take it as an act of war and try to wipe us out in return. Perhaps they think we killed Larn, too. Humanity has been showing these little creatures too many bad examples, especially in the misuse of force. We should give them something better to imitate…"

The Captain sealed her lips with a kiss, smoothed her hair tenderly, and pressed her gently back on to the pillow.

"We shall," he murmured, and she looked trustingly at him. I felt embarrassed and ashamed, and fiddled about with my globular helmet. The Captain straightened up.

"Put it on," he said to me. "We're going out."

Presently we stepped out on to the Moon again. A fusillade of tiny shells greeted us. We heeded them not, but went to the back of The Pioneer and set our shoulders to the wheel—or, rather, to the covers of the wheels. Straining and pushing, we got the great vehicle moving slowly—dreadfully slowly, despite the fact that the lesser gravitation had lifted five-sixths of its weight from it.

Previously the Captain had set the front wheels by wrenching the steering-wheel round, so that as we inched the ship along, the battery of rocket-tubes began to swung away from the model city and point out over the empty field of plants. We puffed and struggled for nearly twenty minutes, and most of that time the shells exploded all around, spurting up little fountains of soil and chips of rock, and scoring bright patches on the bulging side of the ship. But, miraculously, not a splinter touched us.

In time the bombardment ceased, and the little people just stood at a safe distance and watched us. I like to think that they were beginning to comprehend what we were doing, and that another feeling was filtering in to oust the animal hate from their minds. But perhaps the brutal truth was they had run out of ammunition.

Be that as it may, we continued to shove unmolested. All the time some lines from a play kept floating about at the back of my mind, but I could not seem to pin the words down.

At last we had pushed the ship many yards from the town, with its tail pointing obliquely away. The gases could do no harm now, except to some of the plants, which could not be helped. We looked our last at the fantastic city and its army of occupation that must soon perforce retreat before the coming night. Then we climbed back into the ship.

Clemence was sitting up now, and it was clear that she would never allow her wound to bother her overmuch. Her eyes were shining, and her elated smile absolved us of all our sins. Contritely, without a word, we took our seats at the control-panel. The Captain turned the switch. Came the jerk of the recoil, and away we went rushing over the ground.

It was then, as the level floor of the crater fled beneath our wheels, that those elusive, yet so familiar words of Portia came at last into the forefront of my consciousness.

> *The quality of mercy is not strain'd;*
> *It droppeth as the gentle rain from heaven*
> *Upon the place beneath...*

When I looked again the ground was gone. The rocky plain, the Lilliputian town, the dead crater city of the long-forgotten Gend, and Larn sleeping in his lonely tomb—all had vanished like the figments of a dream, and we were speeding out towards the promise of a green bubble floating in the vastness of space, the ball that was our home and the home of our kind.

NOTHING HAPPENS ON THE MOON

Paul Ernst

One of the psychological problems that astronauts will have to deal with is the loneliness and isolation of space. This not only affects those undertaking long distant journeys in the future such as to Mars and beyond, but also those venturing to and staying on the Moon. Astronaut Scott Kelly, who spent 340 consecutive days on the International Space Station during 2015–16 reported that even though he had comrades nearby, each day usually had an acute sense of isolation because he could see the Earth and knew his family was there, but they were to all intents inaccessible. How much worse would it be, therefore, if you were isolated on the Moon.

The first writer to tackle this in any detail was Paul Ernst (1899–1985). He was a prolific writer for the American pulp magazines and was best known for writing the adventures of the superhero The Avenger for the pulp of that name between 1939 and 1942. Ernst was a capable writer, and went on during the 1940s and after to write successfully for the high-paying slick magazines, but his early attempts at science fiction, starting in 1930, were formulaic and uninspired. However, Ernst responded to the challenges of John W. Campbell, Jr., who took over editing Astounding Stories *in 1938 and who began to revolutionize the field. It was Campbell who encouraged newcomers soon to be giants of the field such as Robert A. Heinlein, Isaac Asimov, Eric Frank Russell, L. Sprague de Camp and A.E. van Vogt. "Nothing Happens on the Moon" shows the writing capabilities of Ernst when working with the best editor the field had yet had.*

THE SHINING HALL OF THE FULL EARTH FLOATED LIKE A smooth pearl between two vast, angular mountains. The full Earth. Another month had ticked by.

Clow Hartigan turned from the porthole beside the small air lock to the Bliss radio transmitter.

"RC3, RC3, RC3," he droned out.

There was no answer. Stacey, up in New York, always took his time about answering the RC3 signal, confound it! But then, why shouldn't he? There was never anything of importance to listen to from Station RC3. Nothing of any significance ever happened on the Moon.

Hartigan stared unseeingly at the pink cover of a six-month-old *Radio Gazette,* pasted to the wall over the control board. A pulchritudinous brunette stared archly back at him over a plump shoulder that was only one of many large nude areas.

"RC3, RC3—"

Ah, there Stacey was, the pompous little busybody.

"Hartigan talking. Monthly report."

"Go ahead, Hartigan."

A hurried, fussy voice. Calls of real import waited for Stacey; calls from Venus and Jupiter and Mars. Hurry up, Moon, and report that nothing has happened, as usual.

Hartigan proceeded to do so.

"Lunar conditions the same. No ships have put in, or have reported themselves as being in distress. The hangar is in good shape, with no leaks. Nothing out of the way has occurred."

"Right," said Stacey pompously. "Supplies?"

"You might send up a blonde." said Hartigan.

"Be serious. Need anything?"

"No." Hartigan's eyes brooded. "How's everything in Little Old New York?"

Stacey's businesslike voice was a reproof. Also it was a pain in the neck.

"Sorry. Can't gossip. Things pretty busy around here. If you need anything, let me know."

The burr of power went dead. Hartigan cursed with monotony, and got up.

Clow Hartigan was a big young man with sand-red hair and slightly bitter blue eyes. He was representative of the type United Spaceways sent to such isolated emergency landing stations as the Moon.

There were half a dozen such emergency landing domes, visited only by supply ships, exporting nothing, but ready in case some passenger liner was crippled by a meteor or by mechanical trouble. The two worst on the Spaceways list were the insulated hell on Mercury, and this great, lonely hangar on the Moon. To them Spaceways sent the pick of their probation executives. Big men. Powerful men. Young men. (Also men who were unlucky enough not to have an old family friend or an uncle on the board of directors who could swing a soft berth for them.) Spaceways did not keep them there long. Men killed themselves or went mad and began inconsiderately smashing expensive equipment, after too long a dose of such loneliness as that of the Moon.

Hartigan went back to the porthole beside the small air lock. As he went, he talked to himself, as men do when they have been too long away from their own kind.

"I wish I'd brought a dog up here, or a cat. I wish there'd be an attempted raid. Anything at all. If only something would *happen*."

Resentfully he stared out at the photographic, black-and-white lunar landscape, lighted coldly by the full Earth. From that his eye went to the deep black of the heavens. Then his heart gave a jump. There was a faint light up there where no light was supposed to be.

He hurried to the telescope and studied it. A space liner, and a big one! Out of its course, no matter where it was bound, or it couldn't have been seen from the Moon with the naked eye. Was it limping in here to the emergency landing for repairs?

"I don't wish them any bad luck," muttered Hartigan, "but I hope they've burned out a rocket tube."

Soon his heart sank, however. The liner soared over the landing dome a hundred miles up, and went serenely on its way. In a short time its light faded in distance. Probably it was one of the luxurious around-the-solar-system ships, passing close to the Moon to give the sightseers an intimate glimpse of it, but not stopping because there was absolutely nothing of interest there.

"Nothing *ever* happens in this Godforsaken hole," Hartigan gritted.

Impatiently he took his space suit down from the rack. Impatiently he stepped into the bulky, flexible metal thing and clamped down the headpiece. Nothing else to do. He'd take a walk. The red beam of the radio control board would summon him back to the hangar if for any reason anyone tried to raise RC3.

He let himself out through the double wall of the small air lock and set out with easy, fifteen-foot strides toward a nearby cliff on the brink of which it was sometimes his habit to sit and think nasty thoughts of the men who ran Spaceways and maintained places like RC3.

Between the hangar and the cliff was a wide expanse of grey lava ash, a sort of small lake of the stuff, feathery fine. Hartigan did not know how deep it might be. He did know that a man could probably sink down in it so far that he would never be able to burrow out again.

He turned to skirt the lava ash, but paused a moment before proceeding.

Behind him loomed the enormous half globe of the hangar, like a phosphorescent mushroom in the blackness. One section of the half globe was flattened; and here were the gigantic inner and outer portals where a liner's rocket-propelled life shells could enter the dome. The great doors of this, the main air lock, reared halfway to the top of the hangar, and weighed several hundred tons apiece.

Before him was the face of the Moon: sharp angles of rock; jagged, tremendous mountains; sheer, deep craters; all picked out in black and white from the reflected light of Earth.

A desolate prospect... Hartigan started on.

The ash beside him suddenly seemed to explode, soundlessly but with great violence. It spouted up like a geyser to a distance of a hundred feet, hung for an instant over him in a spreading cloud, then quickly began to settle.

A meteor! Must have been a fair-sized one to have made such a splash in the volcanic dust.

"Close call," muttered Hartigan, voice sepulchral in his helmet. "A little nearer and they'd be sending a new man to the lunar emergency dome."

But he only grimaced and went on. Meteors were like the lightning back on Earth. Either they hit you or they missed. There was no warning till after they struck; then it was too late to do anything about it.

Hartigan stumbled over something in the cloud of ash that was sifting down around him. Looking down, he saw a smooth, round object, black-hot, about as big as his head.

"The meteor," he observed. "Must have hit a slanting surface at the bottom of the ash heap and ricocheted up and out here. I wonder—"

He stooped clumsily toward it. His right "hand," which was a heavy pincer arrangement terminating the right sleeve of his suit, went out, then his left, and with some difficulty he picked the thing up. Now and then a meteor held splashes of precious metals. Sometimes one was picked up that yielded several hundred dollars' worth of platinum or iridium. A little occasional gravy with which the emergency-landing exiles could buy amusement when they got back home.

Through the annoying shower of ash he could see dimly the light of the hangar. He started back, to get out of his suit and analyse the meteor for possible value.

It was the oddest-looking thing he had ever seen come out of the heavens. In the first place, its shape was remarkable. It was perfectly round, instead of being irregular as were most meteors.

"Like an old-fashioned cannon ball," Hartigan mused, bending over it on a workbench. "Or an egg—"

Eyebrows raised whimsically, he played with the idea.

"Jupiter! What an egg it would be! A hundred and twenty pounds if it's an ounce, and it smacked the Moon like a bullet without even cracking! I wouldn't want it poached for breakfast."

The next thing to catch his attention was the projectile's odd colour, or, rather, the odd way in which the colour seemed to be

changing. It had been dull, black-hot, when Hartigan brought it in.
It was now a dark green, and was getting lighter swiftly as it cooled!

The big Clock struck a mellow note. Time for the dome keeper to
make his daily inspection of the main doors.

Reluctantly Hartigan left the odd meteor, which was now as
green as grass and actually seemed to be growing transparent, and
walked toward the big air lock.

He switched on the radio power unit. There was no power
plant of any kind in the hangar; all power was broadcast by the
Spaceways central station. He reached for the contact switch which
poured the invisible Niagara of power into the motors that moved
the ponderous doors.

Cr-r-rack!

Like a cannon shot the sound split the air in the huge metal
dome, echoing from wall to wall, to die at last in a muffled rumbling.

White-faced, Hartigan was running long before the echoes died
away. He ran toward the workbench he had recently quitted. The
sound seemed to have come from near there. His thought was that
the hangar had been crashed by a meteor larger than its cunningly
braced beams, tough metal sheath, and artful angles of deflection
would stand.

That would mean death, for the air supply in the dome would
race out through a fissure almost before he could don his space suit.

However, his anxious eyes, scanning the vaulting roof, could find
no crumpled bracing or ominous downward bulges. And he could
hear no thin whine of air surging to escape from the fifteen pounds
pressure in the hangar to the almost nonexistent pressure outside.

Then he glanced at the workbench and uttered an exclamation.
The meteor he had left there was gone.

"It must have rolled off the bench," he told himself. "But if it's on the floor, why can't I see it?"

He froze into movelessness. Had that been a sound behind him? A sound, here, where no sound could possibly be made save by himself?

He whirled—and saw nothing. Nothing whatever, save the familiar expanse of smooth rock floor lighted with the cold white illumination broadcast on the power band.

He turned back to the workbench where the meteor had been, and began feeling over it with his hands, disbelieving the evidence of his eyes.

Another exclamation burst from his lips as his fingers touched something hard and smooth and round. The meteor. Broken into two halves, but still here. Only, *now it was invisible!*

"This," said Hartigan, beginning to sweat a little, "is the craziest thing I ever heard of!"

He picked up one of the two invisible halves and held it close before his eyes. He could not see it at all, though it was solid to the touch. Moreover, he seemed able to see through it, for nothing on the other side was blotted out.

Fear increased within him as his fingers told him that the two halves were empty, hollow. Heavy as the ball had been, it consisted of nothing but a shell about two inches thick. Unless—

"Unless something really did crawl out of it when it split apart."

But that, of course, was ridiculous.

"It's just an ordinary metallic chunk," he told himself, "that split open with a loud bang when it cooled, due to contraction. The only thing unusual about it is its invisibility. That *is* strange."

He groped on the workbench for the other half of the thick round shell. With a half in each hand, he started toward the stock room, meaning to lock up this odd substance very carefully. He suspected he had something beyond price here. If he could go back to Earth with a substance that could produce invisibility, he could become one of the richest men in the universe.

He presented a curious picture as he walked over the brilliantly lighted floor. His shoulders sloped down with the weight of the two pieces of meteor. His bare arms rippled and knotted with muscular effort. Yet his hands seemed empty. So far as the eye could tell, he was carrying nothing whatever.

"What—"

He dropped the halves of the shell with a ringing clang, and began leaping toward the big doors. That time he *knew* he had heard a sound, a sound like scurrying steps! It had come from near the big doors.

When he got there, however, he could hear nothing. For a time the normal stillness, the ghastly, phenomenal stillness, was preserved. Then, from near the spot he had just vacated, he heard another noise. This time it was a gulping, voracious noise, accompanied by a sound that was like that of a rock crusher or a concrete mixer in action.

On the run, he returned, seeing nothing all this while; nothing but smooth rock floor and plain, metal-ribbed walls, and occasional racks of instruments.

He got to the spot where he had dropped the parts of the meteor. The parts were no longer there. This time it was more than a question of invisibility. They had disappeared actually as well as visually.

To make sure, Hartigan got down on hands and knees and searched every inch of a large circle. There was no trace of the thick shell.

"Either something brand-new to the, known solar system is going on here," Hartigan declared, "or I'm getting as crazy as they insisted poor Stuyvesant was."

Increased perspiration glinted on his forehead. The fear of madness in the lonelier emergency fields was a very real fear. United Spaceways had been petitioned more than once to send two men instead of one to manage each outlying field; but Spaceways was an efficient corporation with no desire to pay two men where one could handle the job.

Again Hartigan could hear nothing at all. And in swift though unadmitted fear that perhaps the whole business had transpired only in his own brain, he sought refuge in routine. He returned to his task of testing the big doors, which was important even though dreary in its daily repetition.

The radio power unit was on, as he had left it. He closed the circuit.

Smoothly the enormous inner doors swung open on their broad tracks, to reveal the equally enormous outer portals. Hartigan stepped into the big air lock, and closed the inner doors. He shivered a little. It was near freezing out here in spite of the heating units.

There was a small control room in the lock, to save an operator the trouble of always getting into a space suit when the doors were opened. Hartigan entered this and pushed home the switch that moved the outer portals.

Smoothly, perfectly, their tremendous bulk opened outward. They always worked smoothly, perfectly. No doubt they always would. Nevertheless, rules said test them regularly. And it was best to live up to the rules. With characteristic trustfulness, Spaceways had recording dials in the home station that showed by power markings whether or not their planetary employees were doing what they were supposed to do.

Hartigan reversed the switch. The doors began to close. They got to the halfway mark; to the three-quarters—

Hartigan felt rather than heard the sharp, grinding jar. He felt rather than heard the high, shrill scream, a rasping shriek, almost above the limit of audibility, that was something to make a man's blood run cold.

Still, without faltering, the doors moved inward and their serrated edges met. Whatever one of them had ground across had not been large enough to shake it.

"Jupiter!" Hartigan breathed, once more inside the huge dome with both doors closed.

He sat down to try to think the thing out.

"A smooth, round meteor falls. It looks like an egg, though it seems to be of metallic rock. As it cools, it gets lighter in colour, till finally it disappears. With a loud bang, it bursts apart, and afterward I hear a sound like scurrying feet. I drop the pieces of the shell to go toward the sound, and then I hear another sound, as if something were macerating and gulping down the pieces of shell, eating them. I come back and can't find the pieces. I go on with my test of opening and closing the main doors. As the outer door closes, I hear a crunching noise as if a rock were being pulverized, and a high scream like that of an animal in pain. All this would indicate that the meteor *was* a shell, and that some living thing *did* come out of it.

"But that is impossible.

"No form of life could live through the crash with which that thing struck the Moon, even though the lava ash did cushion the fall to some extent. No form of life could stand the heat of the meteor's fall and impact. No form of life could eat the rocky, metallic shell. It's utterly impossible!

"Or—*is* it impossible?"

He gnawed at his knuckles and thought of Stuyvesant.

Stuyvesant had been assigned to the emergency dome on Mercury. There was a place for you! An inferno! By miracles of insulation and supercooling systems the hangar there had been made livable. But the finest of space suits could not keep a man from frying to death outside. Nothing to do except stay cooped up inside the hangar, and pray for the six-month relief to come.

Stuyvesant had done that. And from Stuyvesant had begun to come queer reports. He thought he had seen something moving on Mercury near his landing field. Something like a rock!

Moving rocks! With the third report of that kind, the corporation had brought him home and turned him over to the board of science for examination. Poor Stuyvesant had barely escaped the lunatic asylum. He had been let out of Spaceways, of course. The corporation scrapped men suspected of being defective as quickly as they scrapped suspect material.

"When a man begins to see rocks moving, it's time to fire him," was the unofficial verdict.

The board of science had coldly said the same thing, though in more dignified language.

"No form of life as we know it could possibly exist in the high temperature and desert condition of Mercury. Therefore, in our judgment, Benjamin Stuyvesant suffered from hallucination when he reported some rocklike entity moving near Emergency Hangar RC10."

Hartigan glanced uneasily toward the workbench on which the odd meteor had rested.

"No form of life *as we know it.*"

There was the catch. After all, this interplanetary travel was less than seventy years old. Might there not be many things still unknown to Earth wisdom?

"Not to hear the board of science tell it," muttered Hartigan, thinking of Stuyvesant's blasted career.

He thought of the Forbidden Asteroids. There were over two dozen on the charts on which, even in direst emergency, no ship was supposed to land. That was because ships had landed there, and had vanished without trace. Again and again. With no man able to dream of their fate. Till they simply marked the little globes "Forbidden," and henceforth ignored them.

"No form of life as we know it!"

Suppose something savage, huge, invisible, lived on those grim asteroids? Something that developed from egg form? Something that spread its young through the universe by propelling eggs from one celestial body to another? Something that started growth by devouring its own metallic shell, and continued it on a mineral instead of vegetable diet? Something that could live in any atmosphere or temperature?

"I *am* going crazy," Hartigan breathed.

In something like panic he tried to forget the affair in a great stack of books and magazines brought by the last supply ship.

The slow hours of another month ticked by. The full Earth waned, died, grew again. Drearily Hartigan went through the monotony of his routine. Day after day, the term "day" being a strictly figurative one on this drear lunar lump.

He rose at six, New York time, and sponged off carefully in a bit of precious water. He ate breakfast. He read. He stretched his muscles in a stroll. He read. He inspected his equipment. He read. He exercised on a set of homemade flying rings. He read.

"No human being should be called on to live like this," he said once, voice too loud and brittle.

But human beings did have to live like this, if they aspired to one of the big posts on a main planet.

He had almost forgotten the strange meteor that had fallen into lava ash at his feet a month ago. It was to be recalled with terrible abruptness.

He went for a walk in a direction he did not usually take, and came upon a shallow pit half a mile from the dome.

Pits, of course, are myriad on the Moon. The whole surface is made up of craters within craters. But this pit was not typical in conformation. Most are smooth-walled and flat-bottomed. This pit was ragged, as if it had been dug out. Besides, Hartigan had thought he knew every hole for a mile around, and he did not remember ever seeing this one.

He stood on its edge looking down. There was loose rock in its uncraterlike bottom, and the loose rock had the appearance of being freshly dislodged. Even this was not unusual in a place where the vibration of a footstep could sometimes cause tons to crack and fall.

Nevertheless, Hartigan could feel the hair rise a bit on the back of his neck as some deep, instinctive fear crawled within him at sight of the small, shallow pit. And then he caught his lips between his teeth and stared with wide, unbelieving eyes.

On the bottom of the pit a rock was moving. It was moving, not as if it had volition of its own, but as if it were being handled by some unseen thing.

A fragment about as big as his body, it rolled over twice, then slid along in impatient jerks as though a big head or hoof nudged at it. Finally it raised up from the ground and hung poised about seven feet in the air!

Breathlessly, Hartigan watched, while all his former, almost superstitious fear flooded through him.

The rock fragment moved up and down in mid-space.

"Jupiter!" Clow Hartigan breathed hoarsely.

A large part of one end suddenly disappeared. A pointed projection from the main mass of rock, it broke off and vanished from sight.

Another large chunk followed, breaking off and disappearing as though by magic.

"Jupiter!"

There was no longer doubt in Hartigan's mind. A live thing had emerged from the egglike meteor twenty-seven days ago. A live thing, that now roamed loose over the face of the Moon.

But that section of rock, which was apparently being devoured, was held seven feet off the ground. What manner of creature could come from an egg no larger than his head and grow in one short month into a thing over seven feet tall? He thought of the Forbidden Asteroids, where no ships landed, though no man knew precisely what threat lurked there.

"It must be as big as a mastodon," Hartigan whispered. "What in the universe—"

The rock fragment was suddenly dropped, as if whatever invisible thing had held it had suddenly seen Hartigan at the rim of the pit. Then the rock was dashed to one side as if by a charging body. The next instant loose fragments of shale scattered right and left up one side of the pit as though a big body were climbing up and out.

The commotion in the shale was on the side of the pit nearest Hartigan. With a cry he ran toward the hangar.

With fantastic speed, sixty and seventy feet to a jump, he covered the ragged surface. But fast as he moved, he felt that the thing behind him moved faster. And that there *was* something behind him he did not doubt for an instant, though he could neither see nor hear it.

It was weird, this pygmy human form in its bulky space suit flying soundlessly over the lunar surface under the glowing ball of Earth, racing like mad for apparently no reason at all, running insanely when, so far as the eye could tell, nothing pursued.

But abysmal instinct told Hartigan that he was pursued, all right. And instinct told him that he could never reach the hangar in the lead. With desperate calmness he searched the ground still lying between him and the hangar.

A little ahead was a crack about a hundred feet wide and, as far as he knew, bottomless. With his oversized Earth muscles he could clear that in a gigantic leap. Could the ponderous, invisible thing behind him leap that far?

He was in mid-flight long enough to turn his head and look back, as he hurtled the chasm in a prodigious jump. He saw a flurry among the rocks at the edge he had just left as something jumped after him. Then he came down on the far side, lighting in full stride like a hurdler.

He risked slowing his speed by looking back again. A second time he saw a flurry of loose rock, this time on the near side of the deep crack. The thing had not quite cleared the edge, it seemed.

He raced on and came to the small air-lock door. He flung himself inside. He had hardly got the fastener in its groove when something banged against the outside of the door.

The thing pursuing him had hung on the chasm's edge long enough to let him reach safety, but had not fallen into the black depths as he had hoped it might.

"But that's all right," he said, drawing a great sigh of relief as he entered the hangar through the inner door. "I don't care what it does, now that I'm inside and it's out."

He got out of the space suit, planning as he moved.

*

The thing outside was over seven feet tall and made of some unflesh-like substance that must be practically indestructible. At its present rate of growth it would be as big as a small space liner in six months, if it weren't destroyed. But it would have to be destroyed. Either that, or Emergency Station RC3 would have to be abandoned, and his job with it, which concerned him more than the station.

"I'll call Stacey to send a destroyer," he said crisply.

He moved toward the Bliss transmitter, eyes glinting. Things were happening on the Moon, now, all right! And the thing that was happening was going to prove Stuyvesant as sane as any man, much saner than the grey-bearded goats on the board of science.

He would be confined to the hangar till Stacey could send a destroyer. No more strolls. He shuddered a little as he thought of how many times he must have missed death by an inch in his walks during the past month.

Hartigan got halfway to the Bliss transmitter, skirting along the wall near the small air lock.

A dull, hollow, booming sound filled the great hangar, ascending to the vaulted roof and seeming to shower down again like black water.

Hartigan stopped and stared at the wall beside him. It was bulging inward a little. Startled out of all movement, he stared at the ominous, slight bulge. And as he stared, the booming noise was repeated, and the bulge grew a bit larger.

"In the name of Heaven!"

The thing outside had managed to track him along the wall from the air lock, perhaps guided by the slight vibration of his steps. Now it was blindly charging the huge bulk of the hangar like a living, ferocious ram.

A third time the dull, terrible booming sound reverberated in the lofty hangar. The bulge in the tough metal wall spread again; and the two nearest supporting beams gave ever so little at the points of strain.

Hartigan moved back toward the air lock. While he moved, there was silence. The moment he stopped, there was another dull, booming crash and a second bulge appeared in the wall. The thing had followed him precisely, and was trying to get at him.

The colour drained from Hartigan's face. This changed the entire scheme of things.

It was useless to radio for help now. Long before a destroyer could get here, the savage, insensate monster outside would have opened a rent in the wall. That would mean Hartigan's death from escaping air in the hangar.

Crash!

Who would have dreamed that there lived anywhere in the universe, on no matter how far or wild a globe, a creature actually able to damage the massive walls of a Spaceways hangar? He could see himself trying to tell about this.

"An animal big enough to crack a hangar wall? And invisible? Well!"

Crash!

The very light globes, so far overhead, seemed to quiver a bit with the impact of this thing of unguessable nature against the vast semisphere of the hangar. The second bulge was deep enough so that the white enamel which coated it began chipping off in little flakes at the bulge's apex.

"What the devil am I going to do?"

The only thing he could think of for the moment was to move along the wall. That unleashed giant outside must not concentrate too long on any one spot.

He walked a dozen steps. As before, the ramming stopped while he was in motion, to start again as he halted. As before, it started at the point nearest to him.

Once more a bulge appeared in the wall, this time bigger than either of the first two. The metal sheets sheathing the hangar varied a little in strength. The invisible terror outside had struck a soft spot.

Hartigan moved hastily to another place.

"The whole base of the hangar will be scalloped like a pie crust at this rate," he gritted. "What can I—"

Crash!

He had inadvertently stopped near a rack filled with spare power bulbs. With its ensuing attack the blind fury had knocked the rack down onto the floor.

Hartigan's jaw set hard. Whatever he did must be done quickly. And it must be done by himself alone. He could not stay at the Bliss transmitter long enough to get New York and tell what was wrong, without giving the gigantic thing outside a fatal number of minutes in which to concentrate on one section of wall.

He moved slowly around the hangar, striving to keep the invisible fury too occupied in following him to get in more than an occasional charge. As he walked, his eyes went from one heap of supplies to another in search of a possible means of defence.

There were ordinary weapons in plenty, in racks along the wall. But none of these, he knew, could do material harm to the attacking fury.

He got to the great inner doors of the main air lock in his slow march around the hangar. And here he stopped, eyes glowing thoughtfully.

The huge doors had threatened in the early days to be the weak points in the Spaceways hangars. So the designers, like good engineers, had made the doors so massive that in the end they were stronger than the walls around them.

Bang!

A bulge near the massive hinges told Hartigan that the thing outside was as relentless as ever in its effort to break through the wall and get at him. But he paid no attention to the new bulge. He was occupied with the doors.

If the invisible giant could be trapped in the main air lock between the outer and inner portals—

"Then what?" Hartigan wondered.

He could not answer his own question. But, anyway, it seemed like a step in the right direction to have the attacking fury penned between the doors rather than to have it loose and able to charge the more vulnerable walls.

"If I can coop it in the air lock. I might be able to think of some way to attack it," he went on.

He pushed home the control switch which set the broadcast power to opening the outer doors. And *that* gave him an idea that sent a wild thrill surging through him.

A heavy rumble told him that the motors were swinging open the outer doors.

"Will the thing come in?" he asked himself tensely. "Or has it sense enough to scent a trap?"

Bang!

The inner doors trembled a little on their broad tracks. The invisible monster had entered the trap.

"Trap?" Hartigan smiled mirthlessly. "Not much of a trap! Left to itself, it could probably break out in half an hour. But it won't be left to itself."

He reversed the switch to close the outer portals. Then, with the doors closed and the monster penned between, he got to work on the idea that had been born when he pushed the control switch.

Power, oceans of it, flooded from the power unit at the touch of a finger. A docile servant when properly channelled, it could be the deadliest thing on the Moon.

He ran back down the hangar to the stock room, and got out a drum of spare power cable. As quickly as was humanly possible, he rolled the drum back to the doors, unwinding the cable as he went.

It was with grim solemnity that he made his next move. He had to open the inner doors a few inches to go on with his frail plan of defence. And he had to complete that plan before the thing in the air lock could claw them open still more and charge through. For all their weight the doors rolled in perfect balance; and if the unseen terror could make dents in the solid wall, it certainly was strong enough to move the partly opened doors.

Speed! That was the thing that would make or break him. Speed, and hope that the power unit could stand a terrific overload without blowing a tube.

With a hand that inclined to tremble a bit, Hartigan moved the control switch operating the inner doors, and instantly cut the circuit again.

The big doors opened six inches or so, and stopped.

Hartigan cut off the power unit entirely, and dragged the end of the spare power cable to it. With flying fingers he disconnected the cable leading from the control switch to the motors that moved the portals, and connected the spare cable in its space.

He glanced anxiously at the doors, and saw that the opening between them had widened to more than a foot. The left door moved a little even as he watched.

"I'll never make it!"

But he went ahead.

Grabbing up the loose end of the cable, he threw it in a tangled coil as far as he could through the opening and into the air lock. Then he leaped for the power unit—and watched.

The cable lay unmoving on the airlock floor. But the left door moved! It jerked, and rolled open another six inches.

Hartigan clenched his hands as he stared at the inert cable. He had counted on the blind ferocity of the invisible terror; had counted on its attacking, or at least touching, the cable immediately. Had it enough intelligence to realize dimly that it would be best to avoid the cable? Was it going to keep on working at those doors till—

The power cable straightened with a jerk. Straightened, and hung still, with the loose end suspended in midair about six feet off the air-lock floor.

Hartigan's hand slammed down. The broadcast power was turned on to the last notch.

With his heart hammering in his throat, Hartigan gazed through the two-foot opening between the doors. Gazed at the cable through which was coursing oceans, Niagaras of power. And out there in the air lock a thing began to build up from thin air into a spectacle that made him cry out in wild horror.

He got a glimpse of a massive block of a head, eyeless and featureless, that joined with no neck whatever to a barrel of a body. He got a glimpse of five legs, like stone pillars, and of a sixth that was only a stump. ("That's what got caught in the doors a month ago—its leg," he heard himself babbling with insane calmness.) Over ten feet high and twenty feet long, the thing was, a living battering-ram, painted in the air in sputtering, shimmering blue sparks that streamed from its massive bulk in all directions.

Just a glimpse, he got, and then the monster began to scream as it had that first day when the door maimed it. Only now it was with a volume that tore at Hartigan's eardrums till he screamed himself in agony.

As he watched, he saw the huge carcass melt a little, like wax in flame, with the power cable also melting slowly and fusing into the cavernous, rocky jaws that had seized it. Then with a rush the whole bulk disintegrated into a heap of loose mineral matter.

Hartigan turned off the power unit and collapsed, with his face in his hands.

The shining ball of the full Earth floated like a smooth diamond between two vast, angular mountains. The full Earth.

Hartigan turned from the porthole beside the small air lock and strode to the Bliss radio transmitter.

"RC3, RC3, RC3," he droned out.

There was no answer. As usual, Stacey was taking his time about answering the Moon's signal.

"RC3, RC3—"

There he was.

"Hartigan talking. Monthly report."

"All right, Hartigan."

A hurried, fretful voice. Come on, Moon; report that, as always, nothing has happened.

"Lunar conditions the same," said Hartigan. "No ships have put in, or have reported themselves as being in distress. The hangar is in good shape, with no leaks."

"Right," said Stacey, in the voice of a busy man. "Supplies?"

"You might send up a blonde."

"Be serious, please. Supplies?"

"I need some new power bulbs."

"I'll send them on the next ship. Nothing irregular to report?"

Hartigan hesitated.

On the floor of the main air lock was a mound of burned, bluish mineral substance giving no indication whatever that it had once possessed outlandish, incredible life. In the walls of the hangar at the base were half a dozen new dents; but ricocheting meteors might have made those. The meteoric shell from which this bizarre animal had come had been devoured, so even that was not left for investigation.

He remembered the report of the board of science on Stuyvesant.

"Therefore, in our judgment, Benjamin Stuyvesant suffered from hallucination—"

He would have liked to help Stuyvesant. But on the other hand Stuyvesant had a job with a secondhand-space-suit store now, and was getting along pretty well in spite of Spaceways' dismissal.

"Nothing irregular to report?" repeated Stacey.

Hartigan stared, with one eyebrow sardonically raised, at the plump brunette on the pink *Radio Gazette* cover pasted to the wall. She stared coyly back over a bare shoulder.

"Nothing irregular to report," Hartigan said steadily.

WHATEVER GODS THERE BE

Gordon R. Dickson

One of the great dramas of the Apollo era was with Apollo 13, the mission in which astronaut Jack Swigert uttered the immortal words "Houston, we've had a problem." The incident occurred on 13 April 1970 when an electrical fault caused an oxygen cylinder to explode causing a number of systems to fail. As a consequence the three astronauts, Swigert, James Lovell and Fred Haise, had to abort the Command Module and transfer to the Lunar Module which now became their lifeboat. In one of the most remarkable trips ever made by humans, the lunar module orbited the Moon, reaching the farthest point from Earth humans have yet travelled, and successfully returned to Earth on 17 April. It was one of those moments when many on Earth collectively held their breath and hoped.

Placing astronauts in danger and working out how to rescue them is meat-and-bread to most science-fiction writers. It is what brings not only drama and tension to a story but also a degree of scientific expertise in solving a problem. In the following story Gordon R. Dickson (1923–2001) applies his creative thinking to just such a problem of whether the survivors of the first lunar expedition can find a way of getting back to Earth following an accident on landing.

Canadian born, but resident in the United States since he was thirteen, Dickson majored in creative writing at college and made his first sale in 1950. He was one of the few people in science fiction at the time to be a full-time writer from the start.

A T 1420 HOURS OF THE EIGHTH DAY ON THE MOON, MAJOR Robert L. (Doc) Greene was standing over a slide in a microscope in the tiny laboratory of Moon Ship Groundbreaker II. There was a hinged seat that could be pulled up and locked in position, to sit on; but Greene never used it. At the moment, he had been taking blood counts on the four of them that were left in the crew, when a high white and a low red blood cell count of one sample had caught his attention. He had proceeded to follow up the tentative diagnosis this suggested, as coldly as if the sample had been that of some complete stranger. But, suddenly, the scene in the field of the microscope had blurred. And for a moment he closed both eyes and rested his head lightly against the microscope. The metal eyepiece felt cool against his eyelid; and caused an after-image to blossom against the hooded retina—as of a volcanic redness welling outward against a blind-dark background. It was his own deep-held inner fury exploding against an intractable universe.

Caught up in this image and his own savage emotion, Greene did not hear Captain Edward Kronzy, who just then clumped into the lab, still wearing his moonsuit, except for the helmet.

"Something wrong, Bob?" asked Kronzy. The youngest of the original six-officer crew, he was about average height—as were all the astronauts—and his reddish, cheerful complexion contrasted with shock of stiff black hair and scowling, thirty-eight year old visage of Greene.

"Nothing," said Greene, harshly, straightening up and slipping the slide out of the microscope into a breast pocket. "What's the matter with you?"

"Nothing," said Kronzy, with a pale grin that only made more marked the dark circles under his eyes. "But Hal wants you outside to help jacking up."

"All right," said Greene. He put the other three slides back in their box; and led the way out of the lab toward the airlock. In the pocket, the glass slide pressed sharp-edged and unyielding against the skin of his chest, beneath. It had given Greene no choice but to diagnose a cancer of the blood—leukaemia.

Ten minutes later, Greene and Kronzy joined the two other survivors of Project Moon Landing outside on the moon's surface.

These other two—Lt. Colonel Harold (Hal) Barth, and Captain James Wallach—were some eighty-five feet above the entrance of the airlock, on the floor of the Mare Imbrium. Greene and Kronzy came toiling up the rubbled slope of the pit where the ship lay; and emerged onto the crater floor just as Barth and Wallach finished hauling the jack into position at the pit's edge.

Around them, the crater floor on this eighth day resembled a junk yard. A winch had been set up about ten feet back from the pit five days before; and now oxygen tanks, plumbing fixtures, spare clothing, and a host of other items were spread out fanwise from the edge where the most easily ascendible slope of the pit met the crater floor—at the moment brilliantly outlined by the sun of the late lunar "afternoon". A sun now alone in the sky, since the Earth at the moment was on the other side of the moon. A little off to one side of the junk were two welded metal crosses propped erect by rocks.

The crosses represented 1st Lieutenant Saul Moulton and Captain Luthern J. White, who were somewhere under the rock rubble beneath the ship in the pit.

"Over here, Bob," Greene heard in the earphones of his helmet. He looked and saw Barth beckoning with a thick-gloved hand. "We're going to try setting her up as if in a posthole."

Greene led Kronzy over to the spot. When he got close, he could see through the faceplates of their helmets that the features of the other two men, particularly the thin, handsome features of Barth, were shining with sweat. The eighteen-foot jack lay with its base end projecting over a hole ground out of solid rock.

"What's the plan?" said Greene.

Barth's lips puffed with a weary exhalation of breath before he answered. The face of the Moon Expedition's captain was finedrawn with exhaustion; but, Greene noted with secret satisfaction, with no hint of defeat in it yet. Greene relaxed slightly, sweeping his own grim glance around the crater, over the hole, the discarded equipment and the three other men.

A man, he thought, could do worse than to have made it this far.

"One man to anchor. The rest to lift," Barth was answering him.

"And I'm the anchor?" asked Greene.

"You're the anchor," answered Barth.

Greene went to the base end of the jack and picked up a length of metal pipe that was lying ready there. He shoved it into the hole and leaned his weight on it, against the base of the jack.

"Now!" he called, harshly.

The men at the other end heaved. It was not so much the jack's weight, under moon gravity, as the labour of working in the clumsy moonsuits. The far end of the jack wavered, rose, slipped gratingly against Greene's length of pipe—swayed to one side, lifted again as the other three men moved hand under hand along below it—and approached the vertical.

The base of the jack slipped suddenly partway into the hole, stuck, and threatened to collapse Greene's arms. His fingers were slippery in the gloves, he smelled the stink of his own perspiration inside the suit, and his feet skidded a little in the surface dust and rock.

"Will it go?" cried Barth gaspingly in Greene's earphones.

"Keep going!" snarled Greene, the universe dissolving into one of his white-hot rages—a passion in which only he and the jack existed; and it must yield. "Lift, damn you! Lift!"

The pipe vibrated and bent. The jack swayed—rose—and plunged suddenly into the socket hole, tearing the pipe from Greene's grasp. Greene, left pushing against nothing, fell forward, then rolled over on his back. Above him, twelve protruding feet of the jack quivered soundlessly.

Greene got to his feet. He was wringing wet. Barth's faceplate suddenly loomed before him.

"You all right?" Barth's voice asked in his earphones.

"All right?" said Greene. He stared; and burst suddenly into loud raucous laughter, that scaled upward toward uncontrollability. He choked it off. Barth was still staring at him. "No, I broke my neck from the fall," said Greene roughly. "What'd you think?"

Barth nodded and stepped back. He looked up at the jack.

"That'll do," he said. "We'll get the winch cable from that to the ship's nose and jack her vertical with no sweat."

"Yeah," said Kronzy. He was standing looking down into the pit. "No sweat."

The other three turned and looked into the pit as well, down where the ship lay at a thirty degree angle against one of the pit's sides. It was a requiem moment for Moulton and White who lay buried there; and all the living men above felt it at the same time. Chance had made a choice among them—there was no more justice to it than that.

The ship had landed on what seemed a flat crater floor. Landed routinely, upright, and apparently solidly. Only, twenty hours later, as Moulton and White had been outside setting up the jack they had just assembled—the jack whose purpose was to correct the angle of the ship for takeoff—chance had taken its hand.

What caused it—lunar landslip, vibration over flawed rock, or the collapse of a bubble blown in the molten rock when the moon was young—would have to be for those who came after to figure out. All the four remaining men who were inside knew was that one moment all was well; and the next they were flung about like pellets in a rattle that a baby shakes. When they were able to get outside and check, they found the ship in a hundred foot deep pit, in which Moulton and White had vanished.

"Well," said Barth, "I guess we might as well knock off now, and eat. Then, Jimmy—" his faceplate turned toward Wallach. "you and Ed can come up here and get that cable attached while I go over the lists you all gave me of your equipment we can still strip from the ship; and I'll figure out if she's light enough to lift on the undamaged tubes. And Bob—you can get back to whatever you were doing."

"Yeah," said Greene. "Yeah, I'll do that."

After they had all eaten, Greene shut himself up once more in the tiny lab to try to come to a decision. From a military point of view, it was his duty to inform the commanding officer—Barth—of the diagnosis he had just made. But the peculiar relationship existing between himself and Barth—

There was a knock on the door.

"Come on in!" said Greene.

Barth opened the door and stuck his head in.

"You're not busy."

"Matter of opinion," he said. "What is it?"

Barth came all the way in, shut the door behind him, and leaned against the sink.

"You're looking pretty washed out, Bob," he said.

"We all are. Never mind me," said Greene. "What's on your mind?"

"A number of things," said Barth. "I don't have to tell you what it's like with the whole Space Program. You know as well as I do."

"Thanks," said Greene.

The sarcasm in his voice was almost absent-minded. Insofar as gratitude had a part in his makeup, he was grateful to Barth for recognizing what few other people had—how much the work of the Space Program had become a crusade to which his whole soul and body was committed.

"We just can't afford not to succeed." Barth was saying.

It was the difference between them, noted Greene. Barth admitted the possibility of not succeeding. Nineteen years the two men had been close friends—since high school. And nowadays, to many people, Barth *was* the Space Program. Good-looking, brilliant, brave—and possessing that elusive quality which makes for newsworthiness at public occasions and on the tv screens—Barth had been a shot in the arm to the Program these last six months.

And he had been needed. No doubt the Russian revelations of extensive undersea developments in the Black Sea Area had something to do with it. Probably the lessening of world tensions lately had contributed. But it had taken place—one of those unexplainable shifts in public interest which have been the despair of promotion men since the breed was invented.

The world had lost much of its interest in spatial exploration.

No matter that population pressures continued to mount. No matter that natural resources depletion was accelerating, in spite of all attempt at control. Suddenly—space exploration had become old hat; taken for granted.

And those who had been against it from the beginning began to gnaw, unchecked, at the roots of the Program. So that men like Barth, to whom the Space Program had become a way of life, worried, seeing gradual strangulation as an alternative to progress. But men like Greene, to whom the Program had become life itself, hated, seeing *no* alternative.

"Who isn't succeeding?" said Greene.

"We lost Luthern and Saul," said Barth, glancing downward almost instinctively toward where the two officers must be buried. "We've got to get back."

"Sure. Sure," said Greene.

"I mean," said Barth, "we've got to get back, no matter what the cost. We've got to show them we could get a ship up here and get back again. You know, Bob—" he looked almost appealingly at Greene—"the trouble with a lot of people who're not in favour of the Project is they don't really believe in the moon or anyplace like it. I mean—the way they'd believe in Florida, or the South Pole. They're sort of half-clinging to the notion it's just a sort of cut-out circle of silver paper up in the air, there, after all. But if we go and come back, they've *got to* believe!"

"Listen," said Greene. "Don't worry about people like that. They'll all be dead in forty years, anyway.—Is this all you wanted to talk to me about?"

"No. Yes—I guess," said Barth. He smiled tiredly at Greene. "You pick me up, Bob. I guess it's just a matter of doing what you have to."

"Do what you're going to do," said Greene with a shrug. "Why make a production out of it?"

"Yes." Barth straightened up. "You're right. Well, I'll get back to work. See you in a little while. We'll get together for a pow-wow as soon as Ed and Jimmy get back in from stringing that cable."

"Right," said Greene. He watched the slim back and square shoulders of Barth go out the door and slumped against the sink, himself, chewing savagely on a thumbnail. His instinct had been right, he thought; it was not the time to tell Barth about the diagnosis.

And not only that. Nineteen years had brought Greene to the point where he could, in almost a practical sense, read the other man's mind. He had just done so; and right now he was willing to bet that he had a new reason for worry.

Barth had something eating on him. Chewing his fingernail, Greene set to work to puzzle out just what that could be.

A fist hammered on the lab door, "Bob?"

"What?" said Greene, starting up out of his brown study. Some little time had gone by. He recognized his caller now. Kronzy.

"Hal wants us in the control cabin, right away."

"Okay. Be right there." Greene waited until Kronzy's boot sounds had gone away in the distance down the short corridor and up the ladder to the level overhead. Then he followed, more slowly.

He discovered the other four already jammed in among the welter of instruments and controls that filled this central space of the ship.

"What's the occasion?" he asked, cramming himself in between the main control screen and an acceleration couch.

"Ways and means committee," said Barth, with a small smile. "I was waiting until we were all together before I said anything." He held up a sheet of paper. "I've just totalled up all the weight we can strip off the ship, using the lists of dispensable items each of you made up, and checked it against the thrust we can expect to get safely from the undamaged tubes. We're about fifteen hundred Earth pounds short. I made the decision to drop off the water tanks, the survival gear, and a few other items, which brings us down to being about five hundred pounds short."

He paused and laid down the paper on a hinge-up desk surface beside him.

"I'm asking for suggestions," he said.

Greene looked around the room with sudden fresh grimness. But he saw no comprehension yet, on the faces of the other two crew members.

"How about—" began Kronzy; then hesitated as the words broke off in the waiting silence of the others.

"Go on, Ed," said Barth.

"We're not short of fuel."

"That's right."

"Then why," said Kronzy, "can't we rig some sort of auxiliary burners—like the jato units you use to boost a plane off, you know?" He glanced at Greene and Wallach, then back at Barth. "We wouldn't have to care whether they burnt up or not—just as long as they lasted long enough to get us off."

"That's a good suggestion, Ed," said Barth, slowly. "The only hitch is, I looked into that possibility, myself. And it isn't possible. We'd need a machine shop. We'd need—it just isn't possible. It'd be easier to repair the damaged tubes."

"I suppose that isn't possible, either?" said Greene, sharply.

Barth looked over at him, then quickly looked away again.

"I wasn't serious," Barth said. "For that we'd need Cape Canaveral right here beside us.—And then, probably not."

He looked over at Wallach.

"Jimmy?" he said.

Wallach frowned.

"By golly, Hal," he said. "I don't know. I can think about it a bit…"

"Maybe," said Barth, "That's what we all ought to do. Everybody go off by themselves and chew on the problem a bit." He turned around and seated himself at the desk surface. "I'm going to go over these figures again."

Slowly, they rose. Wallach went out, followed by Kronzy. Greene hesitated, looking at Barth, then he turned away and left the room.

Alone once more in the lab, Greene leaned against the sink again and thought. He did not, however, think of mass-to-weight ratios or clever ways of increasing the thrust of the rocket engines.

Instead, he thought of leukemia. And the fact that it was still a disease claiming its hundred per cent of fatalities. But also, he thought of Earth with its many-roomed hospitals; and the multitude of good men engaged in cancer research. Moreover, he thought of the old medical truism that while there is life, there is hope.

All this reminded him of Earth, itself. And his thoughts veered off to a memory of how pleasant it had been, on occasion, after working all the long night through, to step out through a door and find himself unexpectedly washed by the clean air of dawn. He thought of vacations he had never had, fishing he had never done, and the fact that he might have found a woman to love him if he had ever taken off enough time to look for her. He thought of good music—he had always loved good music. And he remembered that he had always intended someday to visit La Scala.

Then—hauling his mind back to duty with a jerk—he began to scowl and ponder the weak and strong points that he knew about in Barth's character. Not, this time, to anticipate what the man would say when they were all once more back in the control cabin. But for the purpose of circumventing and trapping Barth into a position where Barth would be fenced in by his own principles—the ultimate ju-jitsu of human character manipulation. Greene growled and muttered to himself, in the privacy of the lab marking important points with his forefinger in the artificial and flatly odorous air.

He was still at it, when Kronzy banged at his door again and told him everybody else was already back in the control cabin.

When he got to the control cabin again, the rest were in almost the identical positions they had taken previously.

"Well?" said Barth, when Greene had found himself a niche of space. He looked about the room, at each in turn. "How about you, Jimmy?"

"The four acceleration couches we've still got in the ship—With everything attached to them, they weigh better than two hundred apiece," said Wallach. "Get rid of two of them, and double up in the two left. That gets rid of four of our five hundred pounds. Taking off from the moon isn't as rough as taking off from Earth."

"I'm afraid it won't work," Kronzy commented.

"Why not?"

"Two to a couch, right?"

"Right."

"Well, look. They're made for one man. Just barely. You can cram two in by having both of them lying on their sides. That's all right for the two who're just passengers—but what about the man at the controls?" He nodded at Barth. "He's got to fly the ship. And how can he do that with half of what he needs to reach behind him, and the man next to him blocking off his reach at the other half?" Kronzy paused. "Besides, I'm telling you—half a couch isn't going to help hardly at all. You remember how the G's felt, taking off? And this time all that acceleration is going to be pressing against one set of ribs and a hipbone."

He stopped talking then.

"We'll have to think of something else. Any suggestions, Ed?" said Barth.

"Oh." Kronzy took a deep breath. "Toss out my position taking equipment. All the radio equipment, too. Shoot for Earth blind, deaf and dumb; and leave it up to them down there to find us and bring us home."

"How much weight would that save?" asked Wallach.

"A hundred and fifty pounds—about."

"A hundred and fifty!" Where'd you figure the rest to come from?"

"I didn't know," said Kronzy, wearily. "It was all I could figure to toss, beyond what we've already planned to throw out. I was hoping you other guys could come up with the rest."

He looked at Barth.

"Well, it's a good possibility, Ed," said Barth. He turned his face to Greene. "How about you, Bob?"

"Get out and push!" said Greene. "My equipment's figured to go right down to the last gram. There isn't any more. You want my suggestion—we can all dehydrate ourselves about eight to ten pounds per man between now and takeoff. That's it."

"That's a good idea, too," said Barth. "Every pound counts." He looked haggard around the eyes, Greene noticed. It had the effect of making him seem older than he had half an hour before during their talk in the lab; but Greene knew this to be an illusion.

"Thank you," Barth went on. "I knew you'd all try hard. I'd been hoping you'd come up with some things I had overlooked myself. More important than any of us getting back, of course, is getting the ship back. Proving something like this will work, to the people who don't believe in it."

Greene coughed roughly; and roughly cleared his throat.

"—We can get rid of one acceleration couch as Ed suggests," Barth continued. "We can dehydrate ourselves as Bob suggested, too; just to be on the safe side. That's close to two hundred and fifty pounds reduction. Plus a hundred and fifty for the navigational and radio equipment, There's three hundred and ninety to four hundred. Add one man with his equipment and we're over the hump with a safe eighty to a hundred pound margin."

He had added the final for a minute it did not register on those around him.

—Then, abruptly, it did.

"A man?" said Kronzy.

There was a second moment of silence—but this was like the fractionary interval of no sound in which the crowd in the grandstand suddenly realizes that the stunt flyer in the small plane is not coming out of his spin.

"I think," said Barth, speaking suddenly and loudly in the stillness, "that, as I say, the important thing is getting the ship back down. We've got to convince those people that write letters to the newspapers that something like this is possible. So the job can go on."

They were still silent, looking at him.

"It's our duty, I believe," said Barth, "to the Space Project. And to the people back there; and to ourselves. I think it's something that has to be done."

He looked at each of them in turn.

"Now Hal—wait!" burst out Wallach, as Barth's eyes came on him. "That's going a little overboard, isn't it? I mean—we can figure out something!"

"Can we?" Barth shook his head. "Jimmy—. There just isn't any more. If they shoot you for not paying your bills, then it doesn't help to have a million dollars in your debts add up to a million dollars and five cents. You know that. If the string doesn't reach, it doesn't reach. Everything we can get rid of on this ship won't be enough. Not if we want her to fly."

Wallach opened his mouth again; and then shut it. Kronzy looked down at his boots, Greene's glance went savagely across the room to Barth.

"Well," said Kronzy. He looked up. Kronzy, too, Greene thought, now looked older. "What do we do—draw straws?"

"No," Barth said. "I'm in command here. I'll pick the man."

"*Pick* the man!" burst out Wallach, staring. "You—"

"Shut up, Jimmy!" said Kronzy. He was looking hard at Barth. "Just what did you have in mind, Hal?" he said, slowly.

"That's all." Barth straightened up in his corner of the control room. "The rest is my responsibility. The rest of you get back to work tearing out the disposable stuff still in the ship—"

"I think," said Kronzy, quietly and stubbornly, "we ought to draw straws."

"You—" said Wallach. He had been staring at Barth ever since Kronzy had told him to shut up. "*You'd* be the one, Hal?"

"That's all," said Barth, again. "Gentlemen, this matter is not open for discussion."

"The hell," replied Kronzy, "you say. You may be paper CO of this bunch; but we are just not about to play Captain-go-down-with-his-ship. We all weigh between a hundred-sixty and a hundred and eighty pounds and that makes us equal in the sight of mathematics. Now, we're going to draw straws; and if you won't draw, Hal, we'll draw one for you; and if you won't abide by the draw, we'll strap you in the other acceleration couch and one of us can fly the ship out of here. Right, Jimmy? Bob?"

He glared around at the other two. Wallach opened his mouth, hesitated, then spoke.

"Yes," he said. I guess that's right."

Kronzy stared at him suddenly. Wallach looked away.

"Just a minute," said Barth.

They looked at him. He was holding a small, black, automatic pistol.

"I'm sorry," Barth said. "But I am in command. And I intend to stay in command, even if I have to cripple every one of you, strip the ship and strap you into couches myself." He looked over at Greene. "Bob. *You'll* be sensible, won't you?"

Greene exploded suddenly into harsh laughter. He laughed so hard he had to blink tears out of his eyes before he could get himself under control.

"Sensible!" he said. "Sure, I'll be sensible. And look after myself at the same time—even if it does take some of the glory out of it." He grinned almost maliciously at Barth. "Much as I hate to rob anybody else of the spotlight—it just so happens one of us can stay behind here until rescued and live to tell his grandchildren about it."

They, were all looking at him.

"Sure," said Greene. "There'll be more ships coming, won't there? In fact, they'll have no choice in the matter, if they got a man up here waiting to be rescued."

"How?" said Kronzy.

"Ever hear of suspended animation?" Greene turned to the younger man. "Deep-freeze. Out there in permanent shadow we've got just about the best damn deep freeze that ever was invented. The man who stays behind just takes a little nap until saved. In fact, from his point of view, he'll barely close his eyes before they'll be waking him up; probably back on Earth."

"You mean this?" said Barth.

"Of course, I mean it!"

Barth looked at Kronzy.

"Well, Ed," he said. "I guess that takes care of your objections."

"Hold on a minute!" Greene said. "I hope you don't think still you're going to be the one to stay. This is my idea; and I've got first pick at it.—Besides, done up in moonsuits the way we are outside there, I couldn't work it on anybody else. Whoever gets frozen has got to know what to do by himself; and I'm the only one who fits the bill." His eyes swept over all of them. "So that's the choice."

Barth frowned just slightly.

"Why didn't you mention this before, Bob?" he said.

"Didn't think of it—until you came up with your notion of leaving one man behind. And then it dawned on me. It's simple—for anyone who knows how."

Barth slowly put the little gun away in a pocket of his coveralls.

"I'm not sure still, I—" he began slowly.

"Why don't you drop it?" blazed Greene in sudden fury. "You think you're the only one who'd like to play hero? I've got news for you. I've given the Project everything I've got for a number of years now; but I'm the sort of man who gets forgotten easily. You can bet your boots I won't be forgotten when they have to come all the way from Earth to save me. It's my deal; and you're not going to cut me out of it. And what—" he thrust his chin at Barth—"are you going to do if I simply refuse to freeze anybody but myself? Shoot me?"

Barth shook his head slowly, his eyes shadowed with pain.

Rocket signal rifle held athwart behind him and legs spread, piratically, Greene stood where the men taking off in the rockets could see him in the single control screen that was left in the ship. Below, red light blossomed suddenly down in the pit The moon's surface trembled under Greene's feet and the noise of the engines reached him via conduction through the rocks and soles of his boots.

The rocket took off.

Greene waved after it. And then wondered why he had done so. Bravado? But there was no one around to witness bravado now. The other three were on their way to Earth—and they would make it. Greene walked over and shut off the equipment they had set up to record the takeoff. The surrounding area looked more like a junkyard than ever. He reached clumsy gloved fingers into an outside pocket of his moonsuit and withdrew the glass slide. With one booted heel he ground it into the rock.

The first thing they would do with the others would be to give them thorough physical checks, after hauling them out of the south Atlantic. And when that happened, Barth's leukemia would immediately be discovered. In fact, it was a yet-to-be-solved mystery why it had not shown up during routine medical tests before this. After that—well, while there was life, there was hope.

At any rate, live or die, Barth, the natural identification figure for these watching the Project, would hold the spotlight of public attention for another six months at least. And if he held it from a hospital bed, so much the better. Greene would pass and be forgotten between two bites of breakfast toast. But Barth—that was something else again.

The Project would be hard to starve to death with Barth dying slowly and uncomplaining before the eyes of taxpayers.

Greene dropped the silly signal rifle. The rocket flame was out of sight now. He felt with gloved hands at the heat control unit under the thick covering of his moonsuit and clumsily crushed it. He felt it give and break. It was amazing, he thought, the readiness of the laity to expect miracles from the medical profession. Anyone with half a brain should have guessed that something which normally required the personnel and physical resources of a hospital, could not be managed alone, without equipment, and on the naked surface of the moon.

Barth would undoubtedly have guessed it—if he had not been blinded by Greene's wholly unfair implication that Barth was a glory-hunter. Of course, in the upper part of his mind, Barth must know it was not true; but he was too good a man not to doubt himself momentarily when accused. After that, he had been unable to wholly trust his own reasons for insisting on being the one to stay behind.

He'll forgive me, thought Greene. He'll forgive me, afterwards, when he figures it all out.

He shook off his sadness that had come with the thought. Barth had been his only friend. All his life, Greene's harsh, sardonic exterior had kept people at a distance. Only Barth had realized that under Greene's sarcasms and jibes he was as much a fool with stars in his eyes as the worst of them. Well, thank heaven he had kept his weakness decently hidden.

He started to lie down, then changed his mind. It was probably the most effective position for what time remained; but it went against his grain that the men who came after him should find him flat on his back in this junkyard.

Greene began hauling equipment together until he had a sort of low seat. But when he had it all constructed, this, too was unsatisfactory.

Finally he built it a little higher. The moonsuit was very stiff, anyway. In the end, he needed only a little propping for his back and arms. He was turned in the direction in which the Earth would raise over the Moon's horizon; and, although the upper half of him was still in sunlight, long shadows of utter blackness were pooling about his feet.

Definitely, the lower parts of his moonsuit were cooling now. It occurred to him that possibly he would freeze by sections in this position. No matter, it was a relatively painless death.—Forgive me, he thought in Barth's direction, lost among the darkness of space and the light of the stars.—It would have been a quicker, easier end for you this way, I know. But you and I both were always blank checks to be filled out on demand and paid into the account of Man's future. It was only then that we could have had any claim to lives of our own.

As Greene had now, in these final seconds.

He pressed back against the equipment he had built up. It held him solidly. This little, harmless pleasure he gave his own grim soul. Up here in the airlessness of the moon's bare surface, nothing could topple him over now.

When the crew of the next ship came searching, they would find what was left of him still on his feet.

IDIOT'S DELIGHT

John Wyndham

The "Space Race" was part of the Cold War between the United States and the Soviet Union. It began in 1955 when both nations declared they would place a satellite in orbit around the Earth in the International Geophysical Year in 1957. The Russians beat the Americans to it with Sputnik 1 on 4 October 1957, and beat them again with the first man in space, Yuri Gagarin, on 12 April 1961. There were many other firsts along the way culminating in the United States landing the first men on the Moon on 20 July 1969. It was the Russians who landed the first spacecraft on the Moon, Luna 2, in September 1959 and the Russians also took the first photographs of the far side of the Moon with Luna 3 in October 1959.

This rivalry, which spurred on the desire for space exploration more than any other incentive could achieve, was firmly in the mind of writers at that time. John Wyndham considered what might happen if the Russians, Americans and British each had a base on the Moon and a nuclear war erupted between the two great powers on Earth.

Wyndham, whose real name was John Beynon Harris (1903–1969), is best known for such books as The Day of the Triffids *(1951),* The Kraken Wakes *(1953) and* The Midwich Cuckoos *(1957), but he had been selling science fiction since 1931. The following story comes from a series Wyndham wrote, collected as* The Outward Urge *(1959), which follows generations of the Troon family through the conquest and exploration of space.*

THE MOON A.D. 2044

I

There was a double knock on the alloy door. The Station-Commander, standing with his back to the room, looking out of the window, appeared for the moment not to hear it. Then he turned, just as the knock was repeated.

"Come in," he said, in a flat, unwelcoming tone.

The woman who entered was tall, well-built, and aged about thirty. Her good looks were a trifle austere, but softened slightly by the curls of her short, light-brown hair. Her most striking feature was her soft, blue-grey eyes; they were beautiful, and intelligent, too.

"Good morning, Commander," she said, in a brisk, formal voice.

He waited until the door had latched, then:

"You'll probably be ostracized," he told her.

She shook her head slightly. "My official duty," she said.

"Doctors are different. Privileged in some ways, on account of being not quite human in others."

He watched her come further into the room, wondering, as he had before, whether she had originally joined the service because its silky uniform matched her eyes, for she could certainly have advanced more quickly elsewhere. Anyway, the uniform certainly suited her elegant slenderness.

"Am I not invited to sit?" she inquired.

"By all means you are, if you care to. I thought you might prefer not," he told her.

She approached a chair with the half-floating step that had become second-nature, and let herself sink gently on to it. Without removing her gaze from his face, she pulled out a cigarette-case.

"Sorry," he said, and held the box from the desk towards her. She took one, let him light it for her, and blew the smoke out in a leisurely way.

"Well, what is it?" he asked, with a touch of irritation. Still looking at him steadily, she said:

"You know well enough what it is, Michael. It is that this *will not do*."

He frowned.

"Ellen, I'll be glad if you'll keep out of it. If there is one person on this Station who is not directly involved, it is you."

"Nonsense, Michael. There is *not* one person. But it is just because I am the least involved that I have come to talk to you. Somebody *has* to talk to you. You can't afford just to let the pressure go on rising while you stay in here, like Achilles sulking in his tent."

"A poor simile, Ellen, *I* have not quarrelled with my leader. It is the rest who have quarrelled with theirs—with me."

"That's not the way they see it, Michael."

He turned, and walked over to the window again. Standing there, with his face pale in the bright earthlight, he said:

"I know what they are thinking. They've shown it plainly enough. There's a pane of ice between us. The Station-Commander is now a pariah.

"All the old scores have come up to the surface. I am Ticker Troon's son—the man who got there by easy preferment. For the same reason I'm *still* here, at the age of fifty-five years over the usual grounding age; and keeping younger men from promotion.

I'm known to be in bad with half-a-dozen politicians and much of the top brass in the Space-House. Not to be trusted in my judgment because I'm an enthusiast—i.e., a man with a one-track mind. Would have been thrown out years ago if they had dared to face the outcry—Ticker Troon's son, again. And now there's this."

"Michael," she said calmly. "Just why are you letting this get you down? What's behind it?"

He looked hard at her for a moment before he said, with a touch of suspicion:

"What do you mean?"

"Simply what I say—what is behind this uncharacteristic outburst? You are perfectly well aware that if you had not earned your rank you would not be here—you'd have been harmlessly stowed away at a desk somewhere, years ago. As for the rest—well, it's mostly true. But the self-pity angle isn't like you. You *could* simply have cashed in and lain back comfortably for life on the strength of being Ticker Troon's son, but you didn't. You took the name he left you into your hand, and you deliberately *used* it for a weapon. It was a good weapon, and of course it made enemies for you, so of course they maligned you. But you know, and hundreds of thousands of people know, that if you had not used it as you did we should not be here today: there wouldn't be any British Moon-Station: and your father would have sacrificed himself for nothing."

"Self-pity—" he began, indignantly.

"Phony self-pity," she corrected, looking at him steadily.

He turned away.

"Would you like to tell me what the proper feeling is when, at a time of crisis, the men that you have worked with, and for—men that you thought had loyalty and respect, even some affection, for you, turn icy cold, and send you to Coventry? It certainly is not the time to feel pride of achievement, is it?"

She let the question hang for a moment, then:

"Understanding?" she suggested. "A more sympathetic considera-tion of the other man's point of view—and the state of his mind, perhaps?" She paused for several seconds.

"We are none of us in a normal state of mind," she went on.

"There is far too much emotion compressed in this place for anyone's judgment to be quite rational. It's harder for some than for others. *And* we don't all have quite the same things uppermost in our minds," she added.

Troon made no reply. He continued to stand with his back to her, gazing steadily out of the window. Presently, she walked across to stand beside him.

The view outside was bleak. In the foreground an utterly barren plain; a flatness broken only by various sized chunks of rock, and occasion-ally the rim of a small crater. The harshness of it was hard on the eyes; the lit surfaces so bright, the shadows so stygian that, if one looked at any one part too long, it dazzled, and seemed to dance about.

Beyond the plain, the mountains stuck up like cardboard cutouts. Eyes accustomed to the weathered mountains of Earth found the sharpness, the height, the vivid jaggedness of them disturbing. Newcomers were always awed, and usually frightened, by them. "A dead world," they always said, as they looked on the view for the first time, and they said it in hushed voices, with a feeling that they were seeing the ultimate dreadful place.

Over the horizon to the right hung a fluorescent quarter-segment of the Earth; a wide wedge bounded on one side by the night line, and serrated at the base by the bare teeth of the mountains.

For more than a minute Troon gazed at its cold, misted blue light before he spoke. Then:

"The idiot's delight," he said.

The doctor nodded slowly.

"Without doubt," she agreed. "And there—there we have it, don't we?"

She turned away from the window and went back to the chair.

"I know," she said, "or perhaps I should say, I like to think I know what this place means to you. You fought to establish it; and then you had to fight to maintain it. It has been your job in life; the purpose of your existence; the second foothold on the outward journey. Your father died for it; you have lived for it. You have mothered more than fathered, an ideal: and you have to learn, as mothers learn, that there has to be a weaning.

"Now, up there, there is war. It has been going on for ten days—at God knows what cost: the worst war in history—perhaps even the last. Great cities are holes in the ground; whole countries are black ashes; seas have boiled up in vapour, and fallen as lethal rain. But still new pillars of smoke spring up, new lakes of fire spread out, and more millions of people die.

"'The idiot's delight,' you say. But to what extent are you saying that because you hate it for what it is; and to what extent are you saying it for fear that your work will be ruined—that there may come some turn of events that will drive us off the moon?"

Troon walked slowly back, and seated himself on a corner of the desk.

"All reasons for hating war are good," he said, "but some are better than others. If you hate it and want to abolish it simply because it kills people—well, there are a number of popular inventions, the car and the airplane, for instance, that you might do well to abolish for the same reason. It is cruel and evil to kill people—but their deaths in war are a symptom, not a cause. I hate war partly because it is stupid—which it has been for a long time—but still more because it has recently become *too* stupid, and too wasteful, and too dangerous."

"I agree. And then, too, of course, much of what it wastes could otherwise be used to further Project Space."

"Certainly, and why not? Here we are at last, close to the threshold of the universe, with the greatest adventure of the human race just ahead of us, and still this witless, parochial bickering goes on— getting nearer to race suicide every time it flares up."

"And yet," she pointed out, "if it were not for the requirements of strategy we should not be here now."

He shook his head.

"Strategy is the ostensible reason perhaps, but it is not the *only* reason. We are here because the quintessential quality of our age is that of dreams coming true. The truly wishful dreams, the many-minded dreams are now irresistible—they become facts.

"We may reach them deviously, and almost always they have an undesired obverse: we learnt to fly, and carried bombs; we speed, and destroy thousands of our fellow men; we broadcast, and we can lie to the whole world. We can smash our enemies, but if we do, we shall smash ourselves. And some of the dreams have pretty queer midwives, but they get born all the same."

Ellen nodded slowly.

"And reaching for the moon was one of what you call the truly wishful dreams?"

"Of course. For the moon, first; and then, one day, for the stars. This is a realization. But there—" He pointed out of the window at the Earth, "—down there they are seeing us as a hateful silver crescent which they fear—that is the obverse of this particular dream.

"You're very eloquent," said the doctor, a little wondering.

"Aren't you, on your own subject?"

"But would you be telling me, in an elaborate way, that the end justifies the means?"

"I'm not interested in justifying. I am simply saying that certain practices which may be unpleasant in themselves can produce results which are not. There is many a flower which would not be growing if the dung had not happened to fall where it did. The Romans built their empire with savage cruelty, but it did make European civilization possible; because America prospered on slave labour, she was able to achieve independence; and so on. And now, because the armed forces wanted a position of strategic advantage they have enabled us to start out into space."

"To you, then, this Station—" she waved an encompassing hand, "—this is simply a jumping-off place for the planets."

"Not simply," he told her. "At present it is a strategic outpost—but its potentialities are far more significant."

"Far more important, you mean?"

"As I see it—yes."

The doctor lit a cigarette, and considered in silence for a few moments. Then she said:

"There seems to me very little doubt that most people here have a pretty accurate idea of your scale of values, Michael. It would not be news to you, I suppose, that with the exception of three or four— and the Astronomical Section which is starry-eyed, anyway—almost nobody shares them?"

*

"It would not," he said. "It has not been, for years; but it is only lately that it has become a matter of uncomfortable importance. Even so, millions of people *can* be wrong—and often have been."

She nodded, and went on, equably:

"Well, suppose we take a look at it from their point of view. All the people here volunteered, and were posted here as a garrison. They did not, and they do not, consider it primarily as a jumping-off place—though I suppose some of them think it may become that one day—now, at this moment, they are seeing it as what it was established to be—a Bombardment Station: a strategic position from which a missile can be placed within a five-mile circle drawn anywhere on Earth. That, they say, and quite truly say, is the reason for the Station's existence; and the purpose for which it is equipped. It was built—just as the other Moon Stations were built—to be a threat. It was hoped that they would never be used, simply because the knowledge of their existence would be an incentive to keep the peace.

"Well, that hope has been wiped out. God knows who, or what, really started this war, but it has come. And what happened? The Russian Station launched a salvo of missiles. The American Station began pumping out a systematic bombardment. The moon, in fact, went into action. But what part did the British Station play in this action? It sent off just three, medium-weight missiles!

"The American Station spotted that Russian freighter-rocket coming in, and got it, with a light missile. The Russian Station—and, by the look of it, one of the Russian Satellites—thereupon hammered the American Station, which erupted missiles for a time, both local and Earth-bound, and then suddenly went quiet. The Russian Station kept on sending missiles at intervals for a time, then it, too, went quiet.

"And what were we doing while all this was going on? We were sending off three more, medium-sized missiles. And since the Russian Station stopped, we have contributed another three.

"*Nine medium-sized missiles!* Our total part in the war, to date!

"Meanwhile, the real war goes on up there. And what's happening in it? Nobody knows. One minute's news is corrected, or denied, a few minutes later. All we *do* know for sure is that the two greatest powers there have ever been are out to destroy one another with every weapon they possess. Hundreds of cities and towns must have vanished, and all the people in them. Whole continents are being scorched and ruined.

"Is either side winning? *Can* either side win? Will there be anything left? What has happened to our own country and our homes? We *don't know!*

"And we do nothing! We just sit out here, and look at the Earth, all calm and pearly-blue, and wonder hour after hour—day after day, now—what horrors are going on under the clouds. Thinking about our families and friends, and what may have happened to them...

"The wonder to me is that so few of us, as yet, have cracked up. But I warn you, professionally, that if things go on like this, more of us will before long...

"*Of course* the men brood, and become more desperate and rebellious as it goes on. *Of course* they ask themselves what we are here for at all, if not to be used. Why have we not fired our big missiles? Perhaps they would not count a great deal in the scale of things, but they'd be something: we'd be doing what we can. They were the reason we were sent here—so why haven't we fired them? Why didn't we fire them at the beginning, when they would have had most effect? The other Stations did. Why have we still not fired them, even now? Can you tell us that?"

She ended, looking at him steadily. He looked back at her, just as steadily.

"I don't plan the strategy," he said. "It is not my job to understand top-level decisions. I am here to carry out the orders I receive."

"A very proper reply, Station-Commander," commented the doctor, and went on waiting. He did not amplify, and she found the continuation thrown back on her.

"They tell me." she observed, "that we have something like seventy major missiles, with atomic warheads. It has frequently been pointed out that the earlier the big blows fall, the more effective they are in destroying the enemy's potential—and in preventing retaliation. The aim, in fact, is the quick knock-out. But there our missiles still rest—unused even now."

"Their use," Troon pointed out again, "is not for us here to decide. It is possible that the first inter-continental missiles did what was required—in which case it would simply be waste to launch these. It is not impossible, either, that if they are held in reserve there could be a point when our ability to continue the bombardment might be decisive."

She shook her head.

"If the strategic targets have been destroyed, what is there left for decisive bombardment? These aren't weapons for use against armies in the field. What is worrying our personnel is, why weren't our weapons used—on the right kind of targets, at the right time?"

Troon shrugged.

"This is a pointless discussion, Ellen. Even if we were able to fire without orders, what should we aim at? We've no idea which targets have been destroyed, or which are only damaged. Indeed, for all we know, some of the target areas may now be occupied by our own people. If we had been needed, we should have had the orders."

The doctor remained quiet for a full half minute, making up her mind. Then she said, forthrightly:

"I think you had better understand this, Michael. If there is not some use made of these missiles very soon, or if there is not some intelligible statement about them from H.Q., you are going to have a mutiny on your hands."

II

The Commander sat quite still on the corner of the desk, looking not at her, but towards the window. Presently:

"As bad as that?" he asked.

"Yes, Michael. About as bad as it can be, short of open rebellion."

"'Mm. I wonder what they think they'll get out of that."

"They aren't thinking much at all. They're worried sick, frustrated, feeling desperate, and needing some kind—any kind—of action to relieve the tension."

"So they'd like to unhorse me, and poop off major atomic missiles, just for the hell of it."

She shook her head, looking at him unhappily.

"It's not exactly that, Michael. It's—oh dear, this is difficult—it's because a rumour has got round that they *should* have been sent off."

She watched him as the implication came home. At length, he said, with icy calmness:

"I see. I am supposed to have the other Nelson touch—the blind eye?"

"Some of them say so. A lot of the rest are beginning to wonder."

"There has to be a reason. Even a Commanding Officer must be supposed to have a motive for dereliction of duty amounting to high treason."

"Of course, Michael."

"Well, I'd better have it. What is it?"

Ellen took a deep breath.

"It's this. So long as we don't send those missiles we may be safe: once we do start sending them we'll probably bring down retaliation, either from the Russian Station, if it still exists, or from one of their Satellites. Our nine medium missiles haven't been a serious matter—not serious enough to justify them into provoking us to use our heavies. But, if we *do* start to use the major ones, it will almost certainly mean the end of this Station. Your own view of the primary importance of the Station is well known—you admitted it to me just now... So, you see, a motive can be made to appear...

"The American Station has almost certainly gone; possibly the Russian, too. If we go as well, there will no longer be anyone on what you called the 'threshold of the universe.' *But,* if we were able somehow to ride out the war, we should be in sole possession of the moon, and still on the 'threshold'... Shouldn't we?"

"Yes. You make the motive quite uncomfortably clear," he told her. "But an ambition is not necessarily an obsession, you know."

"This is a closed community, in a high state of nervous tension."

He thought for some moments then:

"Can you predict? Will it produce a revolution, or a mass-rising?" he asked her.

"A revolution," she said, without hesitation. "Your officers will arrest you, once they have plucked up the courage. That could take a day or two yet. It is a pretty grim step—especially when the C.O. happens to be a popular figure, too..." She shrugged her shoulders.

"I must think," he said.

He went round behind the desk and sat down, resting his elbows on it. The room became as quiet as the construction of the Station permitted while he considered behind closed eyes. After several minutes he opened them.

"*If* they should arrest me," he said, "their next move must be to search the message-files—(a) to justify themselves by finding evidence against me, and (b) to find out what the orders were, and whether they can still be carried out.

"When they discover that, except for three sets of three medium missiles, no launching orders have been received, there will be a panic. Such of my officers as may have been persuaded into this will be utterly shattered—you can't just apologize to your C.O. for arresting him as a traitor, and expect it to be left at that.

"There will be just one hope left, so someone more decisive than the rest will radio H.Q. that I have had a breakdown, or something of the kind, and request a repeal of all launching orders. When that brings nothing but a repetition of the same three sets of three, they'll be really sunk.

"Then, I should think, there will be a split. Some of them will have cold feet, and be for taking the consequences before matters get even worse; a number of men are bound to say 'in for a penny, in for a pound,' and want to launch the missiles, anyway. Some will have swung back, and argue that if H.Q. wanted launchings they would have said so—so why risk a further act of wanton insubordination which will probably bring enemy reprisals, anyway.

"Even if good sense and cold feet were to win, and I should be released, I should have lost much of my authority and prestige, and there would be a very, very sticky situation all the way round.

"On the whole, I think it would be easier for everyone if I were to swallow my pride and discourage my arrest by anticipating their second move."

He paused, contemplating the doctor.

"As you know, Ellen, it is not a habit of mine to reflect aloud in this manner. But I think it would do no harm if some idea of the probable results of my arrest were to filter round. Don't you agree?"

She nodded, without speaking. He got up from the desk.

"I shall now send for Sub-Commander Reeves—and I think we will have Sub-Commander Calmore as well—and explain to them with as little loss of face as possible that, the changes of war being what they are, and the chances of leakage now being nil, I am lifting security on messages received. This is being done in order that all senior officers may fully acquaint themselves with the situation, in readiness for any emergency.

"This should have enough deflationary effect to stop them from making that particular kind of fool of themselves, don't you think?"

"But won't they just say that you must have destroyed the relevant messages?" she objected.

"Oh, that one wouldn't do. There's service procedure. They will be able to compare my file with the Codes Section's files, and that with the Radio Section's log-book, and they'll find they all tie up."

She went on studying him.

"I still don't understand why our missiles have not been launched," she said.

"No? Well, perhaps all will be revealed to us one day. In the meantime—suppose we just go on obeying our orders. It's really much simpler.

As the door closed behind her, he continued to stare at it for fully a minute. Then he flipped over a switch, and requested the presence of his Sub-Commanders.

With the interview over, Troon allowed a few minutes for the officers to get clear. They had gone off looking a little winded, one carrying the message-file, the other his signed authority of access to the code files, in a bemused way. Then, feeling the need for a change, he, too, left his room, and made his way to the entrance-port. In the dressing-room the man on duty jumped to his feet and saluted.

"Carry on, Hughes," Troon told him. "I'm going outside for an hour or so."

"Yes, sir," said the man. He sat down and resumed work on the suit he was servicing.

Troon lifted his own scarlet pressure suit from its pegs, and inspected it carefully. Satisfied, he shed his uniform jacket and trousers, and got into it. He carried out the routine checks and tests; finally, he switched on the radio, and got an acknowledgement from the girl at the main instrument desk. He told her that he would be available for urgent calls only. When he spoke again his voice reached the duty man from a loudspeaker on the wall. The man got up, and moved to the door of the smaller, two-man airlock.

"An hour, you said, sir?" he inquired.

"Make it an hour and ten minutes," Troon told him.

"Yes, sir." The man set the hand of the reminder-dial seventy minutes ahead of the clock. If the Station-Commander had not returned, or had failed to notify an extension by then, the rescue squad would automatically be summoned.

The duty-man operated the lock, and presently Troon was outside; a vivid splash of colour in the monochrome landscape, the only moving thing in the whole wilderness. He set off southward with the curious lilting moon-step which long service had made second nature.

At half a mile or so he paused, and made a show of inspecting one or two of the missile-pits there. They were, as they were intended to be, almost invisible. The top of each shaft had a cover of stiff fibre which matched the colour of the ground about it. A scatter of sand and stones on top made it difficult to detect, even at a few yards. He pottered from one to another for a few minutes, and then stood looking back at the Station.

It was dwarfed and made toy-like by the mountains behind it. The radar and radio towers, and the sun-bowls looking like huge artificial flowers on the top of their masts, gave a rough scale; but for them it would have been difficult to judge whether the Station itself was the size of a half-inflated balloon, or half a puff-ball. It was hard to appreciate that the main body was a hundred and twenty yards in diameter at ground level until one looked at the corridors connecting it with the smaller, storage-domes, and remembered that the roofs of those corridors were four feet above one's head.

Troon continued to regard it for some moments, then he turned round, pursued a zig-zag course between the missile-pits, and when he was hidden from the Station by a rocky outcrop, sat down. There he leaned back and, in such modified comfort as the suit allowed, contemplated the prospect dominated by the bright segment of Earth—and also the shape of the future in a world ruined by war.

Looking back on his life, it was only those years before he was twelve that appeared sunlit and halcyon. He, his mother, and his grandfather had then lived quietly and happily in a roomy cottage. They had their friends and neighbours; he had his own school friends in the village; beyond that small circle they had been, except for his grandfather's reputation as a classical scholar, unnoticed and unknown. And then, in the September of his thirteenth year had come the break-up.

A man called Tallence had somehow stumbled across the story of Ticker Troon and the missile, and had applied to the authorities for the lifting of the security ban. After twelve years there was no good reason for silence—and, indeed, had been none for some time. Four Satellite Stations had for several years been known to be in position—the British one, two fair-sized Russian ones, and the huge American one. The existence of space-mines was no longer a secret, nor was the fact that all the Stations now carried means to combat them. Tallence, therefore, had managed to carry his point and, presently, to produce his book.

It was a good book, and the publishers spared nothing on the publicity that launched it; the conveniently timed citation of a posthumous V.C. for Ticker Troon helped, too; and the book went straight into the epic class. It was filmed, televised, digested, and strip-treated until, a year later, there was scarcely a man woman or child outside the Soviet Empire who did not know of Ticker Troon and his exploit.

For his son it had been all very exciting at first, but the excitement of being a public figure had soon worn off. The sense of being watched became distasteful. The feeling that he was expected to be exceptional weighed upon him at school, and only slightly less when he went up to Oxford. The house that his mother had

accepted with a feeling of reluctant obligation never had the quality
of home that there had been in the cottage. His mother seemed to
be forever socially busy now; his new interests were not shared by
his grandfather; it seemed impossible to remain unreminded for
an hour that he was the son of Ticker Troon—and that was rather
like finding one had Sir Francis Drake, Lord Nelson, or the National
Gallery, for a father.

His discovered fascination with the problems of space made it
worse; as if a part of him had turned traitor and conspired to draw
him away from his old interests, and deeper into his father's shadow.
An unquenchable curiosity had sprung alight in his mind, and presently he had been forced to admit that though his father's qualities
might be beyond him, he had certainly inherited his one passionate
interest. With that once decided, he had been willing to set about
using his name to further it, and he had entered the Service.

III

Troon's first brush with the politicians had followed the announcement (a premature announcement, in point of fact) that the Russians
were about to set up a Moon Station. The immediate effect of this
was that the Americans, who had got into the habit of regarding
the moon as a piece of U.S.—bespoken real estate that they would
get around to developing when they were ready, were shocked into
intense activity. The press wanted, as usual, to know Lieutenant
Troon's views on the situation. He had them ready, and they made
their first appearance in a responsible Sunday newspaper with an
influential circulation.

He was well aware of the situation. A Moon Station was not a
thing that could be set up for just a few million pounds. It could not

but entail an expenditure that the government would be alarmed to contemplate, and he knew that the official policy would be to discourage any suggestion of a British Moon Station as a frivolous and profligate project, minimizing, or brushing aside, all arguments in its favour.

In his short article, Troon had mentioned the advantages to strategy and to science, but had dwelt chiefly upon prestige. Failure to establish such a Station would be a turning point in British policy; it would amount to the first concrete confession that Britain was content to drop out of the van; that, in fact, it was now willing to admit itself as a second-or third-rate power. It would be public confirmation of the view, held in many circles for some time now, that the British had had their day, and were dwindling into their sunset; that all their greatness would soon lie with that of Greece, Rome, and Spain—in their past.

Troon's first carpeting over the matter was by his C.O. He then trod a number of ascending carpets until he found himself facing a somewhat pompous Under-Secretary who began, as the rest had done, by pointing out that he had broken Service regulations by publishing an unapproved article and then worked round by degrees to the suggestion that he might, upon reconsideration, find that a Moon Station had little Strategic superiority to an armed Satellite Station, and that if the Americans and Russians did build them, they would be wasting material and money.

"Moreover I am able to tell you confidentially," the Under-Secretary had added, "that this is also the view of the American authorities themselves."

"Indeed, sir," said Troon. "In that case it seems odd that they should be doing it."

"They would not be, I assure you, but for the Russians. Clearly, the moon cannot be left entirely to Russian exploitation. So, as the Americans can afford to do it, they are doing it in spite of their views on its worth. And since they are it is not necessary for us to do so."

"You think, sir, that it will do us no harm to be seen standing on American feet instead of on our own in this enterprise?"

"Young man," said the Under-Secretary severely, "there are many pretensions which are not worth the price they would exact. You have been unpatriotic enough to suggest in print that our sun is setting. I emphatically deny that. Nevertheless, it has to be admitted that whatever we have been, and whatever we may yet be, we are not, at present, one of the wealthier nations. We cannot afford such an extravagance for mere ostentation."

"But if we do keep out of this, sir, our prestige cannot fail to suffer, whatever arguments we may advance. As for the American denial of strategic value, I have heard it before; and I continue to regard it as a wool-pulling. A Moon Station would be far less vulnerable, and could mount vastly greater fire power than any Satellite Station."

The Under-Secretary's manner had become cold.

"My information does not support that statement. Nor does the policy of the Government. I must therefore request you…"

Troon had heard him out politely and patiently. He knew, and he was sure that the Under-Secretary must know, too, that the damage already done to the declared policy was considerable. There would be a campaign for a Moon Station certainly. Even if he were publicly to reverse his views, or even if he were to remain silent, the newspapers would enjoy tilting at those who had brought pressure to bear on him. He had only to behave circumspectly for a few weeks while the campaign gathered force, to refuse to give opinions where he had been ready to give them before, and perhaps look a little rueful in his silence… There would have been a campaign in some of the popular papers in any case; the main effect of his making his views known early was that in the public mind he appeared as the Moon Station's most important advocate.

In a few weeks, feeling among the electors had become clear enough to worry the government, and produce a rather more conciliatory tone. It was conceded that a British Moon Station *might* be considered, if the estimates were satisfactory. The prodigious size of the estimates which were produced, however, came as a shock which sharpened the divided opinions.

At this point, the Americans took a kindly hand. They had apparently changed their views on the value of Moon Stations, and, having done so, felt that it would be advantageous for the West to have two such Stations to the rival's one. Accordingly, they offered to advance a part of the cost, and supply much of the equipment. It was a generous gesture.

Presently there was a rumour in circulation that the wrong kind of thinking—to put it at its least slanderous—was going on at high levels, and that there was actually in existence a scheme by which a Station could be established at a cost very considerably under half the present estimates; and that Troon (You know, son of Ticker Troon) thought well of it.

Troon had waited, quietly.

Presently, he found himself again invited to high places. He was modestly surprised, and could not think how the proposal came to be connected with his name but, as a matter of fact, well, yes; he did happen to have seen a scheme… Oh no, it was quite an error to think it had anything to do with him, a complete misunderstanding.

The idea had been worked out by a man called Flanderys. It certainly had some interesting points. Yes, he did know Flanderys slightly. Yes, he was sure that Flanderys would be glad to explain his ideas…

The American and Russian expeditions seemed, in so far as their claims had ever been sorted out, to have arrived on the moon simultaneously; the former landing in Copernicus, the latter in Ptolemy—both claiming priority, and both consequently announcing their annexation of the entire territory of the moon. Experience with the Satellite Stations had already shown that any romantic ideas of a *pax coelestis* should be abandoned but, as each expedition was highly vulnerable, both concerned themselves primarily with tunnelling into the rock in order to establish strongholds from which they would be able to dispute their rights with greater confidence.

Some six months later, the smaller British expedition set down in the crater of Archimedes, with the Russian six hundred miles away beyond the Apennine Mountains to the south, and the American four hundred miles or so to the north-east. There, in contrast with their intensively burrowing neighbours, they proceeded to establish themselves on the surface. They had, it was true, one drilling-machine, but this, compared with the huge tunnelling engines of the others that had cost a good many times their weight in uranium to transport, was a mere toy which they employed in sinking a series of six-foot diameter pits.

The Flanderys Dome, essentially a modification of Domes used in the Arctic for some years, was a simple affair to erect. It was spread out on a levelled part of the crater floor, coupled with hoses, and left to inflate. With only the light gravity of the moon weighing down its fabric, the outer casing was fully shaped at a pressure of eight pounds (Earth) per square inch, at fifteen it was perfectly taut.

Then the contents of the various rockets and containers went into it through the airlocks, or the annuli. The air regenerating plants were started up, the temperature controls coupled, and the work of building the Station inside the dome could begin.

The Americans, Troon recalled, had been interested. They reckoned it quite an idea for use on a moon where there did not happen to be any Russians about; but on one where there were, they thought it plain nuts, and said so. The Russians themselves, he remembered with a smile, had been bewildered. A flimsy contrivance that could be completely wrecked by a single, old-fashioned h.e. shell was in their opinion utter madness, and a sitting temptation. They did not, however yield to the temptation since that would almost certainly precipitate untimely action by the Americans. Nevertheless the presumption of a declining Power in arriving to settle itself blandly and unprotected in the open while two great Powers were competing to tunnel themselves hundreds of feet into the rock was a curious piece of effrontery. Even a less suspicious mind than the Russian could well have felt that there was something here that was not meeting the eye. They instructed their agents to investigate.

The investigation took a little time, but presently the solution forthcame—an inconvenient clarification. As had been assumed, the pits that the British had been busily drilling at the same time that they built their Station into the Dome, were missile-shafts. This was similar to the work being done by the other two parties themselves—except that where the Americans also used pits, the Russians favoured launching ramps. The more disturbing aspect of it came to light later.

The British system of control, it appeared, was to use a main computing-engine to direct the aim and setting of any missile. Once the missile had been launched, it was kept on course by its own

computor and servo systems. The main computor was, unlike the
rest of the station, protected in a chamber drilled to a considerable
depth. One of its more interesting features was that in certain conditions it was capable of automatically computing for, and dispatching,
missiles until all were gone. A quite simple punched-card system was
used in conjunction with a chronometer; each card being related
to a selected target. One of the conditions which would cause this
pack of cards to be fed to the computor was a drop in the Station's
air-pressure. Fifteen pounds per square inch was its normal, and
there was allowance for reasonable variation. Should the Dome be
so unfortunate, however, as to suffer a misfortune sufficient to reduce
the air-pressure to seven pounds the missile-dispatching mechanism
would automatically go into action.

All things considered, it appeared highly desirable from the
Russian point of view that the Flanderys Dome should not suffer
any such misadventure.

During the years that had intervened between the establishment of
the Station, and his succeeding to command of it, Troon, who had
rapidly become something of a selenologist himself, had nursed
from the time of the landing an ambition to see and record something of the moon's other side. According to rumour, the Russians
had, within a year of their arrival sent an ill-fated expedition there,
but the truth or otherwise of the report remained hidden by the
usual Slav passion for secrecy. It was one of Troon's regrets that
exploration would have to wait on further development of the jet-
platforms, but there was no reason to think that the invisible side
held any surprises; photographs taken from circling rockets showed
no more than a different pattern of the same pieces—mountains,
"seas," and craters innumerable.

The regret that exploration must fall to someone else was no more than minor; most of what he had wanted to do, he had done. The establishment of the Moon Station was the end to which he had worked, manoeuvred, and contrived. He had given Flanderys the idea of the Dome, and helped him to work it out; and, when that looked like being rejected for its vulnerability, he had briefed another friend to produce the solution of automatic reprisals which they had called Project Stalemate. It was better, he had thought then, and still thought, that the affair should appear to be a composite achievement rather than a one man show. He was satisfied with his work.

He had almost reconciled himself to handing over the command in another eight months with the thought that the Station's future was secure, for, however much it might be grudged as a charge on the armed forces, the discovery of rare elements had given it practical importance, the astronomers attached great value to the Station, and the medical profession, too, had found it useful for special studies.

But now there had come this war, and he was wondering whether that might mean the end of all the Moon stations. If this one survived, would there be the wealth, or even the technical means, left to sustain it when the destruction was finished? Was it not very likely that everybody would be too busy trying simply to survive in a shattered world to concern themselves with such exotic matters as the conquest of space…?

Well, there was nothing he could do about that—nothing but wait and see what the outcome was, and be ready to seize any opportunity that showed.

Troon got up, and walked out from behind the rock. He stood for some moments, a lone scarlet figure in the black and white desert, looking at his Moon Station. Then, picking his path carefully between the missile-pits, made his unhurried way back to it.

IV

At the end of dinner he asked if he might have the pleasure of the doctor's company at coffee in his office. Looking at her over the rim of his cup, he said:

"It would seem to have worked."

She regarded him quizzically through her cigarette smoke.

"Yes, indeed," she agreed. "Like a very hungry bacteriophage. I felt as if I were watching a film speeded up to twice natural pace." She paused, and then added: "Of course, I am not familiar with the usual reactions of Commanding Officers who have been suspected of treason and stood in some danger of lynching, but one would not have been surprised at a little more—er—perturbation..."

Troon grinned.

"A bit short on self-respect?" He shook his head. "This is a funny place, Ellen. When you have been here a little longer your own sense of values will seem a little less settled."

"I have suspected that already."

"We realized when we came here that there would be particular problems, but we could not foresee all of them. We realized that we'd need men able to adapt to life in a small community, and because they would be restricted almost all the time to the Station, we had them vetted for claustrophobic tendencies, too. But it did not occur to anyone that, out here, they would have to contend with claustrophobia and agoraphobia at the same time. Yet, it is so; we are shut in, in a vast emptiness it made a pretty grim mental conflict for a lot of them, and morale went down and down. After a year of it the first Station-Commander began to battle for an establishment of women clerks, orderlies, and cooks. His report was quite dramatically eloquent. 'If this Station,' he wrote, 'is required to keep to its present establishment then, in my considered opinion, a complete collapse of morale will follow in a short time. It is of the utmost importance that we take all practical steps which will help to give it the character of a normal human community. Any measures that will keep this wilderness from howling in the men's minds, and the horrors of eternity from frost-biting their souls, should be employed without delay.' Good Lyceum stuff, that, but true, all the same. There was a great deal of misgiving at home— but no lack of women volunteers; and when they did come, most of them turned out to be more adaptable than the men. And then, of course, the patriarchal aspect of the C.O's job came still more to the force. It is no sort of a place for a disciplinarian to build up his ego; the best that can be done is to keep it working as harmoniously as possible.

"I have been here long enough to take its pulse fairly well as a rule, but this time I slipped up. Now, I don't want that to happen again, so I'd be glad of your further help to see that it doesn't. We've dislodged this particular source of trouble but the causes are still there; the frustrations are still buzzing about, and soon they are going to find a new place to swarm. I want the news early, the moment they look as if they have found it. Can I rely on you for that?"

"But, seeing that the cause—the immediate cause, that is—is H.Q.'s failure to use us, I don't see that there is anything here for them to concentrate the frustration on."

"Nor do I. But since they cannot reach the high-brass back home, they will find something or other to sublimate it on, believe me."

"Very well, I'll be your ear to the ground. But I still don't understand. Why—why *doesn't* H.Q. use these missiles? We know we should be plastered, wiped out, in an attempt to put the main

computor out of action. But most of the men are past caring about
that. They have reached a sort of swashbuckling, gotterdamerung
state of mind by now. They reckon that their families, their homes,
and their towns must have gone, so they are saying: 'What the hell
matters now?' There is still just a hope that we are being reserved
for a final, smashing blow, but when that goes, I think they'll try to
fire them themselves."

Troon thought a little, then he said:

"I think we have passed the peak of likelihood of desperate
action. Now that they are sure that no firing orders were received,
they must most of them swing over to the proposition that we are
being conserved for some decisive moment—with the corollary
that if our missiles are not available when they are called for, the
whole strategy of a campaign could be wrecked. After all, could it
not come to the point where the last man who still has ammunition
holds the field? For all we can tell, we may at this very moment be
representing a threat which dominates the whole situation. Someone
could be saying: 'Unconditional surrender *now*. Or we'll bomb you
again, from the moon.' If so, we are a rather emphatic example of
'they also serve…'"

"Yes," she said, after reflection. "I think that *must* be the intention.
What other reason could there be?"

The jangle of the bedside telephone woke Troon abruptly. He had
the handpiece to his ear before his eyes were well open.

"Radar Watch here, sir," said a voice, with a tinge of excitement
behind it. "Two ufos observed approaching south-east by south.
Height one thousand; estimated speed under one hundred."

"Two *what?*" inquired Troon, collecting his wits.

"Unidentified flying objects, sir."

He grunted. It was so long since he had encountered the term that he had all but forgotten it.

"You mean jet-platforms?" he suggested.

"Possibly, sir." The voice sounded a little hurt.

"You've warned the guard?"

"Yes, sir. They're in the lock now."

"Good. How far off are these—er—ufos?"

"Approximately forty miles now."

"Right. Pick them up televisually as soon as possible, and let me know. Tell switchboard to cut me in on the guard's link right away."

Troon put down the telephone, and threw back the bedcovers. He had barely put a foot on the floor when there was a sound of voices in his office next door. One, more authoritative than the rest, cut across the babble.

"Zero, boys. Open her up."

Troon, still in his pyjamas went through to his office, and approached his desk. From the wall-speaker came the sound of breathing, and the creak of gear as the men left the lock. A voice said:

"Damned if I can see any bloody ufos. Can you, Sarge?"

"*That,* "said the sergeant's voice patiently, "is south-east by south, my lad."

"Okay. But I still can't see a bloody ufo. If you—"

"Sergeant Witley," said Troon, into the microphone. A hush fell over the party.

"Yes, sir."

"How many are you?"

"Six men with me, sir. Six more following."

"Arms?"

"Light machine-gun and six bombs, each man, sir. Two rocket-tubes for the party."

"That'll do. Ever used a gun on the moon, Sergeant?"

"No, sir." There was a touch of reproof in the man's voice, but one did not waste ammunition that had cost several pounds a round to bring in. Troon said:

"Put your sights right down. For practical purposes there is no trajectory. If you do have to shoot, try to get your back against a rock; if you can't do that, lie down. Do *not* try to fire from a standing position. If you haven't learnt the trick of it, you'll go into half a dozen back somersaults with the first burst. All of you got that?"

There were murmured acknowledgements.

"I don't for a moment suppose it will be necessary to shoot," Troon continued, "but be ready. You will not initiate hostilities, but at any sign of a hostile act you, Sergeant, will reply instantly, and your men will give you support. No one else will act on his own. Is that clear?"

"Yes, sir."

"Good. Carry on now, Sergeant Witley."

To a background sound of the sergeant making his dispositions, Troon hurried into his clothes, He was almost dressed when the same voice as before complained:

"Still I don't see no bloody—yes, I do, though, by god! Something just caught the light to the right of old Mammoth Tooth, see…?"

At the same moment the telephone rang. Troon picked it up.

"Got the telly on them now, sir. Two platforms. Four men on one, five on the other. Scarcely any gear with them. Wearing Russian-type suits. Headed straight this way."

"Any weapons?"

"None visible, sir."

"Very well. Inform the guard."

He hung up, and listened to the sergeant receiving and acknowledging the message, while he finished dressing. Then he picked up the telephone again to tell the switchboard:

"Inform the W.O.'s mess that I shall observe from there. And switch the guard link through to there right away."

He glanced at the looking-glass, picked up his cap, and left his quarters, with an air of purpose, but carefully unhurried.

When he arrived at the W.O.'s mess on the south-east side, the two platforms were already visible as shining specks picked out by the sunlight against the spangled black sky. His officers arrived at almost the same moment, and stood beside him, watching the specks grow larger. Presently, in spite of the distance, the clear airlessness made it possible to see the platforms themselves, the pinkish-white haze of the jets supporting them, and the clusters of brightly coloured space suits upon them. Troon did not try to judge the distance; in his opinion, nothing less precise than a rangefinder was any use on the moon. He clicked-on the hand mike.

"Sergeant Witley," he instructed, "extend your men in a semicircle, and detail one of them to signal the platforms down within it. Control, cut my guard-link now, but leave me linked to you."

"Guard-link cut, sir."

"Is your standby with you?"

"Yes, sir."

"Tell her to search for the Russian intercom wave-length. It's something a little shorter than ours as a rule. When she finds it, she is to hold it until further notice. Does she speak Russian?"

"Yes, sir."

"Good. She is to report at once if there is any suggestion of hostile intention in their talk. Cut me in on the guard-link again now."

The two platforms continued smoothly towards them, dropping on a long slant as they came. The sergeants' men were prone, with their guns aimed. They were deployed in a wide crescent. In the middle of it stood a lone figure in a suit of vivid magenta, his gun slung, while he beckoned the platforms in with both arms. The platforms slowed to a stop a dozen yards short of the signaller, at a height of some ten feet. Then, with their jets blowing dust and grit away from under them, they sank gently down. As they landed, the space-suited figures on them let go of their holds, and showed empty hands.

"One of them is asking for you, sir, in English," Control told him.

"Cut him in," Troon instructed.

A voice with a slight foreign accent, and a trace of American influence said:

"Commander Troon, please allow me to introduce myself. General Alexei Goudenkovitch Budorieff, of the Red Army. I had the honour to command the Moon Station of the U.S.S.R."

"Commander Troon speaking, General. Did I understand you to say that you *had* that honour?"

He gazed out of the window at the platforms, trying to identify the speaker. There was something in the stance of a man in a searing orange suit that seemed to single him out.

"Yes, Commander. The Soviet Moon Station ceased to exist several earth-days ago. I have brought my men to you because we are—very hungry."

It took a moment for the full implication to register, and then Troon was not quite sure.

"You mean you have brought *all* your men, General?"

"All that are left, Commander."

Troon stared out at the little group of nine men in their vivid pressure-suits. The latest intelligence Report, he recalled, had given the full complement of the Russian Station as three hundred and fifty-six. He said:

"Please come in, General. Sergeant Witley, escort the General and his men to the airlock."

v

The General gazed round at the officers assembled in their mess. Both he and his aide beside him were looking a great deal better for two large meals separated by ten hours of sleep. The lines of hunger and fatigue had left his face, though signs of strain remained.

"Gentlemen," he said, "I have decided to give you an account of the action at the Moon Station of the U.S.S.R. while it is fresh in my mind, for several reasons. One is that I consider it a piece for the history books—and for the military experts, too. Another is that, although it appears to have brought the campaign in this theatre to a close, the war still continues, and none of us can tell what may happen to him yet. With this in mind, your Commander has pointed out that knowledge carried in a number of heads has a better chance of survival than if it is restricted to two or three, and suggested that I who am in a better position to give the account than anyone else should speak to you collectively. This I am not only honoured but glad to do for it seems to me important that it should be known that our station fell to a new technique of warfare—an attack by dead men."

He paused to regard the faces about him and then went on:

"What you call in English the booby-trap—something which is set to operate after a man has left it or is dead; a kind of blind vengeance by which he hopes to do some damage still—that is nothing new; it is one would imagine, as old as war itself. But a means by which dead men can not only launch, but can press home an attack—that, I think, is new indeed. Nor do I yet see where such a development may lead."

He paused again, and remained so long looking at the table in front of him that some of his audience fidgetted. The movement caught his attention, and he looked up.

"I will start by saying that, to the best of my knowledge, all life that still exists upon the moon is now gathered here, in your Dome.

"Now, how did this come about? You are no doubt aware in outline of the first stages. We and the American Station opened our bombardments simultaneously. Neither of us attacked the other. Our orders were to disregard the American Station, and give priority to launching our Earth-bound missiles. I have no doubt that there orders were similarly to disregard us. This situation persisted until, of our heavy missiles, only the strategic reserve remained. It might well have continued longer had not the Americans, with a light missile, destroyed our incoming supply-rocket. Upon this, I requested, and received, permission to attack the American Station, for we had a second supply-rocket already on the way, and hoped to save it from the same fate.

"As you know, the use of heavy, ground-to-ground missiles is not practicable here, nor would an attempt to use our small reserve for such a purpose have been permitted. We therefore retaliated with light missiles on high-angle setting to clear the mountains round the Copernicus crater. Again as you will know, the low gravity here gives a wide margin of error for such an attempt, and our missiles were ineffective. The Americans attempted to reply with similar missiles, and they, too, were highly inaccurate. There was slight damage to one of our launching ramps, but no more.

"Then, one of our Satellite Stations which chanced to be in a favourable position dispatched two heavy missiles. The first they reported as being two miles off target; for the second, they claimed a direct hit. This would seem to be a valid claim, for the American Station ceased at once to communicate, and has shown no sign of life since.

"A reprisal attack on our own Station for the American Satellite was to be expected, and it came in the form of one heavy missile which landed within a mile of us. Our chief damage was fractures in the walls of the upper chambers, causing a considerable air-leakage. We had to close them off with bulkheads while we sent men in spacesuits to caulk the larger fissures and spray the walls and roofs with plastic sealing compound. The area of damage was extensive, and the work was hampered by falls from the roof, so that I decided to remain incommunicado, in the hope of attracting no more missiles until we had stopped the leaks. It was to be hoped, too, that now the Satellites had been brought into the action ours might succeed in crippling the American with their wasps by the time we had made good."

"Wasps?" somebody interrupted.

"You haven't heard of them? I'm surprised. However, it can do no harm now. They are very small missiles, used in a spread-out flock. A Satellite can easily meet one, or several, ordinary missiles with counter-missiles and explode them at a safe distance, but with missiles that come to the attack like a shoal of fish, defence is difficult, and some will always get through—or so it is claimed."

"And did they, General?" Troon asked. He gave no indication of knowing that the British Satellite which his father had helped to construct, was disabled, and nothing had been heard from the American Satellite since the second day of hostilities."

The General shook his head.

"I cannot say. By the time we had our leaks repaired and our mast up again, there was a message from H.Q. saying that it had lost touch with our Satellites…"

His earlier formality had eased, and he went on more easily, as a man telling his story.

"We thought then that we had, as you say, come through. But it was not yet certain that there would be no further attack, or that more cracks in the roof might not open, so we kept our suits handy. That was very fortunate for some of us.

"Five earth-days ago—that is four whole days after the American Station was hit—the man on television watch thought that he caught a glimpse of something moving among the rocks on the crater floor to the north of us. It seemed improbable, but he held the masthead scanner on the area, and presently he caught another movement—something swiftly crossing a gap between two rocks—and he reported it. The Duty-Officer watched, too, and soon he also caught a snatch of movement, but it occurred too rapidly for him to be sure what it was. They switched in a telephoto lens, but it reduced the field of view, and showed them nothing but rocks, so they went back to the normal lens just in time to see what looked like a smooth rock appear from the cover of one ordinary jagged rock, and slither behind another. At this point the Duty-Officer reported to me, and I went down to join them in the main control-chamber.

"We alerted the guard to stand by with rocket-tubes, and went on watching. The thing kept on dodging about, suddenly shooting out of a black shadow, or from behind a rock, and vanishing again. There was no doubt that it was gradually coming closer, but it seemed in no hurry to reach us.

"Somebody said: 'I think there must be two of them.' The appearances and disappearances were so erratic, that we could not be sure. We tried radar on it, but at that angle and among so much broken rock, it was practically useless. We could only wait for the thing to reach more open ground, and show itself more clearly.

"Then there was a report from the guard of another moving object, somewhat further west. We turned the scanner that way, and observed that there was indeed a similar something there that dodged about among the rocks and shadows in the same, unidentifiable way.

"Over an hour went by before the first of them reached the more open ground at a range of eleven kilometres from us. But even then it was some time before we could get a real idea of it—for it was too small on the normal lens to show detail, and too erratic for the telephoto to follow it. Before long, however, there were three of the things all skirmishing wildly about the crater floor with sudden rushes forwards, sideways, any direction, even back, and never staying still long enough for us to make them out clearly in the crosslight.

"If our armament had included short-range bombardment missiles, we should have used them at the first sighting, but they were not a weapon that had seemed reasonable equipment for a Moon-Station, and we could only wait for the things to come within practicable range of the portable rocket-tubes.

"Meanwhile they continued to dash hither and thither zig-zagging madly about the crater floor. It was uncanny. They made us think of huge spiders rushing back and forth, but they never froze as spiders do; their pauses were no more than momentary, and then they were off again; and one never could tell which way it would be, They must have been travelling quite thirty or forty metres to make an advance of one metre, and they were in an extended line so that we could only get one, or perhaps, for a moment, two of them, on the screen at the same time.

"However, during the time it took them to cover the next two kilos we were able to get better views and impressions of them. In appearance they were simple. Take an egg, pull it out to double its length, and that is the shape of the body. Put long axles through it near the ends, and fasten tall, wide-tyred wheels on them—tall enough to give it a good ground clearance. Mount the wheels so that they have a hundred and eighty degrees of traverse—that is, so that the treads can be turned parallel with the lines of the axle, whether the wheels themselves are before or behind the axle. And you have this machine. It can move in any direction—or spin in one spot, if you want it to. Not, perhaps, very difficult once you have thought of the idea. Give it a motor in each wheel, and an electronic control to keep it from hitting obstacles. That is not very difficult, either.

"What is not so clear, is how you direct it. It was not, very clearly, by dead reckoning. We thought it might be responding to our radio, or to the rotation of radar scanner, or to the movements of our television pickup, but we tested all those, and even switched off our screen for some minutes, but the guard outside reported no effect. Nor was it detecting and seeking any of our electric motors; we stopped every one of them for a full minute, without emanation result. It was just possible that the things were picking up an emanation from our power-pile but that was well shielded, and we already had decoy radiators to deflect any missiles that might try that. I myself think it probable that they were able to detect, and to respond to, the inevitable slight rise of temperature in the Station area. If so, there was nothing we could have done about it."

The General shrugged, shook his head, and frowned. He went on:

"What we faced, in essence, was a seeking missile, on wheels. Not difficult to construct, though scarcely worth attempting for use in a simple form—too easy a target for the defence. So what those Americans had done, the frightening thing they had done, was to introduce a random element. You see what I mean? They had put in this random stage, and somehow filtered the control through it…"

He thought again for a moment.

"Machines do not live, so they cannot be intelligent. Nevertheless, it is in the nature of machines to be logical. The conception of an illogical machine seems to be a contradiction in terms. If you deliberately produce such a thing, what have you? Something that never existed in nature. Something alien. What you have done is to produce madness without mind. You have made unreason animate, and set it loose. That is a very frightening thing to think about…

"But here, among these not-quite-machines that were scuttering about the crater floor like water-boatmen on a pond, there was a controlling thread of ultimate purpose running through the artificial madness. Their immediate actions were unpredictable, insane, but their final intention was just as sure as the bomb that each was carrying in its metal belly. Think of a maniac, a gibbering idiot, with one single continuing thread of intention—to murder…

"That is what those machines were. And they kept on coming with short, or very short, or not so short crazy rushes. They darted and dodged forward, sideways, backwards, obliquely, straight, or in a curve; one never knew which would be next-only that, after a dozen moves, they would be just a little closer.

"Our rocket men opened fire about five kilos. A sheer waste, of course; one could as well have hoped to hit a fly on the wing with a peasshooter. Mines might have stopped them—if they did not have detectors—but who would have sanctioned the use of valuable rocket-space to bring mines to the moon? All our men could do was to hope for a lucky shot: Occasionally one of them would be hidden for a moment or two by the burst of an explosion, but it always reappeared out of the dust, dodging as crazily as ever, Our eyes and heads ached with the strain of trying to follow them on the screen, and to detect some pattern in their movements—I'm sure myself that no pattern existed.

"At three kilos the men were doing no better with their shooting, and were starting to show signs of panic. I decided that at two kilos we would withdraw the men and get them below.

"The things kept on coming, as madly as ever. I tell you, I have never seen anything that frightened me more. There was the dervish-like quality of the random madness, and yet the known deadly purpose. And all the time there was the suggestion of huge, scuttering insects so that it was difficult not to think of them as being in some alien way alive...

"Some of the rocket bursts did succeed in peppering them with fragments now and then, but they were not harmed. As they approached the two kilo line I told Colonel Zinochek, here, to withdraw the patrol. He picked up the microphone to speak, and at that moment one of the things hit a rocket bomb. We saw it run right into the bomb.

"The explosion threw it off the ground, and it came down on its back. The diameter of the wheels was large enough to allow it to run upside down. It actually began to do so, but then there was a great glare, and the screen went blank.

"Even at our depth the floor of the chamber lifted under us, and cracks ran up two of the walls.

"I switched on the general address system. It was still live, but I could not tell how much of the Station it was reaching. I gave orders for everyone to put on spacesuits, and stand by for further instructions.

"One could hope that the explosion of one machine might have set off the others, but we could not tell. They might have been shielded at the moment, or, even if they were not, either, or both of them might have survived. Without air there is not the usual kind of blast and pressure-wave; there is flying debris, of course, but what else? So little work has been done on the precise effects of explosions here. Our mast had gone again so that we were without radar, or television. We had no means of telling whether the danger was over, or whether the machines were still scurrying about the crater floor like mad spiders; still working closer...

"If they were, we reckoned that it should take them about thirty-five minutes to reach us, at their former rate.

"No half-hour in my life has been as long as that one. Once we had our helmets on, and the intercoms were working, we did our best to learn what the damage was. It appeared to be fairly extensive in the upper levels, for there were few replies from there. I ordered all who could to make their way down to the lowest levels, and to stay there.

"Then there was absolutely nothing we could do but wait... and wait... and wait... Wondering if the things were indeed still skirmishing outside, and watching the minute-hand crawl round...

"It took them—or it—exactly thirty-one minutes...

"The whole place bounced, and threw me off my feet. I had a glimpse of cracks opening in the roof and walls, then the light went out, and something fell on me...

"I don't need to go into details about the rest. Four of us in the control-chamber were left alive, and five in the level immediately above. None of us would have survived had the rock had earth-weight—nor should we have been able to shift it to clear a way to the emergency exit.

"Even so, it took us four earth-days to get our way through the collapsed passages. All the Station's air was gone, of course, and we had to do it on dead men's air-bottles, and emergency rations—as long as the rations lasted—and with only one two-man inflatable chamber between us to eat in.

"The emergency exit was of course, at some distance from the main entrance, but even so, a part of the roof of the terminal chamber had fallen in and wrecked one of the platforms there; fortunately the other two were scarcely damaged. The outer doors of the airlock were at the base of a cliff, and though the cliff itself had been a shield from the direct force of the explosion, a quantity of debris had fallen in front of the doors so that we had to blast them open. That gave us a big enough opening to sail the platforms through, and avoid any radio-active contamination—and, I think, by reason of the airlock's position, any serious exposure to radiation ourselves."

He looked round at the group of officers.

"It has been chivalrous of you, gentlemen, to take us in. Let me, in return, assure you that we have no intention of making ourselves a liability. On the contrary, there is a large food store in our Station. If the cisterns have remained intact, there is water; also there are air-regeneration supplies. But we need drilling gear to get at these things. If, when my men are rested, you can let us have the necessary gear, we shall be able to add very considerably to your reserves here."

He turned to the window, and looked at the shining segment of Earth.

"—And that may be as well, for I have a feeling that we may be going to need all the supplies we can collect."

When the meeting was broken up, Troon took the General and his aide along to his own office. He let them seat themselves, and light cigarettes before he said:

"As you will understand, General, we are not equipped here to deal with prisoners of war. I do not know your men. Our Station is vulnerable. What guarantees can you give against sabotage?"

"Sabotage!" exclaimed the General. "Why should there be sabotage? My men are all perfectly sane, I assure you. They are as well aware as I am that if anything should happen to this Station it must be the end of all of us."

"But might there not be one—well, let us call him a selflessly patriotic man—who might consider it his duty to wreck this Station, even at the cost of his own life?"

"I think not. My command was staffed by picked, intelligent men. They are well aware that no one is going to *win* this war now. So that the object has become to survive it."

"But, General, are you not overlooking the fact that we, here, are still a fighting unit—the only one left in this theatre of war."

The General's eyebrows rose a little. He pondered Troon for a moment, and then smiled slightly.

"I see. I have been a little puzzled. Your officers are still under that impression?"

Troon leaned forward to tap his cigarette ash into a tray.

"Perhaps I don't quite understand you, General."

"Don't you, Commander? I am speaking of your value as a fighting unit."

Their eyes met steadily for some seconds. Troon shrugged.

"How high would *you* place our value as a fighting unit, General?"

General Budorieff shook his head gently.

"Not very high, I am afraid, Commander," he said, and then, with a touch of apology in his manner, continued: "Before the last attack on our Station you had dispatched nine medium missiles. I do not know whether you have fired any more since then, therefore the total striking power at your disposal may be either three medium missiles—or none at all."

Troon turned, and looked out of the window towards the camouflaged missile-pits. His voice shook a little as he asked:

"May I inquire how long you have known this, General?"

Gently the General said:

"About six months."

Troon put his hand over his eyes. For a minute or two no-one spoke. At length the General said:

"Will you permit me to extend my sincere congratulations, Commander Troon? You must have played it magnificently."

Troon, looking up, saw that he was genuine.

"I shall have to tell them now," he said. "It is going to hurt their pride. They thought of everything but that."

"It would, I think, be better to tell them now, "agreed Budorieff, "but is not necessary for them to know that *we* knew."

"Thank you, General. That will at least do something to diminish the farcical element for them."

"Do not take it too hard, Commander. Bluff and counter-bluff are, after all, an important part of strategy—and to have maintained such a bluff as that for almost twenty years is, if I may say so, masterly. I have been told that our people simply refused to believe our agents' first reports on it.

"Besides, what was our chief purpose here—yours, mine, and the Americans'? Not to *make* war. We were a threat which, it was hoped, would help to prevent war—and one fancies that all of us here did do something to postpone it. Once fighting was allowed to start, it could make really very little difference whether our missiles were added to the general destruction or not. We have all known in our hearts that this war, if it should come, would not be a kind that anyone could win.

"For my part, I was greatly relieved when I received this report on your armament. The thought that I might one day be required to destroy your quite defenceless Station was not pleasant. And consider how it turns out. It is simply because your weapons were a bluff that your Station still exists: and because it exists, that we still have a foothold on the moon. That is important."

Troon looked up.

"You think so, too, General? Not very many people do."

"There are not, at any time, many people who have—what do you call it in English?—Divine discontent? Vision? Most men like to be settled among their familiar things, with a notice on the door: 'Do Not Disturb.' They would still have that notice hanging outside their caves if it were not for the few discontented men. Therefore it is *important* that we are still here, *important* that we do not lose our gains. You understand?"

Troon nodded. He smiled faintly.

"I understand, General. I understand very well. Why did I fight for a Moon Station? Why did I come here, and stay here? To hold on to it so that one day I could say to a younger man: 'Here it is. We've got you this far. Now go ahead. The stars are before you...' Yes, I understand. But what I have had to wonder lately is whether the time will ever come for me to say it..."

General Budorieff nodded. He looked out, long and speculatively at the pearl-blue Earth.

"Will there be any rocket-ships left? Will there he anyone left to bring them?" he murmured.

Troon looked in the same direction. With the pale earth-light shining in his face he felt a sudden conviction.

"They'll come," he said. "Some of them will hear the thin gnat-voices crying... They'll have to come... And, one day, they'll go on..."

AFTER A JUDGEMENT DAY

Edmond Hamilton

One of the driving forces behind the exploration of space, besides the hope of finding extraterrestrial life, is to ensure the continuation of the human race, should any disaster affect the Earth. In 2010 Stephen Hawking warned that with rising population levels and finite resources, let alone wars and the inevitable nuclear threat, if humankind wanted to ensure its future it would be necessary to expand into space. He reckoned we had a deadline of two centuries.

The following story, written nearly fifty years before Hawking's comments, considers exactly that problem: what would people in a lunar colony do if they discovered a virulent plague was wiping out humanity on Earth.

Edmond Hamilton (1904–1977) was one of the great science-fiction pulpsters of the 1920s and 1930s. He earned the nickname "Earth Wrecker" because in story after story, following his first sale in 1926, he came up with endless ways to destroy the Earth, and save it at the last moment. There were invaders from space, other dimensions and, of course, the far side of the Moon from where dangerous turtle-men arrive in flying saucers (in 1929). Hamilton's reputation long endured—in the early 1940s he wrote a long series about the adventures of space hero Captain Future—but he had started to rein in his excesses as early as 1930, and produced far more thought-provoking stories than he is usually credited. This increased in his later years, as the following story shows.

M ARTINSEN LOWERED HIS HEAD SO THAT HE WOULD NOT see the window and the Earth. He looked instead at the complex bank of telltales across the room from him. He looked at them for a long time before he really saw them, and noticed that one had changed. A tiny red star had appeared in that section.

He reached and punched a button on the desk, and then leaned and said into an intercom,

"Ellam, Sixteen is coming in."

There was no answer.

"Ellam?"

He knew his voice was searching through every part of the Station, down the gleaming metal corridors, into the small laboratories and the rock supply-caverns below. He waited, but there was still no answer from Howard Ellam.

Martinsen made a tired sound, between weariness and anger, and rose to his feet. He thought he knew what had happened, though he had taken precautions against it. He walked across the room and started down a corridor, a rumpled, soiled figure in the coverall he had not changed for days, his grizzled-grey head held up, but his shoulders sagging and his feet scuffing the plastic floor.

No sound broke the silence except the gentle purr of the aerators. There was no one in the Station but Ellam and himself. Carelli had taken the two others of the staff back to Earth with him weeks before, in one of the two emergency-ferries.

"I'll be back," he had told Martinsen, "as soon as I get things untangled down there. You and Ellam stay and handle the Charlies as they come in."

Carelli hadn't come back. Martinsen felt now that he never would come back, he or anyone else. They still had the second ferry. But they also had their orders.

He walked along in the silence, remembering when he had first walked this corridor, tingling with excitement and anticipation, his first ten minutes inside Lunar Station. How he had thought of the work he would be doing here, of the importance of that work to everyone on Earth, now and in the future. The future? My God, that was a laugh.

He went on through the silent rooms and passages until he found Ellam. He was sitting. Just sitting. He looked normal, except for the fact that he hadn't shaved, but when Martinsen saw the glassiness of his fixed stare, he looked around until he found the bottle of pills, half-spilled across a table.

Martinsen sighed. There was no liquor in the Station, but there were tranquilizers. He had thought he had found and hidden them all, but apparently Ellam still had a store. Well, that was one way to take catastrophe. Wrap your mind up in cotton-wool so you can't think about it. He put the pills in his pocket. There was nothing he could do but leave Ellam to come out of it.

He went back to C Room and sat there, watching the little red star slowly change position on the board as Probe Sixteen returned toward the Moon. The other probes, all recalled at the same time, would be coming in during the next few days, until all the Charlies had returned. And then?

He found that he was staring up at Earth again. How many people were still alive there? Many? Any? He thought of calling again but there was never any answer any more, and later would be just as good.

It was very much later when he finally went down to communications and tried to call. He put it through three times, and waited after each time, but there was no answer. Not a flicker.

The anger rose again in Martinsen. *Everybody* on Earth couldn't be dead. Not everybody. The A-Plague might have swept the globe and wiped out hundreds of millions, but surely someone down at Main Base would have survived, and why didn't that someone answer?

But that someone still living at Main Base… would he be able to answer if he wanted to? He just might not be able to utilize the complex communications instruments. The whole little staff here in the Station had, as a matter of course, been taught how. But that certainly did not apply to all the thousands who had worked at Main Base, and if the survivors didn't know…

Martinsen shook his head. Even if that had happened, even if Carelli had found Main Base depopulated when he went back down there, still, Carelli could have called and said so. Unless… unless Carelli and Muto and Jennings had been hit by the A-Plague before they had had time to find out what conditions were, and to get back to Communications and call back. But if that had happened, it meant that the A-Plague was triumphant over Earth and all its billions.

It was funny, in a way, Martinsen thought. For decades, people had been afraid of atomic destruction. It was nuclear war they had feared most, but also they had been afraid of fallout and what it might do to their bodies. But nuclear war had never happened, and fallout had been cut to a safe level. The only trouble was that a level that did not affect human bodies might very well affect other and smaller bodies. Like the bodies of bacteria.

A series of radioactive-induced mutations had occurred in a species of hitherto not-very-harmful bacteria. The scientists had finally wakened up to what was going on. But by then it was too late, the most fearful bacteria in the world's history had appeared and were spreading, and the A-Plague was let loose. Its first incursions, with previously unheard-of high mortality rates, had been in South America. The world health organizations had taken alarm. There had been swift measures of quarantine, concentrated searches for a vaccine. But it was too late for all that, and the messages that came through to the five horrified men in Lunar Station were of cities, then countries, then whole nations going silent. Until Main Base, too, went silent.

And five men were left marooned in Lunar Station, and after Carelli and Jennings and Muto went back down, there were only two men, and one of them kept doping up on pills to forget a wife and kids, so you might say he was alone, with a dead or dying world down there, and...

"Knock it off," Martinsen told himself. "You can cry later."

The telltales showed more little red stars, more probes approaching the Moon. The beautiful, slim metal ships in which no human had ever ridden yet, were returning. They had quested to the nearest stars and their planets, moving in overdrive, and those in them had walked under the radiation of strange suns. But the quest had been suddenly interrupted, a hyperspace signal had flung an abrupt command, and now the probes were coming back in.

He thought it was probably all for nothing. What use was it to record carefully all the knowledge the Charlies would bring back with them, if there was nobody left alive on Earth to use it? But Carelli had left him responsible and he couldn't just sit and throw away the rewards of the whole project.

Cybernetic-Humanoid And Related Life Study, was the project's name. CHARLS, it was more often called, and of course the cyborgs that went out in the probes were at once nicknamed Charlies. And after a time, after Probe 16 had automatically made its landing and entered the reception hangars of Lunar Station, Martinsen heard the soft footsteps of Charlie Sixteen in the passageway, going quietly toward the analysis laboratories.

Martinsen got up and went to the labs. On the spot that had his number painted on the floor, Charlie Sixteen stood silent and unmoving. Martinsen started his preliminary examination, and despite his conviction that it was all for nothing now, he was quickly caught up in the routine.

"Heart-pump, kidneys, cardio-vascular system, all look good," he muttered. "Looks like more calcium mobilization than we expected, but it'll take time to find out. Let's see how your hypothalamus reacted, Charlie," Charlie Sixteen stood and said nothing, for he could not speak. Neither could he hear, nor think. He was not a man, but a mechanical analog of humanity used to study the effect of unusual environments on a pseudo-human body. Cyborgs, they had been called from the first one in the early 1960's—cybernetic organisms.

He looked grotesquely like a man with his skin off, for through his transparent plastic tissues you could clearly see his artificial heart-pump, the clear tubes of his arteries and veins, the alloy "bones", the cleverly simulated lung-sacs, visible for close study through an aperture in the rib-cage that gaped like a ghastly wound. People who first saw cyborgs always found them horribly lifelike, but that first impression always faded fast, and a cyborg after that was no more lifelike than a centrifuge or a television set.

The staff at Lunar Station had had toward the Charlies something of the attitude of a window-dresser handling clothes-mannequins.

But these mannequins were far more than stiff wax figures. They could walk, could obey the commands programmed into their electric nerve-systems. These mannequins were not made to stand in shop windows, but to plumb the stars. In the probes, at accelerations no human frame could endure, they would be sent to the worlds of foreign suns, and would walk those worlds and breathe their air and react to their gravitation, and then the probes would bring them back again to Lunar Station and the men there would ascertain the effects of the alien environments on these human analogs.

It had taken a long time for the Station staff to get the cyborgs ready and programmed to act as humanity's scouts into the stars. And during that time the men had humorously given them the Charlie names, in the way in which one had given a car or a boat a name, and had made small jokes about Charlie Nine being brighter than the others, and Charlie Fourteen being a coward who didn't want to go to the stars, and the like. And now, to the infinitely lonely Martinsen, the joke became almost reality, and he talked to the cyborg he was examining as to a living man.

He had gone to the hangars and had got from Probe 16 the tapes that held a record of the faroff coasts which that slim metal missile had explored. He had run through the tapes, first the visual ones that showed the tawny-red desert on which Charlie Sixteen had walked beneath two shadowed moons, and then the tapes on which the sensor instruments had recorded all the physical data of that world. He pondered certain points in those records, and had returned to his examination of Charlie Sixteen, not even hearing the muted metallic sounds from the hangars that told of two more probes making their automatic return and re-entry.

"I *think*," he told Charlie Sixteen, "that you're a slightly damaged cyborg. Consider yourself lucky that that's all… if you were a man, you'd be dead."

Consider yourself lucky, Charlie! If you were a man, you'd know, and think, and remember and…

Martinsen pushed that thought out of his mind and went on with his examination. Charlies Eight and Eleven had come in by the time he finished with Sixteen, walking silently into the lab and then standing moonless on the painted numbers where their programming ended. Martinsen got the tapes from their two probes and started on them, unwilling to stop work even when the hours passed and he grew tired, unwilling to be back to the chair and sit and look at Earth.

"Now why is your temperature down six degrees?" he muttered to Charlie Eight. "You went in and out of hypothermia perfectly the first time, but the second time you didn't come quite back to normal, and…"

"Are you out of your mind, talking to a Charlie?"

Howard Ellam's voice cut across, and Martinsen turned to find Ellam standing in the doorway, his eyes red-rimmed, his body swaying a little, but looking awake enough.

"Just thinking aloud," Martinsen said.

"Thinking?" Ellam jeered. "Things have got bad, all right, when we start talking to cyborgs."

"I'd as lief talk to a Charlie as to a man coked up on sleep-pills," flared Martinsen.

Ellam stared at him and then laughed. "Want to hear a sick joke? The last two men in the world were locked up together, and what happened? They got cabin-fever."

He laughed and laughed and then he stopped laughing. He said dully, "I'm sorry, Mart."

"Oh, forget it," said Martinsen. "But forget about us being the last two men, will you? No plague, not even an A-Plague, takes everyone. There's always a few survivors."

"Sure, there's always a few survivors," said Ellam. "Kill off all the whooping-cranes, and there still turns out to be a few survivors, for a little while. But they're finished, as a species. We're finished."

"Bull," said Martinsen without conviction.

He went doggedly on with his examination of the Charlies, his notations of their reactions to specific environments. Ellam, as though regretting his outburst, helped him set up the bio-instrumentation, and the measuring of effects. Mineral dynamics was Ellam's special field, and he was quick and precise in this. More probes, more missiles homing from the shores of infinity, kept coming in. Presently all but five of the eighteen Charlies stood in the lab.

"Charlie Six hit it lucky," said Ellam, after a while. "There's a world out there at Proxima that would be just fine for humans. If there were any humans to go there."

Martinsen made no answer, but went on with his work. Presently, with a what's-the-use shrug, Ellam quit and went out of the lab.

Martinsen supposed he had gone back to his pills. But when he finally stopped working, too tired to be accurate any longer, and went back through the Station, he found Ellam sitting in C Room looking up through the window at Earth.

"Never a light," said Ellam. "It used to be we'd see the lights that were cities, through the little refractor, but it's all dark now."

"The lights may be out, but people are still alive," said Martinsen.

"Oh, sure. A few of them. Sick and dying, or afraid they'll soon be sick and dying, and all the already dead around them."

"Will you *please* knock it off?" said Martinsen.

Ellam did not answer. After a moment Martinsen turned away. He did not feel like sleeping now. He went back to the labs.

He had turned out the lights there when he left. He walked back in, dull with fatigue, and the bar of light from the passageway struck in through the dark rooms and littered off chrome flanges and bars, and showed the quiet faces, rows and rows of them, of the Charlies standing there, each on his number, not moving, not making a sound. And of a sudden, after all his long familiarity with them, a horror of them struck Martinsen and he stood shivering. What was he doing in this place upon an alien world, with these unhuman figures, all looking toward him from the shadows? He was a man, and this was not a place for men. Things had gone too fast. Once he had been a boy in a little Ohio country town, and its quiet streets and white houses and old elms and maples must be still much the same, and oh God, he wanted to go back there. But there would be nothing there but death now, man had gone too far and too fast indeed, he was trapped here with unhuman travesties who stood silently looking at him, looking and looking…

He switched on the lights with a shaking hand, and suddenly there was a change, the Charlies were just Charlies, just machines that had never lived and never would live. Nerves, he thought. It had better not happen too often, for if it did he would end up running and screaming through the Station, and that was no way for a man to end. He could take pills like Ellam, but work was a better anodyne. He worked.

For days he worked, making the routine examination of every Charlie, noting everything down and not asking himself what eyes would ever read his notes. And when all that was done, and he knew more about the worlds of foreign stars than man had ever known before, he set himself to repair those Charlies that had been damaged by radiation, poisonous atmospheres, or abnormal gravitation.

Sometimes Ellam would help him, when he was not in a state of semi-stupor from his pills. He usually worked in heavy silence, but one time when the repair of Charlies was almost completed, Ellam asked,

"What's it all for, anyway? Nobody will ever be sending these Charlies out again."

"I don't know," Martinsen answered. And then, after a moment, "Maybe I will."

"You? The Station will-be dead and you with it before they'd ever get back."

"I wasn't thinking of having them come back," Martinsen answered vaguely.

An unusual sound of some kind awoke him later from his sleep. He sat up and listened and then he realized its origin. It came from the hangar of the emergency ferries.

Martinsen ran all the way there. His heart was pumping and he had an icy dread on him, the fear of being altogether alone. He was in time to catch Ellam before Ellam had got the little ferry set up for its automatic launch.

"Ellam, you can't go!"

"I'm going," said Ellam stonily.

"There's nothing but death waiting on Earth!"

Ellam jeered. "What's waiting here? It may be a little longer in coming, but not much."

Martinsen gripped his arm. He had come almost to hate Ellam, during these last days, but now suddenly Ellam was infinitely precious to him as the last defence against ultimate solitude.

"Listen," he said. "Wait a little longer, till I get the Charlies all repaired. Then I'll go with you."

Ellam stared at him. "You?"

"Do you think I want to be left alone here? Anyway, it's as you say, just a matter of time if we stay here. But I have one more thing I want to do."

After a moment Ellam said, "All right, if you're going with me. I'll wait a little while."

Martinsen had no illusions about the implications of his promise. The chances were that he and Ellam would both die of the plague very soon after they reached Earth. Still, death there was only a very high probability, whereas it was a certainty here when the Station machinery stopped operating. And that being so, there was not much room for choice.

But the resolution that had been forming in him was suddenly, sharply crystallized now. Ellam would not wait too long, he knew. He would have little time to do the thing he wanted to do.

He set to work furiously in Communications, preparing master-tapes. The first one was an audio-visual vocabulary tape in which the visual picture of a thing or an action was conjoined with Martinsen's speaking the noun or verb that defined it. It would not be a very large vocabulary but it would contain the key words, and he thought that with it an intelligence of any reasonably high level could quickly advance to expanding interpretations.

He was engaged in finishing this vocabulary-tape when Ellam came into the Communications room and watched him puzzledly for a while. Then he said puzzledly,

"What in the world are you doing?"

Martinsen said, "I'm going to send the probes and Charlies out, before we leave."

"Send them where?"

"Everywhere they can go. Each one will take with him a copy of the tapes I'm preparing."

Ellam said, after a moment, "I get it. Messages in bottles from a drowning person. In other words, the last will and testament of a dying species."

"I still don't think our species will die," Martinsen said. "But even if it lives, it's bound to slip back... maybe a long way and for a long time. Everything shouldn't be lost..."

"It's a good idea," said Ellam. "I'll help you. Here, give me the mike." And he spoke mockingly into it, "This is the deathbed message of a race who were such damn fools that they managed to kill themselves off. And our solemn warning is, don't ever learn too much. Stay up in the trees."

Martinsen took the microphone away from him, but he sat brooding after Ellam had left. After all, there was truth in the bitter assertion that man was responsible for is own destruction. But was it the whole truth?

He suddenly realized his inadequacy for this task. He was no philosopher or seer. He was, outside of his own specialized field of science, a thoroughly average man. How could he take it upon himself to decide what was important to tell, and what was not? Yet there was no one else to do so.

The documentary factual knowledge, the science and the history, were what he began with and they were not so terribly difficult a problem. The Station contained a large microfilm library, and it was easy enough to set up the microfilm equipment so that selected factual knowledge fed directly onto the tapes. But there were also music, art, literature, many other things, and some of all that must survive. He felt more and more overwhelmed by the task as he muddled along trying to make his selections.

How did you evaluate things? Were Newton's Laws of Motion more important than Mozart's quartets? Were the Crusades more worthy of being remembered than Plato's Dialogues? Could he throw away forever the work of long-dead master artists, just because there was no room for a picture of the Parthenon? So much had been done in the world, so many causes valiantly fought, so much beauty created, so much toil and thought and dreaming, how could one pick and choose?

Martinsen went doggedly on with it, and when the last master-tape was finished he knew how faulty and wretched a job he had done. But there was no time to try again.

He sat for a while, looking at the last tape. He felt somehow that he could not let this imperfect record end without adding his own small word.

He said, after a little while, into the microphone, "The thing that has happened to us was of our own doing. But it came not so much from evil as from fecklessness."

He brooded for a moment and then went on. "We inherited curiosity from the ape, and curiosity unlocked many doors for us. The door of power, the door of space. And finally, if all perish, the door of death. Let this be said of us, that we preferred the risk of disaster to the safety of always staying still. But whether this was good or bad, I do not know."

Wearily, he shut off the machine. There was nothing left to do but to run the master-tapes through a duplicator until there was a full set of duplicate tapes for each of the eighteen probes. Then he went to the laboratory where the Charlies were.

Ellam, because he was impatient to get this done and leave, had agreed to program the Charlies. He looked almost cheerful now as he worked with Charlie Three. The endplates of the electrical "nerves" had been removed, and a chattering instrument was feeding code into the cyborg's memory-banks, code-signals that were orders. Orders about course in space, orders covering the landing on any planet which looked habitable or inhabited, orders on delivering the tapes only if certain conditions that indicated civilization were present, orders to go on to other stars and other possible planets if they were not. The probes had an almost unlimited range in over-drive, and some would go far indeed.

"Charlie Three is going to Vega," said Ellam. "And from there, if necessary, on to Lyra 431, and maybe a lot farther. He's going to see things, is Charlie Three. They all are."

Martinsen felt a pang of regret. Once men had thought that in time they too would see those things. But it was not to be, and the cyborgs would go in their place, weird lifeless successors of man.

He thought of a poem he had read during his rummaging of the library. What was it Chesterton had written?

> *"For the end of the world was long ago,*
> *And we all dwell today as children of a second birth,*
> *Like a strange people left on Earth,*
> *After a judgment day."*

The cyborgs were not people and instead of being left on Earth they were to fare into the wider universe. Yet, stillborn and lifeless though they were, they were yet in a sense the children of men, carrying out to unguessable places the story of their creators.

The programming was finished. There was a wait. Then, at the ordered moment, the cyborgs walked quietly out of the laboratory, one after another.

From the window in C Room, Martinsen and Ellam watched as the probes took off. They raced into the sky as though eager to go, vanishing from view as they went rapidly into overdrive to cross the vast and empty spaces.

Where would be the final ends of the Charlies? Some might perish in whirlpools of strange force, in unthinkable cosmic dangers. Others might ironically become the idols or gods of savage, ignorant minds. It could be that in time some would drift to other galaxies. But sometime, somewhere, one at least might deliver his message to those who could decipher it. The music of Schubert might be heard by alien ears, the dreams of Lucretius pondered by alien minds, and the human story would not pass without leaving its imprint on the universe.

The last probe was gone. Martinsen looked up at the globe of Earth, and then he took Ellam gently by the arm.

"Come on, Howard. Let's go home."

THE SENTINEL

Arthur C. Clarke

Clarke's "The Sentinel" is the obvious story to close this anthology. Originally published in 1951, it was one of the stories that fed into the development of Clarke's collaboration with Stanley Kubrick, the revolutionary film 2001: A Space Odyssey *(1968). It poses that profound question of what we might yet discover on the Moon and what that will mean for the whole of humanity.*

Arthur C. Clarke (1917–2008), along with Robert A. Heinlein and Isaac Asimov, were regarded by many as the "Big Three" writers of science fiction in the 1950s and 1960s. He may have seemed like the latecomer of the three because his first professionally published story, "Loophole", appeared in 1946, whereas both Asimov and Heinlein had debuted in 1939. In fact Clarke beat them both to it. He not only had short stories in amateur magazines as early as 1937, but he sold articles to Britain's first science-fiction pulp magazine, Tales of Wonder, *in 1938. The second of these was a call to arms in "We can Rocket to the Moon—Now!". Clarke was an avid member of the British Interplanetary Society and would doubtless have written far more fiction and essays had World War II not intervened. He served as a radar instructor with the RAF. Soon after the War Clarke wrote a revolutionary article, "Extra-Terrestrial Relays: Can Rocket Stations Give World-Wide Radio Coverage" (1945) which forecast, in detail, the geostationary satellite.*

Many of Clarke's early books, starting with Prelude to Space *(1951), considered humanity's expansion into space. These include the novel* A Fall of Moondust *(1961) and the study* The Exploration of the Moon *(1954). Clarke is well known for his quotes, of which perhaps the most* relevant here is the following from The View from Serendip (1977): "I'm sure we would not have had men on the moon if it had not been for Wells and Verne and the people who write about this and made people think about it."

T HE NEXT TIME YOU SEE THE FULL MOON HIGH IN THE SOUTH, look carefully at its right-hand edge and let your eye travel upward along the curve of the disk. Round about two o'clock you will notice a small, dark oval: anyone with normal eyesight can find it quite easily. It is the great walled plain, one of the finest on the Moon, known as the Mare Crisium—the Sea of Crises. Three hundred miles in diameter, and almost completely surrounded by a ring of magnificent mountains, it had never been explored until we entered it in the late summer of 1996.

Our expedition was a large one. We had two heavy freighters which had flown our supplies and equipment from the main lunar base in the Mare Serenitatis, five hundred miles away. There were also three small rockets which were intended for short-range transport over regions which our surface vehicles couldn't cross. Luckily, most of the Mare Crisium is very flat. There are none of the great crevasses so common and so dangerous elsewhere, and very few craters or mountains of any size. As far as we could tell, our powerful caterpillar tractors would have no difficulty in taking us wherever we wished to go.

I was geologist—or selenologist, if you want to be pedantic—in charge of the group exploring the southern region of the Mare. We had crossed a hundred miles of it in a week, skirting the foothills of the mountains along the shore of what was once the ancient sea, some thousand million years before. When life was beginning on Earth, it was already dying here. The waters were retreating down

the flanks of those stupendous cliffs, retreating into the empty heart
of the Moon. Over the land which we were crossing, the tideless
ocean had once been half a mile deep, and now the only trace of
moisture was the hoarfrost one could sometimes find in caves which
the searing sunlight never penetrated.

We had begun our journey early in the slow lunar dawn, and still
had almost a week of Earth-time before nightfall. Half a dozen times
a day we would leave our vehicle and go outside in the spacesuits to
hunt for interesting minerals, or to place markers for the guidance
of future travellers. It was an uneventful routine. There is nothing
hazardous or even particularly exciting about lunar exploration. We
could live comfortably for a month in our pressurized tractors, and
if we ran into trouble we could always radio for help and sit tight
until one of the spaceships came to our rescue.

I said just now that there was nothing exciting about lunar
exploration, but of course that isn't true. One could never grow
tired of those incredible mountains, so much more rugged than the
gentle hills of Earth. We never knew, as we rounded the capes and
promontories of that vanished sea, what new splendours would be
revealed to us. The whole southern curve of the Mare Crisium is
a vast delta where a score of rivers once found their way into the
ocean, fed perhaps by the torrential rains that must have lashed the
mountains in the brief volcanic age when the Moon was young.
Each of these ancient valleys was an invitation, challenging us to
climb into the unknown uplands beyond. But we had a hundred
miles still to cover, and could only look longingly at the heights
which others must scale.

We kept Earth-time aboard the tractor, and precisely at 22.00
hours the final radio message would be sent out to Base and we
would close down for the day. Outside, the rocks would still be

burning beneath the almost vertical sun, but to us it was night until we awoke again eight hours later. Then one of us would prepare breakfast, there would be a great buzzing of electric razors, and someone would switch on the short-wave radio from Earth. Indeed, when the smell of frying sausages began to fill the cabin, it was sometimes hard to believe that we were not back on our own world—everything was so normal and homely, apart from the feeling of decreased weight and the unnatural slowness with which objects fell.

It was my turn to prepare breakfast in the corner of the main cabin that served as a galley. I can remember that moment quite vividly after all these years, for the radio had just played one of my favourite melodies, the old Welsh air, "David of the White Rock."

Our driver was already outside in his space-suit, inspecting our caterpillar treads. My assistant, Louis Garnett, was up forward in the control position, making some belated entries in yesterday's log.

As I stood by the frying pan waiting, like any terrestrial housewife, for the sausages to brown, I let my gaze wander idly over the mountain walls which covered the whole of the southern horizon, marching out of sight to east and west below the curve of the Moon. They seemed only a mile or two from the tractor, but I knew that the nearest was twenty miles away. On the Moon, of course, there is no loss of detail with distance-none of that almost imperceptible haziness which softens and sometimes transfigures all far-off things on Earth.

Those mountains were ten thousand feet high, and they climbed steeply out of the plain as if ages ago some subterranean eruption had smashed them skyward through the molten crust. The base of even the nearest was hidden from sight by the steeply curving surface of the plain, for the Moon is a very little world, and from where I was standing the horizon was only two miles away.

I lifted my eyes toward the peaks which no man had ever climbed, the peaks which, before the coming of terrestrial life, had watched the retreating oceans sink sullenly into their graves, taking with them the hope and the morning promise of a world. The sunlight was beating against those ramparts with a glare that hurt the eyes, yet only a little way above them the stars were shining steadily in a sky blacker than a winter midnight on Earth.

I was turning away when my eye caught a metallic glitter high on the ridge of a great promontory thrusting out into the sea thirty miles to the west. It was a dimensionless point of light, as if a star had been clawed from the sky by one of those cruel peaks, and I imagined that some smooth rock surface was catching the sunlight and heliographing it straight into my eyes. Such things were not uncommon. When the Moon is in her second quarter, observers on Earth can sometimes see the great ranges in the Oceanus Procellarum burning with a blue-white iridescence as the sunlight flashes from their slopes and leaps again from world to world. But I was curious to know what kind of rock could be shining so brightly up there, and I climbed into the observation turret and swung our four-inch telescope round to the west.

I could see just enough to tantalize me. Clear and sharp in the field of vision, the mountain peaks seemed only half a mile away, but whatever was catching the sunlight was still too small to be resolved. Yet it seemed to have an elusive symmetry, and the summit upon which it rested was curiously flat. I stared for a long time at that glittering enigma, straining my eyes into space, until presently a smell of burning from the galley told me that our breakfast sausages had made their quarter-million mile journey in vain...

All that morning we argued our way across the Mare Crisium while the western mountains reared higher in the sky. Even when we were out prospecting in the space-suits, the discussion would continue over the radio. It was absolutely certain, my companions argued, that there had never been any form of intelligent life on the Moon. The only living things that had ever existed there were a few primitive plants and their slightly less degenerate ancestors. I knew that as well as anyone, but there are times when a scientist must not be afraid to make a fool of himself.

"Listen," I said at last, "I'm going up there, if only for my own peace of mind. That mountain's less than twelve thousand feet high—that's only two thousand under Earth gravity and I can make the trip in twenty hours at the outside. I've always wanted to go up into those hills, anyway, and this gives me an excellent excuse."

"If you don't break your neck," said Garnett, "you'll be the laughing-stock of the expedition when we get back to Base. That mountain will probably be called Wilson's Folly from now on."

"I won't break my neck," I said firmly. "Who was the first man to climb Pico and Helicon?"

"But weren't you rather younger in those days?" asked Louis gently.

"That," I said with great dignity, "is as good a reason as any for going."

We went to bed early that night, after driving the tractor to within half a mile of the promontory. Garnett was coming with me in the morning; he was a good climber, and had often been with me on such exploits before. Our driver was only too glad to be left in charge of the machine.

At first sight, those cliffs seemed completely unscalable, but to anyone with a good head for heights, climbing is easy on a world where all weights are only a sixth of their normal value. The real danger in lunar mountaineering lies in overconfidence; a six-hundred-foot drop on the Moon can kill you just as thoroughly as a hundred-foot fall on Earth.

We made our first halt on a wide ledge about four thousand feet above the plain. Climbing had not been very difficult, but my limbs were stiff with the unaccustomed effort, and I was glad of the rest. We could still see the tractor as a tiny metal insect far down at the foot of the cliff, and we reported our progress to the driver before starting on the next ascent.

Inside our suits it was comfortably cool, for the refrigeration units were fighting the fierce sun and carrying away the body-heat of our exertions. We seldom spoke to each other, except to pass climbing instructions and to discuss our best plan of ascent. I do not know what Garnett was thinking, probably that this was the craziest goose-chase he had ever embarked upon. I more than half agreed with him, but the joy of climbing, the knowledge that no man had ever gone this way before and the exhilaration of the steadily widening landscape gave me all the reward I needed.

I don't think I was particularly excited when I saw in front of us the wall of rock I had first inspected through the telescope from thirty miles away. It would level off about fifty feet above our heads, and there on the plateau would be the thing that had lured me over these barren wastes. It was, almost certainly, nothing more than a boulder splintered ages ago by a falling meteor, and with its cleavage planes still fresh and bright in this incorruptible, unchanging silence.

There were no hand-holds on the rock face, and we had to use a grapnel. My tired arms seemed to gain new strength as I swung the three-pronged metal anchor round my head and sent it sailing up toward the stars. The first time it broke loose and came falling slowly back when we pulled the rope. On the third attempt, the prongs gripped firmly and our combined weights could not shift it.

Garnett looked at me anxiously. I could tell that he wanted to go first, but I smiled back at him through the glass of my helmet and shook my head. Slowly, taking my time, I began the final ascent.

Even with my space-suit, I weighed only forty pounds here, so I pulled myself up hand over hand without bothering to use my feet. At the rim I paused and waved to my companion, then I scrambled over the edge and stood upright, staring ahead of me.

You must understand that until this very moment I had been almost completely convinced that there could be nothing strange or unusual for me to find here. Almost, but not quite; it was that haunting doubt that had driven me forward. Well, it was a doubt no longer, but the haunting had scarcely begun.

I was standing on a plateau perhaps a hundred feet across. It had once been smooth—too smooth to be natural—but falling meteors had pitted and scored its surface through immeasurable eons. It had been levelled to support a glittering, roughly pyramidal structure, twice as high as a man, that was set in the rock like a gigantic, many-faceted jewel.

Probably no emotion at all filled my mind in those first few seconds. Then I felt a great lifting of my heart, and a strange, inexpressible joy. For I loved the Moon, and now I knew that the creeping moss of Aristarchus and Eratosthenes was not the only life she had brought forth in her youth. The old, discredited dream of the first explorers was true. There had, after all, been a lunar civilization and I was the first to find it. That I had come perhaps a hundred million years too late did not distress me; it was enough to have come at all.

My mind was beginning to function normally, to analyse and to ask questions. Was this a building, a shrine—or something for which my language had no name? If a building, then why was it erected in so uniquely inaccessible a spot? I wondered if it might be a temple, and I could picture the adepts of some strange priesthood calling on their gods to preserve them as the life of the Moon ebbed with the dying oceans, and calling on their gods in vain.

I took a dozen steps forward to examine the thing more closely, but some sense of caution kept me from going too near. I knew a little of archaeology, and tried to guess the cultural level of the civilization that must have smoothed this mountain and raised the glittering mirror surfaces that still dazzled my eyes.

The Egyptians could have done it, I thought, if their workmen had possessed whatever strange materials these far more ancient architects had used. Because of the thing's smallness, it did not occur to me that I might be looking at the handiwork of a race more advanced than my own. The idea that the Moon had possessed intelligence at all was still almost too tremendous to grasp, and my pride would not let me take the final, humiliating plunge.

And then I noticed something that set the scalp crawling at the back of my neck-something so trivial and so innocent that many would never have noticed it at all. I have said that the plateau was scarred by meteors; it was also coated inches-deep with the cosmic dust that is always filtering down upon the surface of any world where there are no winds to disturb it. Yet the dust and the meteor scratches ended quite abruptly in a wide circle enclosing the little pyramid, as though an invisible wall was protecting it from the ravages of time and the slow but ceaseless bombardment from space.

There was someone shouting in my earphones, and I realized that Garnett had been calling me for some time. I walked unsteadily to the edge of the cliff and signalled him to join me, not trusting myself to speak. Then I went back toward that circle in the dust. I picked up a fragment of splintered rock and tossed it gently toward the shining enigma. If the pebble had vanished at that invisible barrier I should not have been surprised, but it seemed to hit a smooth, hemispherical surface and slide gently to the ground.

I knew then that I was looking at nothing that could be matched in the antiquity of my own race. This was not a building, but a machine, protecting itself with forces that had challenged Eternity. Those forces, whatever they might be, were still operating, and perhaps I had already come too close. I thought of all the radiations man had trapped and tamed in the past century. For all I knew, I might be as irrevocably doomed as if I had stepped into the deadly, silent aura of an unshielded atomic pile.

I remember turning then toward Garnett, who had joined me and was now standing motionless at my side. He seemed quite oblivious to me, so I did not disturb him but walked to the edge of the cliff in an effort to marshal my thoughts. There below me lay the Mare Crisium—Sea of Crises, indeed—strange and weird to most men, but reassuringly familiar to me. I lifted my eyes toward the crescent Earth, lying in her cradle of stars, and I wondered what her clouds had covered when these unknown builders had finished their work. Was it the steaming jungle of the Carboniferous, the bleak shoreline over which the first amphibians must crawl to conquer the land—or, earlier still, the long loneliness before the coming of life?

Do not ask me why I did not guess the truth sooner—the truth, that seems so obvious now. In the first excitement of my discovery, I had assumed without question that this crystalline apparition had been built by some race belonging to the Moon's remote past, but suddenly, and with overwhelming force, the belief came to me that it was as alien to the Moon as I myself.

In twenty years we had found no trace of life but a few degenerate plants. No lunar civilization, whatever its doom, could have left but a single token of its existence.

I looked at the shining pyramid again, and the more remote it seemed from anything that had to do with the Moon. And suddenly I felt myself shaking with a foolish, hysterical laughter, brought on by excitement and overexertion: for I had imagined that the little pyramid was speaking to me and was saying: "Sorry, I'm a stranger here myself."

It has taken us twenty years to crack that invisible shield and to reach the machine inside those crystal walls. What we could not understand, we broke at last with the savage might of atomic power and now I have seen the fragments of the lovely, glittering thing I found up there on the mountain.

They are meaningless. The mechanisms, if indeed they are mechanisms, of the pyramid belong to a technology that lies far beyond our horizon, perhaps to the technology of para-physical forces.

The mystery haunts us all the more now that the other planets have been reached and we know that only Earth has ever been the home of intelligent life in our Universe. Nor could any lost civilization of our own world have built that machine, for the thickness of the meteoric dust on the plateau has enabled us to measure its age. It was set there upon its mountain before life had emerged from the seas of Earth.

When our world was half its present age, something from the stars swept through the Solar System, left this token of its passage, and went again upon its way. Until we destroyed it, that machine was still fulfilling the purpose of its builders; and as to that purpose, here is my guess.

Nearly a hundred thousand million stars are turning in the circle of the Milky Way, and long ago other races on the worlds of other suns must have scaled and passed the heights that we have reached. Think of such civilizations, far back in time against the fading afterglow of Creation, masters of a universe so young that life as yet had come only to a handful of worlds. Theirs would have been a loneliness we cannot imagine, the loneliness of gods looking out across infinity and finding none to share their thoughts.

They must have searched the star-clusters as we have searched the planets. Everywhere there would be worlds, but they would be empty or peopled with crawling, mindless things. Such was our own Earth, the smoke of the great volcanoes still staining the skies, when that first ship of the peoples of the dawn came sliding in from the abyss beyond Pluto. It passed the frozen outer worlds, knowing that life could play no part in their destinies. It came to rest among the inner planets, warming themselves around the fire of the Sun and waiting for their stories to begin.

Those wanderers must have looked on Earth, circling safely in the narrow zone between fire and ice, and must have guessed that it was the favourite of the Sun's children. Here, in the distant future, would be intelligence; but there were countless stars before them still, and they might never come this way again.

So they left a sentinel, one of millions they have scattered throughout the Universe, watching over all worlds with the promise of life. It was a beacon that down the ages has been patiently signalling the fact that no one had discovered it.

Perhaps you understand now why that crystal pyramid was set upon the Moon instead of on the Earth. Its builders were not concerned with races still struggling up from savagery. They would be interested in our civilization only if we proved our fitness to survive by crossing space and so escaping from the Earth, our cradle. That is the challenge that all intelligent races must meet, sooner or later.

It is a double challenge, for it depends in turn upon the conquest of atomic energy and the last choice between life and death.

Once we had passed that crisis, it was only a matter of time before we found the pyramid and forced it open. Now its signals have ceased, and those whose duty it is will be turning their minds upon Earth. Perhaps they wish to help our infant civilization. But they must be very, very old, and the old are often insanely jealous of the young.

I can never look now at the Milky Way without wondering from which of those banked clouds of stars the emissaries are coming. If you will pardon so commonplace a simile, we have set off the fire-alarm and have nothing to do but to wait.

I do not think we will have to wait for long.

STORY SOURCES

All of the stories in this anthology are in the public domain unless otherwise noted on page 4. The following gives the first publication details for each story and the sources used.

'The Sentinel' by Arthur C. Clarke, first published in *Ten Story Fantasy*, Spring 1951, under the title 'Sentinel of Eternity'.

'Sub-Satellite' by Charles Cloukey, first published in *Amazing Stories*, March 1928.

'Whatever Gods There Be' by Gordon R. Dickson, first published in *Amazing Stories*, July 1961.

'Nothing Happens on the Moon' by Paul Ernst, first published in *Astounding SF*, February 1939. No record of copyright renewal.

'A Visit to the Moon' by George Griffith, first published in *Pearson's Magazine*, January 1901.

'After a Judgement Day' by Edmond Hamilton, first published in *Fantastic*, December 1963.

'Dead Centre' by Judith Merril, first published in *Magazine of Fantasy and Science Fiction*, November 1954.

'Sunrise on the Moon' by John Munro, first published in *Cassell's Family Magazine*, October 1894.

'Lunar Lilliput' by William F. Temple, first published in *Tales of Wonder*, Spring 1938.

'First Men in the Moon' by H.G. Wells, this extract first published in *The Strand Magazine*, July and August 1901.

'Idiot's Delight' by John Wyndham, first published in *New Worlds Science Fiction*, June 1958.